Is death really nec

About the author

Judi was born and brought up in Cornwall. She escaped the prospect of spending her working life there in the lower reaches of local government by fleeing to the University College of Wales, Aberystwyth as a mature student. She graduated in 1980 with a degree in History and American Studies.

In 1980 she moved to Milton Keynes where she worked as a project manager for the Open University until 1997, when she left to concentrate on writing full time. She has latterly returned to the Open University fold as a part-time Associate Lecturer, tutoring Creative Writing.

Judi's poetry has been published in a number of British small press anthologies over many years.

Her short fiction has been published in, amongst others, Acclaim (1996), Interzone (1998), The Interpreter's House (1999)and Carve (2004) magazines; also in anthologies including the Independent on Sunday (1997), World Wide Writers (1998), the new writer's Collection (2003) and most recently in two Earlyworks publications - *with islands in mind* (2007) and *The Road Unravelled* (2007).

This is her first published novel.

IS DEATH REALLY NECESSARY?

Judi Moore

Is death really necessary?

Published in 2008 by YouWriteOn.com

First Edition

Published by YouWriteOn.com

For Marilyn, my dear friend, without whom this book would never have been written.

Thanks

My grateful thanks for help with this book go to Crysse Morrison, Victoria Green, Jane Killick, Tom Sefton, Guy Russell and Marilyn Ricci for reading various drafts of what follows and giving valuable advice.

My thanks also to Barrie Jones, Zvi Friedman and Ian McCall for putting me straight on matters of fact; to David Baxter, Steve Rogers and Marshal Anderson for helping me with the vexed question of the future; to Edith Thorne for the loan of her Edinburgh eyrie; and once again to David Baxter for producing cover artwork as quickly as a conjuror can pull a guineapig out of a hat.

All remaining errors of fact and typography are, of course, my own.

Judi Moore

24 October, 2008

IS DEATH REALLY NECESSARY?

1

1.1

On the 31st of January 2039 Teddy Goldstein left Dunster castle on the Caithness coast for the first time in two years. She was on her way to Edinburgh to bury her father. His death had ended a father-daughter war which had degenerated into endless campaigns of petty spites and frustrations.

Teddy was wondering what she had left to live for.

The jetpod ahead of them, carrying her father's coffin, banked sharply as it entered city airspace. Moments later their own jetpod followed suit. Teddy glanced at the other two passengers – her son and his partner, Rory. She saw Ek give Rory's hand a squeeze as the jetpod lurched extravagantly onto its new heading. Rory was a nervous flyer, and the two loved to touch – any excuse would do. The little incident made Teddy smile wanly as she turned back to the window. The huddled roofs of Edinburgh slid beneath her, greasy-grey with rain. Edinburgh was pretty in the snow, but it never got cold enough to snow any more. Rain made the grey slate, granite and encrustations of city pollution that made up the façade of the city look dejected.

Very suitable, then.

The jetpod continued to turn. The city continued to rush by beneath her. It made her feel queasy – but almost everything did these days.

The pilot straightened up, finally, and began to follow the railway lines into the city. The restored and Listed tenement blocks loomed up like cliffs in front of them. Teddy cursed the pilot under her breath. These flyboys were always ex-military, burned out by tours in Afghanistan or the Middle East and craved the old combat rush of adrenalin every time they flew. This one had saved his kamikaze tricks until now, so that the citizens of Edinburgh could hear him power up the boost and watch him make this dangerously steep and completely unnecessary climb. They swept over the old tenements with feet to spare, the blare of their own passage thrown back at them from the stonework. She tutted to herself: it had been a cheap trick and as a result of it she felt *really* queasy.

Now they swooped down over the elegant roofs of New Town, slick in the rain. January was always grey, and January in Edinburgh was one of the gloomiest places Teddy had ever known. She'd spent plenty of nights in underpasses, weeks in cardboard cities: she knew gloomy when she saw it.

It had taken nearly an hour to fly in from Dunster – which Teddy had discovered to be more than enough time for the sort of introspection inevitable when burying your father. Although Rory was the poor flyer, it was her Ek that looked the more miserable of the two. Teddy and her father had started badly and worked at making matters worse for as long as Teddy could remember. But Ek had loved his grandfather. Theo Goldstein was, after all, the only parent Ek had had when he was growing up. Today would be hard on him.

Teddy sighed. She owed Ek. There was a lot that he should know about his mother. But they had to get the old man in the ground before she could think about anything else. Besides, a noisy jetpod piloted by a burnout with a death wish was not the place for the sort of conversation that begins, 'there are some things I've been meaning to tell you'. And, fond as she was of Rory, the conversation she must have with her son was one that should only take place between blood kin.

*****

The noise from the jetpod's engines rose to a scream and everything began to shake. The pilot had reversed thrust for landing. Teddy realised that even the fillings in her teeth were vibrating. Perhaps the train would have been a better bet, after all.

The noise and vibration got still worse and she lost her train of thought. Then she realised that, not only did she feel very sick indeed, she was now starting a brain-stabbing headache. *How appropriate*, her father would have said.

Theo had always been so vital. He had already been over a hundred years old when she returned to Dunster castle two years ago – and far fitter than she. He'd still been putting in sixteen hours a day at The Works then. Most of his veins and arteries were plastic by that time, his heart was plastic, as were his lungs, kidneys and liver – all developed by his beloved company and a boon to private medicine. But this year the little explosions in the blood vessels of his brain had begun and even Gold's Prosthetics had been unable to devise a way of reconnecting the delicate little blood vessels running through that particular organ. The life had gone out of him, week by week: the trips into the Works had become a struggle, then a chore, then impossible.

When the infarctions in his head had rendered him speechless she'd begun to go and see him every evening. He looked so tiny in the hospital bed, flattened by the bedding. Last night the only life in his room had been the tell-tales of the machinery monitoring his vital signs, beeping and winking with counterfeit cheerfulness. The old man in the bed had been waxy white. And now he was gone.

About an hour after she'd gone back to her own rooms the LEDs on the monitors had ceased to flash and the beeps changed to a constant wail. One of the identikit starched white nurses had come and told her, solemnly, that her father was dead.

Teddy hadn't known whether to laugh or cry.

*****

A squall hit her window, peppering the plexi-glass like buckshot. It made her jump, which started her coughing. She was still fighting the cough when they landed. One of the city's podpads was on The Meadows, just across the road from her father's town house in Millerfield Place. They'd brought a wheelchair for her. They were having difficulty getting it through the wet ground to the pad, its motor whined peevishly and its wheels churned mud. They would manhandle her out of the jetpod, then coddle her into the wheelchair and haul her to the house. Then, just as she'd caught her breath, it would all start again: she'd be babied into the limousine and they'd all mope across the city to the synagogue, everybody treating her as if she were a cracked egg. She didn't enjoy being coddled or babied – she'd had enough of that in her childhood. If she had the breath she'd tell them to piss off and stop fussing.

The coughing fit passed at last but she could taste the blood, as if she had licked an iron bar. She kept a wad of wet-wipes pressed to her mouth, just in case. Over the top of it she caught Ek's eye. A smile was out of the question. She winked at him instead, and got the ghost of a smile in return.

It was going to be a bloody day all round.

1.2

She was, indeed, manhandled from wheelchair to limo and back again until she was almost weeping with exhaustion. They got Theo underground in a thick Edinburgh mizzle which enabled the many feet of the mourners to turn the small Jewish section of the cemetery to mud. By the time they finally got back to the house Teddy wanted nothing more than to crawl into some small, dark place where she could close her eyes for a few minutes and didn't have to think about what expression was on her face. But the minute she got inside the house people started coming towards her with their 'sincere condolences' faces in place.

The whole of the ground floor was crammed with people. There were various local dignitaries, and most of the city's powerful Greys. They'd be looking for somebody to reminisce with: some of them had memories of what the world was like before World War II. But most of those present were employees of Gold's Prosthetics. Theo's employees always meant more to him than his own flesh and blood, she thought sourly. He'd seen more of them, for a start. This house, for instance: it had been Theo's *pied-à-terre* during the week. Often he'd work through the weekend and not get back to Dunster at all. He'd bought the castle for show, but Edinburgh was where he'd made his dough. The house still reeked of Theo's preferred way of living: polish and cabbage. The smell would never go. Teddy wondered what the Will said, whether she'd be able to sell the horrid place. This was, after all, the place she'd been brought to when …

She was glad of the distraction when George Barrie, the family solicitor, pussyfooted up to her. Didn't people ever retire any more? Barrie couldn't be more than ten or twelve years younger than her father. That made him something like ninety. He looked disgustingly spry. But then, everyone looked disgustingly spry these days. Except herself.

'Miss Goldstein. How are you, hnh? So good to see you again. My condolences, of course, most sincere, hnh. Bearing in mind, hnh, your own state of … hnh. Would it be possible to, hnh, deal with the business of the Will today? All interested parties are here, d'you see? And I thought you might prefer not to … hnh … return to Edinburgh proximately, being as you are, yourself … hnh?'

She doubted that Theo had left her anything more than a curse and a pittance. She had to admit that his sense of family duty was exemplary; he'd kept her all these years. Even when she was living rough in London he'd never cancelled the credit card that she'd stolen when she absconded. Teddy began to realise that very little spite could be directed at someone who was dead.

Yes, spite was wasted on the dead. You couldn't make the dead miserable, nor score points off them, nor ignore them pointedly. There was going to be a big gap in her dreary day by day schedule now that Theo was gone. She was, she was astonished to discover, going to miss him. She was going to have to find something else to do with her time now that he wasn't available for her to vent her spleen on any more.

She sighed audibly, causing poor Barrie to look even more crestfallen than he had, hitherto, looked embarrassed. There isn't a polite way of saying to the daughter of the old bastard you've just buried 'you look like shit. We'll be planting you next. Let's get this Will read before we have the Final Testaments of the Goldstein family backing up'.

But the contents weren't going to improve with time and there was much truth in Barrie's stumbling assessment of her condition.

'Why not,' she said. 'I don't know where we'll find a quiet spot to do it, though.' She looked around for Ek and Rory: they always knew what to do. Rory was hovering around Ek, his hand fluttering around Ek's shoulder and arm, not quite touching him, but wanting to so much. The sight made her smile: they were good together. Not only did they care deeply for each other, they looked out for each other. Rory hated to fly. Ek was burying his Opa. But they'd be all right – they had each other. She felt a tear begin to well up and shook her head angrily. Bathos and self-pity. And envy. Be glad for them. And she was. And jealous as hell.

She waved at Rory, who caught her eye at once, made his excuses (with a hand on Ek's arm) and came over. Rory would find them a quiet place.

1.3

Fifteen minutes later George Barrie shepherded the last of the, as he put it, 'interested parties' into the kitchen and shut the door behind him. As if burying the old bastard hadn't been bad enough, there was this to be got through as well. At least now she didn't have to be pleasant to all those black-clad people swarming through the house. She barely remembered most of the mourners.

She wondered whose house it would be, after the Will had been read. Someone from The Works probably. Maybe it was to be sold and the proceeds put into one of the benefit funds he ran for his workforce.

Rory had organised an ill-assorted sufficiency of chairs. A lot of people seemed to have expectations, all of them from The Works, except herself and Ek. There were a dozen people squashed around the old kitchen table, looking at each other over discarded bits of salad, dirty bowls and dishes, screwed up cling film - the remains of Ailsa's preparations for the funeral buffet.

Barrie sat himself at the head of the table and moved out of his way a greasy bowl that seemed to have contained something fishy. He pulled out his compad, put in his earpiece and looked at them expectantly. Those assembled got theirs out too and there was the usual flurry of hands to ears. Barrie made a couple of keystrokes with his stylus and Theo's face popped up on their little screens: his voice resonated in their ears. This was a shock. Teddy had been expecting words to scroll up the screen. To see Theo again so soon after his death was a bit spooky … he looked so well on the little screen. This Will must have been made before he was taken ill. Before all those little explosions in his brain, he had never been sick a day in his life, had only taken time off work for what he liked to call his 're-plumbing' operations. He'd been commuting weekly to Edinburgh, putting in sixteen hour days, just as he always had; the fittest nonagenarian you'd find for looking. Six months later he was vegetative, bed-ridden, the light gone out of him. To linger like that for another eight months – that had been cruel. What had been more cruel, to Teddy, was the way in which his, obviously terminal, illness had scuppered her own plans. She had wanted Theo to watch her die, not the other way around. She had come home to the castle for that. For Theo, or his illness, to twist it round like that had seemed most unfair. To see him on the screen, sprightly and so much healthier than she was herself, underlined the mess she had got herself into. She fought back tears, felt a hotness in her throat that could herald another bout of coughing, and wished heartily for a very large scotch. She took a couple of seconds to regain some sort of composure, then looked up defiantly. She looked like hell, but she was alive and Theo wasn't. If she hung on to that fact she'd get through his last insults equably enough.

As her father's voice continued to whisper in her ear she looked around the table. Barrie was looking down at his old-man's hands, clasped in front of him on the messy table. A model of discretion was George Barrie. He was also a very able lawyer. There were few people in the world that Teddy trusted. Her father had never been one of them. Barrie was. Angus Frasier, Gold's Managing Director, was another. He was a bluff, avuncular man – a 'safe pair of hands' her father had always called him. Morag Cuthbertson was there too. She was head of Research and Development at The Works.

Theo had used this last opportunity to enumerate his achievements at Gold's and Morag was looking very pleased and proud, as well she might. Teddy hadn't realised just how small its beginnings had been. She knew that Uncle Saul had begun crafting wooden legs and glass eyes at The Works, trading as Goldstein's Prosthetic Eye & Limb Co., during the First World War. Business was, not unnaturally, brisk then and he'd done well. Theodore Goldstein and his family had left Germany just before the Second World War, when Theo was a toddler. Theodore *père* (the family name was not, in Teddy's opinion, an attractive one – especially as she had been saddled with it too) had been a doctor in Berlin. When the internment problem had been sorted out Saul gave Theodore employment at The Works. Saul's artisan skills benefited greatly from Theodore's medical knowledge: Saul retired in 1947, having made another fortune. He'd gifted the business to Theodore, upon whom he'd come to rely completely.

When Theo inherited the business from his father in the Nineteen Sixties he renamed, and refocused, it as Gold's Prosthetics. In the Eighties he'd begun to concentrate on development of robotic limbs, improving and honing until, in the early part of the new century, he began to develop bio-mechanical organs and eyes. Now, to lose a limb or an eye was no longer a disability – if you could afford a Gold replacement.

As the technology improved the limbs and eyes they produced set the standard in the field. When cellular cloning had been banned in the Twenty Twenties Gold's received a new lease of life: the way forward had to be bio-mechanical in the absence of cloning options.

Now Theo was detailing the progress of his last project: Nanonics. In the early Thirties a few estates of houses had been built using nanites (*grown*, was the phrase the builders used) but stood empty. The press took credit for that. If there was a scary story (and there were many) connected with nanites, then the press ran it. If a scratching in the walls should turn out not to be rats or mice, but leftover nanites still doing whatever it was nanites did ... nobody trusted the tiny machines. Nobody wanted a world built with nanites. Theo, however, believed that Nanonics had enormous medical potential and well-funded research at The Works went ahead with considerable publicity. Theo maintained that he had been very close to a major breakthrough when one too many firebombs in the post had made him, reluctantly, put the project into mothballs. He was speaking of it here as the next, major medical breakthrough.

She didn't know much about Nanonics – had never taken any interest in anything connected with The Works. But something was nagging at her. What was it about Nanonics that could be important? Surely the whole project was so monumentally unpopular that no-one in their right mind would ever start it up again?

There were sharp intakes of breath around the table and she realised she had missed something. She paused the D-vid and ran it back until the words sounded familiar again. Glancing up she noticed that everyone was looking at her. The only one who looked less than outraged was Ek: he just looked worried.

Her father's voice said:

I know this will deeply disappoint my loyal employees, but I have decided, with regret and after a great deal of deliberation, not to leave The Works in your care.

My daughter Theodora is the proper heir and it is to her that I leave my shares in the business. She shall have The Works to do with as she sees fit. You might, quite reasonably, hope that she will sell it back to you. Mr Barrie has all the necessary documentation ready for her signature, if she chooses to wash her hands of the business as she has washed her hands of her family. You will, of course, have to come to your own arrangements about what might be a fair price for it.

It pains me to break my promise to you in this way. But I find that, even now, I cannot ignore my duty to my family.

So, that was what had made them suck their teeth.

What the hell had made him do such a thing?

To Ekhah, the son I should have had, I leave Dunster castle, Dunster Home Farm and all the buildings, livestock, leases, tenancies, rights and duties pertaining thereto. He loves the property and has become an excellent farmer. I shall have no fear for the land or the people who live on it while he is Laird.

Well, that was true enough.

The D-vid wittered on, her father's face tiny in front of her, but she couldn't take it in.

She tried to pull the important information together: The Works to her, everything else to Ek, crumbs to the rest of the people around the table who had had such expectations. Dear old Barrie had ushered them all in here just to hear that. Teddy snuck another look up under her lashes. Eleven pairs of eyes were fixed on her: nine pairs looked distinctly unfriendly.

No wonder.

1.4

The little screen blanked. Theo had nothing more to say: nor did anyone else, apparently. The Will-reading party began to break up.

As Barrie was gathering his things together, Teddy realised there was something she'd missed, in all the excitement.

'Who gets this house, Mr Barrie?'

'Hnh? Oh, you do, my dear. It goes with The Works.'

Bloody hell – he'd stuck her with this house that she'd always hated, as well as the business. She'd been wrong about Theo: he'd found a way to be even more vindictive from the grave than he'd been when he was alive.

Teddy made her way slowly upstairs to her old room. She needed to rest. Soon she would have to give up on stairs, but today that childhood room was the closest thing she had to a haven and she struggled up them as best she could. Once there she lay on the bed and looked at the childish things on the walls, the dolls on the dressing table, the greasy old hair-ribbons hanging over the mirror. Hellfire! The whole house was like a mausoleum. How appropriate.

She didn't doze, although she badly wanted to. Something was running around her mind. Theo's Will had given her the germ of an idea. While she lay propped up on the bed, too bright of eye and too flushed of cheek, she worked on it.

Teddy was dying. If you had money – and there had always remained a monetary thread between her and her father – it was quite hard to find things to die of in the Twenty-Thirties, but multi-drug resistant tuberculosis was certainly one of them. If you added a previous AIDS infection to the virulence of the tubercular bacilli, the resulting debility was usually fatal inside a year. Teddy had been diagnosed for eight months.

There was no point in new lungs. Theo himself had had a pair of what Gold's slang called their 'plastic bags', and had tried very hard to find a way for her to receive a pair when her TB was diagnosed as drug-resistant. The problem was that she had no immune system left to speak of after the AIDS and the swingeing course of treatment she had undergone to cure that. A cold could kill her. The tiny alteration in chemistry which a transplant would require was easily overcome even by the very sick, so long as they still had some kind of T-cell count. She didn't. No new lungs.

But Nanonics ... Tiny machines, smaller than a bacterium. Tiny *killer* machines: wasn't that was how they worked? You gave them a target and they homed in on it, like sharks in a feeding frenzy, sucking out of each target the single thing they were programed to destroy, rendering it harmless. Theo had been right - the potential benefits of Nanonics to people like Teddy were enormous.

Of course, the netpapers had concentrated on the 'killer' aspect. They'd blazoned their belief that a new, unstoppable, plague would result if Nanonics were used in the population. The big pharma-corps had played their part. AIDS remedies were extremely lucrative, even now that the AIDS pandemic was finally under some sort of control. Their opinions on the possible dangers of nanonic treatment had been alarming and taken up with enthusiasm by the netpapers. Theo had gone to great lengths to provide evidence that would allay public fears, but plain speaking and documentation were no match for hysteria.

Theo had been close to getting Nanonics to work. And now that he was dead Teddy found she had nothing left to die for.

1.5

The next morning they flew her back to the castle: from mausoleum to prison. It didn't matter. Ek was there, and Rory. And she had nothing else to do but watch the waves crash in from the North Sea and the gloomy little village down in the bay go about its business.

For seven days after the funeral, a good Jewish girl was supposed to sit *shiva* for her father: grieve and remember. Teddy was not a good Jewish girl. The way she had grown up – first isolated in a Scottish castle, then on her own in London – hadn't been conducive to the development of a belief system. She recognised a cultural pull; the need to find humour in the very worst of situations and solace in adversity. That she should question the value of such traits she recognised as Jewish in itself.

However … She covered the mirrors – no hardship there – and lit the great *ner daluk* candle that the *chevra* had left for her. Then she played Theo's will again; her last contact with the dead. On the screen he was vital, aggressive: exactly as he had been in life. *Why did you leave me The Works, the thing you loved more than me? I never understood what you did there. You knew I had no interest in it. Why did you do this thing? And did you really expect me to sell your life's work the same day we buried you? I'm more your daughter than that. You had a reason, didn't you? I'll find it, you bastard. I will.*

And finally, after watching the D-vid many, many more times and thinking deep into several nights when sleep wouldn't come, she believed she'd got it.

She commed Angus Frasier,

'I'm not going to sell, Mr Frasier. I'd rather you told them – they'll take it better from you … I know they'll be dreadfully disappointed. I'm sorry about that.'

'Ah.' There was a lengthy silence, then Frasier's slow, dark brown voice said. 'Well, if you want me to remain I'll do the best I can for you, same as I did for your father.'

'I know you will, Mr Frasier. I appreciate it. My only instruction, for now, is that I'd like everyone to have a bonus. It should be substantial. You decide what's appropriate.'

'Are you sure you want to be bothered with all this?'

The warm, peaty brogue in her ear sounded concerned. It almost brought her to tears.

'I must.' She gave a wry, choking little laugh which came out all wrong. 'I think I've worked out why my father left me the business. I've sent you through a list of the files I'll need – I'll have to do a lot of reading to get myself up to speed. While I'm doing this I absolutely cannot deal with distractions. It's going to take every bit of strength I have – and I must finish it soon, or I never will. I'll be in touch again as soon as I know myself what needs to be done.'

'Good luck to you then, lass. I'll wait to hear from you.'

She broke the connection. He had treated her like a sensible adult – not many people did that. She hoped she was going to be able to justify his apparent faith in her.

What she believed she'd found was something Theo could never have done while he was hale and in control of the business. It would have seemed pure madness to his Board. Procedures had to be followed. Although he was the major shareholder, he always abided by his Board's decisions. They would have voted him down on this, sadly but firmly. But when he turned his shares over to the resentful, dying daughter who knew what crazy stunt she'd pull? Theo knew: he'd set her up for this. The message was clear to her now. *If you want to live, here – I offer you life. But you'll have to work for it.*

Quietly, systematically, Teddy began to put it all together. She trawled through the files she'd requested from Frasier, she downloaded everything she could find about Nanonics, she pulled papers off the Nets on multi-drug resistant tuberculosis, and bought an on-line medical dictionary.

When she was more confident of the terminology she began a correspondence with her doctor, getting from him the locations of yet more papers on M-RTB, and the names of experts in other relevant fields.

She reviewed Gold's employment records and balance sheets.

Her activities seemed to her to be *shiva* in spirit, if not letter – and went on for much longer than the seven days required. She no longer believed that he had expected her to sell the business back to the employees. He knew she always took the hard path. It was, indeed, the path he had always chosen himself. Finally he had managed to make The Works important to her too. Theo would not be there to see, but if Gold's had to be run into the ground to achieve her purpose then she would do it.

It took her more than two months; long past *shiva* and into spring – a spring that she had hardly expected to see. Outside the castle the sea became skittish in the spring gales, a green haze began in the sheltered places and birds began to sing sweet nothings to each other. Inside, she read until her eyes were gritty with screen-time, and the mass of information she had gathered began to make less sense instead of more. By the time she had finished, her movements were almost completely restricted to the old Nursery which she had made her apartment. She slept in an oxygen tent. Sod's Law provided that, as the work became more complex, she was reduced to maybe ten useful minutes in each hour to absorb and process what she had amassed, but finally she had her plans laid.

It was going to be a race against time: she might have left it too late to start living.

1.6

On the 10th of April 2039 Teddy made the trip into Edinburgh once again.

There hadn't been a corporeal meeting of Gold's Board for more than twenty years, but she wanted them all to see her and the true state of her health, to make eye-contact with the people she was about to ask such a lot of, without white-outs or side-cons. Face to face; the old way.

The Boardroom smelled of the hot dust thrown out of the re-activated heating system. An enthusiastic gale cast needles of rain and sleet against the big windows, the draught came in round the frames and stirred the old velvet curtains. Her ride down in the jetpod had been bumpy. She'd spent enough time staring at weather coming in from the North Sea to know an all-day storm when she saw one. It looked like the ride home would be just as bad.

She was already standing, ready to speak. Standing wasn't her best activity any more - she had an oxygen bottle at her side in case it was too much for her. Her knees were trembling and the palms of her hands were slick with sweat against the polished mahogany table top.

It was ten minutes after the hour and they were still straggling reluctantly into the room. They settled down at the far end of the table, near Angus Frasier. Their antipathy was palpable. She could guess what they were thinking. Was she capable of deciding the future of the company? Was she mad? Everybody said she was mad. Had she sold it to some Japanese i-corp? What did she want from them? Their questions hung in the air like moths looking for a flame to throw themselves into. It was all Teddy could do to keep from laughing out loud.

The last one to come in was Sara Prosser (Teddy recognised her from the picture in her personnel file). Dr Prosser wasn't a member of the Board. People looked up at her with curiosity. Teddy realised she'd better get on with it, before anybody made the proper connections.

She was here to tell her father's people that she was going to run Gold's – into the ground if necessary – until it provided what she needed and what her father had wanted more than anything else in his life. There was considerable risk involved in what she was about to propose – much of it, certainly, to herself; but some of it to them. She'd give it to them straight, as her father would have done, and hope they'd be able to deal with it. But she wasn't about to take no for an answer

She had notes prepared on her compad, and the feed set up in her earpiece. She cued it. Then she leaned forward and began to speak.

'Is death really necessary?'

This wasn't what she had planned to say, but it was what came out of her mouth. The feed whispered in her ear, useless now. She had missed that wave and was riding another. She pulled the earpiece out and continued:

'You'll be wondering what could prompt me, of all people, to ask that question. After all, I'm not long for this world – you can all see that.'

She lifted a thin hand from the table top and rested it shakily on the oxygen cylinder beside her.

'But that's the thing: I don't want to die. I thought I did.' An ironic smile twisted her face. 'I went to considerable trouble to turn myself into this wasted wreck. But I was wrong. I want to live.'

She paused for breath and briefly considered using the oxygen. But she had their attention now; she could manage for a little longer.

'And that gives us – you and me – a wonderful opportunity.'

That intrigued them.

'I want to use the magnificent research and development facilities you - we - have here to find a cure for the multi-drug resistant tuberculosis that is killing me. We are going to use Nanonics, the project dearest to my father's heart of the many wonderful medical innovations he enabled here, and we are going to offer a new generation of pathological remedies to the world.'

She heard a small collective gasp. They hadn't expected that. Everybody had been right: Theodora Goldstein *was* barking mad if she intended to involve Gold's in Nanonics again.

'There is no cure for M-RTB. There isn't even effective treatment. As its name implies, the bacteria which have infected my lungs and throat have mutated – not necessarily in my body – to preserve their life. They are more cunning than the strongest antibiotics we have. They have a natural, primeval urge to survive. I have come to understand this urge.

'Unfortunately, for me and the many others like me, Gold's marvellous replacement organs are of no use. I have no immune system – AIDS destroyed that. Without a strong immune system rejection is still a major issue. A transplant would kill me quicker than the TB is doing. For those without an immune system – and there are many struggling with that legacy of the AIDS pandemic – there has to be another way.'

She could feel the cough begin to tickle, knew that when it came it would be explosive, probably bloody, and would make it impossible for her to continue. She had them now, she must keep going. She sipped a little water from the glass in front of her, fought the urge to cough and went on.

'When my father became ill, without his drive and belief in it, his nano-technology project was ended. I understand why. But much good work had been done and the trials were extremely promising – as Dr Prosser here can testify.'

Poor Dr Prosser. She looked up with a haunted expression. Teddy felt a pang – she really should have told Prosser what she was planning. But Prosser might have been unable to contain herself and let something slip out ahead of time. It would have given the Board time to plan a counter-stroke, which was the last thing Teddy wanted.

Prosser was the last remaining member of Gold's Nanonics research team. The others had been let go as soon as it became clear that Theo wouldn't recover. Teddy had found comms between Frasier and Cuthbertson discussing what to do with Prosser. In the end they'd moved her sideways into Robotics, but because only her first degree was in Robotics – and that was ten years out of date – they hadn't been able to give her much to do.

Nanonics was finished – everybody had said so. The letter bombs sent to Gold's made the point rather forcefully. Despite Prosser's splendid resume her applications for other positions hadn't yielded so much as an interview. Nanonics acquired a stigma which stuck to each and every one of the research team. They were glorified technicians now, all of them: Teddy had checked. Gold's being the old-fashioned firm it was, Prosser at least was drawing the same salary as she had when she'd been doing cutting-edge work. Sometimes the honourable way of doing business still worked, even in the middle of the twenty-first century.

'Nanonics was the essence of the post-industrial age. My father believed – as do I – that Nanonics really was the Next Big Thing for Gold's. What other direction could be so logical? Currently we make machines – self-repairing, self-regulating – to replace limbs and organs. They are the best on the market.

'But each separate line is tailored to an individual's need and is, consequently, enormously expensive. Our products are bought by those with good health insurance. And the invasive surgery required to implant them is still a dreadful toll on the patient. So, transplants are a last resort.

'How much less stressful for patients, simply to program the target malfunction into a nanite swarm and inject it directly where it is needed. Once in the body it gathers the elements for its own replication directly from the aberrant cells, destroying them in the process, and leaving the patient's internal repair systems to do the rest. The body's own capacity for renewal is remarkable. It was with that capacity in mind that my father called his Nanonics project Self Heal. With nanite help patients could rebuild themselves from within. There would no longer need to be such a thing as 'major surgery'.'

She paused for breath and more water.

'If the development of medical Nanonics had been only a few months further forward when my father had his first major stroke, it need not have left him vegetative. Nanites could have cleared out the blockages in his arteries. He could have lived another twenty productive years, maybe more. And that's not all.'

Around the table now one or two nodded almost imperceptibly at her last remark. They knew it was true. And they knew how close Gold's had been.

'The M-RTB that is killing me is killing more each year now in first-phase industrial countries than AIDS did in the same places at the height of its virulence. It loves the environment created for it by HIV, where the auto-immune system – sometimes of whole communities – has been crippled for generations. M-RTB is, currently, unstoppable.

'Super-viral and super-bacterial infections are increasing in variety and hostility. They mutate quickly: treatments that work today can be ineffective in as little as six months. The old killers like tuberculosis, syphilis, smallpox, malaria, leprosy and Ebola are coming back. They've taken advantage of increasingly dense habitation patterns and, in some cases, global climate change, to resurge in every country, rich and poor. Add in the new killers which have emerged in the past hundred years – variant-CJD, Legionnaires Disease, HIV and AIDS still, the super-viruses I've already mentioned – and the future looks grim. Doubtless more will continue to emerge in the future. Viral and bacterial mutations put an enormous strain on pharmaceutical development, and mutations will only become more savage. Sick people use up expensive resources. Sick people are unproductive, in pain, frightened.'

They knew all this, of course they did. But how else to convince them, except to lay it all out, put it all together, in a way they maybe hadn't thought of before. She was a tyro at this, but she'd done her homework, and she believed what she was saying. She needed to have them believe at least in her belief. That would be enough for now.

'We now use a cocktail of the strongest drugs to knock back infections that a simple antibiotic mould used to overcome. Every drug we use is a poison in its own right. People fear the lack of control they have over nanites. But no drug is risk-free. Even aspirin has side-effects. Nanites – the nanites we are going to develop – will be completely free of side-effects. They will be not only Self Heal, but also Safe Heal.

'Until now super-viruses and super-bacteria like TB would not have been our markets. But the provision of the best artificial limbs, eyes and organs in the world is not enough, not really. I've read the research. We can do this. We can become pro-active. We can get ahead of disease. What a gift to the world that would be.

'We will start with TB – my TB. I will be your lab rat.'

That lifted the eyes around the table. She saw astonishment there.

'There are, I believe, some 15 million ex-AIDS sufferers world-wide, and several times that number whose immune systems were damaged by HIV. Many of them are still taking an expensive cocktail of drugs daily. Many will suffer serious illness even so: many of them will fall ill with M-RTB. That's our first market, and it's a big one. Once other sufferers see what the results of our research do for me, fear of Nanonics should be allayed. One treatment, reasonably priced will enable them to lead a normal life again. They *will* offer themselves for treatment because their options are so limited. By helping them we shall begin to bring Nanonics, with all its potential, into polite society.'

She smiled – this was the best part, the most persuasive.

'What a gift we will give the world, if we can finish what my father started. He didn't champion Nanonics because he was senile, or deluded – but because he knew how good it could be made to be.

'Gold's was close to clinical trials. Dr Prosser can tell us how close.'

All eyes swivelled in Prosser's direction. Prosser seemed to have got over the shock of finding she apparently had a future again. She looked determined. Teddy hoped that her determination was to support the project, not to come up with reasons why Nanonics was best left alone after all.

Teddy scrutinised each of the faces in front of her.

'If we are successful Gold's will thrive and the shares each of you already hold will make you far wealthier than if Mr Goldstein had left the business to you.'

She took a tentative half step back from the table. There was a chair there somewhere. If she could only find it, and not faint.

'Are there any questions?'

Angus looked uncomfortable. Cuthbertson was trying to disguise a scowl. Teddy was well aware that, properly speaking, she should have brought this to Cuthbertson before it got as far as the Board – then Cuthbertson could have talked her out of it. Oh, she'd have dressed it up in technical jargon and made a dainty thing of it, but it would have been a knee jerk no, just the same. This was the only way Teddy had been able to think of that would get past Cuthbertson.

She tried to meet other eyes. People were examining their manicures and compads intently. There were no questions. Everything was, apparently, perfectly clear. The proposal was made, they understood it, they didn't like it. As Teddy looked around the table only one pair of eyes made contact – Prosser, of course.

'What about you Dr Prosser? Do you think this can work?'

Prosser regarded Teddy steadily, shrugged and said,

'Of course.'

There was a subtext to that shrug that Teddy understood perfectly: *if you're going to throw unlimited funds at this and give me a free hand, of course I can do it. I'm not afraid of public opinion, or the opinion of the people here – if I was I wouldn't have chosen to work in Nanonics in the first place.*

Teddy smiled. She and Prosser understood each other.

The silence around the table continued. Finally Angus Frasier cleared his throat.

'I think you can tell from the reticence in the room that your, ah … proposals have come as something of a …surprise. I think I speak for the Board when I say that we would need time to evaluate your presentation.'

Teddy opened her mouth to protest, but he waved his hand. He understood. He had something for her.

'But I know that time is, for you, of the essence. I propose that we give you Dr Prosser who is, after all, our only remaining specialist in the field. We will also allocate such funds as she feels will be necessary to explore the possibilities of a successful outcome.'

Again Teddy made to intervene, again he stopped her.

'For the duration of Dr Prosser's research into this we need stint her nothing. I take it that a period of … shall we say, six months … will be adequate?'

Teddy felt herself redden. He was, in effect, saying that if they hadn't cracked it in six months she would be dead and they could forget all about it. But it was true. He was offering less than she had hoped for, but more than she needed. If she rejected Frasier's compromise her remaining course had to be confrontation. She found she was able to be gracious.

'Thank you, Mr Frasier. That will do nicely.'

Teddy leaned back in her chair and made use of the oxygen. Angus retrieved the meeting from her control and swiftly closed it. A hum of conversation developed in the room as people quickly gathered up bags and compads. Occasionally she would hear a voice raised: the first word was usually 'but', the rest sank back into the general susurration.

Now only Frasier and Prosser remained. Frasier walked up to Teddy's end of the table. Under the circumstances – she had, after all, just challenged his authority in the company that he had managed and for more than thirty years – this was a magnanimous gesture.

'I pray it works for you. Truly.' He put out a hand and just brushed her shoulder with it. Having done so he didn't linger. TB was, after all, contagious.

And then there were two: herself and Sara Prosser.

1.7

When Angus had gone Teddy said,

'Well, how does it feel to have a career again?'

Prosser looked wary.

'I don't think you realise just what a pariah Nanonics is.'

'It's my only hope. It's what my father intended for me to do. I've spent eight weeks trying to get inside the old bastard's head, and I'm certain I'm right.'

Prosser looked taken aback by Teddy's casual disrespect. Gold's had belonged to Theodore Goldstein III, hearts, minds and all. He had been at the helm of Gold's for sixty two years. He had been fair and he had been clever. The staff thought he shat gold and his farts smelled like roses.

'You heard what Angus Frasier just gave us. And I heard you say you could do it. This belongs to us – you and me. Don't tell me you can't find a little enthusiasm for a promotion that puts you at the head of ground-breaking research, with an unlimited budget?'

'It's not that.' Prosser took a breath. 'Quite apart from the fact that Morag Cuthbertson is now our sworn enemy, nobody will touch Nanonics. Nobody will come. Why the hell did you pick on me? The phrase 'poisoned chalice' comes to mind.'

'You're what's left.'

'Thanks very much. The one without the *chutzpah* to find something else to do. The one that's been making the tea for the last year and a half.'

'So what's wrong with having something interesting to do again? It'll have to be quick and dirty – to start with anyway. But you know – and Cuthbertson knows – there could be a Nobel Prize in this for you.

Put up a smokescreen for Frasier and Cuthbertson. Hire whoever you need. Spend what you like. Answer to nobody but me.'

Prosser still wasn't convinced, that was obvious.

'What the hell is it now?'

'You should have told me.' There was a mulish set to Prosser's jaw.

'Yes, I should. I'm sorry. I couldn't. If you'd gone skipping round the department with a smile on your face Cuthbertson would have smelled a rat. Not that it seems there'd have been much skipping or smiling.'

That got a wry grin out of Prosser.

'So, where do we start?'

'Well, it shouldn't take six months. We were pretty close when Morag pulled the plug. She'd been waiting for an excuse after the bottom fell out of nano-construction. And when Mr Goldstein … well, the termination letters went out as soon as we'd heard he wasn't expected to recover. But Angus wouldn't let her shut it down altogether – you know what Gold's is like. The lab's still set up. All the files are here. Nobody took their work with them – you couldn't give it away by that time anyway. I can probably rehire some of the old hands. But I know of one guy – he didn't work here, but he was leading edge when Nanonics was big. We should have had him in the first place but he's not … exactly a team player. I expect he'll be delighted to get the work.

'I'm not going to suck my teeth and tell you it could be months. If I can get this chap to come, I'm certain we'll have something for you in six weeks.'

Teddy grinned wolfishly. She felt elated – and nauseous. She could feel the unhealthy flush burning her cheeks. She was going to have to spend a couple of days in an oxygen tent recovering from this when she got home. And the prospect of the jetpod flight home through the storm appalled her. But right now …

'Find your man.'

'I'm on it.' And Prosser was out the Boardroom door, leaving Teddy wondering what the hell she had just started and whether it was completely insane of her to think that it was going to work.

2

2.1

Gates Hanford had been out to get milk, that most prosaic of errands. It was pretty much the only thing he couldn't e-get. At around half past seven on a dank April evening he was sitting on his bicycle at the top of Highgate Hill. You could see the whole of north London from here. Usually the view was clogged with traffic, which infuriated him and made the stop more pain than pleasure. Tonight he had other things on his mind.

He had only gone to bed a couple of hours before being woken by his neighbours leaving for work. There had been much banging of car doors, boots and bonnets, some agitated shouting and swearing and, finally, a lot of revving: he gathered (this hadn't been difficult because of the volume at which the problem had been discussed) that one of the disgusting, polluting, petrol-based vehicles that cluttered up what used to be the front garden of the house his flat was in had refused to start. He'd felt disorientated and restless because of the disturbance. Unable to get back to sleep he'd decided to sort through the previous day's net-gathers, and had come across a crumb trail.

Nobody left net-crumbs for him any more. They'd used crumb trails in the nano-tech fraternity occasionally back in the day when there used to be such a thing and someone was being head-hunted. It was a curiously old-fashioned thing to come across now.

When he saw which site the posting led to he was even more curious. He followed the trail to the retro 'Girls just wanna have fun' chatroom and picked up an encrypted message from 'Goldie' to 'Beauty', which was in a vaguely familiar cipher. It had taken him an hour to find the right protocol (there were enough clues, but it had been over a year since he'd needed that cryptogram), load and launch it. Then he'd studied what little there was of the message and had spent another couple of hours thinking about it while he did other things. He remembered Dr Sara Prosser. She'd worked for a small but well-funded group up in Scotland somewhere. They'd had some interesting exchanges way back when.

Gates had never been good with women. It was a bit easier if they were colleagues. Actually, he recalled, he wasn't particularly good with colleagues either, of any gender. And it had been a long, long time since he had had any colleagues.

Prosser wanted something quite extraordinary. And she wanted him to go to Edinburgh.

What she wanted had given him an idea.

Finally he'd composed a reply, encrypted and sent it. She'd come back immediately – she must have been sitting by her machine. The way she'd contacted him made it very likely that whatever she wanted from him wasn't particularly legal. The whole thing had appealed immensely to both his pride and his curiosity.

Beauty and Goldie corresponded spasmodically for a couple of hours. Negotiations were tortuous because of the need to encrypt every send and decrypt every get. By midday they'd come to an agreement. Nanonics was on again. It wasn't popular, but it wasn't illegal. He would work on a specific project of six months duration, with unlimited funds: a walk in the park for someone with his skills and talents. She had actually said that – 'a walk in the park'. It had been years since he had walked in a park. A park was far too public. But she had been absolutely firm that he couldn't do it from London. He must come to Edinburgh, and he must come immediately.

Now he was sitting on the top of Highgate Hill wondering what the hell he had let himself in for.

North London was spread out below him, grid-locked. Multi-coloured ribbons of light meandered as far as the eye could see were. Sodium street-lights shone orange along the roads, like sinuous strings of amber beads, beacons for the all-important motor car. Between the amber beads were the denser strings of white and red lights, theoretically transporting their occupants, but actually motionless in the dark, going nowhere. From up here he could see individual commuters inching off the clogged roads, creeping towards their homes. By the time all those people finally opened their front doors and shook the day's work from them they would be too tired to eat, too late to read a bed time story, too numb for love.

It was never truly dark in London. Nor was it ever quiet. The hum of all those engines floated up to him now. Everyone constantly needed to be somewhere else: you had to be right there right, right now. You had to keep up. The irony was that the more people needed to move about to fulfil their many duties, the slower the whole procession became.

People thought the motor car was their personal bit of freedom – one of the few they had left. That absurd bubble of personal transport meant so much to them. It was a lifestyle statement, sexual gratification, cocoon, bullet, coffin, pet, wardrobe, tool box. It alone enabled them, so they thought, to get through another day, taking them to their places of employment so that they could earn the funds to have somewhere to live, something to eat, education, entertainment, medical care.

He knew about medical care. He'd had treatment for three melanomas and an extremely unpleasant super-virus which the doctors hadn't even been able to put a name to. He still had shooting pains in his hands and feet when it was damp – which it almost always was. He could afford very good health care, but he hated and feared the amorphous illnesses that lurked in the air and water of the city and were carried around in the close press of its population. So he'd taken himself out of the rat race.

He sat looking down at the epitome of the mid twenty-first century: stop-go all the way home. It would be like this for another hour yet. When morning came it would be the same in reverse. Traffic was the thrombin that clogged the city's arteries.

He wiped the drizzle off his specs, then pushed off from the kerb and free-wheeled down the hill.

2.2

'I've managed to get an e-line on the man who can give us a real boost on your project. He was in the breaking wave of Nanonics when it was big. He's been harder to find than credit after Christmas, but I left a crumb trail to try and get him curious. And he bit.'

'Why's he so hard to find?'

'Everybody who was ever anybody in Nanonics is hard to find.'

To Teddy's trained eye, Prosser looked shifty.

'You've worked with him before?'

Prosser continued looking shifty and blushed a bit.

'Sort of. There was never exactly a queue of grad students waiting for openings in the field. The rewards were potentially enormous, but Nanonics always had the cachet of a cold turd. There were only ever about ninety of us, spread around a dozen labs – we were a sort of club. We used to post queries for each other on an intranet we set up. Hanford was a big help to all of us. He's probably the best natural nanite programer I've ever come across. It was the programing, towards the end, that had us stumped. You have to be pretty accurate when you're targeting living tissue. Hanford was closer than anyone else to cracking it.

'There's no point in advertising for people to work on this stuff - no-one will apply. I told you we needed him for this as soon as I heard what you wanted. After he left NanoGen he disappeared. If you go through the usual channels, he doesn't exist. There's no record of him anywhere that you can interrogate legally. But curiosity is a big thing with people like us. Fortunately.

'Turns out he's just as flaky as he ever was – and his paranoia is total. Mind you, anyone who worked in Nanonics is pretty paranoid. The old saw's true – the bastards are out to get you whether you're paranoid or not. You heard about the fire bombs? And our e-comms used to get hacked and trashed, until we got wise and started using ciphers.

'But, flaky or not, Hanford really knows his way around this stuff and he's not only got his files, he's got *everything* that Nano Gen did with Nanonics.'

Teddy felt uneasy. When she'd made her bargain with Prosser she hadn't reckoned on including a flaky, paranoid, invisible stranger with stolen intellectual property in the deal. This, then, was the man whose participation meant that Prosser would have 'something for you' in six weeks. Her unease obviously showed: Prosser gave her the hard sell.

'There was stuff in his last paper eighteen months ago that we hadn't even thought of yet. He's the best. If you want a nano cure in time for it to be of any use to you, we have to have him.'

Teddy still looked dubious.

'He really does have the goods.'

'What's his name?' Teddy asked. A simplistic question, but a tangible hook is a good thing to hang hope on.

'Gates Hanford.'

'Will he come, do you think?'

'He said he would.' Prosser sounded a bit grim. 'He'd better.'

2.3

Gates was dejunking. It had taken time to build the exquisite electronic nexus that kept him invisible. To work at maximum efficiency, it required constant updating. If he stopped maintaining it for even a few days it would be useless. He had been reluctant to lose all that work. But in the end he knew there was no room for manoeuvre – he must go and so must his beautifully constructed systems. He would have to trash his whole set-up to go to Edinburgh. But first he had work to do.

The old proverb 'fail to prepare: prepare to fail' was one of his favourites. So before he did anything else he checked out Edinburgh to see how Hanford-friendly it could be made, down-loading detailed maps of the city and investigating, as far as he could at this range, possible places where he and Beauty could go to ground. He had an idea that Scotland and England had diverged somewhat in the last half a century. His researches showed that the divergence had been considerable. He began to think he might actually enjoy Edinburgh.

Next he downloaded all his old research and the rest of the work that NanoGen had done. Then he spent several hours rummaging through Gold's work, comparing it with his own. It looked as though they'd been close to an answer before they shut the project down.

He checked Gold's track record and accounts on the Net. It was as he remembered – it was a well-respected company with plenty of cash and a thriving R & D department which had published several well-received papers – all more than a year old now – on Nanonics. He was still curious about why Prosser was so keen to start a lab now. Nanonics was a dead letter in Britain. There were still labs working, so they said, in the States. But so little came out of America now, who knew what they were working on? Despite his lengthy, fitful e-conversation with Prosser there was still a lot he didn't know – just that the target was organic. That alone was a novelty. Previously he'd been working on inorganic uses. Inorganic applications tended to frighten the newsnets slightly less, so in the end that was all anybody had been able to get funding for. But an *organic* application … what could it be?

Finally he sent an e-shot that he had been longing to send for a long time. It was time for Planet Earth to get a wake-up call. He put an 18 hour delay on it so that he'd be long gone by the time it arrived, just in case anybody took the trouble to try and track its point of origin. Last of all he sent a message to his Green X Group: *get ready*. That should shed any members who just wanted the talk without the action.

The Green X Group had existed, to date, solely as a secure newsgroup on the Net - except for the flashing logo that Gates had put on his jacket. He had set up encryption protocols of Byzantine complexity for it. He had checked rigorously into the background of all those who requested access. Most who showed an interest in the Green X Group seemed to think that it was concerned with road safety. In a perverse sense this was, indeed, true. However Gates was only interested in the few who showed real antipathy towards roads and the disgusting vehicles that rode on them. These he sounded out cautiously, after making rigorous checks on them. The rest found that the site had moved and somehow the new link wouldn't work. Some fifteen of those he had checked out were now admitted to the Green X Group's private space. He had been pleased to find there were people who felt as he did about motor vehicles all over the world: New York, Sydney, Paris, Rome, Madrid, Berlin, The Hague, Beijing, Tokyo, Brasilia, Tel Aviv, Cairo and Johannesburg were all represented. It was a promising spread of interest, but so far all Gates had been able to get them to do was recruit more people like themselves and pay extraordinary attention to security.

He had long been aware that this wouldn't be enough to keep their interest. Terrorism takes time – they understood that. But recruiting and secret passwords weren't what they joined for. Now that he was back in Nanonics he'd be able to give them something to *do*. Quite what that something was he still didn't know, but he did know he was onto something exciting.

Before he started trashing his networks and throwing out physical evidence of his existence, he set up a search on fossil fuels. It might spark an idea or two. He had let it run while he zapped some soup. Sipping the lurid liquid he started looking at the results. What was this? He read with increasing enthusiasm. Carbon, oxygen, hydrogen: the building blocks of life. Damn, it was so obvious! Why hadn't he thought of this before? Of course! Three well-differentiated targets. He only needed one: carbon, obviously. Whatever carbon-based target Prosser wanted him to program was bound to have resonances with that. And petrol was oh so carbon-based. The same generic program, with the target re-specified, should hold good for the hydrogen in fuel cells too. The synergies were astonishing.

He told Beauty what he had found as he dismantled his electronic nexus, strand by strand. Then he packed his CPU, thin-Vs and other peripherals carefully into a bag for transit.

He had only one more task to perform before he could set out for the station. Crooning to her all the while, he set about the delicate task of packing Beauty securely into the large, cardboard bird-carrier he had brought back after one of his skip trips.

2.4

The following night Gates Hanford sat on his bicycle at the top of Muswell Hill. It was muggy and mizzling, as usual. He was appropriately and anonymously enveloped in his yellow cycling slicker and mask.

He had been railing, fruitlessly, against personal transport for so long. Even with all the computing power at his disposal, and little regard any more for the rule of law, he had been unable to find a way to bring the autocorps down. But now he would have the means. He didn't need the considerable salary Prosser had offered him – he would have worked for nothing, just for the lab space, to be back in the game. He hadn't realised how much he'd missed it. He would use the money they were going to pay him, and the facilities, to start the revolution.

What a validation! For years he'd argued that Nanonics was the way to go. Nanites were so versatile. They could be used in paint to slough off dirt, they were a marvellously efficient way to block UV radiation, they could be used to make clothes and glass self-cleaning, they could be placed inside food packaging to measure spoil rates. They could clean up the environment, provide cheap and abundant manufactured materials, even combat diseases resistant to traditional treatments. That had been his area: self-repairing systems. That was why Prosser wanted him, of course. Her project was an intriguing one. But his own project excited him more.

Back in the twentieth century, the fear had been that computers would take over. What actually took over was the car. Unthinking, it sucked life from the organic and had no conscience. His perfect, shining little slaves would have a conscience - *his* conscience, fed to them through his programs.

He had come up here to have one last pre-Armageddon poke at the enemy. This had, after all, been his only actual offensive against cars so far.

He unclipped his rain cape from the handlebars to give himself a bit more mobility, then leaned down to unfasten a long, thin rod from his bike's cross bar. The end of it blazed with a tiny orange spark as a street light caught it. The blazing tip of the wand was a diamond, only industrial, but it needed to be large for his purpose and had been expensive. He reached around to the back of his waistband and fumbled there for a moment. He had riveted LED studs into the back of his rain cape which were wired to a little power pack which he wore on his belt. The studs lit up and began to flash: a big X. It should have been green, but the street lighting turned it a dirty orange.

He'd be on the Convoy Coach to Scotland in a couple of hours. It hadn't taken long to pack – there were only three things he valued: his computer, his bike and his Beauty. He'd spent the afternoon cycling to various local skips, junking anything that could be traced back to him.

He couldn't wait to go. It might be less toxic in the north. It would certainly be more productive.

One last tilt at the bastards, then. He jammed one end of the rod under his bike's back carrier and tucked the middle of it under his arm like a knight's jousting lance, with the diamond tip pointing forwards. Then he pushed off down the hill through the rainy dark, pedalling hard.

He'd got up a good speed now. At this time of night, in this part of the city, the four-wheeled monsters were quiescent, instead of coming at him, blaring their horns, forcing him into the gutter. They lined the residential street on both sides, wedged up onto the cracked pavements, narrowing the road until there remained only just enough room for another of their kind to squeeze between them. More were crammed into what had once been green front gardens. Soon their roar would start again. But he wouldn't be here then. He whizzed past them gleefully, as they glittered under their coating of collected drizzle as if they were something jewelled and precious. Curse them all.

He was free-wheeling now, getting his balance right. Then he stuck the diamond tip out and let it do its work. His triumphant yell and the small sound of paint being scored accompanied him down the hill.

It was a symbolic gesture only. Something more than this would be done, very soon now. Tonight he had marked them. For now that was enough.

2.5

Gates arrived in Edinburgh just before ten in the morning. They weren't expecting him until after lunch the following day. Plenty of time to find somewhere to live: first he would get acquainted with the city. Beauty would not appreciate the tour so, reluctantly, he checked her and his sleeping bag into Left Luggage, with a request that she not be put in a draught.

He had the map of the city which he had downloaded before leaving London. Having scrutinised it he pushed his bike out into the day. It was cool but bright outside: not raining, not smoggy, not muggy. He had decided against bringing his yellow cycle slicker with the flashing green X to Edinburgh – it resided in one of London's skips. He regretted having to ditch it, but he couldn't afford to be caught with it, now that so much more was at stake.

Heart lifting, mask still in one of the bike's panniers, he started pedalling: up Princes Street (they had a cycle lane, that was a nice touch), through the labyrinthine streets of New Town and north to the Botanical Gardens. He had some lunch there. Then he circled back south, down Lothian Road, round the bottom of the castle, along High Street and Canongate. At the bottom of Canongate he turned west again up Holyrood Road and into Cowgate. Somewhere here was the address that Prosser had given him to report to.

Cowgate was a deep, desolate canyon. The slab sides of the buildings reared up seven and eight stories tall. Most of the windows had blinds, or even whitewash, obscuring them. Hardly anyone was about on the street. This looked like his kind of place. Most of the buildings seemed to contain night clubs, tiny struggling e-businesses, or university departments.

He smiled when he found the address he was looking for – a graphic representation of the company's core prosthetics business was attached to the stonework on the third storey: an old, articulated wooden leg dangling over space. So this was where he would be working. Apparently admin, production and R & D all inhabited this one building. Unheard of, to be still manufacturing in Britain these days. He knew this was still a family business, how had it avoided buy-out or bankruptcy over the years? The quirkiness of it appealed to him.

He was lucky – the building was genuinely high Victorian. It had escaped the fire at the end of the Twentieth Century. Old buildings had nooks and crannies and dimly-lit, forgotten spaces. Yes, this all looked very promising.

Having found his ultimate destination he turned south onto Candlemaker and mooched for a bit. Shortly he found himself in Bristo Square, with Arthur's Seat looming behind it. How marvellous to find something wild in the city. Glad to have a purpose again, he continued south, making for Salisbury Crags in as straight a line as he could. He finally found an entrance to the park beside the glass expanse of the Commonwealth swimming pool and turned in.

He cycled round the park leisurely and, as the sun was shining, stopped briefly near Duddingston Loch and climbed a little way up the Lion's Haunch with his map. He could see most of the south of the city from here, and a golf course that was probably Prestonfield. There were a lot of golf courses marked on the map, and he was still getting his bearings, so it was hard to be certain.

He found a sheltered gully on the side of the escarpment and dozed for half an hour. Then the warmth went out of the spring sun and the chill in the air woke him. It wouldn't be dark for hours yet, but he'd done all the orientation he needed. He must find somewhere to hole up for a few hours. Below him he could see Edinburgh's rush hour begin, and his heart sank. He could smell the stinking monsters even in this wild place. But there was at least a freshness to the air here.

He scrambled down to the road and unlocked his bike from the crash barrier. He'd go and fetch Beauty from the station, then he'd find a café where she could be warm and he could get something to eat. Then they'd just have to wait until dark.

2.6

It was nearly eleven in the evening. Gates made his way back down into the Cowgate. He pedalled cautiously through the murky gorge, lit only fitfully with street lights, looking upwards once again for the grisly symbol of Gold's business premises. There it was: the jointed wooden leg and foot, gracefully flexed as if about to leap into the sky. He left his bike in shadow about five metres away and grinned up at the sign. Across the road the inevitable cyclops of a CCTV camera winked its baleful red eye. No problem. He wriggled his Super Soaker out of his bedroll and checked the reservoir: plenty of paint. He pumped up the pressure and took aim. A stream of gooey green poster paint mixed with PVA gum sploshed over the lens. So much more satisfying than an air rifle, so silent, so effective. He was glad he hadn't left the Super Soaker in a London skip. He had a feeling he'd be needing it again.

When he had finished with the CCTV camera he returned to Gold's building. It was in darkness, except for one light showing through a fanlight over the main entrance. He risked a quick look through the obsolete keyhole in the imposing front door. There was a large hall with a security guard sitting at a desk. No matter. Gates had long since found ways to enter buildings that didn't involve the production of pass cards and light banter. He went on round the side of the building and soon found what he wanted.

On his return he collected his bike and pushed it up the alleyway to the left of Gold's building. Up here were neither streetlight nor CCTV camera. It was pitchy black after the lit street and Gates had to feel his way cautiously along the iron railings. About ten metres in there was a gap in the railings. Steps led down to a basement level. Gates leaned his bike on the railings and descended. Down here somewhere … Ah: here was the door he'd seen, covered with the dust of years and secured with nothing more than a rusty padlock. Gates pulled a pair of bolt cutters out of his pack. The snap of the metal sounded very loud in the quiet dark. He held his breath for a moment, just in case, then tried the door handle. It turned grudgingly, but the door didn't move. He put his shoulder to it and gave it a good shove. It gave a low groan and swung inwards. Mr Invisible slipped inside.

He had brought a flashlight, but he used it sparingly.

There was a whole suite of rooms down here. The door he had come through opened into a corridor which appeared to run the length of the building. Three doors opened off it. The stuff in these rooms was obviously abandoned, forgotten, just as he liked it. Down the corridor to the right of the door he had come in by were boilers, a lot of pipes and some antique heating controls. There were signs that people came down here to maintain them. They didn't use the door he had come in by though. A faint trail in the dust led towards the front of the building. He followed the trail and came to a flight of steps with a door at the top. He crept up the stairs and tried it. Locked. He returned to his own entrance. It didn't look as though anybody ever came this far. The dust was undisturbed except for his own footprints. He'd find a way of keeping it like that.

Nearest to the door he had come in by was a good big room, with a window below ground level, nicely barred. But its door had no lock. Damn. He checked the next two rooms – neither of their doors had locks either. He had brought a sophisticated swipe-lock with him, but it would be badly out of place here where a padlock was considered security enough. But this was where he needed to be: where he could make full use of Gold's considerable resources. He would find a padlock tomorrow. In the meantime, he would make himself comfortable in the first room he'd tried. He'd just have to trust to luck, tonight, that no-one would find a pressing need to wander around in the basement.

He played his flashlight around the room. There were two big, old-fashioned strip lights on the ceiling to give him the light he'd need. There was a stack of boxes at one end, which reached almost to the ceiling. There was, for some obscure reason, a wash-hand basin on the internal wall, which would be very useful. He wondered if the water was drinkable. He shucked off his backpack. If there was a power point or two under the boxes he was in business. Methodically Gates began to remove the boxes from his room and stack them in the one next door. Towards the bottom of the pile were a dozen or so big bundles of paper done up with string which looked as thought they'd been there for a century or more. They would make a useful sleeping pallet, so he re-stacked them neatly in the corner furthest from the window. He was pleased to find an old but functional double electric socket behind the paper bundles.

The third room, nearest the stairs, had some old office furniture in it. He helped himself to a small, rather rickety, table for Beauty, a couple of chairs and two desks, which he dismantled so that he could carry them down the corridor without banging them into the walls and making a noise.

He'd need to function on normal days and nights for a while, until he'd got all the information he needed from Prosser, then he could go back to working through the night and sleeping in the daytime. Tomorrow morning he would set up his own computer system. Tomorrow afternoon he'd go round to the front door and announce himself, get his pass card, exchange the requisite light banter, meet with Prosser's team and find out what was going on. Had he done that today, bag and baggage, someone would immediately have sorted out a place for him to stay. To then disappear into the grey, virtual murk he preferred would have been difficult.

Tomorrow night he'd worm his way into Gold's systems and start to check out his new idea for Carmaggedon. If that went well, he might be in a position to get off a message to the Green X Group right away.

He plodded back up the outside steps to where he had left his bicycle. He had his sleeping bag strapped to the cross bar and Beauty's box on the back carrier. He undid the bungees around the large box and, awkwardly in the dark and with the box in his arms, inched his way back down the steps.

He positioned Beauty's little table near the power points and carefully stabilised its legs with folded-up papers from one of the bundles. Then he opened her box and placed her gently on the table. He pulled her lamp out of his rucksack, unfolded it and plugged it in. Only when it lit did he breathe a contented sigh. Finally he fetched his bike. He retrieved his sleeping bag from the cross-bar and made his bed on top of the papers he had retained for the purpose. He made one final trip down the dusty corridor with a side panel from one of the dismantled desks and blew dust over his footprints.

He'd slept on the Convoy-coach, and had wasted a lot of the day orientating himself and waiting for dark. He was glad now to be out of sight. His body clock said it was time to start work, but he unpacked his sleeping bag anyway, crawled inside it and did a deep breathing exercise to exorcise the unusual excitements of his day. A very few minutes later he was asleep.

While he slept an e-mail marked <**urgent priority**>, arrived on the Reception screens of media groups and governments world-wide. It had somehow managed to avoid everybody's spam filters. It read:

Wake up Planet Earth!

It's a gift to be simple, it's a gift to be free.

You think you are free. You think you are safe in your personalised transport bubbles. You think you are in control. You are not.

We will free you from the tyranny of personal transport.

We seek harmony with the rhythm of the world.

Green X Group

Most of the receiving operators took one look at the circulation and e-binned it as spam - spam often came with a priority tag. One or two briefly considered it more seriously. But e-threats from obscure terrorist groups were more common than new lottery schemes – and the message gave very little to go on. Security protocols scanning the message threw up only two keywords – 'free' and 'tyranny' - and were unable to link them to any recognised, newsworthy, problem. The message contained no overt threat of violence. One or two bored receivers in the news media passed it to an underutilised junior reporter as potential filler material. A few of the more conscientious government data processors filed it as deep background.

3

3.1

Lox Tuthill was tired. The trouble with information was that there was always more – investigating one strand always led to others, the long fingers of which stretched out and out, finally leading on to a completely different topic, maybe one that he'd been working on the previous week, maybe one that might be useful in the future, or maybe one that just caught his interest. And news nets gobbled up vast amounts of information. They needed to renew content at least every half hour – if only with one story ('this just in'). Keeping his clients fed made him feel like a zoo-keeper constantly scaring up tons of good quality fruit and veg to keep the residents bright-eyed and bushy-tailed.

He'd been trawling and sifting for eighteen hours straight. Apart from a couple of human interest fillers most of what he'd put together for his patrons had been statistics. Some of these left something to be desired, insofar as he'd found some topics that were quite interesting and made up the figures that he applied to them. It really didn't matter. Nobody was going to check his sources. He could have done the work in a couple of hours, nobody would have been any the wiser. If anyone wanted to know where he'd got the information they'd have to spend eighteen hours of their own time tracking where he'd been, what he'd sampled. People had an endless curiosity about statistics: 'there are more miles of canal in Birmingham than there are in Venice.' 'One in eight British couples get married abroad.' '14% of Coca Cola drunk in Britain is consumed at breakfast.' And so Lox kept his beasties fed.

Lox loved information. He couldn't let it alone. He could see why reporters were classed along with whores and lawyers as one of the three oldest professions. He really got off on the deliciousness of *knowing* – and the greater delight in *telling*. The only thing that nagged at him, particularly at times like this when his eyes were burning and his back ached, was that it would be nice, once in a while, to get his information from something other than a computer screen.

He rubbed his eyes, then leaned back and stretched. A couple of vertebrae clicked back into place. He'd just check his messages, in case there was something interesting.

There were 27 messages. Six were from friends, twelve were regular reports, three looked like spam (how the hell were they still getting past his guard-dogs?), five were bills. One was marked <**urgent priority**>. He opened it.

He was disappointed to see that it was only a forward from BBC-Sky-M. Their relationship had often been mutually useful: they knew his penchant for the quirky, he knew which statistical fillers they wanted before they knew themselves. Something had been dumped into the file - an automatic gather - 61 times. It wasn't spam, not exactly. Lox flicked briefly through the mailees' addresses: governments sites; media ditto – the whole world had received this by the look of it, but only at reception level; there were no named recipients. Someone had been keen to have whatever it was taken notice of. The work involved in pulling together a mailing list of this size was considerable. But having gone to that much trouble, whoever had sent it hadn't gone the extra mile and personalised the addresses. Odd.

He opened the message.

Interesting, possibly. Hadn't he been taught the Green Cross Code at school? Something told him that these people had a rather different ethos.

He set up a background check on this Green X Group. They were probably just another set of cranks, but a little more connect time wouldn't hurt.

Search running, Lox stood up and set about re-establishing blood flow to his nether regions. Slaving over a hot computer for eighteen hours was nearly as conducive to deep-vein thrombosis as air travel. Standing up he realised that his guts were cramped into knots. When had he last eaten? He really ought to take better care of himself. To get rid of the pins and needles in his feet he bounced across the room to his bath cubby and chugged back some Refluxess. Was he more hungry than tired? Should he eat first, or sleep? His window wall was polarised; he'd blanked it when he'd started the session. He told the windows to clear. Daylight; a bright sunny morning. It had been sunny when he'd started work the previous afternoon. He felt disorientated, as if time had stolen a march on him – it was a depressingly familiar feeling. He looked out and down, seeking something to prove when he was. Three floors below somebody was walking towards the front of his building, looked up and waved. Lox waved back. He had no idea who it was. It hadn't helped.

The machine beeped at him. It had finished its check. He went back to his work station. Interesting. There were a lot of blocks set up here, a lot of red herrings and dead ends. If he wanted to know who had sent the message he would need to spend serious time on it. In his, considerable, experience, people didn't cover their tracks so completely unless they had something to hide. This might be for real. He felt a flutter in his belly which might be a further complaint from his irritated bowel, or the true excitement of a journalist who was on to something. Compiling statistics was, after all, only something he had been doing while waiting for a proper job to come along.

3.2

It was half past eight in the evening of a very long day and Sara had had her hands in the fume cupboard since lunchtime. That morning the mice had died.

In Sara's experience there was nothing like a little light dissection to take your mind off your missed lunch and overdue supper. She was just opening up the last mouse. Not a squeamish woman, what she had found inside them had, nevertheless, made her guts crawl. She had no idea why their targeting had been so far off, but it was: the nanites were attacking healthy organs as well as diseased ones. The speed with which they did so was awe-inspiring. The team had come up with nothing that could be tested on a human being. In fact, she didn't see any point in testing on mice again in the near future. And all Teddy Goldstein had was the near future.

Sara was furious. Everybody was working at full stretch, putting in eighteen hour days, except Gates bloody Hanford. Akemi was writing up his experiments with Crocodilia stem cells – which had potential, if they had five years to refine it instead of four weeks.

The NanoGen material had looked helpful, but the final leap wasn't forthcoming. The person closest to that research was, of course, Gates. When she had hired him he had intimated that pulling the right conclusions out of the files would be a doddle. But nothing, absolutely nothing, had happened in the three weeks that they'd been working with the figures. The breakthrough they needed was as elusive as ever.

She'd done the eighteen hour days herself – hell, she'd done twenty four hour stretches – interrogating the data from Gold's and NanoGen, running it this way and that, until even the basics didn't make sense any more and the numbers floated through her uneasy dreams when she tried to sleep. She had known from the start that she needed Gates to make the project a success – and she'd certainly acquired his services in theory. But where was the bastard?

His workstation was unused, his presence rare. Personnel didn't appear to have an address for him on file, he didn't answer his comms. Since their first and only f-2-f conversation-cum-interview those wasted two weeks ago she'd hardly seen him – and then only when she was packing up to go home and he was starting for the day. Shift work was one thing, but this was … odd. It was also unfair – she'd promised Teddy that she could help her if they got Gates, and Gates had promised that he could do it, and had gone to the trouble of bringing his illegally obtained research. Why the hell had he done that if he didn't intend to do any work once he arrived? It was a mystery to Sara. She'd never led a research team before. This was a big step up for her, potentially. Now she could see her career about to crash and burn for a second time.

She dry-iced the dead mice, just in case there was still a functioning nanite in one of them, and put them in the lead-lined disposal container. The mice hadn't needed to be done tonight. She'd stayed, hoping that Hanford would put in an appearance. Evening was usually the time he was spotted. Whether that was because he was waiting for everybody else to leave before he arrived, or whether he just worked better at night she didn't know. If he would only show up she would ask him.

What sanctions could you use against someone like Hanford? He'd been hiding in the virtual world for so long that it was quite possible he was unable to function any more in the real one. If she leaned on him too hard he might just disappear.

And then where would they be?

3.3

Teddy got out of bed and made it as far as the chair in her little lounge. She had had a pulmonary bleed the previous evening. It had frightened Ek and Rory half to death when she had started choking and spitting blood half way through dinner. It had frightened her as well: she had never got used to this, most disgusting, aspect of her disease. Every bleed reminded her forcefully that time was short. She might drown in her own blood at any time. She had tried to keep the panic out of her face as they had bundled her upstairs to the blessed oxygen, had tried to be calm when the doctor came and did her best to stabilise the situation. Teddy's pillow was a mess this morning and she had been desperate to get away from the sight and smell of her own blood.

The journey from bed to sofa had seemed endless. She hadn't even detoured via the window. The relentless rolling majesty of the sea and the incongruity of the off shore wind farm whirling away on the horizon held no attraction for her today. The window was open and a sweet May breeze came through it. Unfortunately she was past being helped by fresh air: the oxygen cylinder was set up beside her chair. She reached her goal and buried her face in the mask greedily. She was resisting hospitalisation, or the invasion of white-clad nurse clones such as had tended her father the previous year. But she knew one or other of these scourges was maybe only days away. If Prosser didn't come up with something bloody soon …

The speed and discretion with which Prosser had set up the project was impressive. One floor of The Works – already a Clean Space – had been refurbished in little more than a week. Because it was a sterile environment they could categorise it a Restricted Area. That had been useful. It kept the rest of The Works staff out. Inside that space Prosser was queen. Nobody went in without her say-so, and permission was not forthcoming. Security was vice-tight.

To support Hanford Sara had put together a small team, who had begun to arrive even before the premises were ready. She had obtained Ylena Malinina Guba from a hospital in St Petersburg which had been very keen on the potential medical uses of Nanonics. Ylena had done some very interesting work in the area. Sara had re-hired the two best of Gold's old Nanonics team: Karol Slovensky had been working as an IT tech in a pizza factory on the outskirts of Edinburgh, Frankie Henri had been considering her options in Lille. They had both jumped at the chance to get back in the game. To broaden their options she had persuaded Watanabe Akemi to give them six months of his time. He was a bio-engineer from Japan who had worked in cloning and could manipulate DNA with the facility that a chef employs with ingredients. Sara had also creamed off the two best robotic engineers from the in-house team, Kurt and Adrijana. That made eight. Ancillary lab technicians and data-crunchers brought the strength of the team up to fourteen. Prosser had been so positive about Hanford's contribution that Teddy had been hopeful. The team was working at best speed, using the research abandoned the previous year by Gold's and the NanoGen material as their starting point. Only Teddy, Hanford and Prosser knew how the NanoGen material had been obtained.

Despite the urgency and enthusiasm evident on their floor, Teddy knew that the team, and even Prosser, still had worries about resurrecting Nanonics. People not only feared it *per se*, they also feared what might be done with it should it become available to terrorists. So many cuckoo branches of strange belief systems existed around the world now. What couldn't one of them do with a phial of destructive nanites? But Nanonics was, to use an old tag, her last best hope. Who knew, her determination might even bring controlled use of Nanonics back into the main-stream. And anyway, she had her get-out-of-jail-free card: if the worst came to the worst she would just die on them.

Prosser had her team working on microbial solutions too. Brain-stem cell research had been continued in a desultory way in Japan after Nanonics hit the skids. It wasn't Prosser's field, but Akemi was investigating the use of microbial peptides derived from crocodile tissue, and they were pursuing that in parallel.

But Teddy hadn't heard from Prosser in nearly a week. A week was, for Teddy, a very long time. Why hadn't she been in touch? Teddy suspected the worst.

Prosser was comming now. For once Teddy was prepared to use the vid facility – she needed the extra clues that seeing Prosser's face would give her.

'The team has something for you. Try not to get your hopes up. How do you want to play it? You ought to come in, really. We've set up a room here for you.'

Teddy had been dreading this. The memory of the hospital cot in which her father had died, with its steel bars and bleeping machinery, remained very sharp. It seemed to her that once they got you into one of those things the likelihood was that you weren't going to get out of it alive. But here was hope - a faint hope. If it didn't work she could always come home.

But she knew that wasn't so. Once she was in there, she was in. She might come out walking, healthy, cured; or she might come out in a box. Either way it was decision time.

'Is it nano or bio?'

Prosser hesitated before replying.

'Crocodilia. But it's good. It's been scoring a 65% success factor in tests. The basic structure is quite new. It came out of America via Japan last month. Akemi's contacts back home mentioned it and he tracked it down. We've acquired their data under licence and he's been massaging it night and day to try and get it to give us what we need.' There was a long pause. Teddy could almost hear Prosser wondering how honest she should be with her patient, then: 'I think you should try it. The … other route doesn't seem to be moving as fast as we'd hoped. This may at least give you some temporary remission while I try and put some heat under Hanford.'

It sounded as if Hanford was to be thoroughly roasted. It was a vaguely amusing image.

'And you want to try it on your guinea pig?' Teddy couldn't keep the irritation out of her voice. Extract of crocodile brains was not what she had signed on for. Prosser sighed. Teddy detected the tiniest signs of exasperation in her friend.

'Is there nothing from Hanford?'

'No. To be frank he hasn't been the force I thought he'd be. He seems ... preoccupied. Or perhaps he just can't hack working conventionally any more. He comes in when everybody else is leaving for the night – and they aren't doing that before nine in the evening – and he's not sharing his results like he should. I'm beginning to wonder if he's as good as his reputation. Or perhaps he's just burned out. It happens.'

'Well, find somebody else, then.' That came out sharper than she'd meant it to.

Prosser stared at her intently across the miles.

'Hanford was the best of all of us. I got Frankie and Kurt to come back because they couldn't find proper work – and they were the best of Gold's team. The sort of people we want are hard to get hold of, as I've said before. If they've been able to rebuild their careers they won't give you the time of day when you say the N word. We're offering very generous packages, but money isn't the issue.' Prosser paused for a moment and then asked gently, 'do we really have time to look for another Hanford?'

Teddy thought for a few moments. 'I haven't met him. Maybe I should. Maybe it would make a difference.'

'If you think so, by all means. He's a queer fish though, I don't know that appealing to him is going to make anything happen.'

'Well it can't hurt, can it?'

'No, it can't. Do you want to come here or should I ship him up to you?'

Teddy thought some more. She hadn't been outside her apartment for over a fortnight. Despite her miserable history in this castle, it was the closest thing she had to a home. She feared the steel bars of the hospital bed awaiting her at the facility. She feared the medical procedures Prosser would perform on her. But she feared the death that she could feel inside her more.

There was, of course, a subtext to Prosser's enquiry. If Teddy said she would go to Edinburgh she was, if no more than tacitly, agreeing to try Prosser's treatment. But if she went in to see Hanford, then she'd be doing something practical. This was what her father would have done and, after all, she was only carrying out his final wishes. She needed to be doing *something*. And, as long as she was in Edinburgh anyway, she'd let them shoot her full of crocodile extract on the off-chance that it might do some good.

'I'll come down.'

'OK. When?'

Teddy swallowed hard, hoping to alleviate the lump in her throat. It brought on a coughing fit. When it had passed she realised she had decided on rather more than a visit to The Works.

'Straight away. As soon as Ailsa can organise a jetpod.' She had few secrets from Sara Prosser, so she added. 'I shan't be coming back here. Whatever happens now I'll stay in Edinburgh. Not in the facility, not yet anyway. I'll stay at Millerfield Place. Talk to Dr Choudhry at the hospital and then get someone over there to set up what I'll need. You can try your cure on me as an out-patient. I'm not ready for the steel rat trap yet.'

'OK. I'll sort all that.' Prosser smiled for the first time during the interview. 'You're lucky Hanford isn't already in residence. I did offer it to him as lodgings, but he said he was already fixed up.' There was just a beat while Prosser sought the right words to frame her next question. 'Would you like some company?'

Teddy made a small dismissive noise.

'Well, you can't be there on your own. And I suspect you'd throw things at a nurse. If you throw them at me, I shall throw them back.'

Teddy grimaced.

'I like to get to know my patients, guinea pigs, call them what you like. You're a strange one – Teddy Goldstein and her remarkable mission. I'd like to get to know you better.' Prosser gave it another beat before she said, 'we'll eat pizza at midnight and have girlie chats.'

Teddy's snort of laughter brought on another coughing fit. She waved a smiling Sara off the v-link and commed Ailsa. Teddy knew Sara had manipulated the situation to provide the result she wanted. But the thought of pizza and girlie chats somehow wasn't as repulsive as Teddy had expected. Well, the pizza was, perhaps.

3.4

The streets of Edinburgh weren't as clogged with traffic and pollutants around the clock as the streets of London, but they were bad enough. And every vehicle contained at least one pair of eyes. Gates kept to the shadows.

Tonight he would finally *do* something, instead of wishing and scratching pathetically at his enemies' paintwork and sending e-threats.

Tonight he was going to try out a real weapon against the internal combustion engine.

He pedalled slowly past the entrance to the underground car park of the Balmoral Hotel. The hotel's netsite claimed that the car park was secure, but a glance inside revealed that it was only secured against the illicit removal of cars. The security guard's little booth between the entry and exit booms only looked onto the exit: they weren't interested in what went in, only what vehicles came out. The booms were no barrier at all to somebody wanting to enter or exit on foot. Good.

It was around three in the morning – late enough that the night guard was reading his paper, comfortably settled for the night, expecting neither customers nor trouble. If the man was supposed to patrol he showed no sign of doing so any time soon.

Gates made a left, and stopped at the top of Waverley steps. The steps ran the length of the block which was occupied by the Hotel and Waverley Market. The mall was closed and locked. The steps would be unused at this hour; he could stash his bicycle at the bottom, out of sight. The steps would provide his escape route. He looked around for the CCTV cameras. There was one at the top. There was certain to be another at the bottom, and he must be careful not to miss any others in between. He pulled out his Super Soaker: point and shoot. A satisfying arc of paint blinded the camera. He'd got good at this: he'd had plenty of practice. He leaned his bike against the handrail near the top of the steps then made his way cautiously down the steps, Super Soaker carried commando-style, hunting cameras.

Satisfied that he'd got the lot, he dumped the dripping Super Soaker into the plastic bin-liner that he'd brought for the purpose. Then he went back for his bike, carried it to the bottom of the steps and chained it to the handrail at the bottom. Then he pulled on a headband fitted with a caver's hands-free flashlight, so that he could see to make the rest of his preparations. He retrieved the Super Soaker from its sack, quickly wiped off the paint dribbles and put the rag back in the bin-liner which he stowed in his pack. Next he re-filled and re-primed the water-rifle and shoved it into his backpack as far as it would go. The rest of the things he would need were already distributed in his pockets, especially … He felt around in his jacket pocket. Of course it was still there. He resisted the temptation to pull it out and check it one last time. Either it would work, or it wouldn't. He switched off his flashlight.

He began to work his way back round the block, up North Bridge and round the corner onto Princes Street, returning to the Balmoral's underground garage entrance. He checked that everything was as it had been half an hour before on his first ride-by. The guard was still reading. In the distance Gates could hear happy, drunken Scottish voices, but they didn't seem to be coming his way.

Slipping from shadow to shadow Mr Invisible quickly insinuated himself under the car park's entry barrier, then made his way down the ramps to the lowest of the three levels. He crouched by a wall, and got his bearings. The place was full of big, shiny machines, designed to demonstrate that their owners could afford to consume conspicuously. Ideal. He located the CCTV cameras: point and shoot. Moving into the first, disabled, camera's field of vision he looked around for the next one. He only needed to take out half a dozen. It was soon done. He hadn't been able to resist the temptation to put green paint in the water-rifle. He did manage to refrain from spraying a big green X on the wall. Hubris was what got you caught. The time would come for that kind of message.

The park was cavernous and magnified the slightest sound. He walked on cautiously until he was beside the haunch of largest, shiniest car within his surveillance-free zone. He pulled a phial out of his pocket. He couldn't resist holding it up for a moment. The contents of the phial stirred, glinting silver in the dim strip-lighting. Good. Quietly and gently, so as not to set off the car's alarm, he pried open the petrol filler flap and picked the lock of the cap beneath. The mesh some six inches down designed to prevent impurities getting in with the petrol wouldn't prevent the introduction of what he had in mind – it was far too coarse for that. He tipped a little of what was in the phial into the tank, tapping gently on the little glass tube with his index finger, as if he was salting a boiled egg. He repeated the process with a representative sample of the most luxurious cars in the garage within his dead zone.

He heard a driver operate the boom three floors above him. The car came slowly down the ramps towards him. He hunkered down behind his last victim. The car went past, looking for a vacant space. Gates watched while the driver got out of the car and set its alarm, then walked towards the lift which would take him up into the hotel. The lift doors clonked faintly as they closed. Gates realised he had been holding his breath. Time to go.

He trotted silently up the entrance ramp and swung under the barrier. When he rounded the corner onto Waverley steps he couldn't contain himself. He punched the air and let out a whoop: it had begun.

Time to send the world another message. Time to let them all know that he was serious.

3.5

Another of those curious Green X Group messages had been gathered into Lox's in-box. This one read:

> Wake up Planet Earth!
>
> Your emancipation from motor vehicles is at hand.
>
> Look to the streets of Edinburgh.
>
> You have been warned.
>
> Green X Group

Lox had chased the ISP of the previous message without result. Although his failure had just made him more curious, other things had crept into his schedule and he'd left the Green X people on one of his many back burners. Just in case the point of origin of this message was any easier to nail, he set his tracking algorithm onto it again.

But this time he wasn't going to let it go. Something so well hidden. Something so bizarre. Something was up. What was in Edinburgh? And who might be prepared to stump up his expenses so he could go and find out?

Lox checked his bank accounts. There was barely enough spare in there to take him to Edinburgh under his own steam. He always seemed to have no money, although he also seemed never to have the time to spend any. When his pension, mortgage, health plan, local and national taxes, and the payments on his credit cards – that were always somehow maxed out – had been sucked out of his account every month, there seemed to be an awful lot of month remaining and no money for stuff, like – oh, taking a neighbouring, female hive dweller out for a meal. Lox was fond of football. The MK Dons home ground was less than a mile away. There were always tickets available. But the tickets cost more than the monthly payments on his mortgage, so that was one more place he never went. He stayed home, and crunched statistics. Christ, there ought to be something more to life. A trip to Edinburgh, for instance, would make a very nice change.

Lox knew very well that an Editor will take a story much more seriously if he has already invested something in it. It was a slow news week: he'd been trying to pry something interesting out of the ether for eighteen hours. The nets were struggling – in the past hour he'd seen a story posted about a fat puppy found wedged in a drain, one about a woman who'd had her jaw wired shut and had still not lost any weight (it turned out that she'd been putting chocolate bars through her food processor and then sucking them through a plastic tube that she'd wedged between her teeth), and a tired old rehash of the latest climate change scare. The nets were, in effect, empty. No editor likes an empty net.

It only took three calls before Lox found someone willing to invest. Gray Gardner at RDonLine was more prepared than most to look favourably on articles dealing with the peculiar. Lox remembered providing 'cockroaches ate my baby's toes' for him the previous year. Gardner had been grateful. He reminded Gardner of his track record: would he consider …? He would. The Xs weren't great – but then, in all probability, nor was the story. But the prospect of doing actual reporting in the real world made Lox's blood begin to circulate once more. He was going on assignment!

Revitalised, Lox set his decrypter to track down the message's point of origin. By the time he'd shuttled up there the machinery should have some news for him. His irritable bowel reminded him that he hadn't eaten in almost twenty four hours. Since he wasn't going to get any sleep, he'd better eat something and see if that helped the cramps in his gut. He dialled a pizza and then started picking through the clothes which littered the floor of his room, trying to find something clean enough to be worth packing.

3.6

Later that morning Gates dragged himself heavy-eyed from his nest of paper bundles and scanned the local news nets eagerly. His activities in the Balmoral's car park had gone unnoticed, unremarked. He quickly realised why: something had happened in the United States.

To get anything but the most anodyne reports from America now was rare. People were fearful of what went on behind the McCurtain. At the end of the Second Gulf War the US had withdrawn from the Middle East, not as a righter of wrongs and a purveyor of whuppass, but as a nation with too many of its young men lost without gain. The citizens of America expected more bang than that for their buck. When the lists of those killed in Iraq moved from tens into hundreds and then into thousands the demonstrations had begun to outnumber the yellow ribbons. While American Moms and Dads campaigned to get their children back – and were being beaten with nightsticks and doused with water cannon for their impertinence – American civil liberties took a mortal blow. The European Union had been furious about the whole thing: the chemical weapons never found, the American friendly fire, the torture (which gave everyone involved a bad name), the exorbitant cost of the war extorted from United Nations member states, the US appropriation of Iraqi oilfields, the lucrative contracts for reconstruction allocated only to US corporations.

The US had professed itself sick of all the carping, picked up its ball, went home and shut down its borders in 2010. Trade agreements were annulled, US import tariffs rocketed. The most powerful nation on the planet went into a sulk from which, nearly thirty years later, it had never recovered.

What had seeped out of America since then had been amplified by movies, dissected endlessly by the press – Fortress America wasn't standing for any more international back-stabbing. The next nation that wanted a piece of the US had better be prepared to pay a high price for it. Star Wars was back on, chemical and biological weapons were in development, the American nuclear capability trebled. If there was a way to create mayhem in the world, the world believed that the Americans were working on it.

And now, it seemed, a WMD under development in the USA had gone rogue on them.

Gates should have been upstairs at his official work-station, adapting the silver darlings he had used in the Balmoral's garage for use against his employer's tuberculosis. Instead he spent the rest of the morning and most of the afternoon cruising the newsnets, trying to find out what was at the bottom of the American crisis. A certain word kept turning up: a word which, on its own, was guaranteed to throw the media into a frenzy. When seen in conjunction with 'America' the word was causing complete hysteria on the nets. The word was 'Nanonics'.

This was a good thing for Gates. If fear of Nanonics was, once again, going to become a pandemic, then his actions with the petrol would gain a notoriety out of all proportion to their actual destructive capability – which was, so far, small.

However, that the American snafu should be jamming the nets today was irksome. He had been relying on the local nets to tell him whether what he had put into the petrol tanks last night had had the desired effect. Now, with every net full of Nanonics trouble that he hadn't started, there was nothing for it but to go round to the Balmoral himself and try to find out. Ms Goldstein's cure would have to wait a little longer.

3.7

Lox shuttled in to Edinburgh late in the afternoon. He wasn't hungry. His mistreated digestive system was still working on the pizza he'd stuffed down himself before hurrying out to catch the plane. It didn't matter how often he did it, or how short the trip, he never liked flying. The flight and the pizza together had turned his gut into one hard, knotted ball of pain. He chomped a mouthful of mints, which was the only antacid he'd been able to find inside the airport.

He got the Link into Waverley Station. Trying to ignore the cramps in his belly, he waited in line outside it for a cab and, when it was finally his turn, asked to be taken to the cheapest hotel in a central location. Five minutes later he was getting out again in Shandwick Place. He could have walked it and saved himself the fare, but what the hell – if this was the story his instincts told him it was, somebody would be paying him a great deal of money.

Up in his room he unpacked his compad from its nest of slightly soiled underwear in his carry-on. He set up a local newsnet search based on the message from the Green X Group and, while it was working, scanned the rest of the morning's news.

This was new. Something had happened in America. He'd always felt that the Nanonics saga wasn't finished yet. Who knew what the Yanks were capable of any more – nobody had been allowed in there for years. Those who'd managed to get out had nothing but horror stories about Fortress America. That was one reason why the world was so spooked by nano-technology – everyone was afraid the Americans were still working on it.

One news item gave a link. The link turned out to be a posting from a ex-employee of the lab which had had the … trouble. There had been some suggestion, apparently (although not communicated outside the USA) that the ex-employee had been involved in the melt-down (melt-down?!) in some way. The poor sod was trying to clear his name. When the authorities over there realised that he'd managed to get his posting past the security lock-down there was going to be even more hell for him to pay.

We told them what safeguards the process needed, but they skimped on the set-up costs. There's nothing wrong with Nanonics – its not going to eat cities whole, or people, or anything. It can't if proper controls are in place: it only destroys what it's programed to take in and reproduce with. It was just sloppy programing that led to the accident with the monkeys last year. That wasn't even our company. They called us in as fire fighters. We were able to shut the nanites down fine that time. This time it was poor shielding, pure and simple. But before we could cauterise the problem, somebody had called the National Guard. Then the media got a tip off and were all over the place like, well, nanites.

This was going to be big. Damn. The only good thing about it was that it would probably have most other investigative reporters scrabbling for non-existent US visas, leaving him free to get on with … whatever it was. He needed to concentrate on finding his own story. It was too late to get on board this American thing.

His compad couldn't find anything local about the Green X Group. Frustrated, he pulled up his tracker algorithm and had a look to see how it was getting on with breaking down the their encryption protocols. He had to catch a break soon, surely. The machine told him Estimated time remaining to complete task: three hours. Hellfire. Whoever had set this up was good – very good.

While he waited, he tried a bit of deduction. Something in Edinburgh: something that had already happened. He lay down on the bed while he pondered. When the machine was through with the protocols he'd try the local Nets. He could …

When he woke up it was early evening and the pains in his gut were worse. He knew the only way to appease the cramps was to eat, so he went in search of food. The compad had finally finished its work on the Green X Group's encryption protocols. He tucked it into his pocket – the hotel was a dive, and he didn't want to chance losing it. After he'd appeased his irritable bowel he'd have a serious look at the results it had for him.

In deference to his internal plumbing, which was still objecting to the last fast food he'd eaten on the run, he decided to have a sit down meal. Everything open down his end of Princes Street was all burgers and pizzas. So he worked his way outwards. It would do him good to walk a little and would certainly be no hardship. This was an elegant city. It was a long time since he had done anything other than crunch numbers. Number-crunching didn't involve exercise. It was, indeed, so long since he had walked anywhere that he kept to the flat as much as possible. This narrowed his options considerably as not much of central Edinburgh provided level walking. As usual the pure, physical monotony of the action began to unknot his gut. Why didn't he do this more often?

He worked his way slowly southeast in the general direction of Holyrood Palace, through the pleasant formality of Princes Street Gardens with the glowering mass of the Castle rearing up on his right. The path wended its way up to The Mound and, taking the down-hill option, he meandered on to the George IV Bridge. At the bottom of the bridge he came to a crossroads and, as he was trying to decide which street looked most promising for a man in need of a meal, he heard music. This struck him as a bit odd this early in the evening. So he walked towards the source. Sandy Bell's: a pub, open all day. Here he could get alcohol – short-term balm for an irritable bowel – and, possibly, food too. He went in.

He was too early for food, but not by much, so he decided to wait. The menu board promised haggis and 'neeps, which sounded interesting, if potentially unwise for a man with digestive troubles. He ordered a pint – funny how ordering half a litre had never caught on – and went to sit near the band. For a few minutes he did no more than drink deeply of his beer and listen to the eight or ten instrumentalists playing diddley-I music. At last the pain which had accompanied him the length of Britain disappeared completely. Amazing the power music (and alcohol) had to do that.

From the state of them, it appeared that the musicians had been there all afternoon. It was with some surprise that Lox realised it was Saturday, which made a day's inebriated music-making more plausible. A cautious enquiry revealed that this was the regular Saturday lunch-time session which had, as usual, run over. At last the players began to pack away their instruments and disperse. The last two to go were a fiddle player and the harpist. The harp was beautiful; small enough to be held on the lap, but intricately carved. The girl who was packing it away slid it carefully into its padded case. The other girl snapped her violin case shut and sat back down.

'Did you hear what's happened at the Balmoral?'

'What?' said the harpist, still wrestling to pull the zip of the case round her instrument. The fiddle player stretched over and held it steady for her.

'When the toffies came to get their Mercs and Porsches out this morning none of them would start.'

Both girls laughed.

It seemed that eavesdropping was something that, for a journalist, was like learning to ride a bicycle - you never forgot how. Cautiously he fumbled his compad out of his jacket pocket and tried to pretend that he was checking his diary as he started to make notes.

The fiddle player went on.

'My cousin Callum works in their North British bar. He says the garage has been full of police all day. Nobody's been able to work out why the cars won't go. Not one of the them has a mark on it and none of the alarms went off. They've tested the tanks for sugar and it's not that, but they reckon it must be vandalism all the same. Callum says that Alastair - that's the night guard on the park – is in shit city because of it. Most of the people with faecked cars were supposed to be checking out today but 'cos their shiny motors are all no go, there's no room for the cars of guests arriving today. The manager's mad as hell.'

Still giggling the two girls put on their coats and left.

While he eavesdropped, Lox called up the message from the Green X Group on his compad and put it in a split screen beside the notepad where he was furiously scribbling down the basics of the girls' conversation. When they'd gone he stared at it until his haggis and 'neeps arrived. *Look to the streets of Edinburgh.* Or, perhaps, their car parks?

Lox put away his compad when his haggis arrived. No need to rush. He'd eat – remembering to chew, like the doctor'd told him – have another pint, then walk up to the Balmoral and see if they had a room for tomorrow night, stranded motorists notwithstanding. It still might be nothing, of course, but at the very least there'd be Room Service and a mini-bar, all on expenses.

And whether they had a room or not, he would interview the owners of the mysteriously non-starting cars.

3.8

After supper, Lox strolled up George IV Bridge, down The Mound and back up Princes Street to the Balmoral. There he got what he could from the unfortunate motorists. It wasn't much – two told him to f-off, the rest knew nothing more than that they were stranded, but it was an extra line for his copy. Somewhat under-whelmed by his own rusty interviewing technique and the information it had elicited, Lox decided to have a nightcap in the North British, to see if cousin Callum might still be working. Sure enough, the two musicians who had been in Sandy Bell's were there, chatting to the barman. Despite having been immured with his statistics for so long, Lox was a capable socialiser. It didn't take him long to brush off his skills and introduce himself. He bought each of them a drink and started to pick them clean of information. They seemed flattered to be talking to a genuine journalist. Lox found himself affecting the sort of cigarette induced squint that might have been seen in an old movie like Front Page. Ridiculous – cigarettes hadn't been allowed in public places for more than thirty years. Nevertheless, it was fun being a genuine journalist again.

There was definitely something odd going on – a Porsche, a Mercedes, two Jaguars, a Roller and four SUVs were still stuck in the garage beneath the bar. They'd had mechanics in, but nothing they did made any difference. The symptoms were the same as if somebody had put sugar in the petrol, but they'd flushed the tanks and put more petrol in and still the cars wouldn't go. Tomorrow they were going to be towed. Tonight the garage was a spider's web of police tape. The owners of the cars affected were threatening to sue the hotel. The hotel was furious and had sacked the night-security man. The night-security man was furious – he said it must have been done by a guest because he hadn't seen anybody in there that shouldn't have been, and how the hell was that his fault?

Lox made frequent trips to the loo so that he could enter all of this into his compad without being noticed. It was nearly one in the morning before the girls gathered their instruments and said goodnight to cousin Callum. There was only one other customer – a funny, dirty-looking little man hunched over half a bitter in the corner by the loo, smiling and muttering to himself. When Callum asked him please to drink up he swallowed the last half inch in his glass and scuttled out into the night ahead of them.

Lox wanted very much to have a look in the Balmoral's garage. Fortunately Callum's car was parked in there and he was going to give the girls a lift. As casually as he could, Lox tagged along.

The four of them walked down the 'out' ramp. The new night guard was in his booth and Callum had to show his parking pass. Callum's car was on the bottom of the three levels, and they were accosted on each level by a stern-looking security man. Callum had to show his pass on each level before the security man would let them continue. When the others were piling into Callum's car, Lox lingered with the security man.

'I heard there was some trouble down here, mate.' This wasn't hard to substantiate, and Lox waved vaguely at the 'do not cross' police tape festooning various of the cars parked on this level.

'That's all cleared up now. Bit of vandalism down here, they say. Whoever it was won't get a second chance. There's someone on each of the levels now, just in case.'

'Is this where it happened, then?'

'Yeh. Third level.'

Lox got out his NUJ card.

'Oh, shit – you're press?'

'That's right, mate. It'd be really helpful to me if I could slip take a closer look.'

'No way.'

'Just a quick one.'

'At this time of night? Hell fire, don't you people have homes to go to? They've already sacked one bloke over this. I don't intend to be number two.'

A fifty euro note appeared in Lox's hand. He held it up so that the guard could see the denomination clearly in the wan lighting.

'Oh for Chrissakes … go on, then.' The note was now in the guard's trouser pocket.

'No hassle. And if anyone asks …'

'You haven't been here. Christ.'

The guard went. Very shortly Lox was standing beside a concentrated cat's cradle of police tape surrounding a Rolls Royce. Moments later another security guard loomed out of the gloom. Another fifty Euros changed hands. The security guard hung around. Perhaps he was worried that Lox was the vandal revisiting. Perhaps he fancied a second crisp fifty. Whatever – his presence was, in fact, quite useful. In the way of security guards (who are all frustrated law enforcers) he had quizzed the police with whom he had overlapped earlier in the evening. He didn't know much but, unlike his colleague, he was keen to share what he did know. Another fifty Euros changed hands.

'See they took out the cameras – here, here, here and three more over there. Fine appreciation of angles. They did two cars right here, and then the others further in – but they didn't stray outside the sight-lines of the cameras they'd fixed. Not yobs, if you ask me – too careful by half.'

'What was it all about then?'

The guard shrugged. 'Search me. They don't pay me to second guess the criminal mind. They only pay me enough to stop them doing it again.'

'Do you mind if I look around for a bit longer?'

'Knock yourself out.' The guard mooched towards the ramp up to the next level.

Gingerly Lox stepped over the police tape. Any proper clues would have been taken away. But there might be something …

Looking up at the vandalised camera above him, Lox had an idea. He called to the guard.

'Can I borrow your flashlight, mate?'

The guard returned and hitched his leg over the tape.

'If anyone sees me down here with you …'

'No hassle. I'll just be a sec.'

Lox shone the light on the camera. In the fitful orangey light of the car park's night lights the paint on the camera had looked like dried blood. But when he shone the whiter light of the flash on it, it looked … green.

Lox hunted around until he found a pool of the paint that was still tacky and stuck his finger into it. Then he held his finger right in front of the flashlight. Yep – definitely green.

It was probably just a coincidence that the vandals had decided to use green paint, but all the same …

Tired but happy Lox trudged back up the ramp to street level and made his way down Princes Street to his bed.

3.9

Teddy was now incarcerated in the Millerfield Place house. Sara had had some changes made so that Teddy would be 'comfortable', as Sara put it. A bed-sitting room had been set up in the dining room on the ground floor next to the downstairs loo. Contrary to her initial pitch on the subject, Sara had engaged a cook and a nurse. Teddy sent them both away: food didn't interest her and she wasn't about to allow some white harpy to give her a bed bath. The day she couldn't wash herself she'd go smelly. The two women didn't hold Teddy's too-bright, vehement glare very long before scuttling upstairs to pack.

After they had gone Teddy carried the stuff she had brought with her laboriously up the stairs to the room at the back which had been hers as a child on the rare occasions that she had been allowed to come in to Edinburgh from Dunster. The last time she had slept here had been when she was brought into town for her father's funeral. And before that, when? For her confinement. More than thirty years. Not a lot of memories, then – and none of them good.

It was a child's room, small and dowdy and the bed looked tiny. But it would do. No way was she sleeping in the dining room: it reminded her too much of her father's last months. She was too exhausted to unpack, let her stuff stay where she had dropped it and lay down on the bed to catch her breath. The bed smelled musty. Nobody had thought to air out in here.

She discovered that Prosser had taken over Theo's old room – a large, airy one at the front overlooking The Meadows. The decoration was tatty and old-fashioned there too. There was plenty of Sara evident in the room, hardly anything of Theo except some of his old ties and a pair of leather man's slippers. How strange. The impact that he'd made on the world had been considerable – but made entirely through Gold's Prosthetics. As a human being he hardly seemed to have existed. Now that he was ghostly Teddy felt less antipathy towards him. Indeed, she felt almost tender towards him, now that he wasn't, any more, actually present.

It hadn't really been his fault: events had conspired against Theo from the moment he decided that he wanted a family. He'd been 64 at the time, and getting round to it so late had obviously made it more likely that things would go wrong. First off he'd had to find a woman to marry. He'd chosen his secretary and had wooed her with what must have been frightening intensity. She'd succumbed quickly and the wedding had been a cursory affair at the city's Registry Office some nine weeks later. All those who attended were given a buffet lunch in The Works canteen and expected to return to their desks in the afternoon – including the bride. She got a night at the Balmoral (Teddy found she couldn't even think about what passions might have been unleashed in that one, luxurious, night) and was then whisked away to the castle at Dunster. She was replaced in the office the following day.

By the time Teddy was born poor Maihri was immured in the castle. Theo didn't entertain, so Maihri didn't. Theo had no hobbies, so there was nothing for them to do together. Maihri waited for her husband to come home at the weekends and they tried to make a baby. This dreary routine continued for more than a year before Teddy was conceived.

And, of course, she should have been a boy. Theo carried some ancient prejudices inside him: he wanted to leave Gold's to his son. When Teddy arrived, healthy and squalling, his disappointment was apparently palpable. But there were no more children. Teddy suspected there had been no more attempts. Her poor mother had had no idea what she had let herself in for when she said 'yes' to Theo. When he'd given in to her blandishments and brought her into Edinburgh for the Millennium Hogmanay celebrations she'd absconded just after midnight with the lounge pianist at the Balmoral and had never been heard of again. The wonder was that the marriage had lasted so long.

Theo had been left with an unwanted daughter to raise. Had Ailsa not been engaged to care for the little girl, who knew what might have happened to her. Ailsa had done her best, but little children – like pets – instinctively know when they're not wanted. Teddy had constantly sought attention from her father. When bringing him her latest sploshy painting hadn't worked she'd tried more drastic measures – setting fire to the drawing room curtains had been one, pepper in his coffee had been another. Superglued door handles on a Monday morning had been a regular occurrence. In some way, Teddy remembered, she thought that if she physically stuck her father to the house he might remain in it, and not spend the week in Edinburgh while she languished at Dunster. Nothing had worked. He had become increasingly irritated by her. Classic syndrome. And classic outcome: having failed to engage him in any way she could measure, she'd run away.

Teddy could see all this now. One could say it was too late. Teddy doubted whether there could ever have been any mending of their relationship while both of them lived. However, now he was dead (and she wasn't) she could see, as from a mountain top, the problems they had failed to solve. It wasn't her fault. But it wasn't his fault either. They just hadn't been a lucky family, nor perhaps had they been a sensible one. Certainly they were very alike. Teddy had been surprised to discover that when she returned to the castle two years ago. Her surprise had been reinforced by the contents of Theo's Will. Now she had very little to do but ponder on how bloody alike they were.

She would much rather have turned out like her mother.

*****

Over the course of that first week Teddy wandered all over the house – she even forced her leaden legs up the tiny boxed staircase to the attics – gleaning what she could of her family's history here. It was a sad old house. It suited Teddy very well.

Every night she commed or texted to Ek. Every night he asked her to switch the vid function on. Every night she intended to do so, and finally have that conversation about what had made her abandon him mere hours after he was born. But every night she made some excuse to keep the vid facility off. She couldn't tell him that tale without seeing his face, which would require her to transmit her own - and her face was such a haggard thing. It became a game, almost, between them. She told him she looked like hell, he said he didn't care. She believed him. The excuse was a feeble one, she knew – but none the less real for all that. She wondered if he knew what she was trying to build up to. But despite wanting to tell him, each evening she wouldn't or couldn't turn on the vid.

The new treatment based on crocodilic microbial peptides that Sara had called her in to try was not working. As soon as Sara had explained what they wanted to try Teddy had known it was futile. The massive doses of genetically engineered croc-extract that they were pumping into her made her nauseous, and had almost completely finished off her digestive system. What remained of Teddy's own feeble defences against her tuberculosis were being destroyed by the powerful antigens contained in the treatment. On the tubercular bacilli in her lungs they had no discernible effect. She felt worse, much worse, than she had when Sara had talked her into coming into Edinburgh. Was that really only a week ago? Sara wouldn't even let her drink alcohol. Trapped in her own past, she trekked slowly round the house day after day and felt the nearness of death in a way that she never had before: palpable, certain.

She was still surprised how strong her will to survive had become since her father's death. Poor Ek must miss him – he'd actually liked the old man. Such strange lives the three of them had had, seldom living in the same house even. Ek was the best of them. He was good for what ailed her. He had wanted very much to come with her to Edinburgh.

Instead they talked every night of the commonplace things: how Dunster Lamb was selling, what Ek should buy Rory for his birthday, the twenty new turbines being added to the off-shore wind farm. Their conversations did not mention the future, nor did they talk about the past.

Teddy had been a month shy of her fifteenth birthday when Ek was born. The next morning she had hitch-hiked down to London, with nothing but a Smart Card stolen from her father and the clothes she had worn to the hospital – the horrid, baggy things her father had considered appropriate. The Smart Card was quickly stopped and she had had to reassess her life, wants, needs. She had slept rough and begged for her food. There was a simplicity about that which appealed to her. Nobody cared about your shame on the street, nobody judged you. And they expected you to return the favour. She grew up on the street – something even having a baby had been unable to accomplish previously.

She'd begun to feel she could stand anything, as long as she didn't have to go back to Dunster. But her new way of life took its toll. She began to need more respite than sleep alone could provide, something to keep the cold and the guilt at bay. She needed highs, and they had to be chemical as there was no happiness inside her to provide them. There was company to be had around a fire with a needleful of oblivion. But bad things happened when the drugs hit; beatings, AIDS, hepatitis, pneumonia. She had sought out her share and more; dared the devil to take her. She had done it out of spite. And fear. She wondered if the person she was then could have been a mother to the boy. She wondered as she wandered round the dusty old house. It had been abandoned too. There was a lot of that in her family.

She had been delivered, like a limp and dirty sack, to the public hospital by the police who had found her. The tattered ID she had retained through thick and thin, to be her single triumph when they came to bury her, betrayed her then. The hospital called her next of kin and Theo – inevitably – had retrieved her and incarcerated her once more in the bosom of her family. That had been two years ago, when she was a raddled hag of forty and the little boy she hadn't seen since he was born was twenty-four years old.

Ek came back, to meet his mother, but the opportunity for her to be that to him was gone. She had wept, then, for what she had lost. Surely she and Ek could never have any relationship that wasn't based on hate? But Ek had immediately offered unquestioning, non-judgemental friendship. That had been a novelty. And a comfort. As the best doctors Theo could buy came and went, she learned to love her son.

The doctors could do nothing to halt the progressive clogging of her lungs. It seemed only just: find love and die. Perhaps it was then that she had changed her mind about wanting to die. She had always wanted the things she couldn't have. She could hear her father's voice saying those very words.

She had intended to call Hanford as soon as she got to Edinburgh. But the time went on and, as every day ended, she found she hadn't done it yet. There were a lot of tests, and the injections which made her feel awful, and meals took forever when someone had prepared you something and sat with you while you tried to eat some of it. There were only the long conversations with Ek in the evenings to look forward to.

In between it all she wandered the house like a ghost. She was absorbed in her past – probably for the last time. She carried on taking her extract of croc like a good girl, when should have put her foot down and stopped it. All the strength she had found when her father died seemed to be dissipating. She was in limbo, waiting for something she couldn't define.

3.10

Gates was still furious. He knew it had worked – he'd risked everything to go up there and check it out. The staff were full of it, the police had been there for days. But the cars in the Balmoral's underground garage that wouldn't start had remained unknown to the world at large. It ground at him, twisting his guts. Nothing. Nothing on any of the news nets. It seemed there was little point in starting Armageddon at the same time as the Americans; they were the more newsworthy and that was the end of it. The nets were still carrying the Nanonics escape in the USA. He'd had enough of the media's lynch-mob mentality the last time Nanonics had made the news.

It wasn't even as if the news was being suppressed because the authorities wanted to avoid panic – there was plenty of hysteria on the nets about the thing in the States, and that had been an accident. Had they even worked out yet what he'd done? Nightly visits to the North British – where he was acquiring almost the status of a regular – confirmed it: his best efforts had produced not so much as a whimper, let alone a bang.

It was seldom that Gates was at a loss, but he was now. He debated with himself whether the Green X Group should issue another bulletin to the world. But what could it say? The first message had said it all, and said it well. Anything he put out now would be a damp squib, a whine – 'didn't you notice …'. And they hadn't: the world had not noticed. Something bigger was required. In Gold's basement Gates began to breed many, many more of his tiny soldiers. The next time he told the world to wake up he wanted to be certain that they paid attention.

3.11

Today Teddy had had to accept that she could no longer make the stairs: it had taken her three quarters of an hour to come down them this morning, and that with a great deal of help from Sara. Tonight Teddy would have to sleep in the hospital cot in the dining room. She was to be reduced to shuffling from bed to chair, chair to bed. Currently she was resting on one of the sofas in the sitting room. Most of the furniture in the dining room – the sideboard, the dining table and its twelve chairs – had been shoehorned in here now to make space for her bed to be set up properly. She felt like a lot in an auction. By the door of the drawing room was an electric wheelchair, delivered this morning and already an essential. Sara was preparing yet another dose of croc extract. To say Teddy was feeling cranky was to understate.

'I don't care. The treatments make me sicker than ever. I'm not taking any more croc shit, and that's final.'

'Look, we're weeks away from producing anything nanonic that we can even think of trying on you. Possibly more than weeks.' Sara looked embarrassed. 'We're working eighteen hours a day, sometimes more. But …

'What about Hanford? I thought he was The Man?' Teddy couldn't keep the petulance out of her voice. Prosser had made her a promise back in March: six weeks, she'd said – 'If I can get this chap to come,

I'm certain we'll have something for you in six weeks'. Teddy ran those words in her head when she lay, sweating and sleepless, through the night listening to her lungs labouring to bring her another dawn. Why did nobody ever keep their promises?

'I'm afraid Gates has been something of a non-event.' Sara looked wretched. 'He's never been a presence about The Works, exactly. And we've hardly seen him at all in the past week. He doesn't answer his comms. I've been to Personnel for his home address, to try and get hold of him there. Would you credit it, they don't have one? I can't believe it. Where the sweet creeping hell is he?'

Teddy pushed the oxygen mask from her face long enough to say;

'I'll mail him. Get him to come here. I'll do it right now.' She pulled the mask back down and reached for her compad. She'd do it before she thought any more about it. She'd been thinking about it for over a week, and that hadn't done any good She sent:

> Urgent we speak.
>
> Come to 3 Millerfield Place any time today.
>
> No show, no more dough.
>
> T Goldstein

If Gates didn't deliver in the very near future … well, the very near future was all that Teddy had left.

3.12

Lox's new room at the Balmoral was a huge improvement over his accommodation in Shandwick Place. The bed was queen-sized and comfortable. The draperies matched the bed cover. The furniture all matched, and there was lots of it to house his few, creased and slightly grubby clothes. There was even a thin-V disguised as a picture of the Castle. Indeed, not only was there a bathroom with an actual bath in it, fluffy towels and lashings of hot water, but also a second, smaller sitting room beyond that, which he was using as his office.

He was hoping that his reason for pushing his expense account with RDonLine into the stratosphere was going to turn into the sort of story that would allow him to stay in places like the Balmoral as a matter of course.

Sitting at the desk in his sitting room he scanned the news nets for today's hotties. The Nanonics scare in the States was still top story.

Some actual facts had filtered out in the last couple of days. The nets were still headlining these facts in rotation, having nothing new and not wanting to let the story die. It was rare, these days, for an American story to get so much net time. But he could see why they were flogging it.

There had been, apparently, something that the press was calling The Meltdown. It had taken three days to contain, and only after the problem had been neutralised had any hard information got out of America. You could choose who you believed: 'government sources', 'laboratory sources' or 'expert sources'. The nub of the matter appeared to be that a surprising number of elements essential to the running of any laboratory contain fluorine. A flawed targeting program had caused a batch of test nanites to seek fluorine and, having found it, to reproduce exponentially and seek more. They had made a fine job of it: no cabling, no semiconductor, no fluorescent light tube, no heating element in the furnaces had escaped them. They even ate the Teflon out of the wall coverings. They destroyed the integrity of their Clean Space in nine and a half hours.

When the Clean Space was broached, alarms began to ring. By that time the nanites had left their own environment and were seeking fluorine in the outside world. Researchers tracked them by following the trail of fluorine depredation. New nanites were programed and let loose in the fluorine-seeking swarm in an attempt to switch them off. Eighteen hours later the lab personnel reported they were confident that all rogue nanites had been rendered inactive. Unfortunately, a couple of hours later a sub-swarm turned up in a nearby power plant which had already been checked for contamination. It had apparently been carried in on a policewoman's shoe. The power plant was shut down, causing a brown-out in the city, and the shut-down remedy re-applied. After that the crisis really did appear to be over. But who knew?

Nobody had been hurt by the nanites themselves, although there were some casualties in the 80,000 or so homes which were reduced to minimal power for nearly twenty-four hours.

While the researchers were still trying to find a way to turn their escapees off three worrying factors had been uncovered by the American press: viz, that most preparation of elemental fluorine is done in China (still a law unto itself); that the original swarm had only set off the alarms because they had started nibbling at the seals on the next door nuclear facility; that a surprising number of manufactured items in everyday use contained fluorine, including cookware, food packaging, motor vehicles, clothing and even hair conditioners.

The swarm had, apparently, been able to sense that the neighbouring lab contained depleted uranium hex fluoride left over after experimentation on nuclear fuels. The netpress made much of the mindless, destructive capabilities of this particular nanite swarm, and of nanite swarms in general. Certainly nobody could countenance nanites interfering with fissionable materials. The press was reporting the mishap as a disaster of potentially global proportions, which was why it was still making headlines around the world. The British press had dusted off a plethora of old, largely manufactured, nanite scares from when Nanonics had been used briefly in the British construction industry. Questions were being asked in the European and British Parliaments and in the Regional Assemblies.

And all Lox was doing was looking at petrol tanks in an underground garage in Edinburgh and trying to connect them with a crank e-mail. His rusty old journalist's intuition told him there was Something Big here. Everyone else thought that the Something Big was in the USA. Shit.

3.13

It was after midnight and Sara was helping Teddy get ready for bed. Teddy was gliding across the hall from the downstairs cloakroom in the wheelchair, pulling the oxygen cart behind her and trying not to bang Sara on the shins with it, when the door bell rang. In the gloomy old house it sounded like a knell. The two women looked at each other. Prosser raised an eyebrow in the gloom.

'Shall I get it?'

Teddy nodded and followed slowly after as Sara waved the hall light on and went to open the door. It must be Hanford.

It was. Sara opened her mouth to speak. Teddy was fairly certain they would be sharp words. She put a hand on her friend's arm and lifted her oxygen mask.

'Go on. I'll be fine.'

Prosser retreated somewhere into the bowels of the house. Teddy motored over to the open door, gripped the big brass door handle and peered out into the night: a pale, skinny, slightly grubby little man stood squinting in the glare of the automatic outside light.

'Come in, please.'

The man stepped inside, just far enough so that she could close the door. The effort made her pant. He made no move to help her.

'Come through.'

She motored towards the sitting room, dragging the oxygen trolley, hoping that he was following her. She was half afraid that he would cut and run, but when she reached the doorway he was still with her. She parked next to her usual nest on one of the sofas, heaved herself out of the wheelchair and flopped amongst the welter of cushions and compad games. Ah, that was better.

'Please,' she panted and gestured at the sofa which faced her own, 'sit.' She leaned across the wheelchair for the gasmask and gulped some oxygen.

He didn't sit. He still looked like some kind of nocturnal animal. His dark eyes were big in a thin face. He hadn't shaved recently. His clothes were sludge coloured, shapeless. She took a last breath through the mask and then took it off for politeness. Now she was certain there was a faint odour coming from her guest.

'Would you like something to drink, to eat?'

He still didn't say anything, but now he sat – perched rather – on the sofa opposite hers. It was as if he comprehended her only at one remove; one step behind.

'Thank you for coming.' At this hour, when normal people would be in bed, asleep. But then, they weren't normal people, he and she. She recognised a kindred spirit: someone driven, who could not take the expected path. She couldn't take her eyes off him.

Somewhere in the back of the house Sara lurked. Teddy was glad of that. There was something about Hanford; a *frisson*. She was completely certain that in front of her sat a very dangerous man.

Now that he was sitting Hanford was staring, at her. This, she felt, would do no harm. Let him see the state she was in before she made any pleas to his better nature. Teddy had become easy with silence. She needed all her breath to stay alive and had none left for chatter. When healthy she had never appreciated how much effort, how much exhalation, went into talking. Talking was a luxury for her now.

Hanford finally said;

'You look like shit.'

'Don't I though.'

No pleas, not yet.

'I didn't realise.'

'No reason why you should.'

'I've been a bit … pre-occupied with … something.'

'Ah.'

They were silent again and studied each other, almost hungrily. Teddy could see something in Hanford under the stubble, shapeless clothes and dirt. Something more than just danger.

'It's all done, actually,' he said. 'I just got … sidetracked and let it go. I can program in the target and start tests tomorrow - tonight, if you like. In a month…'

'I haven't got a month.'

'Dr Prosser won't let anything through that's not been tested.'

Sara was her friend, probably her only friend. Sara had her best interests at heart.

'Bugger Prosser.'

'I know it works. There's another project I've been working on in parallel. That works fine. It's just a switch, a simple switch. The only difference is the target. Would you …?'

'Yes.'

There was another silence. Now, however, they were conspirators. Finally Teddy asked;

'When?'

He was silent for a time and she began to wonder whether he was just bullshitting her.

'Like I said there's only the targeting to program in. We won't test. If you can keep Prosser off my back …' He looked up at her. 'Say three days?'

Three days! After all this time. He had made her come this close to death and in three days …

'Thank you,' she said. 'Thank you.'

She wanted to say a lot more, but words were expensive. She got up and shuffled slowly across the little square of rug between their two sofas, leaving the comfort of the oxygen cylinder. She sat down beside him. The smell of him was stronger. Her move, for all that it had cost her dearly, had been a mistake she could see at once. Her proximity made him uncomfortable. He eased away from her until he came up against the arm of the sofa.

'I'm sorry. You're quite right. I'm infectious. I don't know what made me …'

'I should probably go. I've got a lot of work to do.'

He looked at her as if waiting for permission. She had felt, briefly, at ease with this man, but he couldn't wait to get away from her – that was clear.

'Of course. Don't let me detain you.' It came out formal: icy – something learned from her father.

Then Hanford did a surprising thing. He stretched out his hand towards her face. He had, she noticed, beautiful hands, the fingers long and fine. His nails were dirty, but she would have expected no less, given the state of the rest of him. With the tips of his fingers he just brushed her cheek. The finger ends were firm and warm.

'You are a very beautiful woman,' he said. 'Or, you have been.' There was another silence, then: 'You will be again.'

Nobody had ever called her beautiful, even when she was well. The old mechanisms kicked in automatically. Harshly she said;

'I'm almost a corpse.'

He smiled. It was the first smile she'd seen from him. He had a broad mouth, mobile, and good teeth, very white in his stubbled face. He looked very different when he smiled.

'I'm very good at seeing what could be,' he said. 'Why else would I …'

But he didn't finish the sentence. His fingers drifted away from her face. Dangerous, she reminded herself; he's dangerous. But the smile was a glorious thing and she found herself smiling too. This seemed to please him.

'See?' he said.

Her smile became wry.

'No,' she said. 'I don't look in mirrors any more.'

'Oh, but you will. You will.'

He was excited now and stood up. Now that he might be going – and going to do the work she needed him to do – for some contrary reason she wanted him to stay.

'Are you sure you won't have something to eat?'

'No, I don't need anything. I'll get back to it.'

'Will you keep in touch? Please?'

He started towards the hall, then turned.

'Yes,' he said, then, 'I'll see you soon.' But he made no more definite arrangement than that, just drifted into the gloomy hall and disappeared into the shadows. She heard the door open and close.

She found she was absurdly pleased at the prospect of seeing him again.

4

4.1

Gates returned to his lair in Gold's basement and began to work feverishly. He had slightly misrepresented to his strange employer how near he was to a remedy for her. A week would have been ample: with a week he could do much. But he hadn't asked for a week – he'd said he could do it in three days. The scientist in him regretted that. But he'd never seen anyone so sick. All the same, he really didn't know why he was putting himself out for her like this.

Still, while he was saving Teddy Goldstein he could save the world as well. There was a nice irony in that.

Finally, around dawn, he had to admit that he was too exhausted to do more. He must get a few hours sleep before setting up the crucial targeting parameters for Teddy Gold's tuberculosis.

Before crawling into his paper nest he made a shopping list. There was no time for e-shopping, he would have to go and actually buy the things he needed tomorrow, in daylight, with money. With this scary thought running through his mind he checked Beauty's humidity meter and switched off her daylight lamp. Then he wriggled into his sleeping bag.

4.2

The next afternoon, Gates pedalled the streets of Edinburgh feeling distinctly uncomfortable. He seldom went out at all in the daytime if he could possibly avoid it. However, today he had needs which must be met in actual shops during business hours.

He wasn't used to being among so many people. The skin on the back of his neck crawled when he thought of all the eyes, watching him. Nevertheless, it was for people, *en masse*, that he was shopping today. They would thank him in the end, they would understand the great good he had done them.

Most of the shops he passed were selling the usual dross that nobody needed and everybody seemed to want. They were gaudy and teeming with shoppers. It had been difficult to track down a hardware store, but Yell had listed two, still grinding on with a few faithful pre-lapsarian customers providing an illusion of turnover. He had ascertained that most of what he needed could be purchased at Mungo's, down in Pleasance – which wasn't: the road was shabby, the shop small, dark and empty. This was much more his sort of place than the glitzy chains he had passed on the way. He bought two packets of dusters, a pair of wooden barbeque tongs, an extension lead, and a plastic two-litre bucket with a lid.

More pedalling took him to the tropical fish shop in Salisbury Road. He had a brief pang of conscience about the fish meandering about in their tanks. Soon after petrol ceased to drive things electricity would start to fail, in the short term, and those fish would die in airless, chilly water. It was a shame, but innocents were always casualties in war. He might even have to sacrifice Beauty to the cause one day. He must stay strong.

He bought the cheapest starter aquarium in the shop which had a good lid. He wondered about buying a spare while he was here. Projects were coming at him thick and fast these days. It was well to be prepared. But manoeuvring one aquarium and the bucket on his bike was going to be tricky enough.

Thus laden he returned to the basement, and laid his purchases on the table. He removed their needless packaging, balling it up neatly. He'd dispose of that, and the receipts, in the boiler later.

He hefted in another desk from the room full of abandoned office furniture, and sited it carefully so that no direct sunlight would touch it. On this he placed the aquarium. He was glad that Teddy's program and subsequent batch production was to be run upstairs. It wouldn't do to get the two batches cross-contaminated. Even he wasn't sure what the results of that might be.

Next he liberated the building blocks for his new nano farm from Gold's ample stocks upstairs: a fresh tube of fluorine, wafers of silicon and rhodium granules. One of the few joys of being employed again was that the basics were to hand. It was nice not having to cycle half over London retrieving packages from plausible addresses (nobody, these days, would send the kind of things he ordered on-line to a PO Box – too many home-made bombs had been built that way over the years). He'd been helping himself for over a month, signing the book, and nobody had noticed that the stuff was nowhere in the Clean Space.

He didn't usually go up to his official workstation in Gold's lab during working hours if he could help it. His appearance today was an error: Sara Prosser caught him. Various, rather obvious, emotions flitted across her face when she saw him. The first was relief, the second anger, and the third a desire to placate: good.

She omitted the pleasantries. Ordinarily he would have been pleased to get right into whatever it was. But he wondered if this was a good sign.

'What did you promise Ms Goldstein?'

'Wha …?'

'Last night, at the house. That was your last chance, you know.'

'Last chance to do what?'

'Work on this project.'

Bugger – she'd noticed.

'Can you at least give me some figures to look at. A timescale …?'

'Ah – I don't really work that way.'

He was backing away from her, keeping his bag behind his back, like some naughty schoolboy. The saviour of the world shouldn't have to deal with this sort of distraction.

'Well how do you work, exactly?'

And she was moving towards him. She had scented his weakness – his inability to talk to people f-2-f.

'Well, you've probably noticed that I work best at night, when the lab's quiet.'

'I've noticed that you come in then. I haven't noticed any work.'

'Ah. Like I said – I like to have it ready, complete, finished, before I …'

'This is supposed to be a project *team*. Last time I looked it up, team meant a bunch of people who work together and share problems.'

'Look, I *really* don't work that way.'

'So I see. What did you promise our patient?'

The sudden change of subject threw him.

'I told her I'd cure her.'

'Did you put a timescale on that?'

'Yes.'

'Are you going to tell me what it is?'

'No.'

'Can you tell me where you're staying, at least?'

These changes of direction were making him very nervous. He gave her the address of a private hotel in the Dalkeith Road which he'd made a note of on his first day in town in case of this eventuality. It would hold her until she felt a need to get hold of him again. By that time, with luck, both of his tasks would be completed and he long gone.

He was wriggling around the edge of his desk now, open floor was behind him, he made a run for it. 'Must get on, work to do.'

And he was gone.

4.3

Sara stood open-mouthed – she had nowhere near finished with Hanford and now all that remained of his presence was a slight, stale whiff in the air where he had been and a closing door. Teddy had seemed much cheered by her interview with him the previous night and had slept better than usual. Sara had almost been fooled into thinking that the little bastard was going to deliver – but the few words they had exchanged, while he edged backwards and she wanted to grab him by the throat and shake the truth out of him, had not filled her with confidence. What the hell did he mean – 'work to do'? She was standing beside his workstation and he wasn't at it. Was he working at the hotel?

A little niggling voice in the back of her head warned her not to lean on him too hard, if she still wanted to keep him. He wasn't good with people, but he was – or had been – fantastic with nanites. He had made Teddy a promise, both he and Teddy had told her that. There was absolutely no reason to suppose he was going to keep it. And absolutely no way to force him to do so.

The stark truth of the matter was that she was no further forward. And nor, she suspected, was Teddy's cure.

Not ready, yet, to listen to the niggling little voice Sara set off for Dalkeith Road.

4.4

Having shaken Prosser loose, Gates returned with his booty, circuitously, to the basement. He removed his haul carefully from his pockets and arranged it on the new desk. Then he sited the aquarium, plugged it in, and ran the extension lead to the elderly socket on the wall. He had to unplug Beauty's lamp for a while, but there was no help for that.

It didn't take long to seed the new environment. The target was already programed. With a pair of sterilised tweezers he coaxed his recently filched ingredients into the tank, adding the fluorine at the last moment. A deft flick with the tweezers and he clapped the lid back onto the aquarium. The aquarium wasn't ideal – it wasn't truly sterile for one thing. But it was much better than the sandwich box he'd used for his first, experimental, Balmoral Batch.

Two hours later, when he checked, there was a pleasing sensation of scurry in the aquarium. He would leave them to bask and multiply for several hours more. He had other business to attend to upstairs: he needed to adapt what he had been running down here into a program for Teddy. He set his machine to page him when his illicit batch had had another three hours.

Next he composed a stirring message to the Green X Group. He felt energised, hopeful, powerful. She needed him. The world needed him. They would see. They would all see.

It was lunchtime now, and Gates took a moment to check on Prosser's whereabouts before he went back upstairs to work on Teddy's program. The security system showed her, mercifully, logged out: the field was clear for him to start on the targeting parameters for Teddy's program at his official workstation.

This was a new departure, and processing the data was going to take time.

He set up a comparison string on his Gold's computer to make repeated passes through the data which Prosser had extracted from Teddy's infected lungs a couple of weeks before and which had been lying ignored on his desk until now. Each pass through the data honed the targets. As the program was, in effect, refining its own educated guesses with each pass the science was not exact. Each pass took about three hours on their equipment. He should be getting somewhere on Teddy's nanites by morning. On the other hand, it could be days. There was nothing he could do about that – he was seeking a completely new target, and would just have to wait until the program told him that he had what he needed. After all, they weren't going to test this. What he had agreed with her was against all scientific morality and integrity. But since that was what they had agreed to do, he'd better make sure that he had the target right. Not that she was likely to be around to sue if it went wrong. But somehow that wasn't the point.

After the target was set he would need to create the initial batch, which would, in turn, need to breed up a good strong colony. It was going to be bloody tight to get a satisfactory working swarm up to strength in three days.

It was odd that just meeting her had made such a difference. The euphoria which had impelled him to contact the Green X Group began to evaporate. He hoped he wouldn't be too late.

4.5

Lox struggled up out of sleep from a long way down. His tongue felt like a brick wrapped in sandpaper and thick fog occupied the space where his brain used to be. Christ, but those girls could drink. Three days now he'd been on the case, and he still wasn't sure if there was anything here.

The room was way too bright for a man with a massive single-malt hangover. He registered that it was probably a nice day outside as he told the curtains to close. The brocade curtains were so heavy that the automatic track struggled to pull them shut. Lox knew how they felt. The LED on his bedside console refused to come properly into focus, but he managed to read 10:30 off it. Not bad, considering. In the comfortable brocade-induced gloaming he picked himself painfully off the bed and stumbled towards the bathroom. There was a last sachet of Revive in there somewhere.

The Revive and ten minutes in the shower helped. He didn't even try shaving, but did manage to climb into some of his cleaner clothes. Damply dressed (working the towel had proved beyond him) but still rather shaky, he called room service for something to get his blood sugar level off zero. While he waited for his breakfast he checked the news nets. Nanonics still provided all the top stories. The domestic nets led with emergency legislation being pushed through the European legislature, the British Parliament and the Assemblies this week. Nanonics was to be outlawed, finally. The Bill would add it to the substances banned under the Prevention of Terrorism Act 2005, making manufacture or possession of any Nanonic-related materials an offence punishable by life imprisonment. Shit. Whatever had happened in the Balmoral's car park was a pathetic little story compared to this. Every journalist without a hangover was going to have been all over it hours ago.

Work had piled up overnight. He had a stack of e-requests for stats evaluations. It was little surprise to see a message from Gray Gardner, tagged urgent. Sure enough, Gray wanted him either to provide the promised story or get out of the Balmoral Hotel. The e-mail was polite, the next one wouldn't be.

Christ, he'd turned this room into a foetid pit. He told the curtains to open again and the windows to ditto. Below him were the trees and brightly-coloured formal flower beds of Princes Street gardens, which made his eyes see spots. It was a rather better view than he got from his hive apartment in Milton Keynes. For that matter he had more space in this 'room' at the Balmoral than he did in his SSEP-tic little cell for the single self-employed person that he called home. Beneath his feet was a thrum, which he had learned was made by trains entering and leaving Waverley station. If he squinted he could actually see them coming and going through a cutting beside the park. He remembered trains in England – just – but they'd finally disappeared when Branson had his last brilliant idea: the Coachways. Now the huge articulated trailer-coaches were the only things using the old rail routes. The rail tracks were still there, like fossilised skeletons, under the hi-speed, cushion-plas surface that had been laid on top of them.

Lox sighed and leaned his head against the cool glass of the window for a moment. He'd have to find something worth writing about up here, and soon, or his arse was going to be grass as far as Gray Gardner was concerned. He didn't want to upset the relationship: RDonLine had put lot of work his way over the years. Perhaps he could put together something about railways? He could get most of it from e-libraries, sweeten it with a few shots of trains up here, ask a few questions about how local citizens viewed train travel, take a ride on one himself. It was a sad come-down from the story he'd hoped to write – much more the sort of thing he usually did. Perhaps he really wasn't a proper journalist any more, just a compiler of boring fillers for use when news was slow. It was tempting to go and lie down again.

Instead he wandered into his sitting room, with the vague idea of finding something sweet and fizzy in the mini-bar. Even with a big soft sofa, two matching armchairs and a sturdy coffee table in it there was room to have a party on the remaining floor area. Which seemed to be what had occurred there the night before. The contents of the mini-bar, emptied, were scattered over the floor. Gray was going to have apoplexy when this week's bill hit him. Perhaps it was worth pointing out to Gray that this was one of the Balmoral's more modest rooms?

Lox had been sitting in the North British the previous evening, looking for inspiration at the bottom of a pint of beer. At some point Callum's cousin Shona had come in, with Fiona. They had their instruments with them and were on their way to Deacon Brodie's to make muzak for the tourists. He still hadn't got over the ephemeral beauty of the harp Fiona had been playing when he first saw her. The sound it had made matched the look of it so perfectly. The woman who played it matched both. So he'd wangled an invitation to go with them. By the time the girls had packed their instruments away and been paid, they left Deacon Brodie's around midnight. Callum got off at one, so they'd gone back to the North British to keep him company for an hour. Callum was a sociable sort of chap, and residential licensing hours being supremely elastic, the party had repaired upstairs to Lox's room around two and had finally run out of alcohol about four. The

Scots sure knew how to drink. Lox was discovering the hard way that his constitution couldn't take this kind of punishment any more.

His breakfast arrived. He received it monosyllabically and started on it cautiously, prefacing the ingestion of solids with a pint of strong coffee and the extravagantly large glass of freshly-squeezed OJ. He was going to miss the catering in this place.

Finally feeling that he was beginning to catch up with the day, he returned to his sitting room, chucked all the detritus from the night before into the waste bin and sat down to do some work.

His compad reckoned that the original Green X message had come from London. Probably the real PoO was still shielded. The clever bastard had probably set up more than one fantasy trail for the curious. Lox set his compad to run a new tracer to unpick the next set of subterfuges and get him the real PoO. It was still the only lead he had.

4.6

When Gates got back to his basement with the data he needed, his monitoring system was flashing a tell-tale. This had been happening a lot in the past couple of days. One of his keywords was 'Nanonics' and, of course, with the lab escape in the States the word was everywhere. He ignored it – it wouldn't tell him anything he didn't already know. He got on with testing his latest batch of little silver darlings.

By five he was about ready to go back upstairs and check on Teddy's program. He'd better just check on that tell-tale. What was the point of creating a state-of-the-art security system if you didn't use it? He brought up the news gather.

It wasn't American this time, it was British. The same information was coming in as top story from all the news nets. Parliament had passed emergency legislation outlawing Nanonics.

The details didn't matter. Upstairs an illegal application was running. Fuck! Why hadn't he checked when he first saw the tell-tale? He should know enough by now to trust his instincts – and his instincts were programed into his monitoring equipment, that's what it was bloody-well for!

He ran back upstairs. The Clean Space was in uproar. Prosser was prowling, overseeing the end of the project, making sure that everything was powered down.

'Gates! Have you got anything running?'

'No. No, nothing.'

'Well you should have had. Anyway, switch everything off. We've been shut down.'

'Why?'

'Don't you read the news? I've had a Directive. As of midday today anything nano-based is no longer legitimate research. Don't go away. We need to talk about the department's future direction.' She gave him a look.

'I'll be right back,' he said. And scurried off to his workstation.

4.7

Prosser sounded tearful.

'Teddy, I'm so sorry – they've closed us down.'

'They? Who? What do you mean?'

'Nanonics has been outlawed, with immediate effect. Emergency legislation. I got the call this afternoon. I'm so sorry. I'll redirect everything into the croc cell research. I know you hate it, but if we concentrate completely on it, perhaps we can catch a break.'

Teddy couldn't think of anything to say. The croc shit was months away from producing anything useful, if it was ever going to. She had days. Just when she'd managed to galvanise Gates …

'Gates's stuff too?'

'He says he didn't have anything running. If he did, we've shut it down. We had to shut everything down. They're taking this thing in the States really seriously. God knows when – if ever – they'll let us start it up again. They're sending inspectors later this afternoon to make sure we've complied and I'll ask them, of course. But …'

'There's no point in trying to make my project a special case, appealing to their better natures?'

'They don't have better natures. Oh, Teddy …'

'Don't keep saying you're sorry.' Teddy couldn't keep the irritation out of her voice, but tried to soften it. 'It's not your fault.'

'I'll see you after I've talked to the inspectors. There may be a loophole. We'll think of something. There's been some interesting work done with shark cartilage. I'll get someone onto that. Try not to … '

'Yeh.' Teddy ended the call and threw her compad across the room. They'd been so close to an answer, she and Gates. But it was to be death after all.

4.8

The next morning was a bright, clear June delight, Gates could see that even through the dusty, barred windows of his basement. The daylight made him sneeze – he wasn't used to it. He wriggled out of his sleeping bag. There was half a can of flat cola on the floor beside him. He drank it for the caffeine. He was too excited to eat.

Trembling slightly from the adrenalin rush, he pulled on surgical gloves and fetched the two packets of dusters, wooden tongs and plastic bucket which he had bought. He took them over to the aquarium and lifted off the lid. With the tongs he lifted up a duster and held it over the tank. The silvery contents of the aquarium writhed gently. Cautiously, so as not to create a nano-tsunami, he lowered the duster into the tank and wiped it gently backwards and forwards. Then he lifted it out again, jiggling it carefully over the tank so as to shake off anything loose. Mustn't waste any. They weren't replicating at maximum capacity yet because the swarm was still small. They wouldn't breed optimally until their programed diet was available. He deposited the duster carefully in the bucket. He repeated the process with the rest of the dusters. Six Weapons of Mass Destruction were now lodged in his bucket. Gravely he fixed the lid back on. It was a testament to his skill that he could keep petro-carbon focussed nanites in a plastic bucket made of petro-carbons. Hellfire, but he was good. Finally he got out his map of Edinburgh and selected his targets.

Seeding individual petrol tanks had worked very well, but it had also demonstrated that it would take far too long to bring a city to a halt that way. He was going to visit a representative sample of the city's petrol and LPG pumps and give them a nice wash and brush up. He must deal with at least one of each company's facilities. Two would be better. That should start a chain reaction that would be unstoppable.

4.9

When Gates cycled into the first filling station he could hear birds singing – the first time he could remember hearing birds for years. The very leaves on the trees looked cleaner, greener. He was going to help the birds and the leaves.

Not a demonstrative sort of person as a rule, Gates found himself so invigorated by the green and the birdsong that he whistled cheerfully as he got off his bike next to the cashier's window. It was good cover anyway. He held up his bucket, and a duster which hadn't been anywhere near the bucket, and pointed to the pumps. The attendant looked surprised. Gates gestured at the back room where, he assumed, the manager – tool of the motor Molochs – lurked. The cashier shrugged: OK. Gates stuck up his thumb. *OK.*

Still whistling he strode to the first pump, pocketing the clean duster as he walked. Carefully he eased the lid off the bucket, extracted an impregnated duster, and began to polish. Such a wonderful silver sparkle did his duster impart to the hose nozzle that it positively glowed in the morning sunlight. Soon all twelve of the pumps, including the one for diesel and the one for LPG, had gleaming nozzles. It would take around half or three quarters of an hour for each little nano swarm to suck enough of what it needed to replicate out of the petrol he'd treated. Some cars would fill up and go on their way – for a little while. But in less than an hour nothing would come out of these pumps. The reservoir below the forecourt would be a pool of something very like molasses in about two hours. When the tanker came to refill the tanks, no matter how carefully they'd washed them out, tiny silvery particles would re-form as soon as they scented fresh food and scuttle back up the hose, into the tanker, back to the refinery, into the very reservoirs of crude oil themselves. Gates's simulation had indicated that to bring the world to a standstill required contamination in fifty cities spread around the world. The process was not strictly timed, it depended on scheduled deliveries and rate of replication. But all should be perfect peace in something between 14 and 28 days. For Edinburgh – for any seeded city – transport would cease to operate in the space of plus or minus twenty one hours. He'd sent out the phials, and strict instructions as to their use, to the Green X Group seven days ago.

4.10

Lox was thinking rather mournfully about Fiona, and her harp. He was going to miss the hard-drinking, hard-playing North British gang. He'd better get packed. He had a jetpod booked for noon and a seat on the twelve-thirty Shuttle. His Editor's invective had become incandescent, and even Lox had to admit that six days was a long time in a five star hotel with no story to show for it.

His system said that the ISP for the second Green X message *was* here in Edinburgh. But he needed more than that. He knew there was a gizmo that security firms and the police used to track computing equipment. Everything was so mobile now, that they'd brought out some bespoke software that worked much the same way that chips did in mobile phones. But the software wasn't available to the GenPub. And it certainly wasn't made legitimately available to journos. Lox was trying to track down a copy on the nets. He'd rubbed e-shoulders with some pretty weird people to do it, and so far he had nothing to show for his slumming. But the last contact he'd made had been hopeful. It was going to cost him a lot of money if his contact came through. Was it worth throwing good money at?

The unstartable cars in the Balmoral's car park had been towed long since: their still furious owners had left using other forms of transport. Lox had interviewed them all. Neither the cars' owners, nor the police, nor Fiona, Shona and cousin Callum in their cups had any plausible theory as to what had happened, or why. The hotel's management was, naturally, keen to put a lid on the whole thing, and its car park was once again open for business. Journalists with their fingers on the world's pulse were turning in topical stories on Nanonics (as his Editor had pointed out in one of his more rational messages). Perhaps there really wasn't anything here.

Groggy still from lack of sleep and days of excessive alcohol intake, he told Reception morosely that he'd wait for his cab in the North British where he intended to have a hair of the dog. He wasn't much looking forward to schlepping back to his solitary e-life in Milton Keynes.

It was a few minutes past noon. Lox was just finishing a Greyfriars' Bobby – something Callum had concocted specially to meet the case Lox specified – when Reception rang through.

'Mr Tuthill? Your taxi, sir. I'm afraid it won't be coming.' Having done the dirty deed with dignity she gabbled out the rest. 'When the drivers came in this morning they couldn't get a single cab to start. It's a bit difficult to know what to say, really. You could take a bus to the airport, sir, but I'm afraid you'll miss your flight.

So, there was a story. Thank Christ for that. While the Receptionist was expressing her regrets Lox started laughing. This was obviously not the reaction she was expecting – nor one she likely to get it from other departing guests to whom she had to impart similar news.

'No problem. Can I keep my room for a few more days?'

'Well, sir, under the circumstances …'

They were keen to have him gone, but he was keener still to stay. It's hard to deflect a jaded journalist who has finally stumbled across a good story.

While they were finding him another room Lox skipped merrily out onto the street. On his way into the North British he had been nursing a thumping head and had been staring at his shoes to avoid the bright sunshine. Had he been less hung over he might have already spotted that his story was right here, on the streets.

It was very quiet outside. It was, actually, rather freaky. The buses were, indeed, running. He realised why as soon as one passed him: it was silent – it must be electric. Fuel-cell powered city cars were still on the streets too. Little else was. A flock of bicyclists rode down the middle of Princes Street. A couple of bits of litter skipped happily down the road in the gentle June breeze. The only empty urban roads that Lox had ever seen had been roped off because of some disaster, natural or man-made. This, he suspected, was another man-made disaster.

Nevertheless, it was going to make marvellous copy.

*****

Fifteen minutes later Lox and his luggage were on their way back upstairs. On the way back up to his new room he pumped the porter for a little local colour to go with what he had. The man had walked to work and was less than happy about having had to do so.

This time the room resembled an opulent broom cupboard, but he didn't care. He pulled out his compad and regarded it with affection. The PoO of the Green X message really must be here, just as his tracer had been saying for the past six days.

With the couple of facts he had, a few seconds footage of an empty Princes Street and some rampant speculation Lox put together a vid-bite for Gray:

> Edinburgh at a standstill
>
> Streets Emptied By Mystery Motor Malady
>
> Five days ago a mysterious malaise immobilised conventionally propelled cars in a private park facility here in Edinburgh. This morning the only cars to be seen are powered by fuel cells. Could the same malady now be afflicting the entire city? Speculation is rife.
>
> Could a cryptic e-mail sent world-wide saying 'look to the streets of Edinburgh' have any bearing on this mystery?

He hoped he was right: that what had happened today was part of the peculiar incident at the Balmoral – and in turn connected to the message from the Green X Group that had brought him up here in the first place. He began to chase the contact with possible access to compad locator software.

Two hours later the software he needed was downloading, and his Smart Card was smarting indeed at the exorbitant amount of credit being extracted to pay for it.

The software safely stored in his own compad, Lox set it running to track the postcode of the compad that had sent the second Green X message. The little screen told him

Estimate 45 minutes remaining to acquire target.

That was more like it. Not only did he now have a target, but it would be acquired inside an hour. Just time to change his shoes and get a bit more familiar with the local geography. In anticipation he spread out his official city map of Edinburgh on the bed. Bloody Data Protection.

Forty five minutes later his compad beeped gently. He seized it eagerly. There was a postcode. He asked it for a proper address but it just kept repeating, rather peevishly,

additional information not available.

OK then. He was a lot further forward than he had been, he'd just have to work with it now. Somewhere down … there. Hellfire, there were a lot of possible locations: that postcode covered the whole of the eastern bit of central Edinburgh. Terrorists didn't look like terrorists, obviously. Where could a terrorist hide in plain sight? There were a lot of businesses in there, and a big chunk of New Town. He thought about this for quite a while – the Greyfriar's Bobby on an empty stomach was making logical deductions difficult.

He needed to narrow things down. He couldn't possibly walk such a big area, not in one day. New Town and Princes Street were rather less likely than … He waved his index finger over the map like a divining rod and finally stabbed down onto the Cowgate, which disappeared into the duvet. How about that for starters? He keyed

addresses for Cowgate, Edinburgh

into his compad and waited while it found an alarming number of entries. Most of them were businesses: but businesses had nooks and crannies where things were stored and forgotten, and he had a hunch that that might be a more likely nest for the Green X Group than a tasteful flat in New Town.

First he would go and talk to the taxi company who had been unable to send him a cab, and then to one of the jetpod companies who weren't able to fly today. Then he would start looking for the physical PoO of that bloody message. He hoped it wasn't going to rain. It being June, and Scotland, he would have plenty of daylight. He rather thought the available daylight might outlast his feet. Gray would want more than that vid-bite he'd sent through. And he'd want it today.

4.11

Lox asked at Reception for the closest taxi firm to the hotel regularly used by guests, recorded the directions the girl gave him and strode off up Leith Street to find it. He had an interesting conversation with the mechanics who'd been trying to make the cabs run again. There was something odd, the man said, about the fuel in them. That was the only thing he could find that wasn't as it should be. There was a lot of sludge in the tank which didn't smell like diesel. When Lox asked if he was going to get it analysed the man laughed. He was going to wash the tanks out with clean diesel, fill them and see if that solved the problem. If it did it was going to take him the whole day to do that for the fleet. No, Lox couldn't have a quick look at the sludge. Nor could he have the dirty rag that the mechanic was wiping his hands with. Didn't he have anything to do except bother busy people? The punctuation the man used for the latter part of this speech was colourful. Lox took the point and departed.

The jetpod people were out at Leith Docks – a nice walk on a pleasant morning. The little heli-jets ran on very high octane petrol – not diesel. When Lox mentioned sludge the mechanics looked at him suspiciously, but agreed that sludge, loosely speaking, described their problem. They, too, had flushed the fuel tanks and lines on one of the jetpods to see if that would clear the problem, but it hadn't. The waste from the tank had been sealed into drums. Lox was pleased to hear it. He toyed with the idea of finessing a sample of it, but then reflected that he probably didn't want to be carrying it around in his coat pocket. Time enough for samples when he was a bit more certain what he was dealing with.

The pilots had nothing to do but shoot the breeze while their machines were being repaired. They would have been very pleased to take him down to The Commercial and tell him all about it over a pint, but it looked as though their combined stories would be useful only as filler material, so Lox schlepped back to the North British for a spot of lunch. He took the precaution of leaving alcohol alone and instead had two cups of strong coffee with his sandwich. God knew when he'd next get something to eat.

Thus fortified, and map in hand, he turned right out of the North British an hour later, and stopped. It really was very quiet. The electric buses ghosted up and down, and occasionally one of the little electric city cars whooshed past and made him jump. Lox wondered how long those would stay out on the streets. Plenty of people would want fuel cell cars, when their own transport wouldn't run. They might not be too scrupulous about how they got hold of them.

People were about and all the shops were open – business as usual, then. Not.

Some youngsters were prancing down the street where the traffic ought to be. They might have been drunk. The kids were playing toreador with the cyclists that had taken over Princes Street, waving shirts in front of them and then jumping aside at the last moment. They were laughing uproariously, the cyclists were swerving nervously. Today this was a novelty. Lox wondered when the joke would wear thin.

A city without cars wasn't right. Lox tried to imagine Milton Keynes without cars. Milton Keynes was *the* city of the car in Britain. It emulated American use of personal petrol-based transport. It had been founded on the ubiquity of the car. It depended on the car for its very existence. It worshipped the car. Lox was a true denizen of Milton Keynes, and he was very fond of cars. They moved you and all your stuff from place to place quickly and without physical exertion. Without cars most people in Milton Keynes would starve inside a week. Of course, he was a long way from Milton Keynes now. He wondered whether its myriad motors were still running. He hoped so. Probably not for much longer, though.

Edinburgh's infrastructure was much older and denser than Milton Keynes', obviously. Things were close together here, rather than a twenty minute drive apart – although you could treble that if you needed to go at primetime. But if nobody could bring food in to the shops here, if emergency services couldn't run …

Lox put in his earpiece and played back what the mechanic at the taxi company had said to him, smiling ruefully at the expletives, as he set off for the Cowgate. Oh, how he missed cars already!

He turned right and went over North Bridge. All the metered parking spaces were empty. He walked on across South Bridge. Below him were the bleak depths of the Cowgate. He spent a few minutes leaning on the bridge, just looking at the buildings that started four and five stories down and rose up past him. Please let it be here …

At the end of the bridge he turned down Chambers Street and, at the south end of George IV Bridge, crossed the road and passed the little statue of Greyfriars Bobby to go down Candlemakers Row into the Grassmarket. He passed three or four bars, all full of people, many already drunk. People were dancing in the street. Everybody was talking about how their cars wouldn't go. Everybody had a theory about the phenomenon. Their talk and laughter was too loud, as if they were trying to drown out the silence where the hum of traffic ought to be. You didn't realise how comforting that hum was until it wasn't there. Traditional Scottish fiddle music pulsed from one bar and electronic modal frenz from another. It all reminded him of an old movie: The Day The Earth Caught Fire.

Lox made his way through the crowds and into the gloomy canyon of the Cowgate.

The Cowgate was a man-made gorge; dark, depressing and sullen. Grime filmed windows, coated doors, lowlighted the stonework that rose up and up as if reaching towards the sun. Lights burned inside the buildings, glimming feebly through the dirt. The activities they lit were muted, private, sinister seeming. At intervals, high in the air, bridges stitched the two sides of the street together. People looking over the parapets were tiny, stick figures. Lox began to feel absurdly hopeful – this looked like the sort of place where terrorists might feel right at home.

Every building had a bank of intercoms at the main entrance - some as many as twelve. Lox sighed and started pressing buzzers.

He found very few people this way, and hardly anyone was prepared to talk to him. They were pre-occupied. Lox understood. Whatever it was that they did behind the crusted-on dirt had been seriously disrupted. If employees couldn't get to work, if deliveries couldn't be received, if goods couldn't be sent – Lox sympathised and moved on.

Lox could hear nothing except pigeons calling to each other, the occasional penetrating beep of a comm in a room with an open window. Litter skittered up and down the empty street. It felt like the end of the world had come. That, Lox told himself firmly, was nonsense. And somewhere here – he tried to keep his spirits up – was a bloody huge story.

4.12

Lox pounded streets, alleys, lanes and the peculiar, Edinburghish alleyways called 'wynds', around the Cowgate for hours. Walking was not something he was used to. When he needed to leave his flat he usually took a cab (there being nothing he needed within what he considered a civilised walking distance). His feet hurt. His calves hurt. His back hurt. This old-fashioned, street-pounding kind of journalism was seriously over-rated.

He gave up ringing intercoms. He wasn't getting any help that way. He would just have to rely on his intuition. Pity it was almost comatose. Pity his feet weren't. He'd probably stood within metres of his quarry at some point already. Were these people too clever for Lox Tuthill? His feet grunted a yes. His pride refused to let him give up yet. There was plenty of daylight left.

He'd been up and down both sides of the Cowgate, and all its tributaries, noting the names of the businesses in his compad, and the com number where he could. He'd peered in through windows and sidled up alleyways to back entrances. He'd riffled through skips (wishing he'd thought to bring a pair of gloves with him). He'd been as systematic as the layout of this ancient part of the city would let him. His street plan had been folded and refolded and was beginning to look distinctly fragile around the area of his search.

But here was an alley he hadn't noticed before. He checked his list – no: he hadn't done this one. His comfortable shoes had started to rub up some big, squelchy blisters. He'd been plodding this weary round for … Having looked at his watch he swore. It was half past eight. No wonder his dogs were barking and his belly growling. It was time to call it a day and go in search of some dinner and a footbath. Nevertheless … this last alley.

Stumbling with tiredness, he lurched into the alley and trod in something squishy that smelled bad. The bowels of Edinburgh could be seriously bleak. The alley took a couple of bends, then he could see another tiny thoroughfare some distance ahead. Nothing opened off the part of the alley that he had trudged up so far, but further along, towards the other street, perhaps … He plodded on.

Now he could see railings, and a break in them. He came opposite the gap, and saw steps leading down. He looked around, there was nothing else at all promising here.

Down the steps he went. At the bottom was a door; padlocked. Nothing surprising there. Idly, Lox hefted the lock in his hand: it was an old-fashioned padlock, but shiny with newness. Perhaps they'd had a break-in. They'd need to make the place secure again. But a padlock was an old-fashioned way to do it. Surely it was just inviting the burglars back? He went on round the building. One corner, two. He guessed he was now opposite the padlocked door. Here was a window and, therefore, some sort of basement. There was a grille to stop people falling into the hole which made the window viable. The glass was, of course, filthy. It was difficult to see what was inside. With a grunt he got down onto his hands and knees and peered in. Beneath the window there was a strange, pale plant. In the corner was a pile of papers with what looked like a sleeping bag on top of them. In between the two was a workstation.

Anyone using a computer that wasn't hand-held these days was crunching serious numbers. This was a machine capable of running a small country. What the hell was it doing in a basement, protected only by a padlock?

The computer was working on something, but the window was too dirty for him to see what. On the desk was a rack of test-tubes. Beside the rack was a small aquarium. This contained something that looked like silvery sand. Lox wondered if he was getting too tired to see straight, or whether it was just a trick of the filthy window: the sand seemed to be moving.

Finally Lox was getting the tingle that told him he was on to something. He fished his compad out of a pocket and took half a dozen pictures. The light was crap and the window was filthy, but he'd run them through a couple of programs when he got back; see if he could enhance the images enough to make out what the computer was doing and what was in the aquarium. His tingle told him that this was something newsworthy. Reason told him that it was probably just an underfunded R & D project relegated to the basement. Lox preferred to trust his tingle.

He made his way on round the building until he came back to the main entrance off the Cowgate itself. An old-fashioned sign with a rather grisly wooden leg swinging beneath it dangled from the third floor. It told him this building housed Gold Prosthetics. The place looked deserted. He banged on the door to be certain. Then he tried it: locked. On the door was an official-looking notice:

CLOSED

By order of the Ministry of Homeland Security under the provisions of the Civil Contingencies Act, 2004 this

building is quarantined until further notice.

Today's date was appended at the bottom.

He'd passed Gold's at least twice: this wooden leg, this notice on this door had been here all the time, on the main drag. He could have saved himself hours of walking if he'd only put it all together. But without that padlock it would never have occurred to him that the leg, or the notice, were significant.

No longer feeling his blisters and grinning broadly he strode purposefully back towards the hotel.

4.13

Lox sat on the edge of the single bed in his new room at the Balmoral. He'd managed to get his shoes and socks off. His bare feet throbbed as he hunched over his compad. He regretted the loss of a second room with a desk. However, under the circumstances a bed to sleep in was as good as he was likely to get.

The images he had taken through the dirty basement window had cleaned up rather well. It was tedious work selecting each segment and blowing it up. The jigsaw he was producing was difficult to arrange, let alone interpret. He was getting a headache that was rivalling the pain in his feet.

The computer in Gold's basement appeared to be running something involving biological data, isolating individual cells and examining their composition. Lox recognised a DNA string when he was presented with one, but the specifics meant nothing to him. Not to worry, he could check them out over the Net later. The pictures he had taken did not enable him to verify whether the silvery stuff in the aquarium was moving or if that had just been a trick of the light and the dirty window. The shots were definitely blurry, but that could be down to any number of infelicities: he'd been exhausted and trembling with excitement when he'd taken them. He wished now that he'd waited a few minutes and taken a second series of pictures for comparison. He might have got a shot of something different on the computer's screen, and possibly have nailed down whether the contents of the aquarium were moving. With a sigh he set up a search for the DNA strand he had captured and went to raid the mini bar. What the hell was in the aquarium?

He took a miniature of Laphroiag into the bathroom with him. His body was demanding alcohol and warm water - and not mixed. One thing you had to say for Scotland; you got a much better standard of whisky. He wondered whether his weary body could stand another bout with Fiona, Shona and cousin Callum. One good jolt of the whisky was enough to provide an answer: of course it could.

5

5.1

Lox had called an early halt to his latest session in the North British. It was only half past one and he was relatively sober.

On the way to his room the 'info waiting' vibrator on his compad started up. He hoped it was the result of his search and not a vitriolic mailing from his editor.

The download took ages. He was sitting on the side of the bed, peering at the little screen, wishing for the zillionth time that he had invested in a fold-out membrane screen for the thing.

Interrogating the information proved more difficult than he had expected. Information is intelligible. This was not intelligible. It had obviously been written by and for people with several higher degrees in the sciences. It was followed by long attributions to learned journals. He tried to think of a keyword that might unlock whatever it was that the machine had found. As he had simply asked it to search on a blown up screenshot of what had been on the computer screen in Gold's basement, this was difficult. It was certainly a DNA formula of some sort – what sort was beyond him, which was why he was searching. He was stuck in a hopeless loop. OK Time to go back to first principles. He keyed 'terrorist', but that brought him nothing. 'Green X Group' brought nothing either; nor did 'silver sand'. He was about to give it up until the morning, when he realised that the god of coincidence was looking after him again.

It was *cars* that were stuck in Callum's garage and now all the *cars* in Edinburgh were fubared. What did cars have in common? Internal combustion engines. Which ran on diesel or petrol. Which in the case of the taxis and jetpods had apparently turned to sludge. Apart from the sludge everything under the bonnet was in perfect working order, which was also what Callum had said was wrong with the Balmoral cars.

He tried petrol. And up came the DNA string. Wow.

He tried 'virus' as a keyword, but got nothing. Feeling euphoric and getting desperate he tried 'pseudo-virus' and found 'Nanonics' hi-lighted. He ran back to the beginning of the paragraph and read;

In the early years of the twenty-first century considerable research was done in the field of Nanonics in an effort to provide an non-invasive means of treating diseases, such as cancer.

Researchers claimed that, once the target was programed, no deviation could occur. However, in clinical trials this was not proven. The BMA decided not to grant a licence, and informed the applicants that they would require much more work to be done on the targeting programs if licences were to be granted for medical use.

The raw materials required to set up a nano-farm are basic in the extreme. Silicon, fluorine, rhodium, (or analogs) a suitable energy source, and a sterile environment to hold the resulting swarm while it multiplies, are all that is necessary. However, in order to animate the swarm a tightly focussed computer program has to be fed to it. No program tested proved entirely target-focussed and it was this that caused the BMA to have doubts. In certain extreme circumstances it proved impossible to shut down the swarm.

European Newsnets have run reports which intimate that, should a nano-swarm 'escape', its self-replicating imperative could cause it to consume everything with which it came into contact that contained traces of the elements used to construct it. Hard evidence for this hypothesis was not proven either.

Public alarm was, however, widespread: as a result of this – and the failure to obtain medical licences – research into Nanonics was officially ended in the European Union in 2037. Following the recent escape of a nano-swarm in America, Nanonics has been outlawed in the UK with immediate effect. It is expected that similar legislation will be enacted EU-wide within the next forty eight hours.

There was more, but Lox had all he needed for the moment. He bookmarked the site and lay back on the bed to let the information he'd acquired fun around in his subconscious for a bit.

So that was what he had seen in the aquarium: a nano-farm. He remembered old newsnet reports about such things in the Twenties. All anti nanites, of course, and they'd been very convincing. Nobody liked bugs. Bugs so small you couldn't see them with the naked eye and that were endlessly self-replicating into the bargain gave everyone the willies. How could you stop them if you couldn't see them? His skin crawled. Of course they didn't really breed, because they weren't alive. They were tiny robots, really. But then, everybody knew how bad bad robots could be from the movies. Nanonics fed those old fears.

It looked like somebody had started all that up again. Shit. This was going to make him a fortune. Any editor apart from Gray at RDonLine would take some convincing but Gray's publication revelled in the weird, thankfully. And when he, Lox, was proved right the world's press would be mobbing him for the story. But his proof would have to be rock solid. One strangely equipped basement with some silver sand and an e-net article were not enough. He had a lot of work to do.

And why had the spooky place with the wooden leg been closed down by the Ministry of Homeland Security, of all people?

5.2

First thing next morning, while he was eating his breakfast, Lox put in his earpiece and ran the latest headlines on the newsnets. The top British news item was the emergency legislation put in place the previous day outlawing Nanonics. There were quotes from the European Ministry at The Hague, the British Ministry of Homeland Security, the Home and Foreign Offices, the Prime Minister and the four Regional Assemblies. They all said the same thing: the essence of it all was that the Americans were playing with some bad toys and the Europeans were locking their own toy cupboard, just in case there was anything nasty in there.

So that was why the Ministry of Homeland Security had nailed a quarantine notice to Gold's front door. So what had Gold's been up to? Something officially sanctioned, by the sound of it. But what about that work station in the basement? Did the Ministry know about that? It had still been running, and the quarantine was already in place. Perhaps it had nothing to do with whatever Nanonics developments were going on upstairs. But in that case, what was in that aquarium?

The strange goings-on in Edinburgh were item two, although Edinburgh didn't get a mention until the third paragraph. The headline read: Major Cities Stopped In Their Tracks. Lox felt slightly sick as he read that London had been paralysed since yesterday morning. Seven other cities were affected: three in the United States (Washington, New York and, of all places, Boise in Idaho); Sydney, Australia; Kyoto, Japan; Bilbao and Split in continental Europe. Nobody had any idea what was going on. Pictures of empty streets and a bunch of half-arsed theories were all that was on offer.

London. For some absurd reason London being stationary seemed more serious than Edinburgh being ditto, despite the fact that he was actually *in* Edinburgh. Well, it was finally official then: there was a problem. And they'd only taken out bloody *London*. Somehow being right wasn't much of a comfort.

The financial reports showed a lot of overnight movement in the automotive sector: optimists saw opportunity and were buying, pessimists saw threat and were selling. It could go either way. Something – fear or excitement, he couldn't tell yet – fluttered up and down Lox's spine. The automotive industry was vital to the global economy. He knew that much, and several Leaders in the financial press told him the same thing. The current, majority view was that the problem could be solved by buying a new car. Lox shook his head as he read. Of all possible scenarios that seemed the least likely. He looked at oil prices. No unusual movement there. Yet.

Everything was starting to fit together. He just hoped that no-one else would put the disparate pieces together before he had them in place himself. This was his big chance. He was closer to an answer than anyone. If only …

But wait a minute. Gold's Prosthetics had been shut down completely. It wasn't just anything on Nanonics – the whole building was quarantined. So what was a computer in the basement doing still running data - and on DNA too. That aquarium must contain a live nano-farm surely? The Ministry obviously didn't know what was going on down there, so that whole application must be well illegal. That was his strap line, right there. He tapped it in while he could still remember it. Then, with the kind of breathless joy that statistics had never been able to instil in him, he pulled up Gold's net site and started searching their research portfolio.

A few moments later he sat back and let out a whoop of triumph. Two years previously the wooden leg people had been working on Nanonics. And he, Lox Tuthill, had proof – albeit rather grainy – that they had still been working on it after Nanonics had been outlawed yesterday. Quite how this married up with the Green X Group and cities grinding to a halt he still wasn't sure. There must be other documents on the computer in that basement which would drop more pieces into place for him. He wondered if Gold's Prosthetics knew what was going on in their basement. He tried phoning them to tell them and hopefully get a comment, but all he got was an automated voice telling him that nobody was currently available to take his call. The system wasn't taking messages either. Not that he wanted to leave one. But it gave a clue that Gold's didn't think they'd be open for business any time soon.

So, how was he to get into that basement?

*****

The com lines to Edinburgh's various police stations were jammed all morning. In the end he camped on the line to the Leith police – an arbitrary decision based solely on his memory of a tongue-twister based on it. He finally got through just as he was sitting down to a light lunch in the hotel's bar. Lox gulped down his mouthful of sandwich and explained that what he had to relate was important. The man he was speaking to was audibly unimpressed. In a Scottish growl that a large dog would have envied, he explained;

'There's urgent, and there's important. But today, unless its urgent *and* important, frankly we couldna care less.'

'Just give me a minute.' Lox wondered how strong to pitch it. 'It's to do with why the cars won't go. I think I know.' He paused. It wasn't for dramatic effect, it was to try and gauge just how freaked the man with the Big Dog voice was going to get when he heard the word 'Nanonics'. 'I think somebody - and I think I know who - is using Nanonics to sabotage petrol.'

To Lox's surprise the man started to bark with laughter. Then he disconnected.

Lox stared at his compad for long moments before ending the call. Yes, that would be one reaction. The man had probably been fielding crank calls all morning. Grimly Lox reset the camp-on facility and finished his lunch. He had a beer. Then he had a couple more.

5.3

By the time he got through again he was back in his hotel room, sleepily regretting the third beer. He levered himself out of the arms of Morpheus to find a warm female brogue on the line. This time he announced who he was upfront.

'Hi, I'm Lox Tuthill reporting for RDonLine. I've been in town investigating a junk e-mail that's been sent round the world by an organisation calling themselves the Green X Group ...'

'I'm sorry sir, as you may know we've been having a bit of trouble with transport today, and I really can't help you with a nuisance mailer just now.'

'No, no – it's not that. Just give me a minute, will you?' Lox found an edge of irritation creeping into his voice. 'The PoO of the e-mail

I've been tracking is here, in Edinburgh. Yesterday I traced it to the Cowgate. And I found something really strange. I think what I saw there may be the reason why you're having that 'bit of trouble with transport'. Somebody has used Nanonics to poison petrol. I tried calling the company, but they're not answering their comms. And somebody really needs to get down there before all the evidence disappears.'

'Nanonics?' Now there was an edge to her voice. He'd pushed the right button with the right person. Finally.

He told her about Gold's, the Notice on the door, the DNA string on the computer, the aquarium and his suspicions about its contents.

As he spoke he realised that he *believed* the aquarium contained a nano-farm, and that previous denizens of that aquarium were infecting people's petrol tanks. Researching and reporting were one thing. Believing what you were writing was something else. The hairs on the back of his neck stirred. Lox realised he was frightened. He ended his diatribe to the warm female brogue,

'I don't know what stops them. Perhaps nothing does.'

His fear, he reckoned later, was what made her take him seriously. She worked for the police. She knew fear when she heard it: and understood it. It was still quite possible that he was nuts, but she could tell he believed he'd seen something, so now she believed he had too.

'Just a moment,' she said. He heard her talking to somebody else, then: 'Can you come down to the Station?'

'Of course. When?'

As he spoke, he realised that he didn't want to go anywhere near that basement and its creepy aquarium again. But it was too late to back out now.

'Right away. I'm not sure we've got anyone free to come out with you, but we'll take a statement for a start.' He was someone she knew now, so she added: 'It's complete chaos here today. We've commandeered every bicycle we can, but it's hopeless. Come in and we'll see what we can do. Ask for Bridie Calder.'

5.4

Within twenty minutes Lox was on his way to Leith Police Station, with as much evidence he could put together.

It was past four in the afternoon by now. But because everything was so odd and it took so long to get anywhere the day felt … elastic, endless. Lox realised from his disorientation just how freaked out he was by all this. He was sure now that he was right.

He asked for Bridie at the front desk. She appeared after about half an hour. She was young. She looked agitated. She brought another woman with her, who might have been a few years older. Neither of them wore uniform. Pity. Lox had a weakness for women in uniform. It would have been nice to be dealing with people possessing a little more *gravitas* than these two girls. But after the Big Dog bark which had ended his first communication with the police he was grateful for what he could get.

They took him into an interview room. Bridie introduced her companion as Detective Sergeant McCall. McCall was trying to look as if she was used to dealing every day with people suggesting possible links between terrorism, nanotechnology and a city full of cars that refused to go. She obviously thought he was out of his mind and only wanted to get back to trying to sort out the chaos that the day's events had caused. Lox tried to remember if he had combed his hair recently. Did he look crazy? He put a hand up to his throat. He hadn't put a tie on that morning, but in all other respects he was dressed well enough to get in and out of the Balmoral without comment. That should be good enough. With a sigh, McCall pulled out a compad and its external microphone and plugged the one into the other. Would he mind repeating what he had told DC Calder earlier? He embarked, once more, on an exposition of what he knew, backing it up with the evidence he had gleaned during more than a week in Edinburgh, of which the highlight was the grainy pix of Gold's basement. It didn't take long, but McCall was visibly impatient; her fingers jumping on the table top. Several times she appeared to be on the verge of stopping him. He began to gabble. It sounded so thin now. He ended with:

'The premises are owned by Gold Prosthetics. I guess that's what they make - there was a wooden leg hanging from the third floor for Chrissakes. I don't know how they're tied into this – but that Notice on the door … you could check with the Ministry.'

McCall looked bored. But Bridie seemed to have taken a liking to Lox. Or perhaps she just didn't want this potential wild goose chase to be her fault. She said,

'We could do that. I could do it now. It wouldn't take a minute.'

Without waiting for a response she dug out her compad and started keying.

'Good. Thank you.' Lox continued. 'We really need to get into that basement. *I've* never seen anything like it.' Lox left hanging in the air the impression that, as a reporter, he'd seen a lot of strange things in his time. He forbore to mention that reporting *per se* wasn't his usual line of work. McCall mellowed a bit.

'I suppose we could get try and get a search warrant. God knows it would be good to get out of the station for an hour or so.' She smiled wanly. 'It's been hell here all day. If it won't go they feel a need to report it. I've got over eight hundred abandoned cars to process.'

Lox said, gently, 'they trust you. You're law and order. They need some of that. They're frightened.' She looked slightly mollified by this, so he continued . 'If I'm right and you catch whoever it is that's doing this – that would be a report worth filing, wouldn't it?'

'*If* you're right it would be instant promotion.' She obviously still didn't believe for a moment that he was. But … 'I can certainly get a search warrant on the basis of what you've shown me, if I can get through to anybody in the Procurator Fiscal's office.'

She pulled out the external mic and made some keystrokes on her compad. She looked at the little screen for a moment or two, then keyed again.

While she was connecting Lox had an idea.

'These eight hundred cars, Bridie – where are they?'

'How do you mean? They're where they stopped.'

'And where is that?'

'All over. One thing that recurs in people's statements is that they've just filled up with fuel, so it's not that they've run out of petrol, or LPG or whatever they're using.'

'Filling stations – so it *is* the fuel.'

Bridie gave him a quizzical look, but McCall had got through to someone in real-time. She looked up at Bridie.

'How should I put this?'

Lox weighed in with, 'How about 'suspected terrorist activity'?'

'No. They won't let a Detective Sergeant handle something like that. They'll want covert surveillance to start with and then an anti-terrorist unit.'

'And how are they going to get an anti-terrorist unit here? They'd have to come in by train. It could take days.' Lox felt that little movement of his neck hairs again. He had a bad feeling about all this, which he was only managing to keep at bay by keeping busy. If there wasn't a way to de-activate what had got into the petrol, they'd be all around the world eventually – even if no more were released. The petrol engine: a thing of the past. Hellfire – there was a headline.

Bridie said: 'Why not tell them you think you have a lead on our transport problem. That's no more than the truth'

McCall made a few more keystrokes.

‘The warrant will be printed at my desk. I’ll just clear it with the Inspector.’

She was through to her superior now. Lox could see the doubts in her mind – her face was flushed and she spoke too quickly. But he’d drawn her in and, for better or worse, she was committed. She waited. She spoke again, thanking her Inspector and signing off. Then she disconnected with a flourish of her right forefinger and said,

‘I’ll go and get that warrant.’

As she stood up Bridie said,

‘Got it. Gold Prosthetics. Owned by Theodora Goldstein. Address - oh, there are two. Ah, one’s in Edinburgh: 3 Millerfield Place.’

‘Cross-check Theodora Goldstein.’

‘On it.’ Her fingers flittered over her compad again. McCall went for the warrant. Gravitas be blowed, they were pretty *and* they were effective: what more could a man ask for? It was something of a novelty for Lox to be on the right side of the law, and to have it pleasing to the eye was a first. He was only too happy to sit back in his chair and see what they could come up with.

‘Ah,’ Bridie said a couple of minutes later. ‘She’s got a record.’

Lox felt a warm glow of vindication.

Bridie was reading and scrolling. Lox moved round her side of the interview table to try and get a look, but the words were moving up the tiny screen too fast. Bridie was obviously practised at this.

‘Nothing recent,’ Bridie said, ‘but a lot of minor stuff before that. Years of it. Let’s see - vagrancy, soliciting, possession of Class A substances, registered addict. I’m downloading a copy of this to DS McCall.’

McCall finally bustled back in, her eyes glued to her compad where Bridie’s forwarded information was obviously appearing. Bridie continued to speed read. She read quicker than McCall. Each woman gave a sharp intake of breath when they’d finished. Bridie finished first, Lox looked the question at her.

Bridie said: ‘She’s only been in control of the company for six months, since her father died. Does that strike anyone else as suspicious?’

She pressed a key on her compad, saving the search and closing the file. Lox couldn’t entirely repress a little grunt of disappointment. He’d have liked a good rummage through the stuff she’d turned up. She grinned at him.

‘Police records, Mr Tuthill. Not available to the press, I’m afraid.’

Nevertheless, she let him look over her shoulder as she delved into the databases. She was good at x-refing and soon had a pretty full picture of what Theodora Goldstein’s life had been like up until 2036:

after that, nothing. She had apparently slipped back onto the right side of the law. Her medical file was particularly interesting. Not only had she been a registered addict last time the police had sight of her, she had also been suffering from M-RTB. That was the last entry, from a hospital in London. Bridie looked up at McCall.

'That's nearly three years ago. She should be dead by now.'

'But she isn't,' said Lox. He started to think aloud. 'Poor little rich girl gets pissed off with her boring life of plenty, runs away from home looking for a way to spice it up and falls in with bad company. When she finally comes unstitched at the seams, the hospital contacts her family so that they can get her medical bills paid. And the family bring her home. But now she's a bird in a gilded cage, bought and paid for.' He looked up at McCall, down at Bridie. 'Is this or is this not the sort of woman who might well have some kind of grudge against society?'

McCall said, 'let's go.'

5.5

Smiling Bridie was snowed under with admin. Lox accompanied the attractive but much less approachable McCall back to Cowgate. McCall kept up a brisk pace which rubbed Lox's blisters back to life. The brittle mood that had been evident on the streets earlier was turning sullen now.

Edinburgh boasted a truly Scottish number of drinking establishments. They passed more than twenty. Each was bursting at the doors with patrons. Most people were drunk. If the dear old dependable car could turn on them so suddenly and completely, what could you depend on? Drink was the other faithful friend, and they had need of a friend tonight.

There would be trouble later. You could see it in the way that groups met, mingled, then split apart suddenly. It was like watching aimless amoebas under a microscope. In another few hours gangs would start to form, then missiles and weapons would be sought. Then windows would start to go and people would be accused of 'looking at me like that' and finally the Police would be sent for. Lox doubted it would do their reputation any good when they turned up on bicycles.

Lox was a cowardly, desk-bound journalist whose only regular exercise was lifting pints of beer and whisky chasers and his companion weighed about fifty kilos wringing wet, although she doubtless had ways of subduing drunks. Lox was glad when they reached their destination unmolested. And his feet were twin areas of misery by the time they stood outside the big, blue wooden door of Gold's Prosthetics.

The building looked as deserted as it had on his first visit. McCall rang the bell anyway.

'I should have brought a Constable with a ram,' she said ruefully.

'There's another entrance,' Lox offered.

'Let's go.'

Lox led her around the side to the padlocked door.

'Hmm. This is new,' said McCall.

Lox had somehow imagined that locked doors would be no barrier to a police detective. He was wrong. Both the door and the padlock were substantial. They had a red-hot search warrant and no way to action it.

'We should have brought the key holder,' said McCall.

'Shoulda, woulda, coulda. If we had, we'd have alerted them to what it is that we think we know about their activities.'

'True enough. Where's this basement, then?'

'At least I can show you that.'

They went on round the alleyway to the basement window. Lox crouched down. He could see nothing. It was nearly nine o'clock in the evening now, and the alley was gloomy. McCall handed him a flashlight and he poked it about awkwardly in the space between the wall and the window until he managed to make it shine inside. The many years' accumulation of grime on both sides of the glass turned the window into a murky mirror. Lox tried leaning down and brushing away the worst of the muck on the outside with his sleeve, but there was more on the inside and matters didn't improve much.

Lox swore and, frustrated, tried to lurch to his feet. The flashlight waved wildly for a moment and then connected with the window. There was a loud crack followed by the tinkle of falling glass.

For a moment everything was still. Then a burglar alarm began to sound at the front of the building. Lox's first instinct was to leg it. He had taken part in enough ill-judged teenage pranks in his time for it to be an automatic response to something breaking and alarms going off. But a moment's consideration convinced him that this was a blessing: a really huge blessing.

Ignoring the distant wailing of the alarm, he hunkered down again and peered through the hole the flashlight had made. Then he threw caution to the winds and smashed out the rest of the glass in the pane so as to make room to stick his head in without cutting his throat on the broken shards. Finally he achieved a fit. It was all there: computer (crunching unidentifiable numbers), phials, aquarium, the bed in the corner, the strange pale plant.

'Here,' he said. McCall took his place at the window.

When they had both had a good look McCall said, 'now we really do have to go and get the key holder – someone has to shut that alarm off, have a look around the place, see if anything's missing.'

'And show us a way into the basement.'

'Exactly.'

5.6

Sara Prosser was making work in the kitchen.

Around midnight Gates Hanford had banged the big old knocker of their front door. Something about their body language suggested to Sara that Hanford and Teddy would rather be alone, so she had gone to tidy up the kitchen. She hadn't heard the front door go again, but Hanford was a genius at coming and going without leaving a trace.

It was now very late. Time for all good patients to try and get some sleep. Sara made her way across the big, dark hall and peered cautiously into Teddy's sick room. She was somewhat relieved to see no Hanford there. 'Has he gone?'

Teddy looked tiny in the bed. A drip snaked up from one arm to an intravenous feed hung on a stand beside the head of the bed. Another fed painkiller into the other arm. A variety of wires led to a bank of monitors behind the bed head. Teddy refused to have them where she could see them.

Teddy put up a hand to the oxygen mask which covered her face and, with obvious difficulty, pushed it slowly up into her hair. In that position the air line looked like as if it was sucking her brains out of the top of her head. Her cheeks had a fierce, unhealthy flush. Her eyes sparkled with fever. She looked obscenely merry, lying in the hospital cot with tubes snaking around her like party streamers: she spoke slowly, her voice breathy and ragged.

'Yes, he's gone. He gave me something.'

'What?'

'Hundreds and thousands.' Sara wondered if her patient was delirious and picked up a thermometer. 'A capsule. Full of shiny silver grains. He's put it in a little box. Like Alice in Wonderland. There's a note in the lid. It says 'this is good for all that ails you'. I think he thought you wouldn't let him see me.'

Sara put the thermometer on her patient's forehead. 'You didn't take it did you?'

Teddy snorted. It made her cough. When the spasm had subsided she gasped out,

'Of course not. What do you think? I'm stupid? I wanted you to see.'

'Thank Christ for that.'

Teddy rummaged painfully about in the bedding, found the little box and opened it. The capsule nestled on a scrap of cotton waste. Something inside it glittered.

'But I'm going to.' The grin that followed this statement was a truly gruesome thing. There was blood on her teeth.

Sara was close enough to grab the capsule out of Teddy's hand. But, kill or cure, this was Teddy's only hope. She had only days left now: possibly hours.

'You know what's in that capsule, don't you?'

Teddy's grin became another coughing spasm. Sara put a hand up to the oxygen mask. Teddy's hand caught her wrist.

'Not yet. Yes, I know what it is. It's a miracle. A most illegal miracle. These little silvery doo-dahs are going to zap the fucking tuberculosis bacilli. Then I'm going to eat up my veggies like a good girl and my lungs are going to heal.' She picked up the little silver capsule. 'This is going to make me well.'

'You're certifiable.'

'Certifiable or dead. I know which I prefer.'

'What makes you think he's finally delivered? He had nothing running when they closed us down. He's done nothing, Teddy. He was a major error of my judgement and I've cursed myself for getting your hopes up every day since he arrived. He's a waste of space. This is probably swarf, or cake decorations.'

'I know he's delivered.'

'How?'

'Because he said so.'

Sara sat down on the end of the bed, as far away from the capsule as she could get. The business in the States had shaken her belief in the value of Nanonics to cure disease. Nanites used fluorine. Human bodies contained fluorine. There had never been a fatality from rogue nanites and she really, really didn't want the first one to be Teddy Goldstein.

'I *really* wouldn't take what he says at face value.'

'What do you mean.'

'He's nuts, Teddy. There may be nanites in that capsule, or sugar granules, or rat poison. The bugs *may* cure you, but it's more likely that they aren't what he says they are. Or they could kill you - eat you from the inside out, with you screaming as they chew through your guts and leave nothing but a hole where your organs used to be.'

'But he's done this,' she held up the little capsule like a talisman.

'Yeh, right. You see why I counsel caution? When Nanonics went belly-up he disappeared – if you remember I had to track him down via a bulletin board and a pre-teen chat room. When I approached him to come and work for you he was so delighted that I think he would have come for nothing. In fact, he did come for nothing – his entire salary has been paid into an off-shore trust with a numbered account: I've no idea what he's living on. He's strange – he knows Nanonics, but he's *extremely* strange.'

'What else is there?' Teddy paused to catch her breath again. 'If I don't do this I'll be dead in a week.' Another pause while she read Sara's face. 'OK, make that a couple of days. You got any better ideas?'

Sara shook her head.

'OK then. You want to watch me take it, or you want to leave? Whatever, I need to put the mask back on in a minute, or I won't be breathing long enough to do anything.' She was panting. Sara could see the truth of what Teddy was saying etched into the pain lines on her face. What right had she to try and talk her out of this, really?

'Take it. Do it now. I'll sit with you.'

Sara put Teddy's oxygen mask back in place. Then she held out her hand and Teddy dropped the capsule into it. Sara put it carefully back in the box and looked at it closely. If this *was* what Hanford said it was, it was a fantastic moment. Sara smiled at Teddy, then fished around at the side of the bed, found the controls and raised the bed so that Teddy was sitting up properly. This was an occasion. There should be dignity. As much as they could muster between them.

She was surprised that Hanford hadn't hung around to see what effect his concoction had. He'd been working towards this, after all, for nearly ten years: maybe longer. And Teddy was the first person prepared - no; call it for what it was, desperate enough – to give him his head.

Sara poured fetched water from the cooler in a paper cup, removed the oxygen mask once more, and handed the cup to Teddy.

'No,' Teddy said.

'Thank God you've changed your mind.'

'It should be scotch. There's some in the cupboard. Please.'

Sara sighed mightily and bent to look in Teddy's bedside cupboard. There was half a bottle of Bell's in there. How the hell had she managed that? Sara fetched a fresh cardboard cup from the water cooler and poured a generous measure.

'Straight?'

'No. Add some water. Same again.' Sara carefully added water from the first cup. She gave it to Teddy. Teddy's hand was trembling and Sara held it steady with her own for a moment before picking up the capsule. She held it out and looked quizzically at her friend.

'Are you really sure?'

'Really.'

'Kill or cure,' Sara said, and handed her the capsule.

'Nothing like a good cliché in moments of crisis,' Teddy croaked. She brought the capsule to her lips, popped it into her mouth, raised the cardboard cup in salute and washed Gates's present down her throat with most of the scotch.

Swallowing it was difficult. Teddy hadn't had anything solid for over a week. Her throat was raw and the effort of getting the capsule down racked her with coughing. Sara wondered if she'd manage to keep it down. When the worst of the fit was over Sara helped Teddy settle the oxygen mask back on and wiped her sweating forehead. She kept on smoothing past necessity, just stroking the lifeless hair. Teddy's eyes closed. She might have been dead already, except for the persistent meeping of the monitor beside the bed.

Sara settled down to wait.

6

6.1

Some three hours later Lox and McCall plodded back to Gold's, accompanied by Mr Angus Frasier, the company's Managing Director, and his security pass.

The streets were becoming alarming. On their way back down to Cowgate they passed a couple of gangs, with bricks and lengths of wood in their hands. The long arm of the law accompanying him was not in uniform, which might have brought their little party to the attention of such people.

By tacit agreement the three ignored the violence around them. They couldn't seem to find anything else to talk about on the walk, however. All were watchful and nervous.

It became obvious about half a klom from Gold's that all was not as it had been there when they left. The alarm was silent. They picked up their pace.

When they arrived Mr Frasier went in the front. McCall should really have gone in with him. And Lox should have stood outside. However, as one, Lox and McCall segued off round the side of the building to the broken window. Lox was delighted to discover that policewomen can be just as curious as journalists. In the basement room a lamp burned, throwing a glow up onto the path. They knelt and peered in. The workstation was gone, everything else – including the strange, pale plant - remained. But it was obvious that whoever had been using the room wasn't coming back.

Lox followed McCall round the building to the basement steps and inched cautiously down them after her. The padlock was gone and the door stood ajar. Damn and bugger. There didn't seem to be any point in stumbling around in the dark any more under the circumstances so he switched on his flashlight. McCall did the same. They went inside.

Only that one room had light spilling under its door. They went up the passage circumspectly. It was a spooky old building – Lox had never completely gotten over that leg dangling over the street – and spooky things had been happening down here. He wasn't sure if he was expecting to be jumped by a gang of fanatics, find half the basement mysteriously eaten away, or trip over a sleeping tramp. Any or all would not have surprised him. The room which had contained so much four hours previously now contained very little. The workstation was gone, the aquaria were empty. But McCall was resourceful. She pulled her compad and an add-on out of her bag.

'DNA tracer,' she said, to Lox's enquiring glance. 'Never leave home without one.' She grinned at him as she plugged the two together. From the taciturn McCall that was a first.

She began methodically to scan the surfaces of the room.

'Whoever was here must have left something - hair, skin flakes, snot, sweat. If it's here this will find it. If we can find it we can tell who was here. Simple.'

McCall crept painstakingly about the room. It looked like this was going to take a while, so Lox wandered off to see if whoever it was had left any more visible traces elsewhere else in the basement.

He looked into every room. None was locked. There was nothing but old, dusty, rotting stuff. Dust lay thick on the floors, undisturbed for years.

But in the corridor it was a different matter. There was a definite line of disturbance running along that. Keeping to the margins of the corridor, Lox followed it. The messed up dust led to a flight of stairs at the front of the building. At the top was a door which had been locked. Someone had recently opened it with a large screwdriver. Much of the door jamb lay on the floor in splinters, as did the screwdriver. Lox stepped over the mess and through the open door.

He was in the main lobby now. It was a grand old space, high and boasting ornate mouldings on the walls and ceiling. On the wall in front of him, above and to the side of the front door, hung the remains of the burglar alarm. A chair stood underneath the alarm and on it lay a hammer. In front of this little tableau stood Mr Frasier, looking glum.

When Frasier stepped forward things scrunched under his feet, and Lox noticed that bits of the alarm were all over the hall. It looked like whoever it was had been pretty weirded-out when he'd come back and found the place screaming. Not so freaked as to leave behind anything useful in the way of computer equipment, software, or nano samples however. Mr Frasier said,

'Just a burglary, that's all,' and gave a hearty sigh.

'I think you'll find that they broke in at the back,' said Lox. 'A padlock's a pretty easy thing to get past.'

'A padlock?'

'Yep, that's what was holding your basement door shut.'

'Good Lord! I had no idea.'

The owner of that peculiar plant back in the basement might have left something of himself on the tools up here. Gingerly Lox picked up the hammer, using a tatty tissue he found in his pocket, and began to retrace his steps, followed by Mr Frasier. As Lox went through the door at the top of the stairs he also retrieved the screwdriver.

McCall showed Frasier the padlock and then shooed him back upstairs to see if anything had been taken. She and Lox were much more interested in what was in the basement than what was upstairs. And explaining what they thought might have been going on down there – and the plant – to Mr Frasier was entirely too complicated an ask.

It took her the best part of an hour to scan the room with the plant in it, and the tools that Lox brought back with him. Then she went and scanned the trail of footprints, the broken door, the chair and the alarm. Finally she switched off the equipment. Slipping it back into pocket and bag, she said:

'Now we need to get back to the Station, so that I can download what we've got and see whose detritus we've picked up. I suppose I ought to go up and have a word with the MD. The chippie ought to be along any time to cover the window and doors – but with the city like it is, who knows?'

The carpenter had come as promised, and was waiting in the lobby with Mr Frasier. McCall gave him his instructions and Mr Frasier said he'd show him where the work was to be done. Then Mr Frasier shook hands with Lox and McCall and thanked them gravely for their trouble. He seemed to think that Lox was a policeman. Lox didn't disabuse him.

Mr Frasier locked the front door behind them as they left. It still wasn't really dark out, although it was nearly eleven o'clock. *Good looting light*, Lox thought morosely. Now that he was faced with the walk back to the police station he realised how very tired he was. And how very close to a good story.

'I need a bath and a drink,' said McCall, 'not necessarily in that order.'

Lox could have murdered a pint himself, to cut the dust and revive his feet. But he knew they were going straight back to the police station, and he knew that he was going to talk her out of stopping at any hostelries they passed. He badly wanted to know what the DNA tracer had picked up. He could almost feel the electronic thrum of credit being transferred to his bank account.

6.2

Teddy's condition hadn't changed for eight hours. Sara sat beside her, waiting for the miracle that Teddy had been so sure of, berating herself for letting Teddy's tubercular euphoria get the better of her own clinical judgment. It was probably mercury or rat poison that the poor woman had taken. But at least she was sleeping, and all the readouts were steady.

At some point Sara was going to have to call a halt to this crazy experiment and run the tests which would demonstrate Teddy's true condition. She'd give it half an hour more, after that ...

A surprisingly raucous dawn chorus had come and gone, and morning was slipping round the edges of the curtains, cold and pale, when Sara finally stood up and stretched her cramped muscles. She needed the loo. After the loo she treated herself to a shower, a change of clothes, a cup of tea and a brief listen to the radio while she was making it. It was good to hear about something outside her own tightly focussed concerns. The news bulletins were about as grim as her own situation. What the hell was going on in the world? London was at a standstill, and they were saying other cities were affected too - even Edinburgh. That explained that extra-loud dawn chorus, then.

What would she do if Teddy needed an ambulance?

*****

Sara picked up her mug. It was, sadly, time for those tests. Carrying her tea, she set off for the dining room again.

When she got there she found Teddy sitting on the side of the bed.

When she saw Sara, Teddy stood up without apparent effort and did a clumsy twirl. Sara hadn't realised just how emaciated her patient had become. The sleeves of Teddy's PJs hung down over her fingers and in between twirls she had to hold the trousers up.

'See? I'm cured.'

Sara discovered she had spilt her tea, when it splashed hot onto her feet and legs. Teddy looked like hell – but she looked like hell standing up. She stood on one leg, then hopped onto the other. She clapped her hands and the lights came on. She clapped them again and the curtains opened. All the room seemed to be in motion.

'I'm starving. Let's make breakfast – eggs and bacon, toast, mushrooms, coffee. Come on.'

Teddy started for the kitchen. Sara stood rooted to the spot. Teddy had been incapable of getting out of bed, let alone standing up. Now she was standing and twirling and hungry. Remarkable didn't begin to describe it. And there was almost nothing in the house to eat. Damn. Sara felt that events had caught her up and blasted past her in the fast lane, horns blaring. She did her best to respond. Following her erstwhile patient across the hall, she said:

'Coffee. We can do coffee. Then I'll have to go shopping. And I should run some tests – see what is actually going on inside you. This is certainly the most remarkable remission I've ever seen. But try not to get your hopes up too much. It could be temporary.'

Teddy danced over to the kitchen window and stared out at the morning. She stretched like someone waking up after a long sleep.

'I'm not getting my hopes up, Sara: I'm better. He's cured me. It's like I've been touched by an angel.'

She brought her arms down and returned to her customary slouch.

'Or, that's what I would say if I believed in any of that crap, which I don't. But he's done it all the same.' She turned to Sara. 'I can go home to Dunster now. Or anywhere.'

'Ah, actually, no you can't,' said Sara.

Teddy's euphoria drained out of her in an instant. 'Why the hell not?'

'I guess you haven't been paying much attention to the news.'

'Damned right. I've been a bit busy dying.'

'Yes. Well, there isn't any transport.'

'We'll hire a jetpod. That's what we usually do.'

'I don't think they'll be flying. Everything's stopped.'

'Oh, that's ridiculous.'

'You'd think so, wouldn't you? But all the same, nothing's moving in Edinburgh.'

'How come?'

'Some sort of sabotage, they think. Petrol, diesel and LPG don't work any more, not in Edinburgh, nor London, nor New York, nor various other cities all over the world – and the number's growing. They were saying it was some kind of virus on the news just now. Only, of course, petroleum can't catch a virus. It's like saying that a building can catch a cold. People have been using up what's in their tanks and when that's gone, as soon as they fill up, some sort of contagion gets in and what's in the tank turns to goop that internal combustion engines can't run on. Why the hell they should pick on Edinburgh is beyond me. New York I could understand. And today of all days …'

'But the jetpods run on something different, don't they?'

'No – it's still petrol, just higher octane. They'll have to put fuel into it to get to Dunster and back, then it'll be grounded too.'

'Check.'

'I will – but do you know what time it is? It's just after six. Nobody at the jetpod office will have a pilot at this hour without a prior booking. Wait a couple of hours. Don't piss everybody off first thing.'

'Ek'll be up. He and Rory'll be milking.'

'Exactly. Wait until they've done that, then give them the good news. Don't piss the cows off.'

Thwarted, Teddy started hopping from foot to foot, like a child whose treat has been taken away. Sara looked at her with concern. The behaviour looked very much like tubercular frenzy.

'So I'm stuck here?'

'Well, you don't have to stay *here*. You can go anywhere you can walk to. It'll do you good to get a bit of gentle exercise. And they say the trains are still running, for the moment. You could go home to Dunster that way.'

'That'd take *ages*. I don't want to be sitting down for hours and hours. I want to *do* stuff.'

Sara tried a laugh which didn't come out too badly, considering. 'If you're that keen on getting out *you* can go shopping for breakfast. I've been living on pizzas recently. If you don't mind, though, I'll run some tests first, see if we can work out what's going on.'

Sara ran the tests and, sure enough, Teddy's tissues displayed no signs of tubercles, the TB bacteria or, indeed, any sign of illness at all. Her liver had been something of a mess before. Now it was as healthy as that of a new-born baby. There was a robust colour in her cheeks - not the fierce fevered flush of the disease, but a pink glow. If Sara hadn't known better she might have thought that the woman was pregnant. Indeed, her hormones were rampant – and Sara knew for a fact that Teddy hadn't had a period for over a year. Everything about her patient exuded health. This was too good to be true. Wasn't it?

Finally Sara ran out of tests. Without admitting anything, she said:

'Well, you'd better have a shower and get dressed if you're going shopping.'

Teddy skipped out of the room and headed for the stairs like a teenager. When Teddy's organs had begun to fail four days earlier Sara hadn't had the heart to leave her for even the brief time it took to fetch something from the chippy or the chinky. Now she realised that the menu Teddy had planted in her mind was making her salivate: when had she last eaten? She began to look forward eagerly to breakfast – and had a few ingredients of her own to add.

She certainly wasn't about to let Teddy go shopping on her own. Even after all those tests Sara was still sceptical. And Teddy had had nothing except what Sara had been able to get into her intravenously for a week. They'd both go. They'd buy bacon and eggs, mushrooms and black pudding, beans and waffles, bread and butter, oh – all kinds of nice things. Sara found she had a sudden hankering for a steak and kidney pudding. Absurd at half past six in the morning.

6.3

Lox had walked with McCall back to Leith Police Station, seen the DNA samples uploaded and learned, without great surprise, that the analysis would take several hours. He hung around for the rest of the night, hoping for a cup of tea at least, but McCall had reverted to type.

As the night got old his adrenalin high turned sour, his feet swelled inside his shoes and his calf muscles tightened into hard knots. In the past eighteen hours or so he'd done a great deal of walking. Fearing that he might be about to seize up solid, and knowing that he had to take his shoes off soon or his feet would explode, he plodded out into the dawn heading for the Balmoral.

Damn, those birds could sing. Lox didn't usually do dawn. In his recent line of work eleven a.m. had been a perfectly acceptable hour to rise at. He found it unsettling to walk through the streets of a city with nothing but the birds for company.

He got back to his room at the Balmoral a bit after six. Removing his shoes was one of the most painful things he had ever done. He had to soak his socks off, and the warm water stung his blisters cruelly. Lox thought longingly of slippers for the first time in his adult life.

He compensated with the mini-bar. At this hour of the morning it was entirely medicinal and it was, after all, on expenses. He could feel the Laphroiag begin coursing towards his lower limbs. Balm was on its way.

Drink in hand he glanced, out of habit, towards his compad. A light flashed 'message waiting' at him. He sighed and wove his way wearily around the bed to answer the summons. A journalist's work was never done.

It was a message from his Editor:

Tuthill: I seem to remember that it was a message from some people calling themselves the Green X Group that convinced me to allow you your jaunt to Edinburgh. In the interests of getting something useable out of it I append another message from them received here, in case it means more to you than it does to us. You can see from the circulation list that it has been sent to the world and his dog. In the light of recent events it is causing rather more interest than hitherto. Make what you can of it.

I should tell you that London traffic is at a standstill. You would oblige me by checking out of that horrendously expensive hotel and finding yourself somewhere B & B until all this blows over. It looks like you're there for the duration, lad.

Gardner

The message was appended:

People of Earth,

Gaia will tolerate your destruction no longer. You know now what her servants can do. Consider your options. This is not a threat, it is a promise: we will not let you destroy our world.

Gaia has said 'enough', and you must listen.

Green X Group

He already knew it was the petrol, but confirmation was always nice. He filed the Green X message in his, now substantial, 'look to the streets of Edinburgh' folder. He wondered if the police had had the sense to take sample swabs around the petrol tanks of the original non-starting cars at the Balmoral. Whatever they'd been checking for at that time would probably not have shown up the real cause of the problem. Now that they knew what they were looking for, they could analyse the samples for it. And, of course, there was the stuff McCall had analysed at Gold's.

The old articles he'd found about public mistrust of Nanonics and the new information about the 'escape' in the States made him pretty certain that if 'Gaia' had any idea what her minions were using to save the world she'd be throwing up volcanoes and tsunamis in a proper strop. But it really was beginning to look as though whoever had been working in Gold's basement was one of 'Gaia's' barking mad minions. That didn't make him feel any better.

He'd better get a personnel listing for Gold's. Then he could get it cross-checked for wackos. If it wasn't so ridiculously early he could get it done by Gray's office. He called the police to see if McCall could put some help his way but, unsurprisingly, she had gone home.

Blessing asynchronous communication, he sent a quick note to Gray Gardner:

> Am gathering information which will prove that the Green X Group are at the bottom of this transport crisis. Preliminary article should be with you tomorrow. I have walked the streets of Edinburgh for eighteen hours straight today (since nothing is moving here either) and am far too <expletive deleted by system> to find anywhere else to stay tonight. Trust me, this is going to be huge.
>
> Tuthill.

He needed to pee. Standing was amazingly painful. His feet instantly became two enormous, throbbing lumps of putty. He minced to the bathroom, trying to find some bit of either foot that he could place on the floor without pain. Then he minced back to the bed and lay down. He'd sleep for a couple of hours. Then he'd write the best story he'd ever written.

6.4

Teddy took her time upstairs. When she came down again she was shining. The clothes she'd found in her old room hung off her: a pair of jeans and a shirt which probably hadn't originally been the overshirt it appeared to be. Her hair was still wet. Her skin glowed.

They made a list – a long list. To list the favourite foods of two hungry people can take a while. Then they realised that, without transport, they'd have to make do with what they could find at the corner shop and carry it all home, so they crossed a lot of things off it. Then they wondered what time the shop opened and Teddy thought it was seven, so they decided to get going as it was now nearly half past.

The early morning seemed to have a zing in it. The grass of The Meadows across the road from the house must have been cut the day before. Sara could smell its grassiness as they walked along beside it.

When they got to the corner shop it was closed. Deflated but increasingly hungry they walked towards the city centre, certain that they'd find somewhere open soon. Several premises had notices stuck to their doors blaming lack of deliveries for their inability to open. The business with the petrol had seemed an inconvenience before. Now they could see it was a serious problem. Finally they had to admit defeat. Teddy wasn't looking so good any more. Her eyes seemed to have sunk into her skeletal face and there were bruised-looking circles around them.

Teddy needed to eat – that was obvious. She also needed to sit down. About half past ten they paused for Teddy to rest in Bristo Square.

'This is ridiculous. For not even a café to be open ... If you don't eat something soon its going to undo all the good ...'

'All the good Gates has done me?'

'I wasn't going to go that far. Hold on there a minute – I'm going to try something drastic.'

Sara made Teddy promise not to go anywhere without her and made her way briskly to the university buildings in the Square. There must be food there somewhere.

6.5

Sara plonked the tatty carrier bag on the table in the kitchen. Teddy was very subdued. They hadn't passed an open shop on the way home either. No matter what had happened to her ... inside, stamina would take time to return. To build up stamina needed good food and plenty of it. The action of those tiny silver granules was probably contributing to her exhaustion. Now that the infection was gone her cells would be working overtime to restore her body. They were doing an amazing job.

Sara had spun an excellent yarn about a diabetic emergency to the staff in the kitchens of the university's refectory. They had given her eggs, bacon a loaf of pappy-looking sliced white bread and a cleaned out plastic yoghurt pot with some margarine in it. Sara had wanted to pay, but they had no facilities to swipe her Smart Card as the refectory was closed til lunch. The staff had worried with her about where the next meal was coming from. The fear in their voices had begun to communicate itself to Sara. As soon as they'd eaten this she would go out and try and find more. The Millerfield Place House didn't have the well-stocked, anti-terror store cupboard that many houses did.

Sara cooked the food and got it onto plates in short order. Teddy was nearly out on her feet. They sat and ate in silence. There was no pleasure in the breakfast after all.

As soon as they had finished Sara suggested that Teddy should have a lie down. She got no argument. She tried to help Teddy into her cot in the converted drawing room, but Teddy wasn't having any of that. They mounted the stairs with Sara almost carrying her patient. Teddy lay on the little single bed in her old room. Sara pulled the duvet over her. Then she went out foraging in earnest. In the pit of her stomach was an uncomfortable knot. She knew it to be apprehension, not indigestion.

6.6

Sara put away the few extra groceries she'd been able to buy and started cleaning. She knew this to be displacement activity. Not that the kitchen couldn't do with a good clean. It had been neglected while she had been taken up with Teddy's decline. It had a smell. It couldn't be healthy. Teddy didn't need any new bacteria at present.

And while she was scrubbing and chucking stuff out she didn't have to think about what she'd seen out on the streets.

She filled three black sacks and put them outside the back door. She tried to remember what day the bins were collected here. Then she realised it was unlikely they'd be collected at all, in the circumstances. Stamping down hard on a general feeling of dread, she made some tea and took a mug up to Teddy. Her patient was sleeping, so Sara left the tea and went back to the kitchen, where she realised she had finally run out of things to do. She sat down at the table, put her head in her hands and wept.

When she heard the thump of the door knocker she was glad of the distraction. Her first thought was that it must be Hanford. Her second thought was that it couldn't be: it was daylight and Hanford was a creature of the night. Who else could it be? Teddy had no friends in Edinburgh, as far as Sara could tell. And for somebody to come now, with Edinburgh frozen and fearful, was surely strange? She went to answer the summons. On the doorstep stood two uniformed police officers.

They would accept no excuses, even though Sara explained that Teddy was sleeping. Ms Goldstein must rise and come with them now. And she was? Ah, Dr Prosser. She would also come down to the station. They would wait. She and Ms Goldstein would kindly refrain from using a comm link; any calls could be made at the station. She wouldn't mind if they had a look around while they waited, would she? Here was a search warrant, in case she did mind.

Sara plastered a smile onto her face, her mind in a whirl. She'd always been a law-abiding person. Faced with two stern and determined police officers she could barely think. To give herself time, she asked them if they would like some coffee while they had their look around. They would.

She scurried out to the kitchen and put the kettle on, trotted upstairs to wake Teddy, told her what was happening, then went down and made the coffee. She delivered two mugs to the officers, now snooping around in Teddy's sick room.

'I'm afraid there's no milk,' she said. There had been no milk to be had anywhere.

While they drank their coffee, she tried to find out what they wanted to talk to Teddy about. Then she tried to find out what they knew about Edinburgh's paralysis. She drew a blank on both. Finally she tried small talk, but the two just slurped up scalding coffee and answered her in monosyllables while they poked about the rest of the downstairs rooms. When they had finished their coffee and were making for the stairs she followed them, to see how Teddy was getting on.

Sara went into Teddy's room and shut the door. The police officers were rummaging around in the airing cupboard on the landing.

Teddy was getting on fine. She looked stick-thin and marvellous – what used to be called 'heroin chic' back in the Noughties.

'What do the police want?'

'They won't say. I suppose it must be something to do with yesterday's shut-down at The Works. It's probably just routine.'

But Teddy wasn't really thinking about the police officers. Sara could tell she was just enjoying being able to breathe and not being in pain. She looked … amazing.

Teddy brushed her hair in front of the mirror.

'The waif look,' she grinned into the mirror at Sara standing behind her and struck a pose. 'I feel *so* good.'

'You look it.'

'Let's go see what they want.'

Teddy bounced out of the door, along the landing, down the stairs and into the hall. Only yesterday Teddy had to have help to push the oxygen mask off her face so that she could swallow Hanford's concoction. *Hanford.* She wouldn't put anything beyond Hanford. This visit from the police couldn't be something to do with him, could it?

By the time Sara joined the others in the hall the police officers had arrested Teddy. Then they arrested Sara too. The charge was production of, or conspiracy to produce, banned substances. It was difficult for Sara to find out whether this was to do with the Notice served on The Works yesterday or something more serious, because Teddy was protesting loudly and dancing about. Sara suspected that her synapses were firing pretty much at random. The police officers, of course, did not know this. As far as they were concerned they were having trouble with a prisoner. They insisted on handcuffing the bouncing Teddy. For good measure they also handcuffed Sara. Sara wanted to cry.

They would have to walk, of course, and it was a considerable hike. Teddy behaved as if she hadn't been outdoors for years. She exclaimed over every flower, bird and sunbeam until even Sara had enough and told her, quietly, to shut up. The police officers watched Teddy curiously. They probably thought she was on something – a breakfast upper, a little speed. Nothing more illegal than smoking a cigarette after breakfast used to be. But all the same, Sara could see it wasn't helping.

With Teddy chastened for the moment, Sara tried to think. The 'banned substances' must be Nanonics – as of yesterday. The police were really on the ball. She'd been rigorous about closing the project down as soon as the Notice had come through. But Teddy, of course, was full of nanites. If they found that out ...

Sara stole a glance at her friend. 'Reborn' was the word that sprang to mind. 'Rebuilt' was more like it. Teddy was a seething mass of tiny biomechanical regulators. It was apparent now that what Hanford had prepared and Teddy had swallowed had done rather more than treat her M-RTB.

Hanford must have continued working on his own after they'd been shut down. Typical. And it would be Dr Prosser, head of the research team, that was going to jail. At least in this scenario Teddy was off the hook. Unless they found out that Teddy was full of the 'banned substance'.

And where was Hanford? Waiting for them in a cell at the police station? Somehow Sara doubted that. In some sense Gates had been on the run for a long time. It was one of the several things he was very good at.

6.7

Around lunchtime Lox returned to the fray. His sleep had been fitful. He had dreamed, vividly, of an army of shiny, silver soldier ants marching inexorably towards him. The second time they woke him up he gave in and got up.

He commed RDonLine for the personnel information he needed on Gold Prosthetics, but got no reply. That was a blow on two counts. If Gray Gardner and his staff hadn't been able to get to their office this morning it was a safe bet that London was ... Lox tried to think of a word that didn't sound like the end of the world. *London.* Shit. He left a message and had a brief look at the newsnets. If London was fubared it would headline. It did:

> London at a standstill!
>
> The people of London are not at work today, because they can't get there. Buses aren't running and the Underground has been closed because of the danger posed by the enormous crowds of people attempting to use it. Private cars ...

There was a lot more in the same vein. Obviously no Data Protection-accredited PA was going to be available to get him Gold's personnel records.

Hacking the kind of information he needed the hard way was going to take hours. And information obtained illegally might hinder the police investigation rather than help. McCall had nice eyes, he remembered – big and grey-green, the colour of the English Channel on a spring day. He should ring her. Gold's files must be her next step too. And he'd ask her about any swabs they had lurking about from the Balmoral thing. Perhaps she'd share information with him under the circumstances.

In your dreams, Tuthill. What the hell was the matter with him? Had he really been out of circulation so long that *any* female was capable of grabbing him by the hormones? *McCall?* She had a manner like rough pumice and the social graces of a lioness that hasn't eaten recently.

But he did need those personnel files. On a whim and a prayer he commed the police station and asked for Bridie.

Bridie was not the sweet and helpful person he remembered.

'I really don't see how I can help you, sir.' The sir came out more like 'sore' with the brogue, which was pleasant to listen to.

'Bridie – it's me Lox, not some nameless GenPub. We're all in this together – we're just looking at it from different angles, is all. If I turn anything up you guys'll be the first to hear. All I need is ...'

'I don't know if they took any swabs from the Balmoral cars, sir. And if there were any taken it would be illegal for me to give you access to them – or to anybody's personnel records that we might happen to have impounded last night. And it would be even more illegal to let you cross-check anything with police files.'

'I'm going to get the information anyway. If you help me it'll be a lot quicker and we can get to the bottom of this whole thing sooner. Get back to normal. That'd be good, wouldn't it?'

'I haven't seen 'normal' since I joined the police. And I was a lot happier when you were just a GenPub, sir. You're going to get me into trouble if I help you. McCall said I wasn't to let you talk me into anything.'

Feebly, and running out of Reasons To Be Helpful, Lox reminded her that she had a lot to do today (it had been her opening gambit when he called) and that if he was crunching the data, she could get on with something else. There was a silence on her end, which became long. Then she broke the connection. Shit.

Lox started hacking.

Three hours later he was wandering the virtual corridors of Gold's personnel files like he owned them. God, he was good.

The artisans and machine minders he dismissed straight away. Most of them had been there since forever and no way would they have the skills and background to do whatever it was the Green X cell inside Gold's was doing. The most obvious place to start was with new scientific appointments. There had been five in the past four months. He started with them. Akemi, Guba, Hanford, Henri and Slovensky. Akemi was a microbial peptides specialist. Guba, Hanford, Henri and Slovensky were into … Nanonics! The research that had got them shut down was recent, then.

He was pleased to see that Gold's still gave psych tests to its new scientific appointees. Lox settled down to scrutinise their CVs in conjunction with the tests. Now, what would the documentation look like for a wack-job attempting to pass as sane?

But hang on. There was no psych profile for this Hanford. Just the one word: *pending.* Lox pulled up the man's CV and his employment history with Gold's. No family, no significant others, no home address, a two year gap in his résumé, hired over the Net with no interview. The last work Hanford had done in his field, according to a gappy CV, had been at the height of the previous Nanonics brouhaha. Since then, nothing. All Lox' instincts told him that Gates Hanford was a man he needed to talk to.

Now, if one was on the run, a loner, possibly a terrorist, and hated other people, where would one go? Lox pondered, his fingers wandering restlessly over the pad of his compad. Where would the bastard go?

He called Bridie again. This time she'd be pleased to hear from him.

6.8

At the police station all was bustle. A lot of dishevelled, dejected people were sitting and standing about. Some of them had blood on their clothes, some sported bandages. It had obviously been a busy night.

Sara expected that they would have to wait with the dishevelled and dejected, but they were hustled right through the security door into an interview room in the bowels of the Station. They'd barely sat down when a detective bustled into the room. One of the uniformed officers who had brought them in left. The other took up station by the door.

The detective didn't switched on a DVD-rec and introduced herself as Officer in Charge Detective Sergeant McCall – to the machine rather than to Sara and Teddy.

McCall stated the time and asked for the full names of the interviewees. The words sounded odd in Sara's mouth as she said them. Neither she nor the words belonged here. She wasn't a criminal.

The McCall person kept right on going.

'Ms Goldstein, you are the owner of Gold's Prosthetics.'

The statement didn't appear to call for an answer, but McCall continued brusquely, 'You will answer please, for the record.'

'Yes,' said Teddy. She looked bemused. In a sense this was the first day of her life – a special day. It was wrong that she should be spending it here.

'We know,' continued McCall, 'that this address has been used until *very* recently for the production of Nanonics. We have evidence, and we have a witness.' Sara thought *Hanford.* It was a good job the camera couldn't read her mind.

'You will respond, please,' McCall said.

'Yes,' said Sara. 'Until it was banned yesterday we were working on a project involving Nanonics. As soon as we got the Directive I closed it down.'

'But you didn't close *all* of it down, did you? What about the research you had running in the basement?'

Sara felt sick. Of course! Hanford's absences from his workstation, the capsule he had brought for Teddy, his day-night inversion – it all pointed to his moonlighting on Nanonics. He was much further ahead with the work than he should have been for the amount of time he'd spent at his desk. Sara thought back to the number of times she had sent people to look for him. Where had he been all those times? In the very building, damn him. And why should he be working in the basement on something which he should have been working on anyway? He'd been working on something else, using Gold's to resource it and as cover.

'What do you want me to say? If you know this then you know more than I do.' Sara spoke sharply.

'You have been directing research into Nanonics at Gold's Prosthetics. And this is the owner of the business.' McCall glared at Teddy. 'Surely *you* ought to know what is being done on your premises and in your name. And *you*,' she turned a Gorgon eye on Sara, 'should know what your staff are doing.'

She had a point. Sara had tried to find the bloody man; to check on what he was doing. As far as she had been able to tell he hadn't been doing anything. But he had been. All the time, by the look of it. Only criminals came into police interview rooms. Only criminals went to jail. Were they criminals? Teddy, glowing with health, straining to be out bounding around, smelling the day, had certainly colluded with Hanford. He had made her well, although he had broken the law to do it. Teddy didn't care. Sara found it hard to care either. The project they had undertaken had been predicated on Nanonics. It was what Teddy had asked them to do at the Board meeting when she had volunteered to be their guinea pig. Death really *wasn't* necessary – they had proved that. Nobody had been harmed, nothing had 'escaped'. Bad timing, that's all it was. But Sara was certain that she and Teddy were going to jail for a very long time.

'What do you want us to tell you?' Sara said, wearily. She wanted this to be over.

'We want to know where Gates Hanford is,' said McCall.

So they knew who they were looking for, and he wasn't in custody. No surprise on either count.

'Aren't we supposed to be allowed one com-call?' Teddy asked.

Sara was surprised at the interruption. Teddy had seemed overcome by events. Sara hadn't even been sure she was taking much of this in.

'Who do you want to call?' McCall, tersely.

'My solicitor.' Teddy was sitting up straighter now. Her hands were clasped before her on the table, not nervously, confidently. She gave McCall icy look for icy look. 'What you say may very well be true, but despite our professional relationships with Hanford – which are a matter of public record – there is no need to assume that we were aware of any … extra-curricular activities of his, and certainly no reason to suppose that we sanctioned them. Either of us. He may have abused our trust. Or,' she smiled, 'you may be clutching at straws to try and explain the recent, strange events in Edinburgh. Whatever – I want to call my lawyer, and I want to do it now.'

McCall sighed. 'Very well.' She nodded at the uniformed officer. 'Get these two booked in. Then give Ms Goldstein her call.'

6.9

Gates sat on a bench in The Meadows. His bike leant on the back of it, panniers bulging, sleeping bag tied to the top of them. He'd slept rough in Holyrood Park the night before. That had been useful. He'd had to leave Beauty behind. She'd have hated a night in the open anyway. He hoped they'd take care of her. He had always known that one day he might have to sacrifice her. And he had lost her in a good cause.

He watched the police come out of the Millerfield Place house with Teddy and Dr Prosser. He watched a team of people in anti-contamination suits go in with some sort of detection equipment. He watched them come out.

As soon as they had gone Gates moved in. He preferred a basement, but in this case he could see that was no good. The only two rooms below ground level both had a window facing out front. Any light would show on the street, any blackout device would look suspicious. It would have to be the attics, further away from prying eyes and easier to make private. The only problem was his bicycle. How to keep it safe and handy? He would be needing it shortly.

For the time being he just walked it nonchalantly round the garden path, and left it in the yard behind the house. He began to look for a way in. There was no simple padlock, but the old Chubb lock made him smile; it was no problem for a man used to 'creating' living spaces. He pulled a small tool kit out of one of the panniers and got started. It didn't take long.

Now he was in the kitchen, or to be more precise, the scullery which led to it. Between the two rooms was a narrow staircase. Of course. Upstairs in the attics was where the servants had lived when these houses were new. And they would need these stairs for delivering warming pans and cups of warm milk to the Nobs at bed-time. Perfect.

On the first floor there were five doors, one of them open. Inside he could see a lot of clothes strewn on the bed, as if somebody had been packing and interrupted. Had she felt that well so soon that she was going to leave? There was no way she could go, hadn't anyone thought to tell her? And anyway, the police had her now.

Had she worked out yet what he had done? By now his little silver saviours would be in every organ, every blood cell, every hair follicle on Teddy's head. Did she know?

He went into the bedroom. She had slept here, probably for years. This was her home. He went over to the bed, softly, as if she was sleeping in it and he didn't want to wake her. These were her things. He knelt down at the side of the bed and slowly thrust his hands into the pile of clothes, getting the smell of her. Then he laid his head on the pillow and closed his eyes. Oh, he hoped she hadn't been going to run from him. Not that he couldn't find her, no matter where she went. She would make a comm-call, a purchase, register somewhere and he would find her. He would go to her and be with her. She was the summit of his life's work – more marvellous even than saving the world from its own stupidity. How could they not see what a wonder he had achieved? 'This is good for all that ails you', oh yes. Gates began to chuckle. The chuckle became a full-blooded laugh. He lay there, laughing and rolling back and forth and clutching the pillow that smelled of her as if it was his lover.

7

7.1

Sara's cell was gruesome. The architecture was twentieth century Brutalist – all whitewashed concrete blocks and tubular steel. There were several rows of glass bricks set high up in what she assumed was the outside wall A little, pallid natural light filtered in through these, making the place look like an aquarium. It had been a glorious June day outside. In here it was chilly. Sara wished she'd thought to pack a bag and put a sweater in it. The two bunk beds, which were most of the furnishings, had their heads in the corner under the glass bricks. A stainless steel loo with no seat or cover and a wash hand basin smaller than a dog's bowl made up the rest. None looked very clean. The toilet was leaking from somewhere. There was no loo paper. The state of the plumbing reminded Sara just what deep shit she was in.

She had been disconcerted to be parted from Teddy, who had been taken elsewhere to call her solicitors. Teddy's sudden competence during the interview upstairs had been a surprise, and extremely welcome. Sara had no ideas of her own as to how they were going to get out of this – or, indeed, how they had got into it – so she was keen to hear Teddy on the subject, now that her friend was fully functional. Perhaps she should have commed her own solicitor? She used the firm her parents did, and they were in England, and that was a long, long way away now.

Sara dearly wanted a cup of tea. The thought of tea inevitably made her want to pee. She looked at the sanitary ware and crossed her legs. Miserable beyond belief, she started to rock gently, hugging herself to try and get warm.

7.2

Gates set up his usual nest of wires, equipment and bedding in Teddy's attic.

It had been a nuisance having to leave Gold's Works. It had been very convenient; he had been able to use their computer power to augment his own. It had been private; nobody had shown the slightest interest in the basement during the time he'd been living down there, until last night. Gates didn't believe in luck. Hanford's Second Law was *always take precautions*. Which is what he had been doing on the park bench opposite Millerfield Place this morning.

Nevertheless, there was nothing he needed to do that was beyond his own resources and although he felt terribly vulnerable perched up in this attic in the sky instead of being snugly below ground, he was sure he could cope with it for the short time that he was going to be here. He got down to business.

The first thing he did was hack the police computer. Their firewalls were absurdly naïve. He ascertained where Teddy was being kept. On her own. Good. Now to match the cell number with a plan of the building … ah, it was in the basement of the new block. How he loved basements. And the new block had windows, not the glass bricks that the old block had. Gates blessed whatever nanny-edict from the EU had made them build the new block with real windows. Glass bricks would have been much more difficult to deal with. But there was a window, and it faced south so it would get the moon: good. Next he cross-checked the plan number of the building with its planning permission in the City Council's records. Ah: he should have expected that – it made things more difficult. But nothing he couldn't handle. He called up Met Office Information. There was a full moon tonight, and it would rise at 0229. Now, what else? Ah yes, suspect's solicitors: e-mail address. He delved into Teddy's rap sheet for that, and was briefly startled at the number of entries it contained. He extracted the address.

He wanted her to know. He couldn't send that kind of information directly. Somebody might pick up on it, but via … what were they called? Barrie, Lewis & Muir. Senior partner: George Barrie. She'd want the best, wouldn't she? She'd always have the best. And who should the message be from? Not himself, certainly. Ah – there was a son: excellent. He thought fast and composed quickly:

> To: GeorgeBarrie@BarLewMuir.co.uk
>
> Re: Teddy Goldstein
>
> I have heard Teddy has taken a turn for the better. I have every confidence that she will live forever. Please tell her that I will see her very soon.

He signed it from Ek and set the words in a greetings card, then he scrambled the mailing protocols so that, should anyone be looking to see where the message came from, the game would not be worth the candle. Unless they were serious. And who would be serious about a son's message of comfort to his mother?

A full moon. He'd wondered about using light-activated swarms in his Green X work, but hadn't needed them in the end. This would be a good opportunity to complete the project. After he'd come back and found the bloody alarm ringing he'd made time to get back into the team's Clean Space and liberate a few last wafers of materials before he packed up his gear and moved on. It was such a shame he'd had to leave his Beauty behind.

Now he'd have a rummage around in the kitchen for something to start a new swarm in.

7.3

Teddy commed her solicitors. They were phased by the lack of transport. The junior to whom she spoke promised action, but couldn't say when it might be forthcoming. Teddy demanded to speak with George Barrie. This was obviously such a shock – usually their only contact with Teddy was when they brought her documents for signature, which she invariably signed without interest of any kind – that the youngster put her through without further question. George, however, was nearing ninety and, although his mind was as sharp as ever, his body was slowing. He promised to talk with the police – some mistake must have been made, Gold's a most reputable firm, sick as she was …etc, etc, but he didn't see how he could possibly get to Leith from Prestonpans as things were. Teddy would not be denied.

'Find a bicycle and get someone competent down here now. I do not intend to spend a day here, not now. I am certainly not going to spend a night.'

'We are, of course, working … hnh… vigorously on your behalf, but ...'

'Buy a bloody bicycle. Put it on my account.'

'My dear Ms Goldstein … hnh, hnh … bicycles are not to be had at any price. We have, hnh, researched such an acquisition. The streets are full of bicycles, the shops are empty of them. People are prepared to do violence for bicycles. The day of the bicycle is here, hnh, but who has one? I have to tell you that this firm does not, and sees no likelihood of procuring same in the near future. It appears that there is, hnh, some kind of war on. This has possibly escaped your notice, as you have been… hnh … sequestered, in the recent past. I will do my best. That is all I can do.'

He disconnected. It left Teddy rattled. He had only stated the obvious, but she realised she had missed something salient: Edinburgh was under siege, nothing could get in or out. Nothing, indeed, could move either far or fast. They had, after all, walked from the Millerfield house to the police station. Usually, in Teddy's experience, they bundled you into a car with a cursory 'mind your head' and the child locks engaged. Teddy had loved the walk – the world had seemed so bright, so fresh. It had given her such an appetite, and all that they'd given her at the police station so far was a cup of horrid grey tea in a polystyrene cup. If she'd had her wits about her she could have made a run for it during that walk. She wondered whether Sara would have been able to keep up with her. The exhaustion that had overcome her while the two of them were out shopping was completely gone. She badly wanted to be doing something – anything – and she hadn't felt like that for more than twenty years.

She tried to calm down. Something sinister was certainly going on. And she had a good idea Gates was at the bottom of it. She wondered where he was. Patently they hadn't caught him yet. Knowing Gates (don't be silly, she told herself, you don't know Gates – but she did: on some primal level) she doubted whether they *would* catch him. Doubted it very much. Hoped it even more. Gates was … someone she cared about. It had been a long time since she had felt that. Not since her re-acquaintance with Ek had she felt close to anyone. Even Sara, good friend that she had turned out to be, didn't engage her like Gates did.

Her musings were disrupted by uniformed police wanting to incarcerate her. The very thought of being locked away, today of all days, was horrific. But she could see there was no help for it and put up only a token fuss.

They passed Sara's cell on their way to the end of the corridor. Teddy could see the name on the panel beside the door. But they kept on going, down another corridor with no windows, and then up some steps. Beside the door at which they stopped was a panel with her name on it.

So, she was really going to jail. This was her punishment for all the bitter years she had wasted. At that moment she came very close to believing in a vengeful God, and her father settling the old scores between them from beyond the grave.

She had no idea what to do about her situation, and George Barrie hadn't been exactly encouraging. She could have done with Sara's calm commonsense right now. She really didn't want to be alone. And she was very, very hungry.

As she thought this a hand on her elbow guided her into the cell. She twisted round and asked,

'Can I at least get something to eat?'

A little push was her only answer. The door of the cell closed heavily behind her and she heard the tumblers of the lock engage: there were a lot of them. It was a very lonely sound.

She found her knees shaking suddenly and sat down with a bump on the hard, narrow bunk – it being the only available surface – banging her head on the top one in the process. Shit.

7.4

To Teddy's relief some food did come. She ate ravenously. Then she availed herself of the sparse facilities. This took accuracy and timing. Afterwards she found there was no paper. She shouted for some, but nobody came.

She found it difficult to be still, and began to pace. From the door to the wall with the window in it was four steps. The other way was only three, because of the bunks. The window was tiny, with an integral security mesh, and set high up in the wall. From what she could see through the mesh, it looked like a bright day outside. She wondered what the time was, but since they'd taken her compad she had no way to tell. She wouldn't be able to com Ek tonight. She'd derived a lot of comfort from that little ritual since she'd come to Edinburgh. She wished she could tell him all that had happened. But it wasn't the sort of thing you could do over a com connection. She hoped he wasn't worrying. He would when he didn't hear from her later.

If they'd let her keep her compad she'd have been on to everyone she could think of who might be able to get her out of here. And there was a chance that Gates might have left her a message. It was he that she trusted to make something happen. Gates would find her. She chuckled. Hardly a knight, and hardly clad in shining armour, but she really wanted to see him again.

The sun was gone from her little window the next time she heard movement in the corridor outside. The overhead light came on in her cell, although it was still broad daylight. Then someone opened the peep-hole in her door and looked in. Teddy pulled a face in that general direction. Apparently satisfied that she wasn't lurking behind the door ready to try and brain any incomer, someone unlocked the door and opened it.

‘About time,’ said Teddy. ‘I need toilet paper.’ She indicated the hook on the wall beside the stainless steel loo. The only response she got from the officer in the doorway was a grunt, which might have meant anything. Then she got something she wasn’t expecting.

‘There’s a package for you.’ It was thrust towards her. It had been prettily wrapped, but was now a ruin, like a broken bird, all flopping flaps and cut ribbon. Someone had sent her a present. It had been defiled by these suspicious ... but nevertheless, someone had sent her a present. She was touched. She was so touched that she was afraid for a moment that she might start to cry.

Having delivered what he’d been told to deliver, the officer retreated and locked the door again behind him. Teddy didn’t hear him go, nor the click of the locking tumblers falling back into place. A present.

There was a note.

Put this on your window sill tonight. The moonlight will make it magic.

There was no signature, but Teddy knew who it was from. Inside the violated wrappings was a little box. It had been taken apart too and roughly re-assembled. In the box, on some cotton wool – which had also been investigated - was a snow dome. She hadn’t seen one of these since she was a child. There was something odd about it – yes: the snow was silver. She shook it thoughtfully and watched as the silver snow swirled lazily and settled on the tiny, old-fashioned house, post box, snowman and Christmas tree in the little hemisphere. Silver snow. To be put on the window sill. When was moon rise? Almost sick with impatience Teddy settled down to wait for her loo roll to come and the moon to shine.

7.5

The loo roll came first, accompanied by George Barrie. She could hear the old man wheezing briskly down the corridor. Teddy felt a pang. However he’d got from Prestonpans to St Leonards Street he had obviously exerted himself to do it. She could hear him huffling on the other side of the door as it was swiped open. As soon as he was inside he handed over the precious toilet paper – single ply, she noted grimly – and started rummaging in his pockets for his inhaler. Three hearty gulps later, a sit down on the lower bunk, and he was ready for action.

To begin with he did a lot of tut-tutting and head-shaking. How had she managed to get … didn't she realise that … very difficult to … Teddy let this wash over her. She hadn't, actually, been expecting George to get here today. And, with the snow dome on her windowsill, she had reason to believe that she wouldn't need his services tomorrow.

However, she probably ought to continue to be outraged and desperate to be at least, bailed; at best, released with the charges dropped. Come to think of it, it would be better to be discharged. To be on the run was an exciting prospect, but possibly not a very practical one. The police, it was true, could not move very fast to recapture her. But then, her flight would be in slo-mo too. That playing field was depressingly level. Better make the most of George. But how to explain her change of health? He was too sharp to bamboozle about something like that. She sat down beside him.

'You are much better than you have been, hnh? I was delighted to get Ek's message. I do not understand how it can be – but I am delighted none the less.'

Ek?

'So, tell me, hnh?'

Innocence must be the best policy.

'I really don't know, Mr Barrie. The police came round this morning and got me out of bed …'

He looked at her properly for the first time. One eyebrow quirked.

'But – moment, forgive me: we are talking miracles here – were you not *unable* to rise from your bed, hnh?'

'They found a treatment. Its been in my system about sixteen hours and, as you can see, I am *much* better.' She gave him a smile as winsome as she could make it.

'Hnh, hnh – and then?'

'They arrested me, and Dr Prosser, and brought us here.'

'And the charge?'

'Producing banned substances, whatever that means.'

'Hnh. I will tell you now what that means. It means they suspect you have been meddling with explosives such as Semtex or C4, weapons-grade plutonium or Nanonics. Those are the only substances which the general public is forbidden to possess. So why should they think such a thing, hnh? And which is it?'

No flies on George. She opened her eyes as wide as possible and looked him straight in the eye.

'We were working on Nanonics, until the Department for Homeland Security pulled the plug on us. They put a Notice on the door, and we shut everything down.'

'Hnh. Then it is possible that this is just an administrative glitch – something happened the wrong way around, hnh? Let us hope so most sincerely. This charge is most serious, *most* serious. The penalty on conviction is life imprisonment – truly life. Governments are very frightened of these substances. Why should the authorities suppose you to be involved, beyond the point at which they closed you down?'

'They say they found something still running, left over from the project, in the basement at The Works. They've connected that with Gates Hanford, I don't know why. He was a member of the project team. Sara says he's an odd-ball. Perhaps he was moon-lighting.'

Moon-lighting. Teddy could barely suppress a chuckle. Indeed her lips did twitch.

'This is not funny. Do you know this Hanford?'

'I've met him,' cautiously, 'once or twice.'

'And Sara Prosser hired him?'

'Yes. Over the Net.'

'Hnh, hnh. So she never met him either – before he came to The Works.'

'No – and she hardly ever saw him then. We were hoping for great things from his research, but Sara said he produced nothing useful for the team.'

'What was his speciality?'

Just like George to cut to the core of the matter. And what should she reply? Could she get away with 'I don't know'? Weak, and hardly plausible.

'Nanonics.'

'Ah. They have evidence of Nanonics in the basement? Do they have DNA traces?'

'I don't know.' She wished she did.

'So what has led them to their conclusions?'

'I don't know that either.'

'Well, hnh, they must disclose what they know to me. I suspect it is not enough to hold you for longer than twenty four hours,' he looked at her hard, 'if what you have told me is true.' The eyebrow quirked again. 'I will see Dr Prosser, hnh, then I will speak with Detective Sergeant McCall, then I will be in touch. Be brave.'

He covered her hand with his own, wrinkled one and smiled at her.

So far so good, then. One way or another she'd be out of here in twenty four hours.

7.6

About fifteen minutes later George was back. There was the usual swiping routine. He hovered in the doorway.

'Ek sent this to us for you. I had my people print it as the police have your compad, hnh? I have, of course, shown it to the police, who have examined it most thoroughly and say that you may have it now, hnh? I thought I would bring it down to you myself. I don't know why he used us. Perhaps your own system at the house is not functioning? Everything has been turned on its head by this, hnh, trouble with the transport. Utilities are becoming unreliable also. I don't think he knows you're here. Should I tell him?'

Teddy scanned the brightly coloured greetings card which George gave her. Why on earth would Ek contact her through her solicitors? Unless …

'No. Don't worry him.' She smiled. 'I'll be out of here tomorrow anyway.'

'So we hope. You should not get your hopes up too high, all the same, hnh?'

She turned it over. The other side was blank. She read the message once more. It certainly wasn't from was Ek. And it was quite different if you read it as being over someone else's signature. She folded the message carefully, and slipped it into the pocket of her jeans.

She thanked George and they said goodbyes again. The door banged shut and the tumblers clicked into place once more. It was a sombering sound. George said she might be out, legally, tomorrow, but Gates obviously didn't think so. She had begun to suspect that there was more – much more – for the police to discover. Gates was free but, despite his care, he was leaving a trail and that trail would lead, in the end, to her. She was, after all, a walking Nanonics farm. Once they worked that out, her confinement would be complete and solitary. They would wear encounter suits just to bring her meals. To live forever, and have the spectre of that forever being spent in jail …

What if the snow dome was just a pretty toy after all? If she didn't get out of here tonight she might well never do so. The tears welled up hot and hard in the back of her throat and she began to cry at last. She wanted Gates.

7.7

Lox had been hunched over his compad, chasing information around the nets, ever since he'd called Bridie for the second time. She had, indeed, been relatively glad to hear from him when she had listened to what he had had to say, but had been maddeningly non-committal about the use his information might be put to and what share in the results he might expect.

When he finally closed the connection and looked up, he was surprised to see it was twilight outside. He was squinting, and there was a familiar gritty sensation behind his eyes which told him that he'd been staring at a very small screen for a very long time. His throat felt dry as a Martian canal and, now that he thought about it, his back hurt. He stood up and stretched out the kinks. His vertebrae went back to their proper places with audible clicks. Christ, he was chewing stats again.

As it was now clear that the stationary Edinburgh traffic was not an isolated incident, he had been browsing for theories about the problem. The phenomenon was now top story around the world. This perhaps should not have surprised him as much as it did. When he analysed his surprise he realised it was more the kind of shock you get from a loud alarm: if he was going to make any impact with his discoveries on the subject he was going to have to go public very soon. A lot of Loxes around the world were doing what he was doing, but so far none of the theories posted were any better than crack-pot. It was quite possible that Lox was still ahead. Then again, it was equally possible that another Lox was sitting at another compad somewhere thinking exactly the same thing. His only advantage was that whatever was happening had started here. And, as far as he could tell from the news that had been posted, he was the only Lox in Edinburgh

One amusing theory he found was that there had somehow been a shift in the Earth's magnetic current which had reversed the vehicles' polarity thus making it impossible to generate the spark necessary to ignite the petrol. Another was that changes in world climate had now caused propellants to overheat and jellify. That theory worried him more. Although its beginning was loopy, its conclusion was on the button: petrol was jellifying – or, to be more accurate, it was turning into a kind of molasses. He knew why. Lox had no qualms about starting a world-wide panic, but he wanted his reputation to be made, not destroyed, in the process. He wished he had the proof to back it up. Sadly the lack of a psych test in a hacked file wasn't it, and Bridie was being bloody coy about sharing.

He told his compad to gather further news on the subject as it broke and went back to those fuzzy pictures he had taken through Gold's basement window the day before. If he could just clean them up then, with the DNA evidence the police had, he could do it – 'official sources have obtained …' would work fine. No names, no pack drill: no injunction.

But then again, if he published, with or without Gates Hanford's name (lawsuits for libel notwithstanding if he *should* happen to be wrong, which he wasn't), the rest of the Green X Group (because there had to be more of them – enough to start these centres of contagion all round the world) would certainly take action, and Christ alone knew what would ensue. They must have more mayhem up their sleeves. The first, and indeed the second, global e-message from them had implied as much.

The 'urgent message waiting' light was flashing. He left off trying to enhance a small fuzzy rectangle and retrieved it. It was from his Editor:

> Tuthill: This in haste and with difficulty. Check 'news breaking'. EU now immobile. USA, Canada, Australia, Japan, parts of Africa, urban India and patches of China nearest Beijing, Shanghai and Hong Kong ditto. Armed guards preventing lorries filling up at oil depots in Middle East, Georgia, Ukraine and Russia. Pipelines closed down and oil wells capped in attempt to halt spread of infection.
>
> Whatever it is, it's spreading like a virus and moving incredibly fast (I do not use hyperbole here – the speed of infection <expletive deleted by system> belief).
>
> Nothing coming out of USA. Think their nano-scare may be at the bottom of all this. Know you don't agree. See also share prices. Stock market crash imminent in my opinion. Is this the end of the world as we know it? Am working from home until then, if you need me.
>
> Gardner

There was nothing there that Lox hadn't already gathered for himself. He e-ed back

> Thanks. Checking. Yes, probably. Noted. Tuthill

Sure enough his compad had a stack of 'news just in' built up just in the time it had taken him to mess around with the photo and read Gardner's message – none of it good. Oil prices were shaky, but shares of motor manufacturers and, to an even greater extent, motor factors and retailers were suiciding. The rest of the markets were sliding in sympathy. Hauliers were, perhaps, worst off. Nothing was moving on the roads. Produce was rotting in containers. Contract deadlines for non-perishables were being missed. It reminded Lox of the Anglo-French produce wars of the last century. Transport companies had gone to the wall then in the time it had taken to resolve them. And those problems had been resolvable. Was this one? It was notoriously difficult to placate fanatics.

Lox built a model to compute how long it would take for global financial markets to crash if the situation wasn't resolved in 1) a week, 2) a month, 3) six months, 4) a year, 5) ever. It did not make cheerful information. In fact he never got past 2). A month in this condition and it was, indeed, the end of the world as they knew it. Scary.

But good for Tuthill in the short term. It looked like the trick was going to be to lash out the story, collect the Euros, spend them on stores and head for somewhere remote (well, anywhere would come into that category soon) to await developments. If his modelling was accurate money wasn't going to be any good in about a fortnight. The dollar and the euro were already falling. Suddenly the rupee and the yen were the global currencies of choice. In fact, anywhere that didn't depend completely on petroleum products for power and transport was the place to put your dosh. Yeh, lay in a ton of tins and load them onto a boat and set sail for somewhere warm.

Something would emerge out of the chaos. They wouldn't slip all the way back to a pre-industrial society. Electricity would still be generated somehow, there would be computers, media of some kind. Lox briefly toyed with the idea of putting money into wind and solar power, while the markets were still operating. But on balance he reckoned he'd rather corner the market in tinned beans. First he'd finish cleaning up that picture, then he'd buy a boat. Or perhaps a horse – they looked so much less effort than a bicycle. He wondered how difficult horses were to load onto boats, and how difficult it was to make either one go in the direction of one's choice as he hunched over his little compad again and brought up the bleary picture he had taken of something in the basement of Gold's.

7.8

It was definitely twilight now and Teddy was becoming agitated. She had put the snow dome on the windowsill as soon as she was alone, intending to watch and see what happened. Then she thought, *the light in here is very bright* – a neon tube which illuminated every corner leaving the inmate nowhere to hide – *what if it sets it off to do whatever it's supposed to do too soon?* So she put it back in the box. Then she got it out again to see if there was any change in the contents, but the swirling silver flakes alarmed her and she put it back into its box once again. But with nothing else to do, and all her hopes pinned on it, she couldn't leave it there. She thought *it and I are kin. It won't hurt me.* So she got it out and cradled it in her hands, determined not to fear it. It wasn't easy: *These might be different bugs. They might not recognise their kin. What if they eat you all up until nothing is left except your silver skeleton?* And back in the box it went. Then another thought occurred to her: *what if I fall asleep and miss moon rise?* So out it came once more. She carried it carefully, so as not to cause any silvery swirls in the little hemisphere, and set it back on the window ledge. Then she hopped up onto the top bunk and sat and stared at the tiny motionless toy.

After a while a bell rang somewhere and the lights went off with an audible clunk. It still wasn't dark – it was never really dark in Scotland around midsummer – so Teddy worried in case the snow dome's contents got started too soon on that account. So she watched it carefully, and watched and waited and …

8

8.1

Teddy woke up cold. She was curled up on the top bunk, wedged against the brick wall at an awkward angle. She had a pain in her neck, her head ached, and her right arm had gone to sleep where she'd pinned it against the wall when she dozed off. Gradually she untangled herself, stretched out the kinks and shook the life back into her hand.

She still felt cold, so she climbed down and pulled the blanket off the lower bunk. There was a reason she'd been up on the top bunk. She wrapped herself in the blanket and tried to remember what it was. It should have been deep night by now – she could tell that much even without a timepiece: it even *smelled* late – and although it wouldn't get really dark in June here, outside was brighter than a midsummer night in Scotland ought to be. Wasn't there an old song about that? How did it go? 'By the light of the silvery moon …'. Shit, yes! The moon. The moon must have risen.

That's why she'd been sitting up there: she'd been waiting for something to happen. She scrambled back up onto the top bunk to look at the little snowscape Gates had sent her and … it wasn't there: neither the toy nor the windowsill remained. There was just a large, neat hole and a great deal of moonlight shining in. Her tiny cousins had done their work. Suddenly she wasn't cold anymore.

She shucked off the blanket and peered at the hole where the window used to be. She was still torn between believing that all nanites were her friends and being terrified that consorting with the wrong kind would start a war within her that could consume her utterly. What had happened? There had been no sound; there was no rubble, no dust. There was, precisely, nothing.

She stretched up towards the hole. That wall had been almost a metre thick. There was a course of bricks on the inside painted a greyish white, then a course of concrete blocks, then a core of steel mesh, then a cavity, then more of the same sandwich facing the outside. Very nice. Very secure. Very gone.

Teddy peered closely at what remained. There was, perhaps, a microscopic busy-ness about the edges of the hole. If she looked away for a minute or two and then looked back she fancied the hole was larger. Fascinated, she made a thumb nail mark in the paint on the inside brick work close to the edge of the hole. Sure enough, like clouds moving across a seemingly windless sky, the ragged edge with its almost invisible flurry of activity moved imperceptibly towards, and then overtook, her little mark. Awed, she knelt there on the top bunk watching Gates Hanford rescue her from jail.

Finally it dawned on her that her escape had been effected some time ago. All she had to do was climb through the hole in the wall and go. In fact, by falling asleep and then becoming mesmerised by the method of her rescue, she might have ruined everything.

She stood up and tried to think. There was nothing to take, nothing to plan. The only thing that bothered her now was touching a working nano swarm in order to get out of jail. She had total confidence in Gates, nevertheless her skin crawled as she wormed her way through the microscopically pulsating hole to freedom.

8.2

Outside was strange; not like night at all, but like being in an old black and white movie. She seemed to be in a sort of garden - a little square of silvered paving enclosed some wizened grey plants in the middle of which a shadowy pedestal trailed blackened weeds. Extraordinary. To her left, at the beginning of her own cell block, was a wall without any windows, startlingly white in the moonlight. She tried to get her bearings. That must be the cell block she'd been walked through to get to hers, the one Sara was in. She wondered if Gates had been able to break Sara out too.

If she turned right instead, she should be able to creep down the side of the block she'd come out of and see if there was a hole in Sara's cell. She did so. It didn't take long to ascertain that the wall was as smooth and as whole as it should have been. Poor Sara.

She could see the main part of the police station: light poured from its windows. The outpouring reminded her that there were almost certainly lights and alarms connected to movement sensors out here. She'd better get moving. But which way? She could see the spikes of a tall fence about ten metres away. She'd have to try and get through it somehow. She set off towards it.

She kept missing her footing in the odd shadows as she hurried away from the cell blocks. Then she stumbled suddenly into black shadows around the side of a little brick building. She stopped in the shadow and allowed her eyes to adjust. Then she took stock.

The fence was all of two metres high and made of metal palisades with jagged tops only a few centimetres apart. A cross bar ran around it about half a metre from the bottom and another about the same from the top. She didn't believe she could climb over it. She couldn't reach the top horizontal to get a grip and pull herself up. Even stick thin as she was, she couldn't slip between the palisades. And it looked much too strong for her to be able to pull the bars apart and get out that way.

Beyond the fence were houses, beyond them she could see that the ground rose steeply: Salisbury Crags. Must be. Holyrood Park; Edinburgh's patch of tame wilderness, a good place to hide – if she could only reach it. She looked to see if there was a gate in the fence, but it seemed to be continuous. About twenty metres further on the fence turned a corner and ran up the side of what looked like the police car park. She crept forward to the edge of the deep shadow. Yes. The fence ran all the way round to the police station. No gate. No weak spots that she could see.

The fence ran away also to the left. She must try that next, see if there was a frailty there. Cautiously she stepped back into the moonlight, slipped around the little building until she could see where the fence went. Mainly what she saw was more Police Station, more lights. It was exactly what you'd expect the cell block of a police station to be: highly secure – all the sightlines were good, everywhere was overlooked. The fence ran along the edge of the park for about ten metres this way, then it turned back in towards the main building where it ran along the side of a little lane. Teddy could see houses on the other side. But she still couldn't see any break in the fence.

She felt very vulnerable in this bright monochrome world. Getting out of the cell was one thing, but how was she to get out of the compound? Hadn't he thought of that? Where was he? It wasn't like Gates to do half a job. She needed to get nearer to the fence. He might be on the other side. If he had micro-thingies that could eat through walls perhaps he had ones that ate fences too? Was that movement? No, just grass waving. But what was that noise, that purring sound? It seemed to be coming nearer, and was suddenly quite insistent. The sound was rising and falling now, as though a muffled engine were straining to do something that was beyond it. She stopped to listen and tried to pin down where exactly the noise was coming from.

It was coming from the tall grass on the other side of the fence.

A few moments later the purring stopped. Then there was a crack, as of stone striking metal; then several more of the same followed by a scraping noise. She peered along the fence's length trying desperately to see where the noises were coming from. Ah, now she had it. Directly in front of her, in fact in the spot least visible from the Station, one shaft out of the fence had been slid across – she could clearly see the wrong angle of it against its fellows. It made a meagre gap - but she was a meagre person. She hurried forward.

The gap was slim indeed, barely more than her hand could span, but the last time she had bothered buying clothes she had shopped in the children's department, and she was sure she could make it. She caught hold of the two stakes on either side of the hole and began to lever herself through.

'Hurry up, for fuck's sake,' came an anxious voice from the darkness.

Having an arm on either side didn't work. She had to retreat and re-arrange. One arm through first, then a leg, then bend that, then wriggle like hell. Somebody caught hold of the arm that was waving around outside the fence looking for purchase, and began to tug. She got pulled off balance and fell awkwardly and painfully half out of the hole. But her other leg and both hips were jammed in the gap.

There was, indeed, some kind of sensor in the garden. Lights came on as she fell and a siren began to bawl. The grip on her arm tightened and someone tugged harder.

'Wait, wait. Stop pulling a minute. We've got to co-ordinate this.'

She could hear panting close by; not her own. Every movement seemed to take an hour. She tried to get upright again, but couldn't get her balance.

'Get me up.'

Someone began to push instead of pull.

'OK. Now get hold under this arm. I've got to dip down to get through, and I can't hold my balance. Hold me up and I can …'

Now that she had some support under her armpit she could move her right foot, the one that was already out. The grip under her arm was rough, but warm; there was a faint odour which she recognised. Gates had come for her.

It was a bit like limbo dancing, only vertical instead of horizontal. Now she had it. She scraped her right hip-bone through and then her left knee. Then Gates gave another heave. She banged her left shoulder as he yanked her out of alignment. But she was through.

'Come on, quick,' he said. 'Your chariot awaits.'

8.3

Sara had fallen into a fitful doze when sirens began to wail and unaccustomed light to sweep back and forth outside the thick glass bricks that served for a window. For a moment, as she came back to full wakefulness, she thought sourly how inconsiderate it was of people to have a party in the small hours without inviting the neighbours. Then she remembered where she was, and realised that all was not well with the powers of law and order. Being normally a law-abiding individual, it surprised her how good that realisation made her feel.

It was frustrating to be incarcerated and not know what was going on. For all she knew this could be the fire alarm and she in danger of being fried alive. Nobody came. She could hear nothing but the siren, see nothing but the search lights.

All at once she knew what was going on. It was Hanford again – bloody Hanford. He had come for Teddy. First of all she cursed him for making things worse: the lights and sirens must mean that they were going to be caught, and if they were caught together the police would never believe that she and Teddy hadn't known what Gates was up to. Next she cursed him for not getting her out too. Finally she wondered how they were getting on …

She strained her ears for any sound outside that wasn't a siren. Nothing. George Barrie had come to see her after he had seen Teddy. He had made it clear that their situation was, as he put it, 'most grave'. He had given her a toilet roll. Strange how one's perception of a thoughtful gift varied with circumstances. Shortly, she supposed, she would be grateful for clean underwear, a bar of chocolate, a toothbrush.

George had been pessimistic. He had pointed out that the whole mess could be construed as her doing. Sara thought back to that first meeting, when Teddy had levered herself painfully to her feet, the oxygen cylinder beside her, and told them all just how sick she was and what she wanted them to do about it.

Sara knew – although she certainly hadn't confessed it to George – that she had relished the opportunity. It had been a chance to make a real difference to medicine and surgery for decades, possibly centuries, to come. There had been oodles of money to fund the research, and a willing guinea pig. It was a researcher's dream come true.

As Teddy had outlined her requirements, Sara had seen the future headlines in her mind's eye. There would be a picture of herself and Teddy smiling and hugging and the first (of many) articles, which might begin: 'Dr Sara Prosser, Head of Research at Gold's Prosthetics in

Edinburgh, embraces the Chief Executive Director whose life she has saved with ground-breaking work. A Nobel Prize is confidently anticipated'. Nice.

If they failed Teddy would die and the research would be quietly shut down. With any luck that would happen before Teddy had bankrupted the company, and the project staff would go back where they'd come from, or segue into improving Gold's already excellent prosthetic limbs and organs. She'd been hanging around Gold's for more than a year on the off-chance that Nanonics wasn't as dead as everybody said. The prospect of helping to get the kinks out of bespoke prosthetics filled her with unrelieved gloom. That was never going to get her into the Lancet, or on the cover of TimeLife. But until Teddy had called that Board meeting Sara had begun to fear that prosthetics was going to be her life's work.

And now she was in jail. She had had no idea how insane Teddy's idea was; how ruthless Teddy would be in pursuit of her goal. Now, it appeared, Teddy was out of jail and she, Sara, was still in it. And, as George had intimated, likely to take the rap for the whole thing. Sara tried to think what 'everything' comprised. It made a long list. The sirens ground on and Sara began to feel very depressed indeed.

8.4

Gates had some kind of vehicle parked on somebody's lawn. Who on earth would want to live this close to a Police Station? Prisoners might flee through your flower beds on a nightly basis. As Teddy thought this, lights came on in an upstairs room. Time to go.

Back inside the compound she could hear commotion. Any moment police officers would be after them. Definitely time to go.

They stumbled the few steps to the eccentric conveyance. Teddy was laughing. She suspected she was hysterical, but it was very funny all the same. Gates' rescue vehicle was a caddy car. He must have stolen it from a golf course – probably the one just up the road at Prestonfield.

'Get in,' he said. 'And stop giggling. Everybody'll hear you.'

She got in. She had every confidence in Gates. He hadn't let her down yet. In fact, he was the only person she could think of who hadn't. Except Ek, of course. And Sara. Poor Sara.

Gates leapt into the driver's side, seized the large steering wheel and stomped on a pedal. The little cart leapt forward, nearly catapulting Teddy out of the back. An angry Scottish voice shouted 'oi' from the house behind them.

'How are we going to get out of here?'

'Same way I got in.' He swung the wheel enthusiastically and the little cart turned full circle in its own length. 'Nippy, isn't it?'

She braced her feet on what passed for a dashboard and hung onto the rail at the side. They purred towards the remains of a chain link fence and through it. Gates wrenched the wheel again and they turned left up a footpath, too narrow for the axle; the wheels skidded in lush grass on either side of the hard-standing. Moments later they bundled onto a metalled road with houses on both sides. Almost immediately they came to what seemed to be a cul-de-sac. Gates drove straight ahead at full speed and Teddy couldn't repress a little scream. But sure enough there was a way through, although a conventional vehicle couldn't have made it.

They now seemed to be cavorting along another residential street. Teddy hoped Gates had some idea of the estate's layout, or this was going to be a short outing. They bore sharply right again into what a moonlit sign said was St Leonards Bank and came to a stretch with houses down the right and only grass and gradient on the other.

'That's where we want to be,' said Gates, gesturing to the wide open spaces on the left. 'There should be a path into it here somewhere.'

'How do you know all this? You've only been in Edinburgh a few weeks.'

'When you're intending to effect a rescue,' he said primly, 'it pays to reconnoitre all possible escape routes. There wasn't much point in breaking you out of jail if I couldn't get you out of town, now was there?'

At that moment the buggy gave a more violent lurch than usual as Gates misjudged the steering and collided with a kerb, throwing her against him. On an impulse she took the opportunity to fling around him the arm she wasn't using to hang on with and kiss him on the cheek. Given the wildness of their ride the gesture became more of an attack than a thank you, but she was glad she'd done it, bruised lip notwithstanding. She was getting used to the smell of him. Almost fond of it. Fond ... hmmm. At the next lurch she extricated herself with as much grace as she could. One thing at a time.

They seemed to be making a tremendous amount of noise. It felt like running a gauntlet. She was surprised lights weren't coming on all down the street as they passed. She shouted,

'Noisy, isn't it?'

'Actually its surprisingly quiet. It just seems loud because we're right on top of the engine. I checked out that very aspect before I nicked it. The hallowed turf of a golf course can't be polluted by loud noises, apparently. They like it peaceful. They use these to suit the ambience, amongst other reasons. Handy, eh?'

He was extraordinary. As they trundled erratically on, Teddy tried to think ahead. After about a hundred metres she realised that the possibilities were rather bleak. She shouted,

'Where are we going next?'

'Into the park.'

'And after that?'

'Ah, that's a bit of a problem. I have to say, medium and long term, I've no idea. In fact, I'm very much open to suggestions.' He took his eyes off the road to look at her and nearly turned them over on another kerb. After he had righted the buggy and resumed something like a straight course, he continued. 'I'm clear on the short term. We're going to put that,' he gestured at the lowering mass of Salisbury Crags moving slowly past them on their left, 'between us and the police. Holyrood Park is a big place. Even in the moonlight they'll be hard put to find us on foot - when we aren't. There's a track at the end here which should get us on to Queen's Drive, so we can go north and find some shadow to lie low in round the back of the Crags or under Arthur's Seat.'

'Surely the police can walk faster than this thing can go.'

'Actually, they can't. This has a top speed of around fifteen kph. A good walker would do about six. Don't knock it until you've tried it. It also has quite surprisingly good pulling power because its low-geared. It only has two – forwards and backwards – but it hauled that upright out of the fence, no problem. Only thing is, I don't know how far it'll go before it runs out of juice.'

'You mean it runs on petrol?' She was surprised. She'd got the distinct impression that Gates had put all the petrol-driven transport in Edinburgh out of commission. And he hated anything petrol-driven.

'No. It's powered by a fuel cell. But it's more than the police have got - unless they have the same idea. You'd think they would, but I'll bet they haven't. And it's a half hour walk from here to Prestonfield to get another one. That's the closest. I checked.'

'You'd better be right. If they catch us they'll lock us both up for the duration.'

'Yep. And the duration will be a long one. It's all in motion now. Everything. They can't stop it. No-one can. Not even me. It's a new world, Teddy. Soon even things like this will stop working. Electricity will fail, for a while. What generates the electricity won't be serviced because the service people won't be able to travel. Everything will have to localise. That's the good part. Then we'll see whether they can re-task fast enough to save some of it. And whether what they save will be the good parts.'

'Save what?'

'Oh - society, culture, quality of life. They'll have to think about all that now. What's worth saving, what should be let go. I've given them the chance to make the choices.'

'Shit, Gates - are you nuts?'

'Some people think so.'

They reached the end of the metalled road. He drove the caddy car up the kerb, between two posts designed to prevent exactly this sort of thing happening, and into a hole in the bushes that looked like something Alice might have used for entering Wonderland. Bushes and brambles started whipping at them.

Teddy screamed and shut her eyes, but they didn't hit anything. Gates wrestled with the wheel for a moment before the buggy settled down on a straight course again. As the little car bucketed down a rough track, he turned to her and resumed their conversation.

'Do you?'

She thought for a moment. What did she think about Gates? Her saviour, certainly. Her friend? Yes. But there was one thing.

'No, I don't think you're nuts - but I do think you should take a bath.'

He laughed. Then stamped on the brake. 'Shit.'

'Well, I'm sorry - but if we're going to be friends I just thought …'

'Never mind about that - washing's going to be a problem for everybody soon. No, I can't see the track. It looked on the map as if it's a way into the park. I hope it is. They'll be pounding up behind us pretty soon. Hang on a minute.'

And he was gone.

8.5

Teddy finally had a chance to catch her breath, and take stock of her surroundings.

The buggy was perched on a little hummock about ten feet below the level of the road they'd come in from. In front of her was a steep path. Behind her, roughly speaking, was Newington within which area lurked the police station. She could hear activity and see flashlights in the gardens of the houses beyond the park to the south east. Lights were going on in the houses. Any minute the authorities were going to erupt into the park and catch sight of a small white golf cart going nowhere. They didn't need flashlights to see it in the moonlight. Suddenly the little conveyance seemed as big as an elephant. She hoped Gates would be quick.

And here he was. He went on past the buggy and peered down the path, then he came back and got in.

'This is now, officially, a footpath - I found a signpost back up at the road. It does go into the park. Its rough and its steep, but I think we can make it.' He grinned. She found it both engaging and reassuring.

They set off again, cautiously this time as Gates forced the little buggy down a rugged track only wide enough for single file walkers. 'Let's hope it takes them a while to work out which way we went.'

'Won't they hear us?'

'Possibly - although this thing really is *very* quiet. The question is, can they work out where the sound is coming from? One of the several good things about the Crags is that they bounce sound around. As far as what they can hear is concerned, we could be anywhere.'

The cart bounced on down. Teddy braced her feet against the dash again, and hung on as well as she could. The worst was soon over. Shortly Gates was wrestling with the steering wheel big-time again to turn the cart onto the metalled road at the bottom. He slowed to walking pace to bump the cart down on to asphalt and Teddy had another anxious moment.

Gates gave the wheel a last flourish as they emerged onto the roadway, and then let out a wild whoop. 'Christ, I love breaking the law.' He started up the slope to their right at full speed, sawing the wheel wildly from side to side and nearly unseating Teddy, who had stopped hanging on when they reached the road.

'Settle down,' she said. 'Concentrate. There are lights behind us. The police may not pick up the sound of a golf cart out on a frolic of its own, but they can certainly hear insane scientists whooping like loons under a full moon. Let's find a place to hide.'

'Right, right.' He quietened down. 'There's a compad under the dash somewhere. Fish it out, will you? Bring up the local maps and let's see if we can find somewhere. It's got GPS, so it should be easy to work out where we are.'

8.6

Teddy fished out the compad. Gates flogged the buggy towards the shoulder of the hill.

She found the local maps and handed the little machine to Gates. Then she had a look around to try and see where they were. What she saw made her gasp. Just on the other side of the little valley that Gates had bumped them down was a phalanx of flashlights. On the end of every flashlight came a Plod. All the police had to do to spot them, surely, was look up. She counted the lights: ten, twenty – maybe twenty five or so. Just the night relief then. How, indeed, were extra police to be acquired? They'd have to walk or cycle in; it would take time. Plod was really plodding tonight. That was something.

As the lights bobbed along she could see that they were stopping to knock on doors. Lights were coming on in the houses backing onto the park. She could actually hear the voices, although not the words. She concentrated hard on one particular interview. She could make out the policeman, and a woman just visible beyond her half-open door. Would she point? No; she had opened the door completely now and stood in the doorway, huddled, confused, half-awake. Teddy could see the woman shake her head. They really did have the police bamboozled. Gates was a genius.

'They don't know where we are,' she said.

'Not yet,' Gates said grimly. He was wrestling with the wheel one-handed, while he tried to interrogate the compad which he'd balanced on the top. 'Wouldn't you know it – we're on a crack in the map!' he said.

'What?'

'Well, with this technology we're running along the edge of the page. Here, hold this, will you?'

He almost tossed the compad at her. Gave the wheel a wrench and stamped on the brake. Then he took the compad back and hunched over it.

Back down at the bottom of the hill Teddy could see an intersection and, in the middle of it, something that looked a bit like a small dead tree. Ah – a signpost.

'Gates?'

'Hmm?'

'Is that the signpost you already looked at?'

'Where?'

'Back down there.'

'No.' He went back to the compad.

'I'll go and look. It might be quicker.'

She got out and trotted back down the road. It felt good to be moving, to have her arms and legs pumping, to feel the blood increasing its tempo as it zinged around her body. It seemed to take no time at all for her to reach her target. Two arms of the sign, pointing left and right, said 'Queen's Drive'. Odd. Two more arms to the front and sort of three-quarters left said 'footpath'. Teddy wasn't sure that a footpath would be wide enough for the buggy. If they were going up the Crags there was likely to be a substantial drop on one side. She didn't particularly trust Gates's driving in a high, narrow place. One mistimed wrench of the steering wheel and they'd be sliding down the Crags with a golf buggy coming down on top of them.

She made her way back up the hill as quickly and quietly as she could.

'It says we're on Queen's Drive,' she panted when she got back to the buggy. 'It says Queen's Drive both ways, so I think it must be circular.'

'Yes, of course!' Gates said. 'Just occasionally I'm really stupid. You've never spent time in here, have you?'

'I was never allowed. I was supposed to be delicate. I spent most of my childhood being coddled at Dunster. When we came into Edinburgh it was usually to take me to see some Specialist or other. That's why we kept the house at Millerfield Place – its just across The Green from the hospital.'

'Let's try the road,' he said. 'It'll put distance between us and them and take us round the back of the Crags. We'll be out of sight. Then we can decide what to do next.'

Down among the houses the flashlights now looked more like fifty than twenty five and were spread all over the estate. It looked as though the police were searching the gardens. As Gates prepared to move them on there came a cry from a house back near where they had started from.

'They've found the hole in the fence. About time.' Gates said.

'Oh shit.'

'That's OK. They still don't know we're not on foot.'

'They soon will. The wheels didn't fit on that path. There are bound to be tyre tracks either side of it.'

'Yeh, I didn't think of that. Shit. We'd better get a move on.'

8.7

They bumbled on up the hill and, sure enough, the Crags began to loom on their left. The buggy veered as Gates looked back at the road. Behind them came a shout.

'They're onto us.'

Teddy could feel him strain as he put his foot down harder on the 'go' pedal. There was no difference to their speed. They were already going as fast as they could. She just hoped it was fast enough. She asked him,

'When does the moon go down?'

'0230. We'll be much harder to find then.'

The shoulder of the Crags was falling, slowly, behind them. They were now out of sight of their pursuers, and in moon shadow. It felt safer, although Teddy knew it wasn't. The moon was still shining as bright as day on the tracks they'd left getting into the park. That glorious full moon had been their benefactor, it would be ironic if it was also their downfall. She asked,

'Are police 'copters still flying?'

'How the fuck would I know?'

Irritation. Fear. Gates was tense, still pressing as hard as he could on the accelerator. The buggy seemed to be going no faster than they could walk.

Her mind began to run ahead of the action. If they managed to hide out in the park – what then? It would be dawn around four. They'd have barely two hours between moonset and sunrise. After that they'd have an endless, Scottish midsummer day to deal with. They had to keep moving, get further ahead of the police if they could. And the buggy was a short term vehicle: it'd run out of juice long before they ran out of daylight. What then - the docks? the roads? the railways? The railways!

'Gates, we're going to have to get out of the Park soon after four – when the sun comes up we'll be sitting ducks.'

'Don't forget there's no traffic.'

'No – even so. We need to get out of Edinburgh.'

'Yes.' It was a cautious agreement.

'You know, we still have railways in Scotland.'

'No shit. I'd forgotten that. Of course you do. *Electric* railways. They should still be running.'

'All we have to do is get to Waverley.' A stretch of water glinted on their right some way ahead. Dunsapie Loch. 'And we're going the wrong way.'

He stopped the buggy.

'We can't be going the wrong way – this road goes all the way round. You're sure they're electric?'

'Yep.'

'Absolutely not diesel.'

'Nope.'

'Only if we're wrong, we're screwed.'

'I know.'

'OK.' He got the map out again. 'Look, we can get out down here, or go round to the Palace.'

'I think we're going to run right into them if we go back round.'

'Right. We'll take our chances on the streets of Edinburgh then.'

He kicked the accelerator and they were off again.

'Of course,' he said, 'the police may have assumed that we'd head back into Edinburgh. They may be watching the station.'

'Or they may be behind us, combing the park as thoroughly as they went through the estate behind the police station.'

'Or they may have instigated a classic pincer movement and be both behind and ahead of us.'

'They're on foot, remember.'

And with that the purring of the little caddy car faded into silence.

'And so are we.'

8.8

It was around two in the morning. Lox was still fully clothed, sitting on the bed in his room, hunched over his compad.

These bloody things were too small for this kind of data gathering: they just gave you a headache. He'd slimmed down the number of hits he'd got on the Net to a under a thousand. Now he could get the machine to read him a summary of them and rest his eyes. He fixed his earpiece and lay back on the bed, to ease the crick in his spine. He was still putting in way too much computer time. But he wondered how he'd feel with no compad to interrogate. That was a possible future now. The way things were going, anything was possible.

He rummaged in his pocket for some antacid tabs, popped a handful out of their strip and began to munch, then said 'go' to his compad. He wasn't going to enjoy this, but he needed to know the worst. He started with 'local'.

Breakdown services are unable to cope with the number of calls they have been getting for home starts and accidents resulting from attempted vehicle hi-jacks. Emergency services are themselves breaking down en route to give assistance.

Fuel-cell vehicles have been particularly vulnerable to thieves in the past few days.

Motorways are deserted.

People are attempting to leave the cities, against official advice, as food supplies become erratic.

The refrigeration units of lorries are failing and food being delivered to stores is spoiling before it can be delivered.

Megamarkets are exhorting people not to panic buy, but admit bread, milk, tinned staples and candles are sold out. Queues for these items are widespread at outlets that still have them.

The USA has closed its borders to foreign goods and nationals. No information is available on effects there of the so-called 'petrol virus'

London experienced an eight hour brown-out last night.

Parisian streets are deserted.

'Eight hours after people would normally be enjoying their evening meals the streets are full of commuters trying to get home. Tempers among the thousands of stranded workers are fraying. From my hotel room balcony I can hear shouts and glass smashing in the distance, which presumably means there is looting is going on not far away. What will the dawn bring? We can only wait and hope. '

Is your journey really necessary? Please do not leave home if you can possibly avoid it..

The British Government and National Assemblies will make statements at 0830 tomorrow. They are expected to declare a State of Emergency.

There was a great deal more in the same vein.

It was after four when Lox pulled out his earpiece and kicked off his shoes. Tomorrow he would write up what he had. He knew what had happened and who was behind it. He was one of very few people, currently, who did. But he doubted that his marvellous exclusive was going to make his fortune any more.

The light had never left the sky tonight, but the long twilight brightened imperceptibly until dawn crept into the sky. The confused birds hadn't stopped chittering all bloody night. A white night, they insisted, was not a time for sleeping. Lox had a nasty feeling that he had spent it listening to the end of his world.

8.9

Teddy and Gates sat for a few minutes in the dead buggy thinking what to do next. Gate said,

'It should have been good for miles more yet. I must have used up a lot of the power trying to pull that stake out at the police compound.'

Although a successful escape looked less likely now, Teddy somehow couldn't believe they were going to be caught. Her head was full of 'what ifs', all of which revolved around ways out of Edinburgh, which got muddled up with the future, which, in turn, got mixed up with the past. Very soon she knew what they ought to do. She said,

'We should go to Dunster. We'd be safe there. We should go to Ek and Rory. There's a farm. We'd be OK.'

'I've been thinking about using the railway. But they're bound to be watching the station.'

'I'd like to go back to the house, pick up my cash card, compad, a change of clothes, stuff like that.'

'They'll be watching that too. And they'll be all over us the minute you use your cash card. I've got actual money. It'll look suspicious to use it for a little while longer, but at least it can't be traced quickly.'

'I still think we should go north.'

'I don't disagree. Once we're out of Edinburgh we'll be hard to track, as things are. But how we get out of Edinburgh … I don't think going to Waverley is a good idea. Let's have another look at that map.'

She fished out the compad and they pored over it.

'Look for green spaces,' he said. 'We've got a head start on them still. They'll have asked the questions, once they realised what we were using to get around. They won't think that we'll need another buggy this soon. If we could find another golf course near enough we might be able to work the same trick again.'

They found one: Craigentinny, to the east of Leith.

'Right, then,' he said. 'We'll shove our faithful steed in the loch, strike off across Whinny Hill and keep St Margaret's Loch on our left. It'll be safer to get off this road, and it should be quicker too. If we step out we ought to be there by dawn.'

'Then what?'

'Well, as I say, after the escape I'd intended pretty much to busk it.'

'We're certainly busking it.'

'We might find a boat.'

'Syrup in the tank?'

'Yeh, that's going to be a major problem.'

'You don't think you might have set things in motion rather the wrong way around?'

'When I, as you put it, 'set things in motion' you weren't a factor.'

'And now I am?'

He looked at her.

'Ah, yes.'

He said nothing else, and she couldn't see enough of his expression in the half-light to know whether his new-found responsibility for her was pleasure or bane for him.

They pushed the golf buggy through an eerie white and grey grassland. Their moon shadows grew longer, then fainter. Patently the moon was going down. It felt colder as the light waned. The chill before dawn, that's what it felt like, when life is at it's lowest ebb. They were sombre and silent; their light-heartedness removed with their transport. They no longer had the advantage.

Finally they got the buggy more or less into the loch and Gates stuck some pulled-up bulrushes in the soft mud around the back of it to hide the tyre tracks and the rump of the buggy, which was still sticking resolutely out of the water.

'It won't take them long to find it, but if we can steal another before they do, we have a chance.'

They started to scramble up Whinny Hill. Clouds finally obscured the moon, now that the light would have been helpful. Then the moon set. It was really dusky now. They stumbled a lot. Teddy didn't tire, exactly, but she began to feel rather hopeless as they trudged on. Her feet began to drag. Then her muscles to ache. It was a very long time since she had been able to take any exercise. The tiny things inside her could keep her body free from disease, but they couldn't tone it. Before long she was breathing hard and had begun to catch her feet in every clump of grass.

But now she could see another stretch of open water. Gates stopped to look at the map and she was grateful for the breather. She couldn't summon the energy to go and crouch over it with him. She sat down with a bump, and felt her feet throb to the rhythm of her heart beat as she lifted each off the ground in turn.

'Good. This is St Margaret's loch,' he said 'We're nearly out of the park. Streets should be easier walking.' He sounded concerned.

'Don't worry about me,' she said. 'I can keep up.'

'I'm sure you can. Don't be offended. I've walked or cycled everywhere since I was a boy. I'm fitter than you. I'm a lot fitter than most people. You've been very sick. It'll take time for your body to build up again.' He turned the torch on her. 'You don't want to do an ankle or something. That can happen when you're tired.'

She sighed. It was only the truth. She'd already come close several times to doing just that.

'I could go and get the buggy and come back for you.'

'No.'

He laughed. 'I didn't think you'd go for it, but I thought I ought to offer.'

She managed a rather wheezy chuckle.

'OK, if that's settled then let's get on with it,' she said and hauled herself to her feet before he could help her. He wasn't going to leave her.

8.10

Lox was dreaming. There was urgency everywhere, yet no movement was possible. Events unfolded in slo-mo, only his mind was working at the proper speed. In frustration he was screaming 'we have to act now!' but nobody could hear him for the ringing.

The ringing was all through his head, interrupting his train of thought, banishing all the ideas he'd had for addressing the crisis, making him forget the copy that he had been working up. Damn. He wished he had written it down. He reached out for his compad to jot it down before it escaped completely, and in doing so woke himself up.

Something *was* ringing – his compad. As he flicked up the lid he looked at the time display: 4.30 a.m. This was unlikely to be good news. One good thing – it was even more unlikely to be his Editor.

It was McCall, although it took him several seconds, in his befuddled state, to work out why an irate female Scot was ringing him at this hour.

'The bloody woman's escaped and there's a hole in the wall of the cell block big enough to drive a car through. If we had a car to drive through it, which of course we don't.'

'Good morning to you too. You've had a busy night, then?'

'Don't try and be funny – it's four thirty in the morning,' she snapped. Lox found her irritation oddly sexy. It must be because he was lying on a bed: most women sounded sexy to Lox if there was a bed in the room. A mental image started to form in which McCall was being funny in a physical way. He shook his head to clear it and tried to concentrate.

'Teddy Goldstein has bust out of jail?'

'Isn't that what I just said?'

'You said something about a hole in the cell block wall. What happened? Did someone blow it up, ram it, what?'

'Not as far as we can tell. It looks as though …' she stopped.

'It looks as though what?'

'You'll laugh.'

'What?'

'As though something ate it.'

He laughed. It was one of two possible responses to information like that. The other was to fill one's trousers. He was wide awake now, and wished he wasn't.

'Nanonics?'

'Of course Nanonics. That's what we arrested her for. The bitch must have had the stuff on her the whole time. Our search procedures obviously aren't up to finding this kind of thing. Nothing showed up when we scanned her - and our scanning techniques can pick up dandruff. This stuff's loose out there and we can't even see it!'

'Whoa there – slow down. Whatever she was carrying the things around *in* would have showed up on a scan.' He thought quickly. 'You didn't pick up Gates Hanford last night did you?'

'No.'

'Well, it's him, then. He's sprung her. What else do you know for certain?'

'She got through the fence at the back into a residential area. Then we think she went into Holyrood Park. After that … we lost her. Under the circumstances, I've called out the mounted section – but only six of them were at the stables, and the others are as stuck as the rest of us.'

'Lost *them*,' he said absently, still trying to work it through. 'You mean she just slipped through the fence? I know she's emaciated, but hell – how far apart are the stakes?'

'No.' McCall's exasperation was, if anything, getting worse. 'The stakes are about twelve centimetres apart. A rabbit would have to breath in to make it through. There was a damaged stake. The rivet through the bottom band had been sprung and about a metre of the stake bent outwards.'

'What's the fence like?'

'Like? It's like two metres of galvanised steel, banded top and bottom and serrated at the top.'

'It wasn't waiting for any repairs? It was sound?'

'It's the perimeter fence of a cell block for chrissakes. It's checked daily.'

'Then she *had* to have had help. Strong help. It must be Gates. How the hell did you manage to lose them? She's sick as a dog and weak as a kitten,' he stopped as the mixed zoomorphisms echoed in his ears. 'Shit. No, I mean neither of them has any experience of this kind of thing. Even if we accept that Hanford is a kind of terrorist he's always been a *virtual* terrorist. The physical stuff would be beyond him. I mean, hell, you've seen the old picture of him from his NanoGen personnel file.'

'No …'

'Well, er, I have. It was taken four or five years and he didn't weigh more than sixty five kilos, wringing wet, back then. If Goldstein weighed sixty kilos she'd look positively healthy. How are people like that going to make a hole in the fence round Leith Police Station?'

There was a silence. Then,

'I wondered why I was calling you, of all people. Now I know. Thank you, Tuthill. You make me think. So. If she'd broken herself out she *could* have stashed a getaway vehicle. But I don't think she knew she was going to be arrested. I *do* think that old wrinkly solicitor of hers is on the level. She hasn't spoken to anyone else who could have helped her. And there are no vehicles running in Edinburgh right now. The whole thing's impossible.'

'I wouldn't use the term 'impossible', if I were you. A number of apparently impossible things have happened in the past week. Impossible is getting to be the thing you do before breakfast.'

'Or the thing you do after dark that's against the law, like breaking and entering.'

'You were there too.'

'OK. Good point well made. *If* she had help, *and* there was getaway vehicle, perhaps the help brought it. Now, what could that be?'

Lox considered this.

'Nothing that runs on petrol, or diesel either probably. But to pull up a paling in the fence like that implies an engine. I mean – we know Hanford is fanatical about bicycles, but that couldn't do the job. It must be an engine. But it's one that doesn't burn fossil fuel.'

'OK – what?'

'I don't know.' Lox was having difficulty concentrating on what McCall was saying. All available computing power was being directed elsewhere. Just before he became completely committed to the problem at hand he made one last sortie into the real world. 'You're at the police station? Should I come over? I can walk it in half an hour and do my thinking on the way.'

'I'll expect you.' She disconnected. Lox didn't notice.

9

9.1

Lox got to the police station shortly after five. The early morning was as fresh and sharp as sherbet. The birds were shouting their heads off. The sky was baby blue with a wispy haze veil laid carelessly over it. It was going to be hot later.

His night fears evaporated in the glorious morning. There was a spring in his step. For one thing he had evolved a plausible theory as to how Goldstein had got away. For another he enjoyed sparring with the caustic McCall. Caustic McCall: he grinned as he walked and wondered what her first name might be.

The police station was buzzing like a hive. While he waited for McCall uniformed officers scurried through the foyer going in, out and in other, less public, directions. He could hear comms ringing; the ones behind the duty desk never stopped. The duty sergeant had three constables back there helping her and still looked harassed. As soon as he said he was a journalist she looked positively panicked. When McCall came to get him the sergeant was mightily relieved to be shot of him. Someone else could let the cat out of the bag; it wasn't going to be her fault.

McCall took him through to her cubby. Lox noticed her hair was mussed and her shirt was rumpled. Patently it had been a long night. She said,

'So, how do you think the bitch got out?'

'Have you got a map?'

She gestured impatiently behind him. It covered most of the wall. Lox turned and began to pore over it. As he wasn't very familiar with Edinburgh's geography it took him a while to get his bearings. McCall made impatient noises as he ran his finger hither and yon. Finally he jabbed his finger at a green area and said,

'See this? You've got them all over the place, but I'll bet good money that this is where Hanford got it from. It's the closest.'

'What is it, and why are you so convinced that Hanford's involved in this?'

Lox was pointing at Prestonfield golf course. McCall got up and joined him at the map. She had to stand rather close to him to see what he was pointing at. Lox was impressed to discover that she smelled nice, despite her beleaguered night.

'I think Hanford used a golf buggy to get her away. They don't use petrol. They're electric. Golf's a popular game, especially in Scotland. You're awash with courses. I suggest you get over there and commandeer the rest of them before somebody else does. They're your best bet for transport. If that's what the fugitives are using, at least you'll be able to cover the same terrain.'

She ran a hand through her already disordered hair and said,

'We've been trying to get hold of fuel cell cars. The public won't volunteer them and the retailers aren't keen to hand them over. As soon as a private one shows up on the streets it either gets stolen or turned over. They'd be better – we'd have a chance of getting ahead of them.'

'I'd take what you can get for now. How much of a head start do they have?'

She looked at the time display on her compad.

'Between four and five hours.'

Lox gave a whistle.

'There's no point in chasing your runaways from here, then. They've got too much of a head start. We need to work out where they might be going.'

'No shit, Sherlock.' She folded her arms and looked at him balefully.

'OK,' he said carefully, 'Sorry. Any ideas?'

'We've sent people round to her place in town and to Gold's Works. We've alerted the patrol at Waverley and we've sent two mounted officers to the Forth Bridge.'

Lox stared at the map for a while, then said,

'They'll figure on that – or he will. They're moving at about, what – I'm guessing now – twelve kph. I should think they've exhausted their original transport by now. These things aren't designed to go all day, just round a golf course. So, they're either on foot, or they've stolen another buggy. How far could they have got in the first one?' He chewed his lip and stared at the map some more. 'How long is a golf course?'

McCall shrugged, but her index finger was already moving towards the com on her desk.

'Murray? You play golf, don't you? How long is the average golf course. Yes. Yes, never mind that. Just a minute, I need to make a note.' The digit moved over to her compad and pecked four times.

'Thanks.' She turned to Lox. 'Not more than seven thousand metres – and that would be a long one.' She cocked an eyebrow at him.

'So, say the buggies can do twice that distance, that's what? Around fourteen thousand metres. OK. What courses are within fifteen kilometres of here?'

McCall rummaged in a drawer and pulled out an old-fashioned pair of compasses with a china graph pencil inserted. She measured fifteen kilometres on the map's key, jammed the point into Leith police station and described two elegant arcs with it.

Lox ran his finger around the chinagraph mark.

'There. Another green space. Craigentinny. Now draw another circle from the edge of this one.'

'I can make a lot of circles like that. Can you narrow it down, Brainiac?'

'One that includes the road bridge.'

She did so. The Forth Bridge was well inside it.

'Have your people reached the bridge yet?'

Her finger jabbed at the buttons on her com again.

'McCall. Have McKendry and Douglas reached the bridge yet? Well ask them.' She drummed her fingers on the desk for maybe half a minute, then, 'shit.'

'They're probably outside your perimeter by now. Especially since you haven't actually established one yet. Can you get hold of officers outside Edinburgh, within jogging distance of golf courses, say up to fifty kloms from here?'

She adjusted the compasses and drew another, larger circle.

'Like that?'

He nodded.

'I'll get right on it.' As she did so Lox stayed where he was, staring at the map, looking for the clue. It was here in front of him somewhere.

'There's something I'm not getting. Something that should be obvious. Can I have a look at her file?'

'Sure. Get Bridie to show you.' She put in her earpiece and gave her compad the names of the two courses they'd identified so far, as she keyed the com again. How the world turned. Twenty four hours ago she had almost arrested him to prevent him looking at that, confidential, police file. He couldn't help a small smile as he set off to find Bridie with *carte blanche* to see whatever he wanted to see.

9.2

By the time Gates and Teddy reached Craigentinny golf course the sun was fully up, and Teddy was exhausted. She slumped onto a convenient bench by the pro shop while Gates picked out a fresh buggy. He went for a clean one, on the assumption that it was probably ready to go out and, therefore, fully charged. There was no key in it. Gates reasoned that the keys were most likely in the Pro Shop, which was, of course, locked.

The security system looked prohibitively sophisticated to Teddy, but for Gates to bypass it was, apparently, as straightforward as opening a TV dinner. He pulled his compad out of a jacket pocket and then rummaged around in another one and pulled out a mare's nest of wires and assorted electronic gizmos: the compad looked bulkier than usual, now that she was looking at it in daylight. She watched him untangle a wire with little croc clips on each end, attach one end of it to the compad and the other to the alarm circuit inside the glass of the door.

'Your compad looks somewhat customised.'

'Of my own devising. It's a bit like a Swiss army knife,' he said, 'only I use it for subverting other people's technology rather than getting things out of horses hooves.'

As it turned out he needed his Swiss army knife as well, to manipulate the lock after he'd by-passed the alarm.

'Lovely,' he said, as the door clicked open obediently at his touch. Teddy roused herself enough to go inside. It wasn't the first time she'd been involved in a little light breaking and entering, but it had been a while. The old pull of the illicit managed to start a little adrenalin pumping around inside her, but it didn't last long.

'I've got to lie down for a few minutes,' she said, as Gates rummaged behind the PoS counter for the right key. He looked at her with concern. Whether the concern was for her welfare or because her weakness was going to slow them down she couldn't tell.

'OK. Just let me sort out the right key and we'll find somewhere.'

'Here's fine.' She could sleep on a rail at the moment.

There were chocolate bars and cold drinks in an auto vend. Looking at them, her mouth filled with saliva so suddenly that it hurt.

'I think something to eat might help.'

'Shit, yes – of course. You need the fuel. You've got to eat. All the time. For a while at least. I should have thought.'

As he spoke he came round the counter to the autovend and swung at the glass front with his elbow. There was a dull clunk. The glass didn't break.

'I wonder if there's anything in the club house?'

Gates compad and penknife came in handy again. Shortly they were making their way quietly through the spike bar to the kitchens. There was bread, and some sort of runny caterer's spread to put on it. Gates went through the refrigerators while Teddy sat on the stainless steel counter. He found ham and cheese, tomatoes and cucumber and a squeezy mayonnaise. He made a sandwich and Teddy started in on it. Even after a few mouthfuls she stopped feeling so peculiar, but sleep washed over her in waves. Almost incapable of speech she gestured with the hand containing the remains of the sandwich.

'Gotta lie down,' she managed, and headed for the main bar, bouncing off the door jamb on the way. The floor here was carpeted and looked most inviting. She lay down and was asleep before her head met the floor.

She awoke to find Gates bending over her.

'We really ought to go,' he said.

'What time is it?'

'Half past eight.'

'Shit. I've been asleep for hours!'

'Yep. I didn't want to wake you, but a cleaner or someone might be along soon. We should go.'

There was a big polystyrene box beside him on the floor.

'I've packed up everything edible in the kitchen. You can eat on the move for as long as this buggy last us. I don't know what we'll do when it dies.'

Teddy was feeling much better for the food and the sleep, but it looked as though, in her current condition, periods of manic energy were going to alternate with slumps. 'I don't want to slow you down and, even with supplies I expect I'll keep getting these energy gaps. It might be safer if we go on with the buggies as long as possible. I guess the slumps are to do with the nanites repairing my system? Will they settle into some sort of maintenance mode?'

'I've never used nanites for this before. But I think that's right – they're working hard right now and need a lot of fuel. When they're done with the major work they should stop burning up everything you eat.'

'Do you have any idea when that might be?'

'None. Sorry. How are you feeling now?'

'I could shift a mountain with a tea-spoon.'

'That good? That'll help. But I think you're right about the slumps. What we need is a regular supply of golf carts. Any ideas?'

'It'd be a good start if we could find some sort of map that shows golf courses. Scotland loves golf, the place is riddled with courses. And where there are courses there are bound to be buggies. Hardly anyone walks round these days.'

'How do you know?'

'There's one at Dunster. Ek and Rory take me there for a drink sometimes. Ek's a member. If we could plan a route from course to course we might be able to get to Perth in the carts, pick up a train there.'

She was on her feet now, strolling around the bar to get some feeling back into her limbs. The floor, in use, had proved harder than it looked when she lay down on it. Behind the bar she noticed the, almost obligatory, collection of whiskies. They looked tempting. She said,

'Fancy one for the road? There's about a dozen decent single malts over here.'

'Hmm.'

She took that as a yes and let herself in behind the bar. She looked for her favourites.

'Islay do you? It's quite a peaty, meaty little number.'

As she looked up for his agreement, she noticed that Gates's attention had been caught by something on the wall. She turned away to pour the whisky, and jumped at the sound of glass shattering. Looking up she saw Gates holding the legs of a bar stool that he had obviously just used to whack a large, framed map on the wall. He put the bar stool down and began moving purposefully around in the wreckage, staring up at the map, scrunching broken glass under his feet.

'Make it a large one,' he said, 'We're in business.'

She made it two very large ones, recorked the bottle and shoved it into the polystyrene box. Then she went to see what he'd found.

Gates was staring at a large map in an ornate frame.

'It's an old map that shows every golf course in Scotland as of …' he peered at the bottom of the map. ' … 1983. How accurate do you reckon it'll be?'

'There may be more now, but there aren't likely to be less. Gates, you're a clever bastard.'

She clapped him on the back and gave him the drink. He shoved it back at her, pulled a chair over to stand on and cut the map out of its frame with judicious slashes of the Swiss army knife. They caught it between them as it fell. Out of the frame, it seemed even bigger than it had done when it was on the wall. Not without difficulty they picked it up and spread it out on the top of the billiard table without tearing it. It was a pretty good fit. When they got it landed Gates took his drink back and they raised their glasses in a toast before drinking deeply. Then they both bent over the map. Finally Gates gestured with his glass.

We could make for the bridge and try this one,' he said.

'The courses all have numbers – I wonder what they're for. Just a minute.' She lifted up the map to try and see if there was anything on the back. There was. But the map was considerably taller than she was. It was taller than Gates too. Between them they worked it off the billiard table and into a more-or-less upright position. Then Gates got up onto the billiard table and held the top edge. The back had information about the courses, arranged in numerical and alphabetical order of the course names. She worked her way down til she found the right number ' … no, not that one. It's only nine holes – or it was in 1983. If there are courses where people are still prepared to walk round, then nine hole courses are the ones. And where walking is the norm there are less likely to be buggies. And they may not charge all of them to go round twice. We don't want to waste time on places that may not be any use.'

'OK. How many holes do they have otherwise?'

'Eighteen. Only two varieties – nine or eighteen. Eighteen holes good; nine holes bad.'

Gates stood on the billiard table holding up the map, while Teddy went from one side of the map to the other, finding courses which took them in the right direction, and then looking up the course codes on the flip side to see if they had the right number of holes. She put what she found into Gates's compad.

Finally she ran out of potential courses.

'OK.' Gates dropped the map and Teddy handed him his compad. He brought up a GPS routing program and made a some keystrokes with the stylus.

'Dunfermline and Kinross.'

'After all that - just the two?'

'I think that's all we need. They're about 25 kloms apart according to this.' He gestured at the compad. 'If the buggies are fully charged they ought to be good for almost exactly that. Kinross is a bit further than that from Perth – almost thirty kloms – but there isn't an eighteen hole course that'll help us between Kinross and Perth.'

'I can walk, as long as we take plenty to eat.'

Gates closed up his compad and began to try and fold the map. Teddy grabbed hold of an edge as it flew up in the air.

He grinned at her and they folded it carefully, like a bed sheet. Then he raised his glass to her. She got the Islay bottle out of the box and pulled the cork with her teeth. Then she refilled both glasses and raised hers in a toast.

'To the simplicity of escape,' she said.

'To anarchy,' he said.

They laughed and drank.

9.3

'I've got it!' Lox was elated. It had taken him a couple of hours – precious hours while the world had been turning and he, Lox, had not – but he had it now. Not only did he know where Goldstein and Hanford were going, he had a picture of it, right there on the screen. 'They're going to Dunster.'

McCall and Bridie came round the desk to look over his shoulder. The screen displayed a picture of a big, white castle with crenellations, arrow slits and all the trimmings.

'Right,' said McCall. 'she only came into the city for treatment. She lives in Caithness.'

'Dunster Castle, Caithness to be precise. I've always wanted to be rich enough to have a two-line address.'

'How are we going to get there, with things as they are?'

Lox turned and looked at her.

'You could always let them go,' he said.

McCall laughed. It was not a pretty sound.

'He's the bastard that caused all this … whatever … with the traffic. And she's the devious bitch that put him up to it. I want them both.' She stepped away from Lox and started to pace. It wasn't a very effective way of alleviating tension as Bridie's cubicle was small, and it wasn't possible to take more than a couple of steps without bumping into something.

'There's always the train,' Bridie said.

McCall stopped pacing.

'Of course. The bloody train's *electric*,' said McCall. 'It should still be running, at least for a while. If they're using golf carts we should be able to overtake them easily on the train.'

Lox was loath to state the obvious but thought he'd better.

'They may decide to take the train themselves once they think they're outside the police cordon.'

'Okay.' McCall was back on form. 'It's quite possible that we and they could end up on the same one.' Her eyes narrowed. 'Now *that* would be just peachy. Bridie, we need to know what trains are running.'

'I'm on it.' Bridie's fingers were already interrogating her compad.

Lox was just considering popping down to the police canteen for a spot of well-earned breakfast when a police constable popped his head into the cubicle.

'Its stopped growing,' he said lugubriously.

'Thank Christ for that,' said McCall. The head withdrew. Lox looked the question at her. 'The hole in the wall of what was Gold's cell in C block. It looks like an elephant-sized mouse has had a go at it. The hole's been getting bigger by about a centimetre an hour. Most of the bloody wall's probably gone by now.'

When McCall had commed him at half past four that morning the hole in Cell Block C had been her opening gambit. Lox was as frightened of nano-tech as the next man, which right now was pretty frightened. Nevertheless, this was his Big Story. His desire for breakfast evaporated. He fought down a sensation like ants crawling over his skin and said,

'Can I see it?'

She shrugged. 'Why not. Bridie, comm me when you know what's running north out of Waverley.'

She shepherded him down into the cells. A and B blocks led out of the Custody Room. The relatively new C block was at the end of B block. McCall swiped her card through the security door between A and B Blocks and led him down a bright, white corridor. There were six cells on either side. Prurient curiosity made Lox scan the names written up beside the doors as they went down the row. At one he stopped.

'Prosser?' he asked.

'Yeh, we picked her up too. She was heading up the research that Hanford used to poison the petrol. She's in this with Goldstein, I'm certain. When I can prove she's involved I shall take enormous pleasure in making sure she's sent down for a very long time.'

'She being the only one left you can take it out on?'

McCall shot him a vitriolic look. 'In this job you learn to work with what you've got.'

They went on to the end of the block and McCall swiped through a second door into C block. She told him that Goldstein had been put in the cell at the end. A breeze wafted down the corridor towards them which had nothing to do with the air-con.

The cell door was closed. McCall swiped her card again. She held it gingerly, making sure she didn't touch the door. The lock mechanism buzzed. McCall put her toe against it, to prevent the lock engaging again, and gestured to Lox.

'There you are. Go in if you want.' She meant 'if you dare'. Patently she wasn't going to if she could decently avoid it. Lox took the point. If this was nano-tech, what parameters was it working to? Would it be content with munching its way through a wall or was it programed to attack everything it came in contact with? Was any of it loose? Was it floating in that breeze that had met them in the corridor? Would it stick to his shoes? Would it get in his hair? Would it eat his brain? But Lox wanted his Big Story badly. And it went against the grain to make it up when the evidence was right there, behind an unlocked door.

He fished around in his pockets looking for something to push the door open with that was disposable. Unfortunately all he had on him were his compad and card wallet.

Cautiously he pushed against the door with the nail of one index finger. The door swung slowly inward. He stepped into the doorway.

'Holy shit!'

As McCall had surmised, most of the cell wall on the far side of the room was gone. The hole had, obviously, grown outwards from one spot and was more or less circular. After it outgrew the wall it had started chewing on the floor, the part of the concrete bench bed nearest the far wall and the ceiling. The 'elephant-sized mouse' analogy was apt.

'What do you think stopped it?'

'I have no idea,' said McCall from the corridor.

'Have you searched it?'

'Sort of. I wouldn't say we'd been thorough. Nobody, including me, wanted to get close to the hole while it was still growing. A relatively large portion of the cell is, therefore … unprocessed. I don't suppose anybody will be any keener now that it's stopped.'

'Do you mind if *I* look around?'

'Knock yourself out. We've been insisting that anyone who's been in here takes a shower afterwards. It might help, it might not; it's the best we can do.'

'Right.' Lox moved into the cell. Behind him McCall made a sound and he turned. She still stood in the corridor.

'Be careful,' she said.

'Count on that.'

Now, what had the police over-looked?

He was surprised to discover just how difficult it was to look at anything properly without touching it. And he *really* didn't want to touch anything. The hair on his head and on his shins began to crawl. Some visceral part of him expected an attack to begin at his extremities. They said it had stopped. Did that mean it was dead, or just inactive? And if it was just inactive, how long was it going to stay inactive for. And what would make it active again – a juicy potential meal? Tuthill steak, for example?

He told himself that there was no reason to believe that he was in any danger. And then he told himself to be bloody quick about whatever it was he was going to do in here. It seemed like a fair compromise.

First he checked the bed. He felt slightly better when he noticed that only the concrete had been eaten away. The blanket and thin pillow were untouched. The pillow had fallen to the ground. He resisted the temptation to pick it up. He did poke around in the blanket with the toe of his shoe, and was gratified to see a piece of paper drop to the floor.

'Look,' he said to McCall.

'OK, don't touch it. I'll get some gloves and something to put it in.'

While he waited he had a cautious look through the hole in the wall. Morning sounds echoed cheerily around the little courtyard outside. Salisbury Crags glowed golden behind the housing estate as the sun settled in to a day's work. Something outside nodded in the light breeze and gave an illusion of movement in the cell. Lox wished fervently that he was somewhere else.

McCall tossed in a pair of gloves and an evidence back. He put the gloves on and retrieved the paper. It said *'Put this on your window sill tonight. The moonlight will make it magic'*.

Now, what the hell did that mean?

9.4

At a sedate pace, Gates and Teddy started north.

They hugged the docks on their way round to the bridge, inching back into Edinburgh, keeping to side streets as much as possible. They gave Princes Street a wide berth, and Waverley Station. Granted, they could have done with a timetable. But if there was one place in Edinburgh where the police would be concentrated, Waverley was certain to be it.

There were people on the streets now that the morning was more advanced. The sight of Gates and Teddy dawdling up the middle of the road in a golf buggy caused amusement. Teddy, feeling festive after her early morning Islay, started waving at people. Gates got her to stop.

'Once they get over how amusing we look they're likely to want the buggy for themselves. And we're supposed to be on the run, remember? Keep a low profile.'

'How the hell can we do that trundling through the capital of Scotland in a golf cart?'

'Try.'

One couple passed them riding double on a horse. Teddy couldn't resist waving at them; they waved back.

As they progressed towards the Forth Road Bridge, Gates waxed lyrical about their current mode of transport. 'Something like this could so easily have been made practical for mass, everyday transport purposes.'

He sounded like a brochure. Teddy tuned him out. It was a beautiful morning, she was high as a kite and they weren't in jail. Reasons to be cheerful: one, two, three.

Gates said, primly, that he wouldn't have had to sabotage petrol-driven transport if people had listened. There were many alternatives to the poisonous petrol, but with each one there was an inconvenience. The biggest inconvenience had always been that it wasn't what everybody else was using. People were lemmings – they all wanted to go the same places at the same time. But, insanely, they all wanted to go by themselves. It made no sense, except that it was human nature.

And to create a new transport infrastructure would take far longer, and far more money, than any government would ever see the benefits of. So, of course, government gave no lead. It remained in thrall to oil because it was easier and because of the huge taxes that could be collected off the back of it. Even here, in Scotland, where they were energy conscious, there weren't many private fuel-cell cars – and a hell of a lot of people still drove to work. Did she remember when they'd voted down congestion charging in the late Twenties? She didn't.

It was no longer the case that the vaults of the oil companies were stuffed with patents for alternative means of production, bought up and left to languish so that nobody knew about them: everybody knew what the alternatives were. Some of them were so ridiculously simple it made him want to weep. But nothing had ever been done. Plenty of lip service had been paid, but no action taken. Until now.

He kept on in this vein for about an hour – the time it took them, with some false turnings, to get close enough to be able to see the Forth Bridge looming over South Queensferry. The sight of it broke his flow. Teddy wasn't sorry.

'Of course,' said Gates as they trundled towards the bridge, 'the police will probably have this staked out as well, if they've been able to get here in time.'

'If they have there's not much we can do. We have to go over this bridge. To go on west to Kincardine bridge will add about fifty kloms to the journey.'

'That's why they'll be here.'

'OK. Let's get as close as we can and then go and have a look, on foot.'

But as soon as they got close enough to have a good look at the bridge it was obvious that nobody was waiting for them. Not at the Edinburgh end anyway.

'Shall we chance it?'

He shrugged and drove on. Sedately, they purred across the bridge. They moved past the stanchions sooo slowly. Teddy found she was leaning forward, urging the little cart to go faster, peering to see the far end of the bridge. It remained strangely indistinct. At last it became obvious that there was a reason why the other end was still invisible – they were, after all, now half way across. There was some kind of mist lying thickly over the last third of it. Shortly they drove into the outer veils of it. It wasn't mist, it was smoke.

As they went on it got denser. Now they were moving at a snail's pace through a choking cloud.

'Christ,' wheezed Teddy. 'I wish we could shut the windows.'

The windshield gave them a little protection. It would have given more had they been moving faster, but Gates had to slow down from their pathetic top speed because it wasn't possible to see anything beyond the front end of the buggy.

'I just hope that this means that anybody at the far end has their hands full already without bothering to look for us.'

'We'll be bloody unlucky if they see us in this.'

They both began to cough as the smoke got thicker and more acrid. Teddy's eyes were streaming now, making it hard to see anything at all. Gates kept rubbing at the wind shield as if it was fogging up, but of course it made no difference. They ricocheted off a kerb and Gates called out,

'Do you think we should stop?'

'No. We can't, not now. We'll hit kerbs before we hit anything more solid. Go on.'

He slowed even more.

'We could walk quicker than this,' he said. 'Perhaps we should leave the buggy?'

This made her nervous. The little carts had been lucky for them so far.

'Just a little bit further,' she said. 'Surely we must be nearly across now.'

And with that came a break in the smoke. They were, indeed, nearly across. She could see, just briefly before the smoke swirled round them again, that what was on fire was the burger franchise at the north end of the bridge. One of the little city cars was parked near the road. Inside the burning building she could see two people brandishing fire extinguishers. Smoke was billowing out of the roof. The two men fighting the fire looked as though they were in uniform. They looked like police.

'I think that car brought police,' she said. 'They're fighting the fire, or somebody is. They look like cops to me. What do you think?'

'I can't see anything much,' he said, and started to cough in earnest.

'I bet they were sent here for us. That means they suspect we're going north. Thank God for this fire. We'd better get a move on in case they see us.'

The words were hardly out of her mouth before they stopped. For a moment she thought that perhaps the buggy's battery had drained already. Then she realised that Gates was still coughing: great hacking whoops which were drawing in more smoke than the air for which his lungs craved.

'Move over,' she said, tugging on his arm.

He shuffled over. She got out and slipped round the other side of the cart to take his place. Somehow the smoke wasn't affecting her as badly – her eyes were stinging and watering, but she wasn't coughing half as badly as Gates. It was simple enough to drive the thing. She stamped her foot on a pedal, discovered it was the brake, stamped on the other and they shot forward splendidly. She kept her foot hard down and they raced past the burger place. Immediately the smoke began to thin. They had been down wind. Another fifty metres and they were out of the smoke completely. She kept going at full speed around the long left hand bend that curled around the burger place and ran up the hill. She risked a look behind and saw that the shoulder of the hill now hid them from anybody at the burning building.

'There,' she said, and stopped.

Gates looked really bad. He was hunched over, still racked with coughing. His eyes were red and streaming; he wiped at them with his sleeves and tried to focus on her. Teddy found that she could see pretty well, considering. And she only had a silly little tickly cough.

'Your colony is working very well,' he wheezed. 'I must get round to giving myself some of the same.'

'You mean, the reason I'm not in as bad a state as you is because of the silver bug things?'

'Your nanites are fixing every bit of damage almost as soon as it occurs. I shall be racked with this for hours. You're already feeling better. Physician heal thyself, eh?' He laughed and paid for his levity with another hacking spasm. Finally, 'where are we?'

'Out of sight of the police. That hill is between us and them.'

'This bodes rather well – except for the breathing and seeing' he gasped for air. 'You'll have to drive.'

So she did. The M90 rose up the hill before them, heading towards Perth and the Highlands. There was nothing on it. There was even a sign: 'Dunfermline 12km, Perth 64km'. She put the pedal to the metal.

9.5

McCall had sent constables to Prestonfield golf club for buggies. The Duty Sergeant and her team were trying to find shops that still had bicycles for sale. They could commandeer what they needed, the State of Emergency having been declared at eight a.m., but soon found you can only commandeer what someone has to give you.

While they waited for some sort of transportation to be available Lox was lolling in McCall's office chair with his feet on her desk, working on his story. Given the trouble he and the rest of the world appeared to be in, it gave him a modicum of satisfaction that he had managed to be of help in the crisis. And that stroke that he had pulled with the golf courses had certainly changed McCall's opinion of him. He was just writing that up now. He wasn't underplaying his part in the deductions the Police had made. Not at all he wasn't.

But what about the larger scheme of things? Petrol-based transport was obviously off the road for the foreseeable future. As soon as it refuelled, not a car, lorry, boat, ship or plane would run. Anything still moving that used petrol was a short-term option – and there seemed to be almost nothing that *was* still moving. When the gauge showed red you were fucked. Big time.

He started to fiddle around with his story, putting it in order, trying out phrases. Under the circumstances his precious story seemed a small thing. Nevertheless, people needed to know the score. Trouble was, there was still a lot of it that *he* didn't know. That ate at him, like nanites running amok. What was that message he'd found on the floor of Teddy's cell about, for a start?

The only one of the gang they still had was Prosser. She must have heard the sirens and commotion. She might not know what the fuss had been about. Or she might have been expecting Gates to come. Perhaps she had expected to be rescued too. If the latter she might be pretty pissed off at being left behind. Perhaps he should have a little chat with Dr Prosser?

McCall came back. She glared at his feet on her desk and he took them off it with what he hoped was a winning smile. There was no reciprocity in McCall's face. Obviously he hadn't risen as far in her estimation as he had thought.

'There are only three buggies ready to use. The rest need recharging. I've got people on it, but it restricts our range.'

'Have you checked the trains?'

'Yes. There's one leaving for the northeast at ten thirty this morning. They don't know how far it'll get. It's probably the last one. They're doubtful that there'll be one coming back here after today.'

'Shit.'

'We're going to be living in a pre-industrial society for a while by the looks of things.'

'I've been thinking …'

'Bully for you. Try not to do it out loud.' McCall jammed her earpiece in and start barking commands at her compad.

'We ought to talk to Prosser.'

'What's this with the 'we'?'

'She might have been expecting to go with them. If so, she'll be really hacked off at being left behind. She might talk now. We're not going anywhere until ten-ish are we? Might as well see what she knows.'

'What's she's prepared to tell us, you mean. It'll probably be a pack of lies; disinformation. Standard terrorist procedure.'

'I don't think she's a terrorist.'

'I do.'

'You got anything better to do?'

McCall gave up looking for whatever-it-was on her compad and pulled out her earpiece. She shrugged and stood.

'Let's go.'

9.6

Gates was still coughing – great hacking barks that didn't seem to shift the smoke, but just irritated his already inflamed airways. He couldn't stop. Teddy fished out a bottle of water for him, but very little of it seemed to go down the right way, and what didn't only made the irritation worse. His eyes still streamed, so did his nose.

'Have you got any tissues in there?' he gasped between coughing fits.

Teddy passed him a handful of paper napkins. He blew his nose and wiped his eyes, but it was a Sisyphean task.

'Are you sure you don't want to stop for a bit?'

'What for?' He said between gasps for air. 'Being stationary won't make me feel any better. Fresher air may help.'

They continued up the deserted motorway. The loudest sound to be heard was Gates coughing. He was beginning to look very ill indeed.

Gates fell into an uneasy doze before they got to Junction 2. Periodically he woke himself up with another coughing fit. The coughing came from deep inside him and sounded as if it was tearing him apart. Teddy put her arm around him so that he didn't fall out of the buggy as he slept.

When she had turned off the motorway and was heading ponderously up the off-ramp she nudged him gently.

'Hmm?'

'If you're up to it I could use a hand with map-reading.'

'Uh-hu.' Even that led to a spasm, but he hitched himself up in his seat and rummaged around weakly for the old map of Scottish golf courses. He spread it out with difficulty, largely obscuring Teddy's view of the road, and hastily pulled it out of the way when she complained, coughing an apology. It was still difficult to remember that there wasn't likely to be anything coming. He tried again.

'Yeh. There are three: one mile north of, two miles west of or right in Dunfermline. Which?'

'Let's go for 'right in'.'

'OK. Pitreavie. Don't take the first right off this roundabout. There should be another about three kloms further on. Keep an eye out for signs.'

She negotiated the roundabout, wondering how she was going to estimate three kilometres without an odometer, then another potential problem occurred to her.

'Are we all right to do this in daylight, d'you think? I mean – I don't suppose anybody's there, but should we wait until it gets dark?'

'It's June. It's Scotland. And, as we found out last night, it won't *get* dark, not really. What do you propose we do until twilight falls? Go shopping?' He tried a laugh, but it came out as a wheezy croak which precipitated another bout of coughing. Afterwards he had difficulty getting his breath.

She ignored the sarcasm: he wasn't well. The sky was blue and cloudless, the sun was bright and on the hot side of warm. She took her jacket off and glanced at her watch: nearly noon. She realised she was hungry again.

'Could you eat anything?'

'No,' he rasped. 'But I'll bet you could – in fact you must. You'll have to eat regularly from now on. Probably about eight meals a day to start with. If my little guys don't get their start-up fuel from the food you eat they'll start taking it from your fat reserves,' he looked at her out of red-rimmed eyes, 'which in your case are minimal. You'll get thinner. Even thinner.' He thought for a moment. 'In fact, if you don't eat enough our little friends might consume *you*.' He thought some more. 'I guess that's the only way you could die now, except for some massive trauma, like having your head cut off.'

'Cheerful! Perhaps we should stop for a picnic breakfast, before we get to Pitreavie?'

'Good idea.' It was as much as he could get out. The way he was fighting for breath concerned Teddy. Smoke inhalation could be quite serious. He was looking worse by the minute. Teddy didn't know what she could do to help him, but one thing was certain: stopping wasn't a good idea at all. Large, regular meals, indeed. She raided the polystyrene box one-handed and munched as they went along. She hoped Pitreavie had a good medical kit.

9.7

McCall had Prosser brought to an interview room.

'You shouldn't even be in the room,' she said to Lox as they made their way towards it. 'I don't know why you're even here.'

He grinned at her.

'We make a pretty good team, that's why. You see some of it: I see some of it. Between us we see most of it.' The grin became rueful. 'Whatever *it* is.'

'I want to keep this on the record,' McCall said. 'That means that you can only observe. You're my *silent* expert. Don't open your mouth. OK?'

Lox opened his mouth to protest, but she was already half way through the door to the interview room. He followed her in.

Dr Prosser looked very sorry for herself. A night in the cells had done nothing for her grooming. She obviously hadn't thought to bring a comb, and her clothes looked as if they'd been slept in which, of course, they had. When she looked up at them from her seat at the interview table Lox could see dark smudges around her eyes. Not make-up: worry and lack of sleep – and possibly tears too. Excellent.

McCall activated the recorder and went through the formalities. Prosser gave her name in a dead little voice which enabled McCall to insist that she repeat it, louder. Prosser looked as if she might cry. McCall got started properly.

'Dr Prosser, last night you were arrested and charged with possession of, and conspiracy to produce, a banned substance. You were arrested together with a Theodora Goldstein. You were asked to reveal the whereabouts of one Gates Hanford.'

McCall looked at her quizzically.

'Yes,' said Prosser.

'I daresay it will come as no surprise to you to learn that Ms Goldstein is no longer in this Station.'

Prosser sat up straighter.

'That's great news – when will I be released?'

'No time soon,' said McCall dryly, 'unless you can eat your way through walls, as Ms Goldstein appears to have done.'

Prosser looked from McCall to Lox and back again. She said,

'Hanford?'

'We believe so.'

'Wow. He's really getting good at this, isn't he?'

There was a silence as those present thought about the implications of Hanford getting 'really good' at targeting nanite swarms. Lox tried to make his face expressionless. He could see that the news of Teddy's escape and Hanford's involvement had perked Prosser up to the point where she was having difficulty keeping a smile off hers. McCall looked grim, but that was nothing new. The Detective Sergeant spoke.

'As you are now the only member of this conspiracy in custody you can be sure that the full weight of the law will be brought to bear upon you. Your only chance of avoiding a lengthy term of imprisonment is to tell us all you know about the jail break. Now.'

'But …'

'I want you to tell us what, exactly, they did and what their plans are now.'

'But …'

'Please don't waste my time, Dr Prosser. Time is of the essence.'

'But … but …'

Prosser sounded like a small two-stroke engine having difficulty starting.

Lox nudged McCall and touched the evidence bag containing the note they had found in the half-eaten cell. Despite the fact that the bag was sealed he touched it very gingerly. McCall pushed it towards Prosser with the tip of one fingernail.

'This was found in Ms Goldstein's cell. Please tell us what it means.'

Prosser leant forward, put her hand on the bag and swivelled it so that she could read what was inside. It didn't look as though she had any fear of the contents. But when she had glanced at the note she took her hand off it pretty smartly.

'Wow,' she said softly. 'I didn't know his research was far enough advanced to enable him to do that.'

Now they were getting somewhere.

'Tell us something you do know,' McCall growled.

This seemed to strike a spark of, probably entirely justified, irritation somewhere inside Prosser. She said,

'I was the project leader – so naturally I was the last person out of the lab. I shut everything down when the Notice came through. I had no idea we were still doing something illegal after that. I had no idea he was living in the basement. I had no idea what he was doing when he wasn't at his workstation. And he wasn't at his workstation very bloody often. What the hell do you want from me?'

She glared at McCall. Lox said, 'just tell us what you know and let's see how it all fits together.' He couldn't keep quiet any longer. Prosser had been a more promising interviewee cowed than irritated. Since impatience was McCall's middle name, Lox could see the interview becoming confrontational in no time flat if something wasn't done to ease matters along. McCall growled something at him that he didn't quite catch, so he put a pleasant smile on his face and beamed it at each woman in turn.

Prosser continued to glare at McCall for a few moments, but seemed to see sense in Lox's request. Now aware of what environment that note had been found in, Prosser picked up the evidence bag carefully by one corner and held it up to the light. There was the faintest shimmer to be seen on the paper.

'Oh shit,' she said and put it down again. She looked at them both. 'I can guess what he's done. I can't say for certain – he's more skilled at this than I am – but it seems to me that he's engineered a batch of nanites that are activated by a particular light source – in this case I suppose it must have been moonlight. Are they still working?'

'No,' said McCall.

'Hmm. But, of course, they'll start working again whenever moonlight strikes them.'

'Oh, shit.' said McCall.

'Shit, indeed,' Lox muttered.

'And were you expecting a delivery like the one Ms Goldstein received?'

'No, of course not. I was playing around when I said I assumed she'd been released. I heard the sirens last night, and it was very likely she was the cause of them. But we didn't talk about anything like this – we didn't have any opportunity. And it's her Gates is … concerned about. Not me. I suspect she was as surprised by events as you were.'

'Pleasantly surprised, I imagine,' McCall said. Lox got them back on track.

'So where would they have gone?'

Prosser thought for a moment.

'The Works? The house? Other than that I really have no idea. How could they go anywhere? There's no transport.'

McCall cleared her throat.

'That is not entirely the case. We believe they made their escape in a … ahem … golf cart. Also, we understand, the railways north are still running.'

'How?' Prosser was obviously surprised at this news.

'They're electric. If the generators fail, so will they. Until then they're still running as long as the drivers can get to work.'

'Oh, well then,' said Prosser, 'She'll go north. To Dunster. Everything's there – her home, her son. You'll never catch her. She must be hours ahead by now.'

A small smile twitched at Prosser's lips as she leaned back in her seat.

9.8

Teddy and Gates had reached Pitreavie. Teddy parked at the end of the private road which led up to it and walked up to make sure there was nobody about. Gates was in such a state now that she didn't want to have to make a run for it. In fact she didn't want surprises of any kind until she had made him comfortable and was reasonably certain that he was getting better. The way he was fighting for every breath frightened her, although she tried not to show it. If this was how she would have been without the nanites inside her she was very glad she had them. If there was a downside to the treatment Gates had given her she certainly hadn't experienced it yet. Why oh why hadn't he set himself up with the same? She didn't know how she was going to treat him without nanonic help.

There was nobody at the club, so she went back to get the buggy. Gates was slumped over onto the driver's seat, and she had to lift him back up before she could get in. He seemed to be unconscious and stank of smoke. She supposed she did too.

She puttered up the shrub-lined drive to the club, steering with her right hand and holding Gates up with her left arm. She parked as near to the main entrance as she could get, which involved driving over a putting green. There were a lot of holes in it with little metal flags stuck in them; she hit a couple but it couldn't be helped. When she glanced back to see what she'd hit, the tyre-tracks of their progress were very evident in the perfect, tight-mown grass, but that couldn't be helped either

Leaving Gates in the buggy she went to look for something to break in with. She didn't have Gates's skill with electronic means of ingress. Around the side of the club she found a big shed containing a panoply of implements for use in the great outdoors. Amongst them was a crow bar. She seized it and hurried back to the main door. She needed access to all areas without aggravation, and the main entrance seemed like her best bet. When she ripped the lock out of this door an alarm was going to go off, and she was going to have to find it before it alerted anybody. And when she found it she was going to have to smash it. She found she was exhilarated by the prospect. This was ridiculous – she was feeling better and better and Gates was getting sicker and sicker. Talk about role reversal.

She felt, actually, Herculean. She jemmied the lock with no trouble at all: one good heave was all it took. Then she trotted nimbly into the club and waited for a couple of seconds. Sure enough an alarm began to ring. She tracked it to a room that said 'Secretary's Office', jemmied that door too, and smashed the bell. But the ringing continued; there must be another one somewhere. She found it in the kitchen and smashed it with a swing that she felt the club champion might have envied. Then she hunted out the control box for the alarm system and ripped it off the wall, just to be on the safe side. When she'd finished she found she hadn't even broken a sweat. Indeed, she was rather sorry nothing else needed smashing. But she had to see to Gates.

Back outside, Gates was still unconscious. Gently she pressed him back into a sitting position, then eased him out of the buggy and half-carried, half-dragged him into the bar. She lay him down on a bench seat, but his breathing began to rattle so she heaved him up into a sitting position instead. She didn't like the look of him at all: his face was grey and his lips were blue. She found a cloth and a bowl in the kitchen and fetched some cold water. She bathed his face and throat, hoping to relieve the inflammation that seemed to be suffocating him.

She wasn't sure how much good she was doing, but he did revive enough to start moaning and then coughing weakly. He flopped over onto his side. She knelt down to try and make sure that he had an airway. While she was there she felt for a pulse. His skin was hot and sweaty and his pulse was way too fast and alarmingly feeble.

They could not come all this way – he could not have done all this for her – for him to end up dead. She wouldn't let him. She shook him gently,

'Gates!'

No response. His head rolled sickeningly. She propped him up again and tried once more, less gently this time, shouting,

'Gates!'

His head stopped flopping. He opened his eyes and tried to focus. It took him several goes, but at last he managed to whisper hoarsely,

'Kiss me.'

Now she was really afraid for him and began to cry quietly, as a child does when it's left alone in a strange, dark room.

'No,' she said. 'You're not going to die. No.' And she wrapped her arms around him tight as tight, hoping to hold his life in with her own new-found strength.

Feebly he fought her embrace.

'Kiss me,' he gasped. 'It's the only thing. It may work … I don't know.'

Now she understood. She held him to her again and kissed him long on the mouth, opening his lips with her tongue, exchanging as much saliva with him as she could. Then she sat cradling him in her arms, hoping for the best.

10

10.1

McCall had Prosser taken back to the cells, then she marched Lox back to her office. As soon as they reached it McCall snugged-in her earpiece and called the Duty Sergeant.

'Apparently what we've got is a nasty case of rogue nanites. Yes, yes – all right, I know. My information is that they'll start chewing at Block C again as soon as the moon rises tonight, so for Chrissakes keep everybody away from that area. What? Yes, move the rest of the people in C Block. Double people up if you have to. Well, just don't tell them!

'Get on to the Department of National Security … their Terrorism Unit. See if they've got anyone local who knows anything about Nanonics. Make sure they understand this is a real threat. Try and get someone here before moonrise or we're really going to have something to show them. At least get them to mail us some sensible advice on what to do.

'My diary says there are fourteen more moonlit nights before the dark of the moon. Check the weather forecasts. A cloudy night tonight would be a big help. Yes, I'll bring the Superintendent up to speed. No, I don't suppose he will, but as he's not here he can go …'

She broke the connection and turned to Lox in one fluid movement. McCall in full flow was a beautiful sight to behold.

'So, she's going north. If she's got any sense she won't try to board the train at Waverley. She'll be heading north independently until she thinks she's outside our perimeter, probably intends to get on at Perth. Pack your toothbrush Tuthill – we're going on a trip.'

'You realise it may be one way?'

That shut her up for a moment. Then,

'I'm going to get them. Even if I can't bring them back. Even if there are no courts left to try them. What he's done is … well, let's just say I'm taking this personally.'

'What are you going to do about Prosser?'

'Small potatoes. Cat's paw. Don't know. Could let her go. Could have her committed for trial – if there was a court working. I'll get someone to check if there is.'

She swivelled and speed-dialled someone.

'Now,' she said, 'if you'll excuse me I've got to explain all this to my Super.'

10.2

Gates was sleeping on the banquette with a chair cushion under his head. A little colour had come back into his face and his lips were no longer that awful blue.

Teddy was eating a proper meal at last – with one eye on her patient. Her appetite seemed unappeasable; as soon as she had finished the substantial sandwich she had made she found herself hankering after chips, ice-cream, biscuits, fruit. The little machines inside her were, indeed, demanding.

Teddy had had trouble with food for many years. It might have started in the days when she had been pronounced 'delicate'. There'd been a lot of screening of what she ate, in case the root cause of the physical symptoms she wasn't able to articulate lay there. And she had been terrified of eating with her father – he insisted that they sat at opposite ends of the long table, cavernous corners of the room disappeared in the darkness. The only sounds were the muttered monosyllables of Ailsa serving, the scraping of the cutlery on the plates, the sound of chewing and swallowing. It all echoed in the high space. Later, in London, food had been hard to get. The drugs meant that sometimes she forgot to eat for days on end. No, food had never been more than a nuisance to her before. But food, it turned out, was wonderful! Who knew?

There was a clock in the bar. Every few minutes she looked up at it. They should be moving on, but she didn't want to wake Gates. She really thought she had lost him. Now they were both of them the same. That was good. It had been … strange, no: frightening, to be the only immortal in the world. And who else should share her condition but the man who had made it possible: the man she loved? What a strange thing to admit to, and in what strange circumstances. But there it was. It would be a long life and a good one and she wanted to share it with him. She couldn't wait to get him home and introduce him to Ek and Rory and Ailsa.

Ek and Rory and Ailsa. And Sara. They were the only other people who cared about her. And they'd left poor Sara in Edinburgh. Edinburgh already seemed like another life.

Ek and Rory: how would it be to see your children getting older – getting older than you. Should she share this with them? Should she even tell them about it? What would they think? Would they want it too, or would they be horrified at what she had become? If they knew it was transmittable would they avoid physical contact with her as if she had contracted some monstrous disease? Another monstrous disease – she'd already had AIDS and tuberculosis. They hadn't shrunk from her then, would they now?

Well, that was worry for another day. She would find the right moment to tell them, or would know it when it came, or would say nothing. The first thing was to get home, then everything would be all right.

10.3

Lox had got as far as the Police Station's foyer on his way back to the Balmoral. He felt fuzzy from lack of sleep. His eyes were gritty and he felt unwashed – as, indeed, he was. He'd checked the morning newscasts while McCall was administering the crisis but had only learned that international motoring matters were moving quickly from bad to bloody awful. Hardly a surprise. He needed a good breakfast, a shower, a change of clothes and some sleep. He was keen to get the breakfast inside him before lunch-time. Back at the Balmoral he could finish tarting up his story and get it off to Gardner without McCall growling at him constantly.

He'd made it as far as Reception when a minor whirlwind erupted behind him.

'If the bastards aren't going to be any more help than that we'd better chuck a tarp over the hole and hope for the best. Do it soon. Try and make sure that no light can get in. Have we got any bio-hazard suits? Well kit a couple of people up with them. I'm sure they'll be fine. Well, it's that or the whole station disappears in a cloud of molecules – or so I'm told. You do that.' McCall disconnected the call and turned her attention to Lox.

'I've been looking for you – don't wander off in future. I've told the Custody Officer she can release Prosser as soon as the train's gone. They're bringing the golf carts over. Come on.'

McCall didn't wait to see if he was following, but lunged at the automatic doors, which only just opened in time. She had faith, she had focus. She had, apparently, unlimited stamina. She also had a nice wiggle in her walk, especially when she was in a hurry. Lox opened his mouth to suggest a change of clothes and a bite to eat, but realised he would be addressing this to a doleful looking constable coming in, probably from golf buggy duty. The constable looked like Lox felt. He gave the man a sympathetic smile and followed McCall out into the bright June day.

Outside three caddy cars were drawn up in a police-neat line. McCall was waiting, with demonstrable impatience, in the one on the left. Lox got in beside her and she galvanised. The buggy shot backwards towards the plate-glass automatic doors they'd just come out of. They got close enough for the doors to glide open before McCall lifted her foot. Over his shoulder Lox saw a couple of people inside leap out of the way.

'Shit, where's forward?'

Lox shrugged. Golf wasn't a game he'd ever had any time for. It involved a lot of walking, of which Lox wasn't fond, and considerable hand-eye co-ordination, which Lox didn't have.

The little cart wasn't over endowed with technology. Under the seat, between the two of them, she found what she needed.

'If I find out which arsehole left it in gear, I'll …'

Lox found the way she rolled the 'r' in 'arsehole' most endearing.

She clunked the switch from reverse through neutral to forward and tried again. They shot forwards narrowly missing an incoming buggy. McCall swung them round that and finally had them pointing in her desired direction. Lox was relieved when all four wheels were once again in contact with the road

'I take it you've got a plan?' Lox said.

'The train.' McCall said. 'It's leaving at ten thirty, possibly. Or it might be later. But if we miss it we're buggered. We need to be there. It's quarter past already. I've told them to hold the train – but I'd rather be there than trust them to do it.'

Lox braced himself with his feet on what passed for a dashboard and hung on as best he could. Goodbye to breakfast, shower, nap, change of clothes. Goodbye, indeed, to his comfortable room at the Balmoral and everything in it. He suspected he wouldn't be seeing any of it again.

10.4

Gates's breathing was much easier now and Teddy felt she could snatch a little sleep herself. It had been a long night, after all. Even with her new found strength and her tiny internal friends fully fuelled she found she wasn't invulnerable. There were still slumps between the highs.

She wanted to stay close to Gates; watch his face as he slept, listen to his breathing. The miracle might not be real, might not last. She didn't know how to test to see if he was properly infected. Gates might know, but until he woke up she wasn't taking any chances.

But for a little while she could let her mind wander. It was a glorious day outside. Bright, clear sunshine poured over the golf course – she could see the beautiful greens of early summer from the big picture window behind the banquette that Gates was lying on. To the north she could see the Highlands beginning, massive and mauvish beneath a sky so blue it brought a lump to her throat. The world was so beautiful. How was it she had had to come so far, be brought so low, before she could see it? The good thing was, she had forever to make up for it.

She wondered about the train they were making for. Even electric trains would be affected by Gates's petrol virus sooner or later. Was the last train speeding north towards Dunster this very minute, while they were stuck here, stymied by Gates's sickness? But it was too grand a day to worry. Things would work out. They always did when she was with Gates. She would sleep, then she would sort them out a fresh buggy. When they reached Perth the train would be there, and would take them home to Ek and Rory and Ailsa. She lay down on the corded carpet beside Gates. Satisfied that he was breathing easily she closed her eyes.

10.5

Sara Prosser stood for a moment and let the beautiful day wash over her. She breathed deeply. The doors of Leith Police Station sighed shut behind her. It was a good sound.

She didn't know why they had let her go. She hadn't been able to tell the hard-eyed McCall woman anything she didn't already know. The threats that the woman had made felt very real. But in the end they'd just handed back her few bits and pieces, and more or less pushed her out the door.

Behind the police station Salisbury Crags loomed large. She smiled. Teddy and Hanford had been scampering around in there last night, apparently, in a golf buggy. Absolute madness – but it seemed to have worked. Outside the police station were several more of the little vehicles. Too late, of course, to do anything about Teddy. Nobody ever seemed able to do anything about Teddy. The woman was a force of nature. Sara laughed out loud. And now she had Hanford as an ally – another dangerous natural phenomenon. What couldn't those two accomplish together? It wasn't her problem any more – that was one good thing, anyway. The laugh died on her lips as she remembered what they had accomplished to date.

And Gates had only come for Teddy. They had left her behind.

She set off for Millerfield Place in a sombre mood.

10.6

As Lox and McCall went down the ramp into the station she'd got out her shield and made Lox hold it out while she yelled at people to get out of the way. Then she'd yelled at the harassed-looking man in the ticket booth until he told her which platform the train was leaving from and had opened the baggage barrier. Squeezing the buggy through that had been interesting. Lox was impressed that she'd managed it. He had been certain they would have to leave it there.

So now they were sitting in the golf cart on the platform and McCall was fuming. Again. They needn't have hurried. There was no information on the monitors and no train. There were lots of people on the platform, milling about aimlessly.

McCall drove up and down the platform, looking for somebody to get a departure time from and staring at every knot of people they passed, just in case Goldstein and Hanford had been stupid enough to try and catch the train in Edinburgh after all and the transport police had somehow missed them. She found neither fugitives nor information.

Lox could see that she was all wound up with nowhere to go. She wanted desperately to make something happen. When they got back to the entrance to the platform she turned the cart around and was about to make another pass. Lox put his hand over her white-knuckled one where it gripped the wheel.

'Save the gas,' he said. 'We'll just have to wait. Let me get you something to eat.'

'It's not gas, I wish it was. If it was we wouldn't be in this mess' she said. Her voice was higher pitched than usual. She snatched her hand away.

Lox made his expression mild, sympathetic. 'There's nothing more you can do,' he said. 'Take it easy for a couple of minutes. Have a cup of coffee. It's been a long night.'

'If I stop now I don't know if I'll be able to start again.' She passed a hand over her face. Lox was relieved to see this sign of weakness in her. He had been starting to think she was as tough as she acted.

'Let go,' he said softly. 'I'll keep an eye out.'

As soon as he said the words he regretted them. He wanted the nap. He wanted coffee and breakfast, and instead he was offering these things to McCall. Well, at least they could both get breakfast. 'Take us to the station buffet.'

And to his surprise she did. The queue for food was long. McCall maintained an agitated silence while they waited. But when they finally got to the serving counter she actually let him buy her something to eat and a cup of tea. They returned to the buggy, and trundled back to the platform where they ate and kept an eye on the monitors.

When they had eaten, to Lox's amazement, McCall's chin dropped onto her chest and she fell asleep. Sleeping in a caddy car took skills McCall did not have: shortly she started to slip sideways out of the buggy. Gently Lox put his arm around her and eased her back to the vertical. But she didn't stop there. Her momentum took her over to Lox's side. Her head slipped down onto his shoulder and there she stayed, snoring gently, until the tannoy woke her up.

Lox had mixed feelings about being used as a pillow. On the one hand it made eating his own breakfast – now brunch – extremely difficult. On the other, her hair smelled nice and the little snuffly snores she emitted were most attractive, revealing a vulnerability that McCall would have denied strenuously had she been awake. It also made a little oasis of peace and quiet in what had been a perfectly bloody twenty-four hours, and was likely to turn into at least thirty-six of the same, if not more. As he lost all feeling in the arm beneath her head, Lox found himself hoping that she might do the same for him later on. God alone knew where they were going to sleep that night.

The tannoy announced that the Scotrail-GNE express to Inverness would be arriving at the platform shortly and leaving at twelve twenty-eight. Then the announcer abandoned his script completely.

'If you're trying to get home, ladies and gentlemen, then don't miss this train. If you're hoping to change for destinations further north than Inverness, and you don't absolutely need to go, then my advice to you is - don't travel. We have electricity at the moment, but if the grid goes down so will the service. Drivers will start to miss their shifts soon, because they can't get to the trains. So this is likely to be a one way trip. Good luck to you all.'

God bless us, every one. Lox looked at McCall, who had come to enough to hear some of the announcement, but not all.

'What did he say?'

'He said if you're hoping to get back to Edinburgh any time soon you shouldn't get on this train.' Lox quirked an eyebrow at her. He had been hoping not only to return to Edinburgh, but also to go home to Milton Keynes before civilisation as he knew it ended. Patently the announcer didn't think much of that plan.

'Are you sure you want to do this? I mean, what about Mr McCall? Won't he be wanting you here, with him, if this is the end of the world as we know it?'

'My husband got his marching orders years ago. McCall is my own name and I'm my own person.'

'I think your Chief Superintendent might have something to say about that. What does he think about this quest of yours?'

'I shall be in constant communication with him.'

'Did you even comm him?' McCall suddenly began to take an unwonted interest in a group of potential travellers on her side of the buggy. 'He has no idea you're doing this, has he? Don't you think you might be more use here, in the circumstances?'

McCall turned and looked him in the eye.

'If things are as bad as you're implying it won't make the slightest bit of difference.'

'And how bad do *you* think things are?'

'Nothing like as bad as they're going to get. Frankly if we're going back to the Dark Ages I'd rather be in the country than stuck in a stinking, disease-ridden city. Think about it.'

Lox thought. She had a point. Cities needed services. Services needed fetching and carrying. Sure, most of the grid was supplied by solar, wind and tidal turbines up in Scotland – they'd had to make the change when the North Sea oil ran out to avoid being held to ransom by England. But whole of the United Kingdom still mainly used petrol engines, and the services that kept the cities sweet and supplied did too. That would stop. If Edinburgh's finest were already reduced to patrolling with bicycles and golf buggies this did not bode well for quelling the riots that were bound to begin as soon as people realised that the present hiccup in their busy, complicated lives was actually their future. 'Get out of town' sounded like a sensible proposal when you considered all the angles.

'He said the train would be in soon. They plan to send it out again at twelve twenty eight.'

'Let's go and negotiate our trusty steed into the baggage car.' McCall slapped the steering wheel lightly.

That nap had improved her temper no end – unless the crisis had unhinged her completely.

They proceeded serenely back up the platform.

10.7

Teddy was woken by someone shaking her. It was Gates. She smiled blearily.

'Are you mad? Anyone could have come in here and caught us.'

Sleepily, she caught his hand where it lay on her upper arm and murmured,

'You're better.'

He squatted down beside her and rocked back onto his heels.

'Apparently. You don't have much experience outside the law do you?'

She sat up.

'Actually, I do. I spent more than five years sleeping rough and avoiding the authorities. I have a reasonable sense of when it's safe. On a scale of one to ten, I'd say this was a eight for safety. Relax.'

He stood up and started to pace.

'I can't.' Having reached the bar he turned and started back towards her. 'Have we got anything to eat?'

'Yes – in that box. There's cheese, ham, some salad stuff, bread and …'

He was in the box already, rummaging. Moments later he was cramming his mouth. It didn't seem to matter what he was eating. Chocolate, bread, an apple and a big lump of cheese disappeared into him in short order.

'You've got them, then?'

He thought about this as he ripped a slice of ham into mouth-sized shreds.

'Looks like it, yes. It's … strange. I feel as though I'm on speed. I need …' He got up again and walked to the window, then back to her. '… to be doing something. I'll go and sort out a new buggy.'

He went. Patently she wasn't the only one who found that being nano-driven took some getting used to. It made her feel almost maternal to watch Gates go through it. And that was another first – she'd never felt maternal before in her life.

When Gates came back he was a bit less hyper. She was sorting out extra provisions for the rest of their journey. Food might be hard to come by later on. She doubted there'd be a restaurant car on the train, and shops would probably be closed. Already lack of deliveries was going to limit what was available, and that was only going to get worse the further north they went. She wondered how Ek and Rory were managing. They grew a lot of their own food, of course. The farm was going to be a real bonus – when they finally got there.

Gates still couldn't sit still. He sat: he stood. Then he settled for pacing up and down between the windows.

'How did you deal with the change?' he asked her, still on the move.

'I was locked up through most of it. I don't think it hit me so hard because I was so ill to start with.'

'Maybe. It's like … being reborn, isn't it? I had no idea.'

'That a good way to put it. Have you seen the colours outside?'

'Yes,' he said, surprise in his voice. 'I never understood beauty before. But now …'

Solemnly he came over to her and took her hand.

'Now I understand beauty very well,' and he bent and kissed her.

10.8

Sara was glad to get inside the front door when she reached Millerfield Place. She didn't like what Edinburgh had turned into since she had been incarcerated. There was a strange juxtaposition of carnival and neglect about the town. No shops were open, but some bars were. There was a great deal of noise coming from inside them. On the streets people moved around in groups for the most part. A lot of them had been drinking, many of them were carrying cans and bottles. The sound of smashing glass had been a regular accompaniment to her walk. She saw several broken shop windows. Rubbish festooned out of wheelies outside shops and private houses. Today should have been bin day, she reflected. They hadn't come. That was an omen. Litter skirled merrily in every street in the light, warm breeze. Soon there would be rats in the streets too.

A lot of people were obviously treating the emergency as an enforced holiday, but there was an edge to their revelry. Their lives had been turned upside down. When they stopped laughing and drinking they'd have to think about that. They'd want somebody to blame. Subconsciously they were working on that as they had this, possibly last, Good Time. When they'd drunk enough they'd take out their frustration on anyone and everything that came to hand.

Sara didn't want to wait around to find out what was going to happen next.

As she slid her ID card through the house-lock she looked back towards the hospital across The Meadows. It was going to be hard in there. Sure, the power would probably stay on, for a while anyway, but deliveries would soon be affected. Did they have stockpiles of clean bedding and fresh dressings, drugs and food? How long would they need to last?

People were going to die – and not just in the hospital – of infection, and maybe malnutrition too. It would be very easy to get sick here soon. She must get to somewhere clean; somewhere with fewer people, where it was less likely that mobs would form and diseases spread. She needed to get to a place where a community might pull together instead of tearing itself apart. Where should she go? Where *could* she go?

Inside the house was silent and gloomy. Sara thought about making a cup of tea, but remembered there was no milk. That was somehow the last straw, and she allowed herself a little cry as she plodded upstairs to her room.

She stuffed a few things into a small back-pack, trying to be survival-minded about it. Then she changed into denim jeans and walking socks and stuffed her feet into her hiking boots. She put on a vest and shirt, jamming a sweater into her bag. Even in June it could get cold in the evenings. Finally she emptied her handbag out on the bed and pocketed the essentials it contained. She wondered how long her debit cards would continue to work. But here was her compad. To be out of touch with everybody, everything, at this particular time had been misery. She didn't put it in the back-pack, but where she could see it as she finished packing.

It had been an automatic thing to come back here: an automatic thing to start packing. But her people were in England, and England seemed like a thousand miles away, another country. Very soon she suspected it really would be. She looked at her compad – she should call home. But what could she say? Nothing that would reassure them.

Teddy had gone north. There were trains running north.

She went down to the kitchen, taking her compad with her, and made a cup of very strong, instant black coffee to buck her up. While she waited for it to cool she composed a message for her mother. Conversation was impossible, but she could do this. It took a surprisingly long time to fashion something. When she'd finished she checked her in-box - there was a message from her parents. It said very much the same things as she had just put in hers: no need to worry about us, hope you're keeping safe, keep in touch, etc etc. They didn't know what to say either. She finished the disgusting coffee and pressed transmit. As her message winged its way to her family she heard the sound of glass smashing in the front room.

Time to go.

11

11.1

Scotland's Responsible Energy Policy meant that snail-mail had gone back onto rail in the mid Twenties. McCall cajoled and bullied the station staff into manhandling their golf cart into the mail van. To get the buggy in, the mail pods would have to come out. Although the contents of the pods were unlikely ever to be delivered to their final destinations, the railway people were understandably reluctant to do this. Lox left her to her negotiations and went in search of more food to take with them. When he returned, laden with fruit, water and sandwiches, the mail pods were stacked on the platform, the buggy was on the train and McCall was sitting in the buggy. The tableau was vaguely reminiscent of Boudicca triumphant. When he tried to get her to come up the train with him to try and find some seats she refused point blank. Their transportation was already attracting vituperative glances from travellers who wanted to use the space it was taking up. No way was she going to risk it being shoved back onto the platform. So Lox joined her in her chariot, got out his compad and tried to concentrate on some pithy conclusions for his story.

It was unlikely that they'd have found seats anyway. The platform was packed solid now. People were getting on and off the train, carrying strange baggage reminiscent of refugees – a bird in a cage, a cowed-looking dog on a lead, a cat in a basket, lumpy looking family treasures wrapped in blankets and coats. Suitcases were everywhere. Little family knots stood about looking miserable. The last train had run in England what – oh, nearly twenty years ago. Was he on the last train to run in Scotland? McCall interrupted his gloomy reverie.

'You stay here with the buggy,' she said. 'I'm going to check the train. They may have got on after all. It's chaos on the platform. Anybody could have walked in.'

'Please yourself, but I think we're ahead of them. And there's no way they could risk Waverley.'

'Don't be too certain. Hanford is clever, and dangerous. Stay alert.'

Lox briefly considered snapping a salute as she slid out of the buggy and tiptoed through the baggage and people filling the mail van.

Watching her, he realised this was going to be a seriously uncomfortable journey. With a sigh he went back to his story.

The train hadn't left at twelve twenty eight. It hadn't even appeared until nearly two o'clock. If the train was this late getting in Heaven alone knew how long it would take to get to Inverness. As Inverness was only the half of it, he was beginning to feel that they were altogether unprepared for this journey, despite the extra provisions he managed to acquire.

McCall was gone a long time and the train still didn't move. Lox went through his introduction and conclusion one last time. He had created eight hundred and fifty pithy words describing the end of the age of the car, with whys and wherefores. Gloomily he encrypted the whole story and sent it to Gardner.

Story completed he should, of course, be on his way back to Milton Keynes, where his hive apartment contained all the things that made life comfortable, where food was delivered to him piping hot and delicious, where the motor car was king – in a word he should be going *home.* Instead he was trying to go north to Inverness and other, even more uncivilised, places. What was wrong with this picture? Of course, all the things he liked about his home were currently unavailable. And he was at least going into the unknown with a most attractive, if spiky, female companion. Feeling distinctly confused, Lox wriggled around on the seat of the buggy until he had achieved a semblance of comfort, and finally allowed his eyes to close.

11.2

By the time Sara had walked to Waverley from Millerfield Place it was nearly half past two. She remembered police persons saying something about the last train north leaving at ten thirty so she was pleasantly surprised to find a train on the northbound platform. She had been hoping for information but here was something much better: transport.

There were hundreds of people milling about. A huge queue at the Information cubby was asking, variously and loudly, about trains to Glasgow, Stirling, the Kyle of Lockalsh, Dundee and Aberdeen. Harassed Scotrail-GNE employees were besieged. Sara looked at the monitor. It was blank. She walked up the train. A lot of people were coming and going along the platform – some running, some in tears. Encampments of large suitcases and strange shaped parcels impeded her progress. A couple of children holding hands looked tensely around for their parents. A dog tied to a bench barked hysterically. Sara threaded her way through the mess. At the first carriage with the doors still open she asked for confirmation from the people crammed in the vestibule. The train was supposed to be going at least as far as Inverness. Good. As she tried to decide what part of the train to try and squeeze into she noticed that at the rear of the train a knot of Scotrail-GNE uniforms were trying to make a ramp to get a golf buggy onto the train. It was just amazing what people felt to be important in times of crisis. You could see sense in taking the family silver and jewellery, but a golf buggy? Golf was going to be way down people's list of priorities for a long, long time.

Sara went on up the train. All the seats were already taken: people and baggage were wedged into every possible space. She went on to the front, hoping to find some niche. The front carriage was as bad as all the others, so she thought she might as well insinuate herself here as anywhere else. Nobody she asked had any idea what time the train would be leaving. It was likely to be a long journey. She found herself a tiny bit of carriage wall, took her pack off and slid down to the floor, drawing her knees up to her chest, trying not to get in anybody's way. Apprehension was palpable around her. What if the train wasn't leaving after all? What if they were all told to get off? What if they had to join another train? It would probably be full already, they wouldn't all get on. People looked around suspiciously, in case others were more comfortably placed or tampering with their luggage. Sara thought briefly about giving up the whole idea. Then she remembered the brick that had come through the window at Millerfield Place.

11.3

Gates and Teddy kissed until her lips began to tingle. She wanted so much to make love to him. The tiny engines inside them both stimulated desire – be it for food, beauty or each other. Passion would provide an outlet for the rush of energy which both of them were experiencing. But there was no bed here, only the rough, not very clean cord on the floor, and she felt that they deserved something better for their first time.

Their bodies demanded to be busy, however, so finally they pulled themselves apart and, by tacit agreement, piled their thievings onto the new cart and consulted the map.

'Back to the motorway, I think. The country roads are nothing like as direct. We want to get as close as we can, although I'm pretty sure we're going to have to do some walking.'

'What time is it?'

Gates got out his compad.

'Fourteen forty two precisely.'

'Afternoon tea in Perth?'

'Absolutely.'

They careered off down the path, Gates sawed crazily at the wheel, making the buggy bounce off the verges. The two of them shouted aloud just for the joy of it. So what if somebody heard them? They were invincible.

11.4

Lox was woken by the jerk of the train pulling out. Looking blearily at his watch he saw that it was half past three. Two minutes later he was asleep again. Seemingly mere seconds later he was shaken roughly awake.

In response to his query McCall told him that the train was making a scheduled stop at Haymarket and hadn't even got out of Edinburgh yet. She told him to keep an eye out of the far side of the train while she checked the platform side. No sooner had he returned to the buggy and slumber once more when she rousted him out again because of an unscheduled stop. They proceeded in this fashion, stop and go, until they finally crossed the Forth and stopped at Inverkeithing. He presumed this latest stop was a problem was points or signals or both. After the many, highly-publicised train crashes and derailments in the early part of the century, fail-safes were legion. The system had only to pose the suspicion of a glitch for the computers to bring everything to a halt. The reason the fail-safes were cutting in so often, and stopping the train, was probably because there was no human available to decide which over-rides were necessary and which should be ignored. In his McCall-induced vigils out of the mail van window he had seen a man clambering down from the train's cab and plodding up the line to a signal box and then again, later, to tinker with points. They must be switching manually. The driver was heroic. He was surprised that the man even had the wherewithal to do this sort of thing himself. If it had been Lox in the driver's seat, he would have thrown in the towel before they'd got this far. He looked at his watch. They had been on the move, loosely speaking, for a little over two hours. He squirmed around on the seat of the buggy once again and tried to relax. The almost-hopeful shuddering of the train ceased and quiet descended. Lox thought, as he drifted back into his much-interrupted nap, that the driver had probably had enough and, having got the train into a station, had abandoned it. Who could blame him?

The train was creeping north so slowly that it was still possible to walk back to Edinburgh. Lox was seriously tempted to do so. At this point he put his foot down and followed this decisive step by getting his head down. He preferred sleep to being awake. Awake he felt depressed. Lox had been an urban creature all his life. Now the world had turned. Not only was he was out of his own place, he would shortly be out of time with the rural world he suspected was soon going to surround him. He had no idea how to forage for food, light a fire, camp out of doors. He had a nasty feeling that all these things were going to be necessary evils where they were going. Wherever that turned out to be.

But McCall still wouldn't let him sleep. Once more she blundered back into their little sanctum, talking at him even before she came in sight of him.

'Not now,' Lox moaned.

'Yes, now,' McCall insisted.

Lox sat up yet again, really cross now.

'Look,' he said, 'I know this train doesn't seem to be going faster than walking pace, but it is. Our fugitives are either on foot, or are constantly having to detour to pick up new buggies. Each buggy has a range of – what did we mark on the map? Fifteen kilometres? There is no way that they can have got this far. We're ahead of them. Relax.'

'I can't.'

'No, not can't. Won't. You think if you switch off for a moment you'll miss something. Well, frankly, what will it matter if you do? We're all going to Dunster – you and I slightly faster than Hanford and Goldstein. At some point, possibly years from now, we may all arrive. Anything may happen to this train – they're obviously missing a lot of support staff. If I was the train driver I would have decamped long ago. I don't suppose you've noticed, peering at the platform with your tunnel vision, but the poor bastard has had to get out and fix every cut-out we've encountered. I don't expect you've been counting, but there have been more than ten. I know because you've woken me up each time we've stopped. I am seriously contemplating walking back to Edinburgh while I still can. If you like I'll move over and you can get your head down. But if you can't be quiet, go away.'

He made room in the buggy, then turned away from her and lay down once more. Still she couldn't rest.

'I'm going to check the train again,' she said, 'in case I missed them.'

Lox's only reply was a grunt.

11.5

Gates and Teddy arrived at Kinross very hungry. They plundered the kitchen of the golf club, stole themselves a fresh buggy and got back on the M90. The new buggy failed about five kloms short of Perth, as Gates had predicted. This was no problem to two of the fittest people in the world. Gates now had the ravenous appetite that Teddy had been contending with, so they had another lunch. After they'd eaten they packed up some bottles of water and fruit in a carrier bag for a between lunches snack. Then they strolled briskly hand in hand along the centre lane of the motorway taunting each other with marvellous menus. Life was good. About an hour and a half later they saw a sign for Murrayshall Golf Club. Ravenously hungry once more they decided on another pit-stop.

'Let's have another lunch, lift one last cart and see if they've got a modern map. It should show where the station is.'

'Do you think they've got salmon?'

'Almost certainly.'

'And sticky toffee pudding.'

'Or Pavlova.'

'Steak and kidney pudding, with sprouts.'

'Just the steak, rare as rare, with onions and mushrooms.'

'And chips.'

'What do you usually eat?'

'TV dinners mostly, when I remember. Food is fuel, or it was. I wonder if this need to gratify my senses is a by-product of the treatment?'

'As opposed to what?'

He blushed. She noticed, laughed gaily and gave his hand a squeeze.

'Love is a large tub of Haagen Daz between two and no spoon?'

'Looks that way.'

They made their way to the kitchen.

11.6

The train was still stuck at Inverkeithy, and Sara was beginning seriously to wonder about getting out and trying to make her own way to Dunster. The only thing that kept her squatting among the crush of people on the train was that she hadn't managed to work out what her own way might be. She could try and get hold of a bicycle and struggle north on that, but the Highlands were ahead and she seriously doubted her ability to pedal very far or fast through that sort of country. The train was now a sweat box, but at least it wasn't hard work. Yet. The atmosphere on board had improved markedly when the train left Waverley. But with every stop it had deteriorated again. Now the passengers were sullen. A young baby was wailing persistently somewhere in the carriage. Sara resisted the temptation to stand up and see if she could do anything to help. She doubted whether she could defend her little niche if she did – or that her interest would be welcome. Even with all the windows open there wasn't a breath of air moving when they were stopped. Sweat slimed the backs of her bent-up knees and trickled down her upper body to soak the waistband of her jeans: her back was glued to the carriage wall with it. Somebody's foot kept kicking her right leg and somebody else's sweat had soaked the shoulder of her shirt where they were pressed together. There was an odour. It was only going to get worse. She was beginning to need to pee. Now that should be an adventure.

At the far end of the carriage there was a commotion: the door into the next carriage had been opened. Someone was calling out 'coming through, coming through'. Willing for something, anything, to break the monotony and discomfort she craned her neck to see what was going on and was surprised to see DS McCall picking her way through the sprawled bodies.

'Ah,' said McCall as she finally found space for her feet near enough to Sara's position not to have to shout, 'Dr Prosser, I presume. How the hell did you get on this train? I left strict instructions that you weren't to be released until it had gone.'

'It was late.'

'Yes, so it was. Damn. I didn't allow for that.'

'Why was it important to you that I didn't catch this train?'

'Why do you think it was important?'

'I've no idea. I only tried the Station on a whim. I didn't know what else to do. Someone chucked a brick through the living room window at Millerfield Place.'

'So …?'

'So I reckoned it was time to get out of Dodge.'

McCall snorted. It coincided with the train giving a jolt as it started to move again.

'Are you seriously expecting me to believe that you haven't arranged to meet Goldstein and Hanford on this train?'

'Well yes, since I had no idea they were on it. Where are they?'

Sara started to get up. As her vague plan had been to go north and find Teddy and Hanford at Dunster she was pleased to think that she had found them earlier than expected. It would certainly be an improvement on spending time with the acidic McCall. The woman's temper seemed to go from frayed to worse. Didn't the cow ever smile?

'I've no idea. I've searched the train from end to end. If they're here I don't know how they're avoiding me.'

Sara muttered, 'something devoutly to be wished', which was covered, fortunately, by the train limping over a set of points. She tried a straightforward request for information, hoping that she might get at least a half-way civil response for once.

'Do you know why the train is going so slowly?'

'Lox says its because the driver has to get out to change signals and points manually.'

'Tuthill is here?' Sara was surprised. She saw an opportunity to wound and took it. 'Don't you go anywhere without that stupid journalist?'

'You'd better come with me,' said McCall grimly, ignoring the barb. Sara wondered momentarily whether the woman had actually brought some thumb screws with her. The invitation was not an attractive one.

'I'm fine where I am, thanks.'

'It wasn't a suggestion.'

Sara had no intention of getting to her feet and going somewhere, anywhere with McCall. Instead she wedged herself slightly further into the press of bodies around her. The man next to her muttered that it might be better for all concerned if she could make up her bloody mind if she was coming or going, Sara ignored him.

'It wasn't a suggestion I was going to take you up on.'

Sara eyed McCall defiantly. McCall glared back.

'I could arrest you again, you know.'

'Could you?' Their conversation was causing some interest among the other passengers. Sara didn't want the people whose body odour she was sharing to believe she was some kind of felon. She pitched her next remark somewhat louder: 'I haven't done anything which would give you grounds for that, and I can think of nobody whose company I would rather be without, in the circumstances.'

That should be clear enough, even for McCall. Interest in their exchanges was now universal within earshot. McCall noticed. She began to twist around in the press of bodies, obviously preparing to depart. The train jolted again and she was thrown against some of the other passengers. Somebody swore, McCall scowled at the owner of the hand she had trodden on and flashed her badge at him. Several people made it plain that it didn't matter who she was, there wasn't room for her here. Sara smiled beatifically at her.

Bested by weight of public opinion McCall retreated back down the carriage. Sara stayed put and pretended interest in her finger nails. Nobody asked her to explain her recent dialogue. She was grateful for that. Nobody would believe any explanation she could provide and, if they did, she would probably be lynched. To think that Hanford had started all this. To think that Teddy was a willing party to it. The world had come to an astonishing pass – and for one, incredible, reason: one woman's desire not to die. There would be deaths because of Teddy's desire – some of the people on this train probably wouldn't make it through the transition. But Teddy wouldn't die. Teddy, she suspected, was now immortal. That was a sobering thought. Somebody – no, not somebody: Gates Bloody Hanford – had made it possible to live forever. That would change everything. It was far more important than Gates's stupid idea of poisoning petrol. She wondered if Teddy realised what she'd started. And whether she understood that people were going to die because of it. She was pretty sure Hanford did.

11.7

Teddy and Gates had decided not to take a final buggy into the town. The silly little conveyance would make them memorable and they wanted to blend in. So they walked.

Teddy was having a wonderful time. It was, probably, the best time she had ever had in her life. Which, she realised, wasn't saying a lot. Of course, there was her new super-humanity to add to the mix: that had certainly added spice to the adventure. And now her lover – soon to be lover, anyway – was as super as she was. Everything was … super as they walked through the outskirts of Perth.

Perth was eerie. The streets were empty. They saw damage to a few shops on their way to the station, but no people. Not so much as a bicycle moved. So much for blending in. If anyone had been detailed to look out for them – well, here they were.

They kept to the pavements, needlessly, as they followed the road signs to the station. They kept in the shadow of buildings as much as possible, despite the lovely sunshine, except where looting damage forced them to step into the road. The silence and emptiness frightened Teddy. It was as though the whole world had stopped, which of course it had. Teddy found, suddenly, that she'd had enough excitement for the time being. She wanted to be somewhere where she could think through all the things that had happened to her and try and make some sense of everything. She suddenly realised that she'd been reborn into a new world and began to wonder what sort of a world it was going to be - and how much of the change was her fault. She wanted to ask Gates if he was certain that his nanites only attacked the specific carbon molecules in petrol. She'd read enough science fiction to know that humans were carbon-based life-forms. Had his nanite swarms gone rogue after all? Was everybody dead? She couldn't frame the question. There were so many answers he could give that would make her fears worse. What if he wouldn't answer her at all? The gloss went off her day.

As soon as they got to the station she stopped worrying. There was life here –too much of it, actually. The ticket office was besieged and it took a long time before they could get to the front. Was there a train going north? Teddy clenched her fists on the counter until the nails dug into her palms painfully. Yes, there was. It was late. How late? The harassed woman didn't know, but several hours certainly. Things were slow. Did they want tickets or not? She had been instructed to inform passengers that the railway could not guarantee a return trip. Gates and Teddy exchanged a glance and a grin. Their luck was holding. Gates bought two singles to Dunster with cash and they shouldered their way back out of the crowd. Looking back at the booth it looked to Teddy as if a riot was not far away. People were frightened. The town was empty, everybody seemed to be here. Where did they all intend to go? Did they think that things were better further north? Further south? Or perhaps it was just the primeval urge to run that impelled them.

'We didn't ask which platform,' Teddy shouted through the din.

'I don't expect there'll be so many trains coming in that picking the right platform is going to be a problem.'

'But they're sure to have trains going south as well. At least one. We don't want to go back where we've just come from, by mistake.'

'Oh I don't know. That might be rather fun. They wouldn't be expecting that, would they?'

Sudden panic gripped her.

'I don't want to go back. I want to go home.' She found she was screaming it at him. Infuriatingly he was grinning at her.

'Sorry. Joke. Bad joke obviously. Not used to them. Must try harder.'

'OK. Platform? Does it say on the tickets?'

'No. Check a monitor.'

Of course. The edgy crowd was affecting her, that was all. Of course you checked a monitor. That's what you always did. She'd caught the crowd's hysteria for a moment, that was all. But they were not a part of the crowd, not really.

She checked the little wounds her nails had made in her palms at the ticket booth. They were gone. Super-human. She grinned to herself. If she was to grab a total stranger and kiss him nobody would think it particularly odd today. But she would be infecting him with something fantastic, that he would pass on to his loved ones, his children – and they to their children. Just like that she could start a super-race. She was a god! She found herself looking about for a suitable candidate as she felt Gates catch hold of her hand.

'Careful,' he said in her ear. 'We don't want to get separated in this crowd.'

They found a monitor which did, indeed, tell them which platform they wanted – although it didn't give a time for the train's arrival, nor its departure. When they reached the platform they could see from the ramp that it was a solid sea of people.

'How the hell are we all going to get on?' she wondered aloud. Gates just gave her hand a squeeze. It wasn't the sort of thing which concerned him. He just dealt with it. She tried to do the same.

Now they were down on the platform. Skilfully Gates eased them between families, round luggage and push-chairs. All at once she understood. He had moved through the world undetected for so long, this was a doddle. She held onto his hand and let him lead her into anonymity.

11.8

Lox was certain that the press in the mail van was less now. People were beginning to get out when they stopped at stations. Very few were getting on. Apparently the urge had been simply to get out of the city.

McCall returned from her search of the train. She was in an even filthier mood than she had been when she set out. Triumphantly she told him that Prosser was on the train – the search had been fruitful after all. Then, to Lox's relief, she finally let the search thing drop and got into the caddy car. Lox made room for her, and showed her the best way to wedge herself in comfortably. Thankfully the woman then stopped talking and shortly dropped off to sleep. She was now snoring softly. Lox was pleased for her – she'd looked out on her feet when she got back.

He had an idea that inside McCall's crusty exterior there was a soft centre. He'd been trying to find it for days now, so it obviously wasn't allowed to show on a regular basis. He was hoping get a glimpse of it when she woke up. In fact he was counting on it. The prospect of being marooned in some hamlet in the north of Scotland with a termagant was not pleasant. The sound of her snoring reminded him of the nap she had taken with her head on his shoulder at Waverley station. Yes, there was a soft spot in there somewhere all right.

While McCall dozed he sat and watched her and thought the sort of thoughts a man thinks when his life is in tatters round his ankles. He noticed that the people in the mail van weren't looking scared to death any more. He realised he wasn't feeling scared either, and wondered why. Something about being on the move, he decided. The old, old urge to flee was being gratified: as long as he was fleeing his nervous system was fine. He wondered how he would feel when they got off the train. Then he stopped wondering because a little tickle of panic promptly returned. The theory was sound. Best not to test it.

It was difficult to tell when the train was pulling into a station. The bloody thing was going so slowly all the time that the change in speed was minimal. So far he had usually found out when people woke him up by shifting around, getting in, getting out, hefting baggage which, a couple of times, had struck him painful blows. But this was surely a station.

There was an echo. He could hear a buzzing, as of bees, which he recognised as the tannoy. And there was activity outside on the platform. This was a proper, main station. It must be Perth. The mail van door opened.

Suddenly he was aware of a solid wall of air coming towards him. It made his ears pop. Looking out at the platform he could see why. Behind the air, pushing it towards him, was a very large, anxious-looking crowd. Very few people were trying to get out. Very, very many were trying to get in. They were shoving each other, ramming each other with luggage, trying to hang on to each other. The murmur of the crowd became angry and frightened shouts. Magnified by the canopy over the station they turned into the roar of a great beast.

This was bad, and at least part of it was coming his way. People were pouring into the mail van. He was just about to wake McCall when she came to all in a moment. Not a good way to wake up. She hung onto him while she oriented herself, and he hung on to her for balance, as the caddy car began to rock in the press of people. When she'd worked out what was going on she braced herself against the dashboard of the caddy car with her feet. He quickly rearranged himself and did the same.

Her first words were predictable

'Are they here? Did you see them?'

He tried to gesture the impossibility of seeing anyone in this crush and almost fell out of the cart. He shouted into her ear,

'No chance. It's a mob out there. We'll be lucky to keep the buggy.'

Luck, actually, had little to do with it. McCall did her Boudicca act again, brandishing her police ID and daring them to go through her. Nobody laid a hand on her, but it was close.

It took an age before everybody had been sardined on board. Finally the train chugged out of the station. McCall and Lox got back in the buggy.

Surrounded by frightened, sweaty people was … interesting. Lox spent the next half hour people watching – circumspectly: tempers in the mail van appeared to be fairly short. He was congratulating himself on his *sang froid* when he remembered he'd passed the point where it was possible to walk back to Edinburgh. It looked as though he really was in this for the long haul.

11.9

On the way to Inverness matters both improved and worsened. The toilet facilities had, of course, backed up before they'd even got as far as Perth. Hardly anybody had thought to bring food or, more importantly, water. The mail van, even with the windows open, was stifling. Every time the train stopped there was a rush for the doors, to get a breath of clean air that twenty people had not already breathed. People started to faint. Children wanted drinks which didn't exist, then whined, then wailed.

One good thing was that the train was not stopping nearly so often any more. Some sort of system must have been put in place to deal with the recalcitrant signals and points. The stops seemed mainly to be scheduled ones now and, although they were long, and the train was still moving cautiously, at least it kept going between stations.

A second good thing was that people were starting to get off at stations again, rather than on. There was still no bare floor to be seen, but the crush wasn't quite as suffocating. And the new passengers were calming down. Those that had water and food shared it around. Children and older folk got the lion's share. A camaraderie began to grow: people started to sing songs. After they pulled out of Blair Atholl, Lox finally got up the nerve to ask if anyone had a pack of cards. Someone had, of course, and Lox was able to idle through a couple of hours dusting off his poker skills. Being, before this, a solitary sort he hadn't had much practice against people, only his compad – against whom he had regularly come out ahead, even with the setting on Max Diff. He found human players, oddly, much easier to read. Sadly none of the players had any cash, nor, indeed, that other time-honoured stake, matches. So they used letters out of the mail bags. After Lox had acquired enough post to start a small sorting office the game lapsed. He started to take notice of his surroundings again. They were just pulling into Dalwhinnie. He consulted the card school: Perth to Dalwhinnie should have taken 69 minutes. It had taken almost four hours. At this rate they wouldn't be in Inverness until midnight.

11.10

In the middle of the train Gates and Teddy were in trouble. They were finding out, the hard way, that their nanites really did need large and regular amounts of fuel, in the form of food. If they didn't get it they got … cranky. Both were suffering badly by the time the train reached Aviemore. Gates kept asking Teddy 'how much longer'. Her increasingly tetchy replies irked him. They were close to their first row.

At Aviemore several people had the idea of getting something to eat and drink from the station buffet. Aviemore had better facilities than most of the little branch stations they had passed. Unfortunately, it being a major winter sports centre, late June was not its busy time. Or the staff hadn't been able to get through. Whatever – the buffet was shut.

Gates got out with the others. He was more than hungry – he was desperate for at least a chocolate bar. The closed buffet enraged him. Teddy watched him shove his way through to the front of the little crowd from the train staring at things they couldn't have. When he reached the front he calmly smashed his fist through the glass. A noisy pandemonium ensued. People were shouting – both encouragement and disapproval – as he continued to smash glass out of the window, blood running down his arm. In his case the injury was temporary; he didn't need to pay it any attention, and he didn't. Soon there was a big enough hole in the window for people to clamber through. Teddy wondered, as she watched the crowd pushing in, what kind of injuries they were sustaining. They were probably trying to emulate him They didn't know that he would heal in minutes. She hoped no-one had sliced through an artery on the way in through the window.

As the train blew its whistle a human chain was passing boxes of stuff out of the Buffet and into the train. Four men burst out through the door carrying a full water cooler, which dribbled and bubbled absurdly as they manhandled it onto the train. They had brought the plastic cups stuffed into their pockets.

Gates was last out. The train was already moving as he jogged towards it. Teddy pounded on the door mechanism until, reluctantly, the door sighed open. He was grinning as she hauled him on board, his face smeared with chocolate. He had a box full of bars under his arm. He ripped it open gave her half a dozen, pocketed a handful himself and passed the rest around. The chocolate melted as they unwrapped it. They ate it quickly and licked their sticky hands. A bottle of water made its way down the carriage and they both took a drink before passing it on. Gates grinned at her. She leaned over and licked some of the chocolate gently from around his mouth. This led to a lingering kiss, which caused a roar of 'way-hey!' to erupt around them and put a stop to any more lovey-dovey nonsense for the time being.

After a while Gates got out his compad and earpiece. After he'd checked the newscasts, smiling and nodding to himself, he said,

'Should we call anybody?'

She thought about it. Poor Sara was still in jail, unless George Barrie had been able to work a miracle. Their compads had been confiscated when they'd been arrested. They might get a message to her via George – but if George knew what they were doing she suspected he would feel duty bound to tell the police.

'You could call Ek. Tell him we're coming home.'

'OK. What's his number?'

'Shit. I've no idea!'

'Oh, come on – he's your son. Surely you can remember …?'

'No. He's on speed dial, I just click and …'

'No prob. I'll access your compad.'

'You can't. The Police have it.'

'That's all right. Just give me a second here and … There we are. Now I'll just copy …'

A moment later he held up the pad triumphantly.

Thoughtfully she took it from him. She ran a sticky forefinger over the number shown there, wondering what to say. There was so much to tell him, it would take the rest of this endless trip and then some. And what if the Police were there already? Unlikely, under the circumstances, but not impossible. She ached to talk to him. It would be wonderful to hear his voice. But it was too much. She couldn't speak to him now. Matters were so complicated all of a sudden.

Instead she pulled the stylus out of its holder and slowly began to press the tiny keys with it:

Dearest Ek,

Coming home. Bringing a very dear friend.

Teddy

xxx

She handed the compad and stylus back to Gates. Gates went on fiddling with it. Teddy stared at the back of somebody's knees and tried to work out what she was going say to Ek when they got home.

11.11

At the front of the train Sara was hot, uncomfortable and bored. She could see just the tops of the mountains out of the window and one mountain – lovely as it may be – looks very much like another from that perspective. She couldn't see where they were when the train stopped. She could, indeed, only tell if it was a station they were stopping at when the doors opened. A station was welcome, as the air in her carriage got renewed. The door didn't open if the train just stopped in the middle of nowhere. They hadn't stopped anywhere official for a long time – too long. She felt nauseous, her head was swimming. Something to do, that was the thing. Something to take her mind off it. She got out her compad, balanced it on top of her steepled knees and put in her earpiece.

There were quite a lot of messages, she was glad to see. This was the distraction she needed. She opened them in order, even the junk mail.

Ek had mailed her:

Sara,

I can't get hold of my mother. Is she worse? Should I come?

That made her smile. How had he thought he was going to get to Edinburgh? News of the petrol virus must have reached Dunster days ago – indeed, the virus itself must have reached them by now. But she was sure that he would try. Where his mother was concerned Ek was unstoppable. She hoped he hadn't set out. If Teddy made it north she would be gutted to find he had gone south. She mailed him:

Ek,

Your mother is <u>well</u>. Stay put.

There was a message from Teddy's solicitor:

Dr Sara Prosser

Congratulations on your release from the Leith Police. Call me as soon as you can.

Geo Barrie

She chuckled over the tongue-twister, but rather thought the urgency had gone off that one and deleted it without reply. The less Geo Barrie knew about developments since last night the better. Sara had left the real world when Teddy swallowed Gates's silver granules (was it really only thirty six hours ago?). It was reassuring to know that the real world was still there. Or it had been when the messages were sent.

As she variously read, replied to and deleted messages the pad beeped to say that she had a call. It was nice to think that somebody cared. Finally.

She brought up vision. The face on the screen didn't surprise her unduly. But she felt it was a sign of things to come that were not necessarily good. It was Gates: he didn't bother with any preamble.

'I'm sorry I couldn't get you out too. I just didn't have the time to get two swarms stable.' There was a pause. 'It wasn't personal, truly.'

'Not a problem. A night in the cells was a … salutary experience. It taught me something. I'm not sure quite what yet.'

'I knew they'd have to let you go sooner or later.'

'Gates, did you intend for all this to happen?'

'Absolutely. I've done what you hired me to do *and* what I came up to Edinburgh to do – two for two. Except for leaving you in jail, bit of a black mark there.'

'Have you still got the formulae?'

'Yes, of course. I downloaded everything onto a Pod. Had to leave my system behind. I'll show you how it's done, if we can find a machine to run it on.'

'I shall hold you to that,' said Sara a tad grimly.

'So where are you, anyway?'

'On the train to Inverness. Where are you?'

'Ditto. Teddy's here.'

'How did you know they'd have to let me go?'

'All their evidence was circumstantial. No DNA traces, no witness to any collusion – nothing.' For a moment he looked almost concerned for her. 'I wouldn't stitch you up like that, Sara.'

'McCall's on the train, by the way. She's been making herself very unpopular shlepping up and down the train looking for you. That Tuthill's here with her.'

'Interesting. Saved from the long arm of the law by the press of humanity. We never even saw her. Well, we'll all go together when we go, eh?'

She quirked an eyebrow at him. He was quiet for a moment, then:

'I s'pose I'm fired?'

'Yes of course.' She grinned. 'Do you care?'

'No.' He grinned back. 'Just making conversation. Which carriage are you in?'

'Right up at the front. McCall was on the move when I saw her. I haven't seen Tuthill. You?'

'Middle. I guess when we get to Dunster we'll find out where we stand.'

'I Guess so. Is there any point in us trying to get together? It's packed here.'

'Same here. Stay put. We'll get together when we finally get off this sweat box. Take care of yourself, OK?'

The little screen blanked.

11.12

Gates was agitated. After fidgeting for some time he said,

'I don't suppose you've got McCall's e-address?'

'Of course not.'

He went quiet again, but continued to wriggle. It was becoming irritating. Finally he said,

'I'm usually the world's best at waiting. But I really need to make something happen. It must be the nanites.'

Teddy was used to him being in control of every situation. For him to confess that he wasn't bothered her a good deal. She was now becoming as agitated as he was. She wondered how much their unease owed to their respective nanite populations making themselves at home.

He was still silent. She presumed that meant he was thinking. At last.

'We can't out run her. I think … I think we should tell her we're here.' This last came out in a rush. He turned to her, excited. 'Yes. We should tell her we're here. There's nothing she can do. She's not armed. How is she going to make any sort of arrest that's going to stick?'

'What the hell are you talking about?'

'Ah, forgot to tell you. McCall's on the train.'

Teddy was horrified.

'If she alerts the police at Inverness they'll arrest us as soon as we get off the train. I suppose you haven't got any more wall-eaters about your person?'

He shook his head.

'We could be there for months – years! Who knows what'll happen to Habeas Corpus, under the circumstances.'

Gates looked deflated.

'I just think we've got to get her on our side, that's all. Change her attitude, get her to want to stay with us. I want to talk to her.'

'Later, perhaps. Not now. Not before Inverness. Please.' She put her hand on his arm. 'Promise me you won't do anything until we're out in the wilds where there isn't a police station.'

12

12.1

They got into Inverness at about eleven. It was still light, which made it feel earlier. But everyone was edgy and tired out from doing nothing, and fretting and sweating on the train for so long.

There was a tannoy announcement and everybody hushed each other while they strained to pick up what it said. For minutes afterwards people tried to confirm what they thought they'd heard: that the train wouldn't be going on tonight. Bolder souls went and enquired of the weary station staff and brought back definite information: the driver was way over his hours as it was. No replacement was available. Further information would be given in the morning. That's all they knew. They were sorry, but there it was.

People began to leave the train. Everyone was tired. Most people had no idea where they were going to spend the night. Gates and Teddy waited as patiently as sheep and stepped meekly out onto the platform when it was their turn. The platform was solid with people. Teddy took hold of Gates's hand. She didn't want to get separated from him in the crush. It would be hard to find one person among so many.

A man pushing a wheelchair was trying to make his way towards the exit. In normal times people would have stood aside for him. But today wasn't normal. He tried shouting, he tried pleading, but he was making no progress. In the wheelchair was a young girl, presumably his daughter, her body twisted with cerebral palsy. She looked exhausted, so pale she was almost grey. Teddy could see fear and tears in her eyes.

Suddenly Gates let go Teddy's hand and wriggled through the crowd the couple of paces necessary to stand in front of the wheelchair. Alarmed, Teddy followed. Gates knelt down in front of the girl. Took her face in his hands, tilted it slight towards him and kissed her full on the mouth.

'What do you think you're doing?' her father shouted. Gates got back to his feet and gave father and daughter a broad grin.

'You'll thank me for that in the morning,' he said. Then he turned to find Teddy. Having caught up her hand again he said, 'now can I go looking for McCall? Please?

'Sure, if you can think where she might be.'

'I'd guess she's blowing her stack at the ticket office about now, waving her badge around in futile fury. Come on.'

The man and his daughter were quickly left behind in the crowd. In moments the people they were passing knew nothing of the incident. Teddy began to wonder if she had hallucinated it.

*****

Gates soon found a woman staring around her in a slightly wild fashion in the queue at the ticket office, put two and two together and walked over to her.

'Are you looking for me? I'm Gates Hanford.'

12.2

McCall's anger, carefully nursed throughout the journey from Edinburgh, was searing hot - so hot that she found it impossible, for a moment, to say anything. Nothing she said could be enough. But something must be said. She spluttered. This angered her further. Finally she managed;

'Gates Hanford, I'm arresting you for …'

'Yes. I thought you'd probably want to do that. If you can just hang on a minute I'll be right with you.' He grinned at her.

'Terrorist!' She bellowed it at him. That was absolutely the word for what he was, what he'd done. She'd hated this man as an abstract for many hours now. Having finally met him she immediately hated his grin and his nonchalance. However, a professional Detective Sergeant did not scream anything as inflammatory as 'terrorist' at a suspect in a crowded railway station. She was trembling with the effort of suppressing her hatred enough to get him into custody.

'You must be McCall. I've heard a lot about you.' His grin got broader. 'None of it good. Have you got handcuffs?' He held out his wrists jauntily.

McCall opened her shoulder bag to get out some wrist restraints, then felt herself blush. That part of her Detective Sergeant's kit appeared to be missing. She must have forgotten to check her bag out before haring off to catch the train. She shook her head. Her hand in her bag was wrapped around her tazer – she just needed an excuse to use it. She wished she knew why this man made her so mad.

Now, what was she to do with him while she found Goldstein? She looked around for a uniform, but the railway police had disappeared. It had been a long, hard day for them; knocking off time had come and gone hours since. They were concentrating on getting this crowd of frustrated and frightened travellers out of the station so that they could close it. The announcement had been quite clear. And although she had felt it was her duty to try and get some sort of priority booking sorted out for the morning she really only wanted a bath and a bed. She felt her anger begin to sag as she thought herself inside their heads. They were tired: so was she. Things were difficult – the unknown was always difficult – and matters were going to get much worse before they got better.

Suddenly the adrenalin that had been her good friend all those long hours on the train deserted her, and all that remained was a jagged headache. She massaged her temples absently while she kept one eye on Hanford and looked around for …

Ah: Tuthill. He'd have to do. She seized Hanford by the elbow and began to work her way through the crowd of unhappy, sometime passengers to where Tuthill was leaning against a pillar looking bedraggled. McCall realised she must look the same way. Glancing at Hanford she noticed that he didn't. The whole thing seemed to be the most amusing joke to him. Bastard.

When she reached Tuthill she said;

'I've got him. You'll have to hang on to him while I find Goldstein.'

'How am I supposed to do that? Have you got any handcuffs? Leg irons?'

'I asked her that,' Hanford chirped. 'Only I didn't think of leg irons. I'm Gates Hanford. Sometime terrorist.' He stuck out his hand in Tuthill's direction.

Feeling as though events had overtaken him some time ago, Tuthill shook the proffered hand and said,

'Lox Tuthill.' He thought for a moment and then said, 'Sometime journalist.' The two men shook. To McCall's relief, Lox then turned his attention back to her, and seemed to be concentrating again. She was anxious to be off after her other fugitive. She didn't want Tuthill to buckle completely until she had both Hanford and Goldstein in custody.

'We could take his belt, pull his trousers round his ankles. That should slow him down,' Tuthill suggested. His eyes were watering and there was the faintest edge of hysteria to his voice that told her he was no more reliable than Hanford.

'I don't wear a belt. They're only held up with faith as it is. Work of a moment, mate. Feel free.'

This last was addressed to McCall. And to her dismay the two men began to giggle weakly.

Trying to whip up something more than exhaustion McCall set off down the platform alongside the silent train, hoping that Goldstein would be as easy to catch as Hanford had finally proved to be.

What she was going to do with them now she had them was, of course, another matter. She needed a secure environment for them. They'd have to be searched to make sure they didn't have any more wall-eating nano-things on them. There'd have to be …

Exhaustion made McCall stumble. There was so much still to do. She felt tears start, so hot and hard that her throat closed over and her eyes were blinded. Why did she have to do all this by herself? Where was the back-up? And anyway, what could she possibly do, now, to bring these people to any kind of justice? The world that she had known was gone. Tomorrow it would be harder just staying alive than today had been. And the day after that it would be harder still, and it would go on getting harder for a while. She couldn't even go home, have a hot shower and flop in front of the Thin-V. All that was gone. The only thing she'd had to hold on to was her pursuit of these two fugitives. Now that she'd caught them her brain refused to look any further ahead. What she was going to do with them after that she had no idea.

Still walking blindly up the platform, she felt somebody take her arm.

12.3

'Are you all right?' It was Sara Prosser. And with her was the Goldstein woman. McCall wiped briskly at her eyes with the backs of her hands.

'Yes. Of course.'

'You look done in. Where are the others?'

This from Goldstein. Why should Goldstein express any concern for her?

'Sara told us you were on the train. Gates wanted to come and find you. I didn't want him to until after Inverness, but I guess he couldn't wait any longer.'

McCall glared at the two of them bleakly. How had control moved so swiftly from herself to the terrorists? But she was so tired.

'What you need is something to eat and drink. Trust me – I'm a doctor!'

Prosser again, absurdly light-hearted. Both Prosser and Goldstein were smiling. Neither of them was taking her seriously. Nothing like this had ever happened to her before but, in front of them, in front of a whole station-full of people, McCall began to weep. Great racking sobs of frustration came and wouldn't stop. How bloody embarrassing.

She was led back towards the exit by Prosser and Goldstein, each with one of her arms tucked through one of theirs. McCall was just glad that nobody she knew – well, nobody whose opinion she cared about anyway – was watching. As they approached Lox and Hanford, still waiting by their pillar, Goldstein proffered a crumpled paper napkin. Mopping herself up as well as she could McCall saw the two men wave. The two women waved back with their free arms. Christ, it was getting like some kind of bloody reunion here. This wasn't what was supposed to happen. Oh, to hell with it - somebody else would have to sort it out.

12.4

Teddy and Sara pressed McCall to eat a semi-melted chocolate bar from Gates's stash while Lox and Gates got the golf buggy out of the mail van. The carriage was several centimetres higher than the platform, and several more centimetres distant from it. They couldn't find anything to bridge the gap, so in the end Gates just drove the buggy out. There was a terrible grating noise as it nose-dived towards the platform, but it seemed to run well enough as he drove it back to the women.

'Three in the cab, two in the dickey,' Tuthill announced cheerily. 'I'll drive. McCall – you're with me. Prosser, you too. You two super-beings can hang on the back.'

'Super-beings?' While she'd been blubbing Tuthill and Hanford had obviously been exchanging news. McCall hoped he was joking, but a sinking feeling told her he wasn't. She'd put her hand on Hanford's arm, she remembered, when she arrested him. Was it catching? She felt her flesh creep and couldn't prevent herself taking the tiniest step back from them.

'It's a long story,' said Hanford. 'It'll make a fine statement. Although what you're going to do with a statement I have no idea.'

'We may yet be glad of a night in the cells,' said Tuthill. 'God knows where else we're going to sleep. I think it's safe to say that Inverness is going to be full.'

Goldstein took charge. She had spent time in Inverness, she said, although not for many years. They'd look farther out. 'We should comm the places I can remember,' Goldstein said. 'Who's got a compad? Mine's still at Leith Police Station. We need directory enquiries. And I need to try and remember hotel names.'

They piled onto the cart and Tuthill got it going. It went very slowly. The battery was going and the load more than it was designed to carry. Teddy began to shout out hotel names, Hanford and Prosser searched for their comm numbers, Tuthill shouted out the names of streets as they passed them, seeking directions. An amicable sort of chaos ensued as they trundled away from the station at walking pace. McCall was squashed on the outside of the buggy's seat next to Prosser, trying not to fall out. She hadn't got out her compad. She didn't want to be a part of this … cavalcade. She was here to keep an eye on her prisoners – on what should be her prisoners. She remembered that she somehow hadn't got around to arresting Goldstein yet. And Hanford hadn't appeared to take his arrest seriously. These two facts galled her greatly. She realised that she was feeling better. She hoped it was the chocolate bar giving her some energy, and not Hanford's super-bugs.

'Anybody doing The Glen?' Teddy called out.

Hanford and Prosser shook their heads, engaged on other calls.

'I'll do it,' McCall sighed and pulled out her pad and earpiece. As she commed Yell she realised that the little task was a comfort. She was doing something, at any rate. Of course, now she was feeling a bit more like herself it was apparent that the place she should be coming was the local police station. She'd do that next. As she waited for the connection she put together in her head what she would tell her local colleagues. Then The Glen answered: there were two rooms available, did they want them?

Suddenly the prospect of food and a bath was all she could contend with.

'They have rooms!' she shouted.

'Take them!'

'They've only got two.'

'Take them!' came again from all sides.

So she took them, and the buggy rolled on its stately way full of hysterical people. McCall pocketed her compad and found she was smiling. She forgot entirely about calling the Inverness police.

12.5

In the bar of the Glen hotel Teddy and McCall glared at one another.

'Why the hell do you still want to arrest us?' Teddy said. 'In case you hadn't noticed, the world's changed. There's no way back to Edinburgh that doesn't involve a great deal of walking. That's no problem for us, but you couldn't keep up. If we run you can't catch us. We don't have to go anywhere with you. If it comes down to it, we are stronger than you – much stronger.

'And what if we let you put us in jail? What makes you think that there'll be any kind of judicial system to try us? Much as you might like to leave us there to rot there's still Habeas Corpus.'

'If the world is going to hell in a hand basket I don't imagine Habeas Corpus will carry much weight. It certainly doesn't with me, currently.' McCall snarled.

'OK. How are you going to feed us?'

'This is the Dark Ages you know. Or it soon will be. What makes you think anyone'd bother?'

There was a satisfaction in McCall's voice that silenced Teddy for a moment. Then she said, rather plaintively,

'You can't just lock us up and throw away the key.'

'Watch me.'

Teddy chose to ignore this sally and said ruminatively. 'Of course you're right. It will be the Dark Ages again in a way: a New Dark Age.'

'Er, actually its going to be more like the Iron Age,' Gates put in, 'if you want to be accurate about it.'

Teddy gave him a sharp look, but it turned into a smile almost at once. Gates smiled back at her toothily

'Iron Age, Dark Age – whatever. Don't you see? Gates has saved the world,' she went on. 'Its not just me he's saved, its everyone. What the hell is the point of arresting the saviour of the world. Or his …' She gave Gates a quizzical look.

'Leman?' he suggested. '*Inamorata*?'

This game appealed to Lox, and Sara got drawn into a lively debate as to the correct terminology for a man and a woman, romantically inclined, who had not slept together (that much was winkled out of them, making Teddy squirm and Gates blush) but who were old enough and (as Lox put it) ugly enough not to be boy- and girl-friend. Gates peeled notes off a substantial bankroll and bought more drinks. He was the only one with any cash – it was, indeed, only a flourish of Gates's wad of cash that had secured them the rooms, as the proprietor of The Glen wasn't having any truck with Smart Cards, the world being the way it was currently. McCall looked less stern as the suggestions became wilder and more ribald. The tensions of the day began to melt away as laughter became general. Finally she herself suggested 'fluffy bunnikins' and giggled along with the rest of them as Teddy and Gates protested.

The rooms available at The Glen turned out to be a small, airless 'family' room under the eaves on the third floor, and a glorified cupboard with a single and a Z-bed on the first. In the bar they tried to establish who was going to sleep with whom. It seemed sensible for the women to take the family room. That left Gates and Lox to sort out who got the Z-bed.

Lox lost the best of three bouts of scissors-paper-stone to Gates and resigned himself to the Z-bed. Gates offered to share the single top-to-toe, but Lox insisted he'd be fine. Whatever was inside Gates, however marvellous it was, Lox still didn't want to get close to it.

On his way to bed, he made a minor detour up to the second floor to go to the loo. He met McCall coming down from the third floor on a similar mission.

There was only the one bathroom on the floor.

'Why don't you use the one on your own floor?' said McCall waspishly.

'Why don't you?'

'Teddy might have …'

'Yeah, and so might Gates.'

Another bout of scissors-paper-stone ensued. Lox lost this as well and spent ten minutes in the corridor, trying not to think about running water, while McCall did what she needed to do. If his bladder hadn't been demanding so much concentration he might have examined his feelings about the nanites inside Gates and Teddy. On the other hand he really didn't want to think about that yet. He might have joked about Super Beings, and Teddy might be right about this being the way of the future, but he wasn't sure he could get to grips with any of it yet. He could have immortality, apparently. But he wasn't up to making a decision of that magnitude tonight. Not ever, if he could possibly help it. There: his mind had just leapt into action all by itself and the decision was made. To be honest the very thought of nanites scared him shitless. He just hoped that nothing crept out of Gates's mouth (or any other orifice for that matter) while they slept and marched across the room to his Z-bed. He imagined something like an army of tiny silver ants. It was as close as he could get. He shivered.

Hell's bell's – he'd come an awfully long way from his safe, productive human hive in Milton Keynes. Tonight he wished fervently that he'd never left it.

12.6

When he got back to the room he found Gates hunched over his compad.

'I don't suppose you've seen this?'

Resisting the impulse to go and look over Gates's shoulder, Lox pulled his own pad out of his jacket pocket. His story had been syndicated world-wide. The news nets were full of it. Teddy and Gates were famous. What they had unleashed on the world was infamous. The word 'Nanonics' was in every banner headline. So was Lox's by-line. That was the first bit of good news he'd had in twenty four hours. He also had an alarming number of new messages. One was from his Editor:

> Tuthill,
>
> am depositing funds in your account while still possible. How you get them out, or spend them, up to you. All rights on your story now taken up. Additional funds from international news nets should be deposited during the course of the day. Well done. I hope you're wrong, but all experience here tells me you're not. See you in the hereafter.
>
> Gardner

Gates couldn't resist going up to the girls' room to tell Teddy – and therefore McCall and Sara as well – that they were now the major international news item. As it was, actually, his story, Lox went with him. The news shifted McCall's mood from the waspish one Lox had already experienced outside the second floor bathroom, to downright homicidal.

'I can't stay here,' she said, and stormed out of the room. Lox followed her.

He caught up with her outside in the hotel's car park.

'You realise,' Lox said, 'that we're here for the duration now?'

McCall didn't say anything, just folded her arms and marched briskly towards the road. Lox had a reason for expressing his thought, and pursued it and McCall.

'If we're going to be here for the duration you could try being a little less … aggressive.'

'Why?'

'Well, wouldn't it be nice to get along?'

'I don't do nice, and I seldom get along with anyone. I'm here under duress –you people abducted me from the station. You should all be in jail. I should have commed the bloody police, not gone joy-riding in a bloody golf buggy. I don't know how this happened. I don't like it, and I don't see any reason why I should pretend that I do.'

McCall gave him a look that seemed to have tears in it.

'OK, fair enough. But *I* didn't abduct you.' Lox was quite happy to be placatory, but determined to get something out of this.

'Perhaps. But it's because of your incompetence that we're here.'

Lox spluttered.

'*My* incompetence?'

'Absolutely. If you'd helped me search the train before we got out of Edinburgh we'd still be there, not here, at the end of the world.'

'Oh, cobblers!' Lox's patience evaporated. She was beautiful, she was standing right next to him, breathing heavily and sweating prettily, breasts rising and falling, and she was completely exasperating.

He tried again.

'If we're going to be stuck here indefinitely you might at least tell me your first name. I can't go on calling you McCall all the time. Nor can everyone else. It looks like …'

'It looks like I don't want to be on first name terms with any of you. Exactly right.'

'Oh, for Christ's Sake!'

McCall started off again, ahead of him this time.

'Have you any idea,' she said, turning to him, 'how long this 'duration' you keep on about is likely to be?'

'No. Sorry.'

She walked on a few steps and stopped again, one hand straying up to stroke the stone of the car park wall. 'To make it through this people will need to become self-sufficient, right?'

'I suppose so. Although it won't take long to put viable alternatives to petrol in place. The vaults of the world's oil corporations are stuffed with them.'

McCall leaned against the corner of the wall.

'Hanford didn't expect a 'viable alternative' to reverse what he's done any time soon.'

'No,' said Lox, surprised that she had considered this. 'And he thought it through very carefully, knowing him – he didn't do this in a fit of pique.'

McCall looked at him sidelong.

'Pique came into it. Don't kid yourself.'

'OK, say it did. You're a city girl. I'm a city boy. Everybody's urban these days. How much did you enjoy it – the gridlock, the fumes, the press of people everywhere, the queues – all that.'

'OK – but there was the good stuff too. You could eat anything you fancied – Chinese one night, Italian the next, Indonesian, Thai. You could buy anything you could imagine, from anywhere in the world.'

'Off the 'Net. I bet you haven't picked out your own groceries in an actual shop for years.'

'No, but it was petrol-driven transport that brought all that stuff into the mix. Don't tell me you didn't enjoy it.'

'Sure I did. The global village was a gas. For a while. But its been out of control for a long time. We need actual villages.'

'Stupid yokels? In-breeding? Roll your own? Please. Urbanisation strengthened the gene pool enormously.'

Lox opened his mouth to ask how she knew so much about it, but McCall pushed off the wall and started towards the hotel.

Purposefully he strode after her, caught her up and planted himself in front of her, forcing her to stop.

'Stop messing about,' she said, trying to side-step him.

'If we're going to be stuck here, together, there's one thing I have to know.'

She knew what he wanted. He saw her face flush. She looked down at her boots.

'All right. It's Winsome.'

'Winsome McCall?'

'Yes. My Dad had … a moment of weakness. Unfortunately it was while he was in the presence of my Birth Certificate. But there's more.'

'Really?'

'I can't use my initials either.'

'Why the hell not?'

'My Dad was a fan of Celtic.'

'So?'

'That went on the Birth Certificate too.'

'The football club? On your Birth Certificate?'

'Yes, you idiot. Do I have to spell it out for you?'

'I think you'd better.'

'I'm Winsome Celtic McCall – W C McCall. Now do you understand why I get along with just the surname?'

'Bloody Hell. Yes, I do. Your Dad was besotted with you, then?.'

'Yes he was, while I was a baby. When I stopped looking cute he wanted another one to play with. When I got in the way he beat me.

When I left home I became McCall. If I was more imaginative I might have called myself something that didn't remind me of my abusive father every day of my life, but I didn't, so there we go.' She shuffled her feet and stared down at them, then she shook herself and lifted her head to glare at him. 'If you can find a reasonable way of rendering Winsome for every day use, I'm your woman. And I warn you now – I don't answer to Winny for anybody.'

Lox grinned broadly.

'I'm sure I'll think of something.'

He realised that his Irritable Bowel hadn't so much as twinged today.

12.7

They had to walk back to the station the next morning. The buggy gave one dying lurch forward when Gates tried it, but wasn't going to take them any further. Gates gave it a little pat as they left it.

There was a train, and it did eventually leave when the driver turned up – on horseback. It was another interminable journey. Lox and Gates helped other passengers with points and signals, which cut out regularly. But the power of positive thinking eventually got them as far as Dunster. Indeed, it looked as though the people hoping to go all the way to Thurso might make it.

At Dunster Teddy skipped off the train like a child and headed out of the station without waiting for anybody else. Gates took off after her and the two of them marched off southwards, up the hill and over the bridge, passing the surprisingly large number of people who'd also got off the train at Dunster, and who also were heading up the hill.

Lox and McCall watched them go. Teddy was setting a brutal pace, but Hanford kept up with her easily.

'I guess that's what being a superbeing is all about,' said Lox.

McCall shrugged and followed them at a much more leisurely pace.

Lox turned to see where Sara had got to and noticed that she was still standing on the platform. She looked worn out. Lox called to her.

'Come on. Last part of the journey. Things'll look better when we get there.'

'Or not.' But when he held out his hand, she took it, and they followed slowly after McCall. McCall waited for them at the bridge. She was awfully pale, and something was dragging her mouth into a really miserable set. When they reached Lox let go Sara's hand and patted McCall's shoulder. He felt there was safety in numbers today.

And their number – the Unenhanced, one might say – was obviously feeling more than a little beleaguered.

'Great bridge this.'

'It's a fucking bridge, is all,' McCall growled.

It was, actually, rather an elegant bridge to find in this isolated spot. And the view was magnificent. The three stood and enjoyed it for several minutes, putting off the moment when they would have to address reality once more.

Below them, in the village, rows of dumpy grey cottages huddled under the wind between the North Sea and the glorious sweep of moorland behind them. The sun was shining. The moors had colours in them that made the writer in Lox itch to write them down, to try and capture their beauty. The bay wrapped around the village like a protecting hand. The low houses looked as though they'd grown out of the ground, with their brown stone walls and slate roofs. It looked like a nice place to live – a good place, where people looked after one another.

He said nothing. They were all standing way outside their comfort zones on this bridge. This wasn't the moment to remind his companions that their future was here. He felt his stomach lurch.

'Come on then,' he said. 'Into the unknown.'

He held out a hand to each of his companions, and the three of them set off once more, trudging dolefully up the hill.

12.8

Teddy found herself jogging down the long drive to the castle for the sheer joy of it. The castle – her father's dreadful folly – had inspired a lifelong gloom in her. But it was a beautiful building in its way. How had she never noticed that before?

The big turning space in front of the house seemed to be full of people. Teddy had intended to pop in on Ed and Rory first, but the sight of all those people made her think she'd better go down to the castle first. As she got closer she could see there were only about fifteen of them, but such a gathering around the front entrance of their remote castle certainly constituted the biggest crowd it had seen since the nineteenth century. What was going on?

Teddy looked for Ailsa, and finally caught sight of her with her back to the big front door trying to shoo the crowd away, as one might cattle that had strayed into the cabbages. It wasn't working. Teddy could see luggage.

Teddy started to jog down the lane, but it wasn't fast enough. She was running now. She had a sudden need to be down there, hugging Ailsa. And she was curious to know what these people wanted. She wasn't even slightly out of breath as she wriggled through the bodies and caught up her housekeeper in a bear hug.

Ailsa shrieked, and kept on shrieking until Teddy caught the old woman's face between her hands and said,

'Ailsa, it's me. It's only me.'

'Good God Almighty, Theodora, I thought you were one of these, set upon me. I was going to call for the Police.' She pulled her fist out of her apron pocket with a compad clutched in it.

'Nobody will come. We're the last to get through. No more trains, Ailsa. Nor cars nor anything. And Ailsa … something wonderful has happened.'

So many words welled up in Teddy's throat that they jammed there and couldn't get through. Tears could though.

Teddy had to content herself for the moment with sobbing happily into Ailsa's neck.

12.9

Sara was about as miserable as it is possible for someone to be who's in a strange place, abandoned by the person she thought was her friend, chivvied along by two others she hardly knows and can't find anywhere private to have a good cry. A refrain echoed in her head as she plodded along with McCall and Tuthill. It went 'what's to become of me?'

Finally the three reached the top of the hill. Ahead of them the road bore to the right, about half a kilometre further on she could see a track with a sign beside it. As they got closer she could see that it read 'Dunster Castle Organic Farm'. By tacit agreement the three of them stopped at the top of the track.

'I suppose this is it?' said McCall.

'Looks like it,' Tuthill said with the awful forced cheerfulness he had been exhibiting all the way up from the station.

They walked through the open gateway. In front of them a lane sloped down towards the sea. To their left was a farmhouse and a couple of barns. They could hear a generator. In the door of the house two men stood, waving cheerily.

'Home, sweet home!' Tuthill said. 'Looks like they've got themselves a pretty nice set-up here. We ought to go over, make ourselves known, fraternise with the natives.'

'They might have a cup of tea,' Sara said wistfully, and set off towards the farmhouse. Lox and McCall followed her.

When they got off the track they could see that it ran steeply downhill towards the sea. From this angle a vista opened up before them. At the bottom of the lane, clinging to the edge of the land, was a castle – an honest to God, gothic castle. In front of it some kind of fete seemed to be in progress. On the landward side of it was an enormous kitchen garden, walled against the weather, produce flourishing in neat, weed-free rows. The three of them stopped, transfixed.

'Holy shit!' said Tuthill.

'It certainly is pretty impressive when you see it for real,' said McCall.

The three of them stood there staring at Teddy's family seat, until Ek and Rory came out into the lane and introduced themselves.

12.10

Rory and Ek were a joy after the rigours of the past two days. Five minutes after they'd been collected from the lane, the three weary – and in one case teasy – travellers, were sitting on the terrace at the back of the farmhouse with a glass of red wine apiece, admiring the view seawards towards the off-shore wind farm. Nearer and below them was a collection of grey slate roofs which was all they could now see of the Goldstein family seat.

Rory reappeared shortly with hunks of fresh-baked bread and a big round cheese which smelt awful. Ek brought out crockery and a couple more bottles of wine.

'Try some – it smells worse than it is. It's our first go at cheese-making. It's from our highland cattle. You need to be a bit tricky to get the besoms to let you milk them. They don't believe they're milch cows, and they're wild as goats.'

'That's the next project – we've got a small herd of British Saanens. They understand about being milked, it's just that getting down so low to do it gives you frightful backache.'

Ek cut bread as Rory pantomimed the after effects of goat-milking. The travellers began to revive.

'Of course people are going to need locally grown staples now – bread, milk, cheese, yoghurt. And we've got bees that give us lovely honey. This crisis, whatever it is, will be the making of us.'

'We'll have to get power for the milk parlour. There'll be too much demand for us to milk by hand.'

'And it takes so long.'

'Not to mention the kicks in the ribs.'

'And the shit in the shoes.'

Ek and Rory laughed uproariously, and this time even McCall joined in.

'How are you going to get a steady electricity supply now?' Lox asked. 'The grid's sure to be more off than it's on.'

Rory gestured towards the sea.

'All those ducky little turbines just keep on turning. This is one of the most productive fields on the coast of Britain – the wind always blows here.'

'And we know where the cable comes ashore,' said Rory with a wink.

More guffaws, during which Ek pulled the cork out of another bottle. As he poured he made another remark which had Lox's eyebrows rising towards his hairline.

'It's been like a party all day. We haven't had such fun since I don't know when. About fifty people have gone down this drive today so far. Look – there's two more turning in now.'

'Daft biddy. It's more like fifteen,' said Rory. 'But we're going to have to get going in a minute. If they're all eating at the Big Hoose tonight we'll have to load up the wheelbarrow with most of McGonagall Mark IV.'

Sara couldn't resist asking.

'McGonagall Mark IV?'

'Last year's bullock. Topped and chopped and laid to rest in the freezer. We identify the biggest bull calf every spring …'

'Cut his bits off and feed him up so he gets nice and plump…'

'… and he gets called …'

'McGonagall!'

'A sweet life, but a short one.'

'And Mark IV's extremely tasty. I hope you lot appreciate him.'

Rory and Ek started talking menus. It made their visitors' mouths water.

'We could do a barbie!'

'It'll have to be stew.'

'Och, who wants to eat stew in June? I'll see what's in the freezer, then I'll com Ailsa, see what she thinks.'

Ek wandered into the house.

'I don't know why they've come,' Rory confided. 'Perhaps they're just looking for a safe place until everything settles down. But it's no bad thing, if they're prepared to stay and work. We shall need more labour on the farm now we can't use the tractor' He turned to Lox. 'We heard your piece on the Scottish newsnet. We know what's happened. And we know who did it. I guess that Teddy and this Hanford chap are heading this way. Well, they will if they've got any sense.'

That reminded the three that cheese and wine at the farmhouse was just a moment of calm in the midst of a crisis. They didn't even know if they'd be welcome at the castle. Their mellow mood evaporated. Sara said,

'I think I'll wander down and try to find out what's happening.'

The other two got to their feet as well.

'What did I say?' said Rory. 'I didn't mean to be a party pooper.'

'It's all right,' said Sara. 'It was nice to forget our troubles for a little while. But we'd better go and see …'

As he saw them out, Rory gave Sara's shoulder an awkward little pat and said,

'I'd like to say 'chin up, it may never happen' – but it has, hasn't it?'

Sara managed a watery smile for him, then strode purposefully off down the lane. It was time for that cry she'd been promising herself.

12.11

Ailsa had escorted a sobbing Teddy into the castle. While Ailsa heaved the heavy, studded door to behind her and shot the bolt, Teddy got a grip on herself. She wiped her eyes and gestured at the door.

'What do they want?'

'I'm sure I've no idea. They've been turning up all day. Ek was here with me earlier, but I sent him up to the farm in case they pestered Rory.'

Typical Ailsa – she'd always maintained that Rory was completely helpless, although he'd once won the ploughing contest at the county show, still climbed Monroes for fun and was a better cook than Ailsa herself. Rory had, however, been an amateur Latin-American ballroom dancing champion in a previous life and had once been unguarded enough to tell Ailsa about it. Ailsa drew her conclusions from that. Teddy grinned. Ailsa continued,

'They've got suitcases and backpacks. One man's brought his bairns. They're all crazies, I reckon.'

Teddy looked out of the window in the hall to see if any craziness was apparent. A miserable-looking boy and girl were kicking stones at each other over by the kitchen garden wall. Where their father was she couldn't tell. Curiouser and curiouser.

Ailsa came and stood behind her at the window. More people were coming down the lane. With a little jolt Teddy realised that she knew these three.

'Do you recognise any of them?' she asked Ailsa.

'No. I surely don't.'

'They're not from the village?'

Ailsa snorted. 'Village people've got more sense.'

'Perhaps they're refugees?' She was thinking out loud now. 'We were all over the newsnets this morning. It said what we'd done, and the how and the why. And it said where the police thought we were going. The nets said to treat us with extreme caution. But I think these people want to be part of it.'

'Us? Part of what?'

'That's a very long story. And you won't believe it when I tell you.' She turned back to the window and watched the little crowd for a little while. 'There's nowhere else for them to go now. They'll have to stay here.'

Ailsa's face opened up like a flower – her eyebrows rose, her eyes grew big and round and her mouth opened. But before Ailsa could try for clarification, Teddy went on.

'We'll organise dormitories. There's loads of room, and beds, and bedding. Feeding them'll be more of a problem, but I'm sure Ek and Rory can help.' She found she was excited. 'Don't you see? We've got our very own kibbutz standing outside, just waiting to be.'

'No,' said Ailsa. 'I don't understand. Not at all. Not any of it. And there'll be no kibbling here.'

Laughing merrily Teddy took her arm.

'Let's go into the kitchen and have a cup of tea. I'll try and tell you what's happened – and what's got to happen next. It's going to be great. You'll see.'

12.12

The castle was amazing. By the time McCall and Lox got to the seaward end of the kitchen-garden wall it loomed over them. The closer they got the more arrow slits and gargoyles they could see. In the space before it …

McCall stopped, so Lox did too.

'Who the hell are all these people?'

Lox said, 'I rather suspect they may be some sort of New Order. Do you remember me saying that we need actual villages to get through this? I'm prepared to bet that these folk aren't from Dunster. I think they've come because Gates and Teddy are here – my piece was all over the nets, remember. They've come to try and be part of whatever it is those two have started. A community this sort of size, growing its own food, pulling together - it might be good.'

'Too small. Not enough biodiversity'

'Oh, that's crap. It used to work fine.'

McCall started towards the castle again, throwing a parting shot over her shoulder as she went.

'You'll be beating the yokels off with a stick if you're going to live here, Tuthill. You're a valuable addition to the gene pool.'

Lox was inordinately pleased that she'd noticed.

12.13

The old iron thistle knocker made a colossal racket on the front door and both Teddy and Ailsa flinched, but a glance through the hall window revealed just the one supplicant: Sara had arrived, looking like hell.

Teddy experienced a small pang of guilt. Sara had been a good friend to her, but had been abandoned, literally, by the roadside. Teddy held that little pang to her for a moment: all these new emotions were such a rush – love, guilt, happiness were all surging through her. It was a new world, no doubt about it.

She chivvied both women into the kitchen, where the yard full of strangers wasn't so disturbing, and made tea – Ailsa was in too much of a dither. While Teddy went through the cosy ritual of cups and milk she explained to Ailsa what had happened, as well as she could. Much of it was news to Sara as well. Teddy slopped a generous measure of cooking brandy into the three mugs, as a restorative for Ailsa and Sara and a little celebration for herself .

Sara looked all in. She obviously felt she was in the way and wanted to be almost anywhere else. Ailsa was not taking to the idea of the kibbutz at all. With the hot brandy coursing through her, Teddy had an almost Olympian view of their plight: it was difficult to assimilate so much change in the time it takes to drink a cup of tea.

'I've been so worried,' Ailsa cradled her tea cup in her hands. 'First there was the news, and it was all bad. Then *you* were in the news yourself, and that was bad too. Then there was no news at all.' She took a sip, and grimaced at the brandy. 'I thought you were dead.'

'And where would have been the surprise in that?' Teddy couldn't resist.

'But that didn't mean I was looking forward to it ye bad wain!' Ailsa began to cry. She'd either had too much brandy or not enough.

'No, of course not.' Teddy put her arms around Ailsa and hugged her hard. 'Daft old thing,' she said fiercely, releasing the woman. But as she stood up she looked Ailsa in the eye, and let her see the truth there.

Almost an hour and most of the bottle of brandy later, Teddy finally felt able to return to the matter of how they were going to feed and accommodate the people outside. She was bracing herself for an argument when Ailsa's compad beeped. On the other end was obviously Ek, with a recipe book in his hand and the contents of the farmhouse's freezer in his head. Ailsa could never resist Ek: she began to smile.

Confident now that everyone would get something to eat, Teddy left Ailsa initiating Sara into the mysteries of her store cupboards and started worrying about where everybody was going to sleep that night.

A major project was standing outside in the yard. It was Gates they had come for – she realised that. She'd never spent much time around people. She was pretty certain Gates hadn't either. They had both slunk through life, avoiding human contact. But a great deal of human contact was going to be needed now. The people outside were going to be a big responsibility. She wondered how good Gates was with responsibility. But Gates was with her, and they were her responsibility too, so that was all right.

But where was Gates?

Through the hall window she could see the sour policewoman and her reporter talking by the garden wall. It might make the woman a bit less sharp if she had something to do. Those two could find out who these people were, what they were good at. By the time that had been done she, Teddy, would have sorted out somewhere for them to sleep. But first she probably ought to talk to them. Herself. Ah.

Taking a deep breath Teddy pulled back the bolt on the front door.

12.14

The main hall was now full of people, giving McCall their details and getting bedding from Tuthill.

Upstairs was, by contrast, deathly quiet. Teddy was wandering the rooms still working out how to fit everybody in. There were five rooms in each of the four towers. The north east tower was her old apartment and only had one bed. She wasn't sure how many beds were in the other towers – she hadn't been fit enough to go up there since she'd come home. The main part of the house had nine bedrooms, not counting her father's. They all had beds – doubles and twins. She had no idea why there was so much furniture when the house had only ever accommodated her father, mother, herself and Ailsa on the top floor. But the main thing was, there was room up here for eighteen in reasonable comfort. Teddy found a compad and started making notes.

At the door of her father's room she stopped. There was a lot of potential here. It was a huge chamber. A family could be comfortable in it if she could get some extra beds moved in. She remembered the man with his children downstairs. Reluctantly she turned the handle of the door and opened it.

The room smelled as it had in her childhood: of dust, pot-pourri and the sea. The old tapestries on the walls rippled an eldritch welcome. The great snowy bed stood, as ever, on its dais, fluffy with clouds of pillows and quilts and – strangely – inviting.

Her father's room. It had always been a place of mystery when she was little.

She went over to the windows. She could feel the wind coming in off the North Sea through the frames. How her father had loved this eyrie.

It seemed somehow sacrilegious to put strangers in here. Anyway, they'd be cold and probably not get a wink of sleep with the tapestries twitching all night long.

That gave her an idea. She had intended to find a cosy little corner of the castle for herself and Gates, but she was having trouble thinking of the right place. She didn't want to return to her old nursery apartment in the tower – she had been so ill there, and so miserable in her childhood. And they were, in a sense, king and queen of something now. It made a perverse sort of sense for them to have this room. She grinned.

12.15

On her way back down the stairs Teddy heard someone hammering enthusiastically with the thistle knocker. More pilgrims? Ailsa appeared in the doorway of the Great Hall, but Teddy called out that she'd go herself. She went on down, checked that the door was bolted and shouted through it,

'What do you want?'

Gates's voice came back to her.

'I'd like to come in, if it's all the same to you.'

With a smile she pulled the bolt and heaved the door open.

'Where the hell have you been?'

'There were too many people about, so I went for a wander. I found the vegetable garden, and met Ek harvesting for dinner. He took me to meet Rory. We had a wee dram to celebrate … and here I am.'

Are there any more of them out there?'

'No, that seems to be the lot – at least for the moment. But listen – I've had an idea what to do with them.'

'Well, I'm glad someone has. I've think I've found everybody a bed for the night, but that's about it.'

'We can start ...'

'A kibbutz?'

'Er …yeh, if you like. But the thing is that everyone who wants to stay here must agree to be part of the ultimate experiment.'

'What ultimate experiment?'

'Immortality. If what I've done is to have any meaning in the greater scheme of things, we have to try. I don't know what sort of faith these people have, whether it's in a god, or in science, or in the capability of the human race to survive no matter what. But this is what I think: we need a cleaner, greener, smaller world. And to survive that we need nanites.'

'*Our* nanites? But if we all live forever …'

'Yeh, yeh. Over-population. That could be a major problem down the line. And I'm going to need everybody's input to work that through. But if we can get the experiment to work here, we can go back into the world with the results and see if anybody else wants to be part of it.'

He was so excited. She steered him towards the small sitting room. It should be quiet there, and the good booze was in the armoire. Teddy was beginning to feel the need for another, this time restorative, drink. In the small sitting room was Sara, sitting in front of the venerable workstation that Ailsa used for the castle accounts.

'Gates! You promised to show me the formulae.'

'I did?'

'You did. You're not a doctor. I am. I need to see what you've done to yourselves. And I need to do it right now.'

'Now. Right.'

Gates rummaged in his trouser pocket and fished out a Pod. He moved towards the computer. Teddy sighed. She had been going to take him upstairs, show him her father's old room, run a bath for him in the ensuite and scrub his back, amongst other things. But what the hell? They had the rest of their lives for all of that.

The end

Lightning Source UK Ltd.
Milton Keynes UK
30 March 2010

152116UK00002B/88/P